LHOSA

SOJOURNER

CAREY ALLEN KRAUSE

Copyright © 2020 by Carey Allen Krause

All rights reserved.

No part of this book may be reproduced in any form or by any electronic or mechanical means, including information storage and retrieval systems, without written permission from the author, except for the use of brief quotations in a book review.

This is a work of fiction. All of the characters and locations are creations of the author and are not intended to represent any actual persons or locations. Some words have been invented for the purpose of storytelling. Any similarity to words found in other creative works is purely coincidental.

Cover art by Alejandro Colucci

Map by the author

For Daniel
who had an idea, and a name…

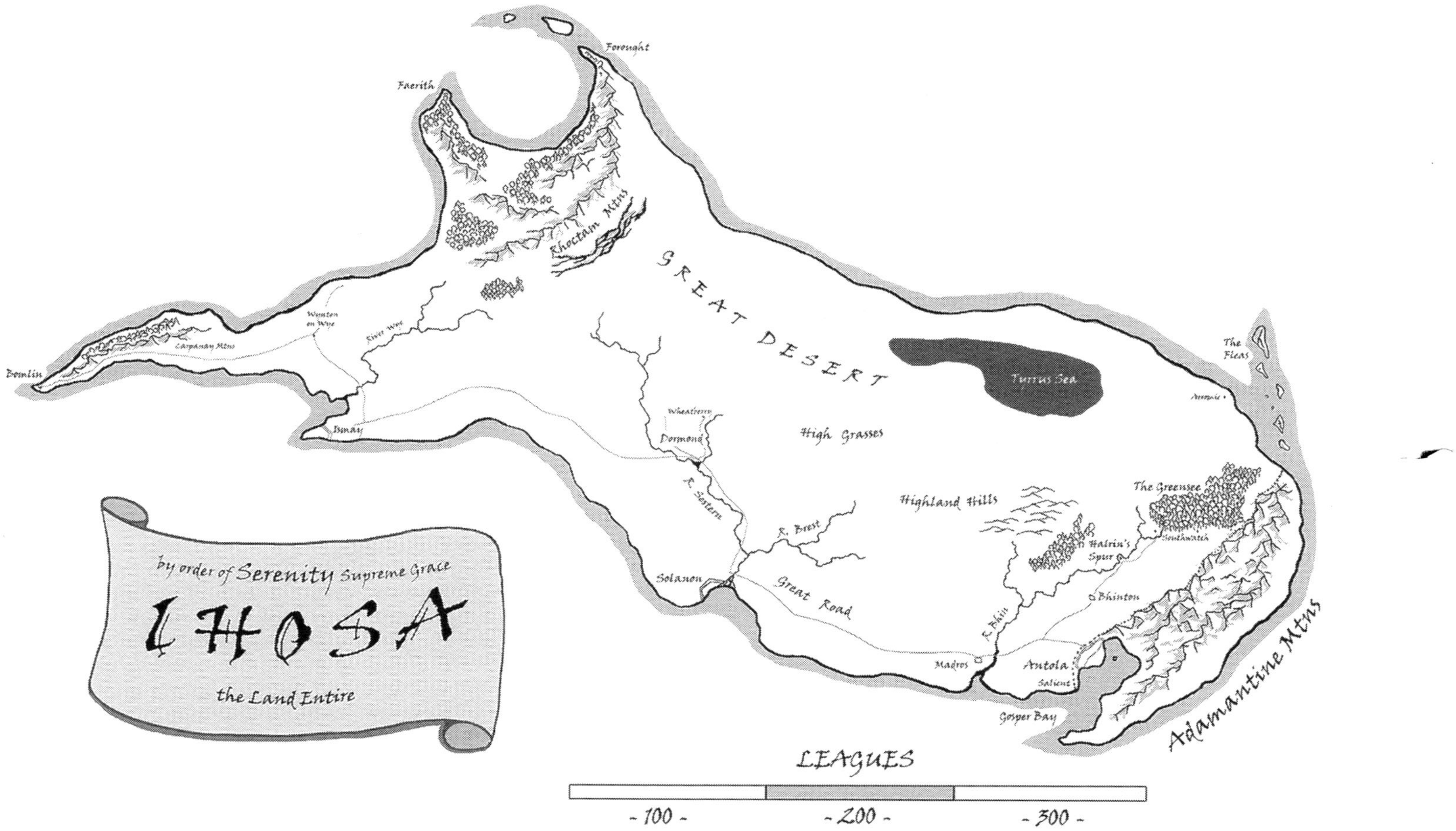
Forought
Faerith
Rhoctam Mtns
GREAT DESERT
Wynton on Wye
River Wye
Carpanay Mtns
Bomlin
Ismay
Wheatberry
Dormond
High Grasses
Tyrrus Sea
The Fleas
R. Sestern
R. Brest
Highland Hills
The Greensee
Southwatch
Halrin's Spur
Solanon
Great Road
Bhinton
R. Bhin
Madros
Antola
Salient
Gosper Bay
Adamantine Mtns
by order of Serenity Supreme Grace
LHOSA
the Land Entire
LEAGUES
- 100 -
- 200 -
- 300 -

FIRST PASSAGE

Our truths exist at many levels. Experiences are tested to become facts; facts are collected to become knowledge; knowledge is shared in stories, which are told and re-told until they become myth. For those of us interested in the history of these things, it is always our goal to unravel the myth and work our way back along the fibers until we are face-to-face with the experience. We hope to re-discover the thoughts of the warriors before a battle became a legend, or retrace the anonymous individual's steps before they became extraordinarily famous. Who were the actual people behind our mythical creations? What were their lives really like? And what myths and antiquities shaped the culture of their world, leading them to believe what they believed? Knowing these things helps us know who they were. Knowing who they were is vital to understanding who we have become.

The Polfre have a saying: "Beginnings have their own beginnings."

—From *The Invention of History* by Robin the Archivist

1

Olei looked up and the Red Eye stared back, an ember burning low in the western sky. It was bad luck to look at the Eye, so they said. Best to keep your gaze on the ground. To gaze at the Eye invited the attention of the Lord Ruhax. He would peer into your thoughts, delve into your heart, and when he failed to find what he sought he would leave behind a measure of pain.

For most people, it made perfect sense that a god would keep watch on them from the sky, but Olei wasn't among them. He had been watching the sky for most of his twelve years. He knew that some things moved fast, such as the Sun and the Sojourner, while other things moved very slow, such as the Eye. But they all moved in predictable ways. Every year the Red Eye reliably appeared two passages earlier than the year before, slipping upward from the eastern horizon and spending the next half year chasing the Sun through the sky, an errant lick of flame seeking return to the mother fire. He could remember when the Eye appeared at the end of Harvest and was overhead all Winter. This year, by comparison, it had not appeared until halfway through the Winter season and was only now disappearing in the west as they approached SummerTop and the start of a new year. Miscarriages and malformations had been the work of the Eye in the past. In the future it would bear the blame for drought and crop failures. Even so, Olei doubted it was the work of the gods. Its movements were as predictable as the movements of the Sun. The gods by contrast were capricious, inscrutable; anything but predictable. And they didn't need the help of lights in the sky to spread fear and misfortune.

There was good fortune in the world, to be sure. The great city of Antola was full of it. But very little made its way north to where he lived in Halrin's Spur. Here, wealth was measured by whether a family survived Winter or not. Olei understood how that kept people focused on the ground in front of them. Perhaps he would spend his adult life doing the same thing. But for now, he wanted to look up as often as he could.

He picked up the two buckets of water and turned down a wide cart path. He had to hold the buckets away from his body not to slosh them, which was tiring. It would be easier to walk home more directly, past the alehouse. But he had good reason to avoid the place. Instead, he struck a track on the south side of the village and followed it toward the river, then home.

The Sojourner had not yet risen. Moving contrary to everything else, it rose in the west and set in the east. Only one night in twelve did it appear on the western horizon right at Sunset, a fingernail gradually emerging from the deep orange sky. The next evening it would not rise until well after dark, and the next not until the middle of the night, always sailing against the wheel of the Sun and stars. On the sixth day it would rise fat and luminous in the west just as the morning Sun rose in the east: two great lights, one on each side of the sky. Six days later it was born again on New Sojourner. A passage: twelve days, one for each of the twelve fingers on his hands. That was a coincidence hard to dismiss.

The world hummed with such resonances, their meaning just beyond perception.

Tonight, Olei wanted to watch the Sojourner rise and fatten until it was a full circle overhead. For that he wanted to be at the highest point he could find. As he trudged home, arms beginning to shake from the weight of the buckets, he planned to do better than the window of his house.

His mother was waiting at their door. "Why does it take you so long? It's getting dark," she said. The interior of their house was even darker than the shadows outside. He set down the buckets and opened a set of shutters. "Olei, no," she said. "It's dangerous."

"There's not enough light in here to see the water jars," he replied, as he filled and covered them in turn. "Besides, it's hot. With the shutters open we can feel a breeze."

"I don't want you going out tonight."

"The drunks don't come to the door anymore. You'll be safe."

"I'm not worried about them. We're too close to the river."

"I'm not afraid," he said, and it was mostly true. His mother, like many of the town's residents, believed stories of roaming bands of raiders who attacked unprotected villages. The Ruhatsi, they called them, demon children of Lord Ruhax. Olei doubted the existence of demons the same way he doubted the divinity of the Red Eye. What puzzled him was how no one else seemed to share his doubt. What use did gods or demons have for a small herding village near the end of the North Road?

Still, he could not help but wonder what hid in the dark beneath the scrubby stand of trees on the other side of the river, looking back at him. But it was that touch of fear that made his night-time prowls an adventure. Halrin's Spur, at the edge of the civilized world, was for Olei the center of an uninspiring existence. He imagined bigger places and greater things.

He looked west above the trees and noticed the Eye seemed to be fading and spreading as it sank toward the far distant hills. He had watched it set on many clear evenings in the past. It never actually seemed to drop below the hills, but rather to melt into a tiny, wavy puddle before evaporating above the horizon.

Reluctantly, he closed the shutters. The room was dark except for the stray beams of a lamp filtering across the alley and through their front room. He slipped to the corner where his mat was unrolled on the floor. He and his mother had been the only occupants of their tiny house since his father had disappeared years before.

Olei lay on his back, listening for the deep breaths that would indicate his mother had fallen asleep. He did not intend to obey. Few nights were as clear as this one promised to be, perfect for sky-gazing. He imagined himself simply rising up and passing through the roof, rising until he could see not only his house but the surrounding houses, mostly mud and thatch, crowded against the eastern bank of the river. The river Bhin, arising far to the northeast, cut a sinuous path in its journey south. Halrin's Spur occupied a bulb of land made where the river turned sharply to the west, and then almost as sharply to the east again.

Looking the other way, Olei imagined he could see the larger, nicer houses and shops surrounding the imposing black walls of the Altarnary. Halrin's Spur was the only village north of Bhinton with an Altarnary of its own. Built of smooth-cut black granite, it was the kind of building he imagined filled the streets of Antola, but it did not fit in here. Perhaps that was the point. It had been built by the Panthea, the religious arm of the Antolan Crown. At the altar inside, the priest occasionally sacrificed small animals to celebrate the gods' protection. It was meant to feel different than their day-to-day world, to remind them that the gods lived close to them but not among them.

For Olei, though, the Altarnary was an excellent observation point for exploration of the sky. He had crept through the building on many previous nights, while the old priest snored. He could traverse the stairs to the roof in complete darkness, where he could lie on his back and gaze at the stars, unseen from below.

He opened his eyes. The lamp from the nearby house had been extinguished. He had fallen asleep. Even so, Olei could easily make out the outline of the window. He padded across the room, silently opening the shutters and hoisting himself through.

The sky was thick with stars. A single candle burned in a chimney outside the foul-smelling alehouse around the corner. Once again, he gave it a wide berth.

He walked familiar paths between buildings, which fed like tributaries into the broad dirt lane in front of the Altarnary. The Curly Top Tavern stood opposite, a decent tavern where a couple of durri would buy a bowl of stew. Behind it was the broad bank of the Bhin, curving west before wrapping itself around the little town.

The massive wood doors in front of the Altarnary would be barred, but Olei's preferred entrance was a back window covered with an easily jimmied shutter. He climbed by feel, pushed open the window, and then dropped like a cat into a kitchen cupboard. There had been a time when the kitchen hearthgrate burned day and night, when the building served as a refuge for travelers and those without enough to eat. But that had been before Olei's time. The old priest made no such efforts. He performed the obligatory sacrifice on SummerTop, but even then, few people attended. Now the hearth sat cold, and the storage boards were empty.

In previous forays through the depths of the building, Olei had found a half-dozen books, some that he could read, and one that was his favorite. To one side of the altar room there was a stairway which led to an upper storage cell, then to a much narrower, steeper set of steps to the roof. He had spent entire nights curled in the little cell with a borrowed candle, reading and re-reading the book. It held stories of great warriors like Donal the conqueror, and tales of great ravenous cats that could disappear into smoke, or black-winged birds the size of houses. In Olei's imagination the Altarnary had once been filled with scenes like those in his book: warriors passing through on great adventures, making their sacrifices and calling for feasts. Now, though, it was a dead, black block of stones in the middle of a flimsy village of thatch and mud bricks.

The Altarnary structure was square, while the altar room itself was a circle of columns crowned by a shallow dome, with a central, open oculus directly over the altar below. He ran lightly up the steps to the roof. There, lying on his back, warmed by the stones of the dome, he could watch the sky in peace.

The star patterns from Winter were already setting in the west. To the south, he could easily pick out the one star that never moved. The rest of the stars circled in greater or smaller arcs around it. He told his mother once that the southern star must still be present in the daytime, just too faint to see against the glare of the Sun. She had looked at him uncomprehendingly.

A fat crescent appeared above the western horizon, then quickly climbed skyward, turning from orange to white. The Sojourner's appearance never lost its excitement. He was fascinated by the speed with which it sailed backward across the sky. He loved the oddness of it. He felt that way himself, sure that he thought differently than the people of Halrin's Spur. He could not imagine himself becoming a bisonman when he grew older. Apprenticing himself to the owner of the Curly Top, or to the tanner, seemed just as limiting. There had to be greater things than that. But his time was running out. He would have to start working somewhere soon. His nights spent dreaming among the stars, he feared, would soon come to an end.

As much as anything, he was reluctant to join the adult world because he worried about his mother. After his father's disappearance, her existence became precarious: a young, unattached woman without family ties to the village. For a few years one of the herders, a bison-sized man named Obo, had taken it upon himself to claim her as his woman. Despite his size, he had been tender toward her and kind to Olei, but his behavior suggested he was fulfilling an obligation rather than an interest. When Obo chose to move back to his hut near the milkhouse, his mother refused to go with him. Before long, the drunks from the piss-smelling alehouse were pounding on their door in the middle of the night. Olei finally decided to resolve the situation himself.

About a year prior, his mother had given him a knife that had belonged to his father. It was an odd thing, with finger-hole rings at the shank that were already too small for his fingers, crafted from a strange brown metal that would not hold an edge. Nonetheless, he carried it with him everywhere, tied to a leather thong around his neck.

He had waited until his mother was asleep, and then, making sure the knife was under his tunic, stole out of the house. This time, instead heading for the Altarnary, he had hidden himself in the shadows. There he waited until one of the drunks staggered out of the alehouse and blundered up to his house. The man stood for a moment in front of the door before he began pounding. Then he took a step back and rammed his shoulder into the door with all his weight. This was something new, and Olei was afraid that the wooden bar inside would not hold. The man slammed his shoulder into the door two more times, then leaned over at the waist, having winded himself. Olei slipped from his hiding place, moving quickly and silently. He jabbed the knife to its hilt into the small of the man's back, surprised at how easily it seemed to penetrate despite its dull edges. Before the man could gasp, Olei darted away and was once again hidden around the nearest corner.

The man's body was found the next morning half a dozen steps from the front door. Sober townsmen, some of whom likely had been drinking partners of the slain man the night before, clucked their tongues over the increased risk from raiders sneaking across the river at night. They chose to burn the body rather than throw it in the river, since it would only pollute the water further downstream. One man thought to ask Olei's mother if she had any idea what had happened. She told him she had heard the frightening pounding, and then nothing, and she hadn't dared open the door until she heard commotion in the morning. She did not tell him about Olei returning through the window a short time after the pounding had stopped.

Shutting off the memory, Olei settled against the stones and watched the Sojourner as it rose higher into the sky. A gentle breeze blew from the north. He found it hard to stay awake, and he began slipping in and out of a dream. In the dream, the people of Halrin's Spur were out of their beds, quietly walking the paths and alleys, murmuring to one another, looking for him.

The scream that startled him awake was close by. A woman had screamed over and over in terror, and then suddenly stopped. Olei felt a wave of panic; he imagined someone had been watching his movements and had chosen this moment to attack his mother. But then he heard another scream from a completely different direction, followed by the sound of a man's angry cries and a child's shrieks. Again, they were suddenly silenced. And then another man's cries, and suddenly the town seemed to explode with screams and cries of fear and pain from every direction.

Olei crawled to the edge of the roof. He could just make out the shapes of dozens of swiftly running figures fanning out through the lanes and alleys. A desperate fear for his mother gripped him. But before he could work up the courage to climb down the ladder into the darkness of the Altarnary, he heard a soft roar and the sky was filled with orange light. In the distance, the milkhouse had burst into flames. Olei watched the fire spread quickly across the thatched roof. Within moments the entire structure was consumed by flames reaching far into the sky. The south side of the dome reflected their orange light. If he stood, he would be as visible as if he were in broad daylight.

He heard a loud *boom* resonate through the Altarnary. He crawled to the front of the roof. The boom reverberated again, this time with cracking sounds, and a third crash was accompanied by the sound of splintering wood as the great doors smashed against the inner walls. Olei watched a few villagers begin to mount a defense in front of the building. When he saw their attackers, he gasped in horror. They fought against creatures with shocking faces and ugly, twisting masses of horn growing from their disfigured heads. The creatures were taller than the tallest villager, and they fought viciously, while seeming to avoid injury themselves.

A horse galloped down the road in front of the Altarnary, carrying one of the hideous raiders. A villager sprang from the shadows and raised an axe. To Olei's horror, the raider was quicker, slashing the man across the neck with a sword. As the man fell, the raider pulled the horse up short, turned, and ran the horse over the body.

Scattered fires were breaking out across the village, mostly toward the river and his home. The raiders were attacking everywhere. He had the sudden feeling that his mother was already dead, and he could do nothing. Until that moment, he had carried a sense of her presence with him, but now it was ripped away, leaving a hole in his chest that he filled with a sobbing gasp for air. He was afraid the raiders would hear him and know where he was.

Then the hole was filled with defiance. He scrabbled around and peeked out to the south, where the milkhouse was fully engulfed. Someone needed to stay alive to bear witness. There was power in witness, the power to later point and say, "*I was there. It was them.*"

A bone-chilling wail split the air nearby. A raider had climbed the ladder and was standing on the far corner of the roof. Olei, terrified, tried to make sense of the silhouette: the creature's skull seemed to grow into tangled loops of bone and flesh. The figure lifted something to its face, and the wail filled the air once again. Olei tried to flatten himself against the stones. He was sure he would be seen if the creature turned around. He closed his eyes tight, that childish reflex that allows one to pretend they are invisible. For a long moment he waited, and then peeked out of one eye. Remarkably, the raider appeared not to have seen him; it was now gazing out across the river. The bizarre bony growths seemed to sway slightly. Then the creature's gaze passed over him as it looked toward the wreckage of the milkhouse. Olei held his breath. Just as quickly, the raider disappeared again down the ladder.

Olei waited for several moments, afraid to move, afraid the creature would suddenly burst onto the roof again. The screams were fewer; the sounds of the raid were fading. His defiance was gradually overtaken by a sense of guilt and shame. The Ruhatsi were real. He had scoffed at his neighbors for their simple superstitions, only to be forced to watch as they were cut to pieces. He lay on his belly, face planted in the stone roof, and sobbed.

Eventually, he worked up the nerve to peek over the nearest edge. The raiders seemed to have vanished. The fire consuming the collapsed milkhouse was already burning lower. Fighting throughout the village had ceased. He decided to wait long enough to be sure the raiders were gone, then run for home.

He waited, and the streets remained quiet. The cries of anguish had disappeared. He waited longer, and the fires burned lower. Whatever warmth the black stone of the Altarnary had absorbed from the Sun was now gone, and he began to shiver. He noticed a glow from the east and wondered if the raiders had started fires far in the mountains, but it was only the Sojourner settling toward the eastern horizon, becoming as orange as fire itself. It gazed sadly down upon the carnage of Halrin's Spur.

When the Sojourner disappeared and the eastern sky began to turn pink, Olei finally worked up the nerve to leave the rooftop. He climbed down and walked quietly to the center of the building. The priest was splayed on his back near the altar, the floor covered with his blood. Olei walked slowly through the battered front doors and onto the steps. Four bodies sprawled on the stone terrace.

The village was silent. Olei expected to see at least a cat or a rat, but nothing seemed to have escaped the night's butchery. He walked carefully out into the street. The man who had been run down by the horse lay on his back, his chest crushed, his head half removed from his neck. Olei walked back toward his little house next to the river. In a village full of the dead, he was now a stranger, the only one moving where stillness was the rule. The door to his house was broken. His mother lay curled in the corner. She possessed that breathless stillness that can only be found in the dead. Even the blood had stopped moving.

Olei sat in the room with his mother until the Sun was bright in the sky. His fear was gone, replaced with hopelessness and shame for not having saved her. He cried, then stopped, then looked at her and sobbed again. Finally, thirst made him stand and uncover one of the water jars. It was full. The raiders had not bothered to disturb the jars; they appeared to have taken nothing but lives.

He drank, then took bread, a pair of onions, and some

dried meat and tied them in a bundle. He made his way back to the Altarnary, where he sat in the altar room until he started to feel sick staring at the body of the priest. He felt better if he was moving, so he hunted until he found the priest's private quarters. He grabbed a couple of hides and one of the priest's cloaks and dragged them back up to the small storage cell at the top of the stairs. By early afternoon he had made a reasonably comfortable nest, which included a stash of additional food.

Later in the day, he heard hoof beats. He crawled out onto the roof and over to the edge. A single rider on a massive horse cantered slowly down from the North Road, surveying the carnage. An arms man, dressed in the uniform of the Crown. Olei almost jumped up to shout to the rider that he was here, that he was the only one alive. But the huge horse had him spooked, and he kept quiet. The arms man rode out of town and no one followed.

High clouds gathered in the northern sky before dark. Olei huddled in his cloak and hides and slept little. The next day it rained. Water slanting through the oculus began to wash away the priest's blood on the floor below.

Four days later, Olei decided he was going to have to leave his refuge soon. He had scrounged enough food to last some time, but he was running out of water. Water from the village well smelled foul. The priest's body filled the Altarnary with a rank smell as well, as did the bodies in the street, which became ever more distorted and inhuman with each passing day. But then, from his perch on the roof, he spied the first group of survivors making their way slowly toward town from the burned wreck of the milkhouse. Olei climbed down and was standing in the doorway when a small handful of men picked their way through the alley and onto the main road. One looked up from the bottom of the terrace and spied Olei in the shadows.

"Precious Alera," he exclaimed. "It's a child."

2

A scraping noise burned through the fog of Olei's dreams. He was awake but tried not to move. The world remained silent. He peeked with one eye. Stars glimmered in a black sky through a single high window. It was still the middle of the night, so he snuggled down into the warmth of his furs, hoping for more sleep.

He heard the scrape again, much closer, and then something was in the room with him, and his furs were flung back.

"Enough dreams," Tobin's voice said, amplified by the stone walls of the small chamber. The click of an ember pot, and a tiny glow silhouetted a tall figure in a cloak. Then the ember touched the wick of Olei's lantern, and the room filled with weak yellow light.

"Who do we serve today?" Tobin said, as he had said every morning for the past two years. "Dress warm and meet me in the kitchen. I want to be moving before daybreak. We can say our prayers along the way."

He turned and started down the stairs. Olei pulled up the furs and gave himself one extra moment, then rose and pulled on double pairs of leggings, followed by his boots. He slipped the knife over his head and tucked it under his tunic. Tobin disliked the knife but had not out-and-out forbade him from wearing it. He grabbed the lantern and pattered down the stairs, crossed the gloom of the altar room, then stopped at the altar. He looked up and could see a handful of tiny stars in the opening above. The altar itself was an ugly thing made of black granite. Olei wondered if it was meant to represent a star, but if so, it was asymmetric and disproportionate, with five rays instead of six, one of which was much shorter than the others.

The one time he had seen Tobin use the altar was for the oblation at SummerTop, the ritual sacrifice. Olei was surprised by how much it upset him to see a small animal killed, considering the massacre he had witnessed the previous year. This morning he completed his own private ritual in front of the altar. He dropped a tiny morsel from his previous night's supper, hoping a mouse would later find it, the altar thus a source of life rather than death. Then he headed down a short flight of stairs toward brightness and the considerable noise of someone lifting and dropping heavy loads. The kitchen was fully lit with several lanterns, so Olei blew his out and set it aside.

"I need six more wheels of cheese," Tobin said, "and four casks of cider. All in the cart, please." The two-wheeled cart filled the middle of the room. A pair of long, well-worn handles pointed to a door in the far wall. Olei had spent many days pushing this cart, and as the handles wore even smoother, his hands had transformed from soft to blistered, then callused and sturdy.

Olei recalled his first trip to the milkhouse, shortly after rebuilding had begun, and how Tobin had traded a half-dozen bottles of ale for the same number of buckets of milk, as well as a smelly burlap bag containing the stomachs of two recently slaughtered calves. Even more vividly, he recalled washing and chopping the stomachs into slippery chunks, which Tobin then instructed him to soak in vinegar. A couple of days later he decanted the resulting greasy liquid, and, following Tobin's orders, added it to a cauldron containing the milk, simmering over a low fire. He assumed he was witnessing Tobin perform rare vitachemical secrets and was surprised and a bit disappointed to find the result of this magic was the formation of curds, which he then helped wash and load into a pair of long-handled wooden presses. Tobin and he completed this exercise ten more times over the next two passages. By the end Olei was doing virtually all the work by memory, while Tobin watched and offered occasional suggestions. He figured his reward for all this work would be ready access to cheese whenever he felt a bit hungry, but now most of that work was going out the door again, and Olei feared he would see little in return.

Tobin must have sensed Olei's unspoken concern. "We will keep enough cheese to survive another Winter. There are only two of us. How much do we need, anyway?"

The remaining two wheels seemed scant resources for two, and of course it was rarely just two, as Tobin often invited whoever passed through the front doors of the Altarnary to stay and eat.

"This cheese is our currency," Tobin said. "We will trade it with those who have other things we want. We keep what little we require, then multiply the value of the rest, until we can care for the greatest number of persons in need."

Tobin disappeared, then returned carrying something stiff, bundled inside an ornate cloth. "We must not forget the Mother," he said. He opened the door leading out of the kitchen. Olei grabbed the familiar handles and pushed to get the cart moving. They headed into the dark alley behind the Altarnary.

Their first stop took them down several twisting tracks to the smoking pits at the edge of their small village. There, Tobin traded four wheels of cheese for an equal number of heavily smoked bison quarters. The slabs of meat and bone were heavier than the cheese wheels they replaced, and afterward Olei had to lean into the cart to keep it moving. The cider they traded for sacks of brown beans and barley, plus two jugs of sorghum syrup. Finally, Tobin directed them toward the well-worn track which ran from town to the milkhouse. Late Summer rains had turned it to mud, which had then dried into crisscrossing ruts that grabbed the cart's wheels and yanked Olei off-balance.

The first rays from the Sun caught the tops of the trees on the far side of the river, turning their yellowing leaves to gold. Olei watched the shadows shrink and hide themselves in the forest as the day took its proper form.

Tobin walked beside him, carrying the Mother like one would a child, enjoying the morning and appearing unconcerned with Olei's efforts.

"We have our own garden, right?" Tobin said.

Olei nodded. Of course they did. Tobin's statement was not a question, but the preamble to a teaching moment.

"We have our own garden, where we grow turnips and onions, and brown beans and tomatoes. From this we eat well all Summer and save some for the Winter. In addition, those in the village who have the means give a measure of their wealth to the Altarnary. Some comes to us as coin, which the Crown's arms men are quick to take as their own when they visit, and which I always have available, lest they decide to collect their debt directly from the people. But we are gifted more than coin. We get bread from the bakery: a day old, too hard for them to sell, but good enough for us. We get apples from our orchard. We get scraps of meat from the bisonmen, but most importantly, we get the milk they believe they can spare. From these gifts we make cider and cheese. Our own time and sweat we give freely, as servants of the gods. Then we trade the cheese and cider to obtain meat and grains of greater value, which finally we take and distribute to those who are most in need. Thus, the Altarnary multiplies its gifts to help our less fortunate brothers and sisters."

Olei maneuvered the cart so the wheels ran on the grass median and to one side of the ruts, making his task easier. "The old priest never gave anything away," he said.

"Easy to disparage the dead," Tobin replied. "They cannot accuse you in turn."

Olei labored in silence. This was not a new conversation. In the days following the slaughter, Olei had found the dead priest's extensive storehouses and had moved a fair amount of it to more secure places known only to him. The overall lack of esteem the survivors of Halrin's Spur felt for their former priest was reflected in the way his body was unceremoniously heaved into the pile to be burned by the riverbank. It did not take long for them to return and plunder the Altarnary's pantries. Olei stood by and watched, occasionally helping. No one recognized him, and, more importantly, no one thought to ask how he managed to survive the next several passages. When Tobin arrived toward the end of Summer, assigned to Halrin's Spur by the Panthea, he seemed to accept that Olei was as much a natural part of the Altarnary as its furnishings. Olei threw himself into his new role as Tobin's guide and assistant and began to believe that he might be able to live in the Altarnary indefinitely.

And then one day, while they worked in the altar room, Tobin had suggested, in an offhanded way, that Olei must have been devastated by the death of the old priest.

"Not me," Olei had said.

"But he must have meant something to you. If not grandfather, then uncle, perhaps?"

Olei had been suddenly wary. "No. My mother…I mean, I worked for him, like I do for you."

"Surprising. The Panthea usually doesn't allow the hire of children. Too much risk of abuse, it seems."

"He was training me. He was training me to be a priest."

It seemed like a terrific answer until it came out of his mouth, after which Olei realized he had stepped onto dangerous ground.

"That's interesting," Tobin said. "Training his own priests. By chance, did he tell you how long that would take?"

"Long time," Olei muttered. He looked at Tobin carefully, trying to discern anything that might reveal the man's age, and thus his own time in training. "Longer than you," he added.

"Well, that could be a very long time, as I'm not a priest," Tobin replied. Olei stepped back, forgetting for a moment the deception he was attempting to weave. "I spent four years at the School for Servants and have my warrant. But, as he must have told you, servants who want to progress and become priests must spend two to four years in additional study and then swear the holy vows. I haven't done that." He looked steadily at Olei. "The Altarnary helps many in need. But it is not a boarding house for orphan children."

Olei felt his fiction collapse around him like the charred timbers of the milkhouse. He was lost. The man before him stood solid and assured of his place in the world, while Olei had nothing: no home, no family, and no place to go from here.

A shaft of sunlight poured through the central oculus onto one of the five arms of the altar, causing flakes in the stone to glitter brightly. By comparison, Olei felt like he was standing at the edge of a black shadow, with no choices except to disappear—or step forward.

"That old priest never gave anything to anyone," he said, trying to sound defiant. "I took things and he never saw me. No one ever sees me. And I don't care. He didn't miss them, and my mother was starving." He waited for Tobin's anger and stiffened himself to take a blow.

Tobin looked at him for a long moment. "Well, he isn't here to give his side of the story, is he?" He put his hands on his hips and stretched his back. "We should get a bite to eat before we tackle the rats in the storerooms, don't you think?" He turned and headed for the kitchen. After a moment, Olei followed. He had been following ever since.

"You said Panthea means all the gods. Why are we only taking the Mother?" Olei asked. The track had become smoother, making it easier to push the cart and still have enough breath to talk.

"The people here, the bisonherders, consider their god to be Alera, the Mother."

"But what about the other gods? Does that mean they don't think they're real, too?"

"For dozens of generations, each of the peoples of Lhosa believed in their own gods, depending on where they lived. But then Serenity the First received the Book of Obligations in his dreams. The book teaches us that all the gods are one family. Still, it's hard to change what people have believed in for a long, long time."

"Maybe the herders don't want the other gods to know about them," Olei said.

"When Serenity called for the Council of Antola, he brought representatives together from all over Lhosa. The gods were one family, he said, and the Eidos, the people of Lhosa, should be one family, too. He formed the Panthea, which teaches respect for the traditions of all gods and therefore respect for the people long associated with each god. The gods have much to give anyone who is willing to learn."

Olei found it hard to picture the gods as a family. And he didn't trust them to give anything without expecting more in return. When Tobin had entered his life, Olei viewed the gods as something to be avoided. But then Tobin just started talking to Olei as if he were continuing a conversation they had shared for years. He fed Olei a near continuous stream of anecdotes about the world and the gods and the work the two of them were doing. At first it all seemed random, but then

Olei began to make connections between the stories, and he realized Tobin was sketching a view of how people and gods connected in the wider world. In fact, Tobin seemed pleased when Olei asked about these connections, which spurred Olei to listen harder and think longer. In the two years since Tobin had taken over administration of the Altarnary at Halrin's Spur, Olei had gone from simply asking questions to pointing out inconsistencies and even contradictions in the stories. He thought at first this might make Tobin angry. But the man just kept talking.

Olei pushed the cart and reviewed what he had been taught. Alera was the wife of Malach, leader of the gods. Bochlus, the god of uncertainty and chaos, was Alera's wayward and troublesome brother. With the gods' protection, the Eidos had lived in peace and freedom throughout Lhosa. But then Lord Ruhax, the Lord Sorceros, created the marauding Ruhatsi. The Eidos were scattered wide across the world, losing sight of the family of the gods. Some worshipped Alera, while others favored Bochlus. But the Eidos who claimed Malach and brought their offerings to him found themselves in his favor. Eventually he made them great, and they ruled the land.

They were good stories, Olei thought, but he was bothered by certain things. If the gods were all one family, how did Lord Ruhax fit in, who seemed to have power over Malach and be nothing but evil? And how could gods be so powerful as to create the Sun and the Red Eye and the Sojourner, and yet not be able to manage affairs among themselves?

Olei's feet were cold and wet inside his thin bisonhide shoes. The Sun was just beginning to warm the heather and dry the heavy dew. His allowed his imagination to drift higher. The Ruhatsi lived at the edge of the desert, far to the north and west of Halrin's Spur, near vast smoking cracks in the ground. The Eidos lived almost everywhere else. Those who lived in faraway places such as Ismay supposedly sounded so different from people in Antola that it was as if they spoke a different language. Their skin was so pale that their veins were visible underneath. Olei looked at his own rich brown skin and felt thankful to have been born in Halrin's Spur.

And then there were the Polfre. Olei, like most people, had always assumed stories about small people whose eyes glowed in the dark were just legends. Then a small, light-brown woman came to see Tobin. She was not even as tall as Olei, but clearly old, with creases in her face and hair the color of rainclouds. She talked with Tobin long into the evening. Olei was kept busy serving them food and cider. At one point the old woman motioned for Olei to step close. She took his hands in hers and he felt a gentle tingle through his forearms. Then she ran one hand carefully over his head. As strange as this was, Olei found it comforting. She smiled at him, and her eyes shimmered in the firelight like luminous spheres. Like a bison's eyes reflecting torchlight, Olei noticed. Later, he thought about how easy it was to accept the existence of the gods, and yet how easily he had dismissed the existence of the Polfre.

They were approaching the milkhouse, which had been rebuilt and was now being enlarged. Tobin unwrapped the bundle he carried, revealing a brightly painted, stylized wooden figure. He wrapped the cloth around his own neck and held the figure aloft. A few adults, all women, looked and began to point in their direction. Their outstretched arms attracted the attention of others, who then gained the attention of those around them. Soon several dozen people were migrating toward the wagon. Olei pushed it into the thick grass beside the track. Tobin motioned for Olei to clear some space in the back of the wagon. He had Olei take the cloth from his neck and drape it over the back of the wagon, and then Tobin carefully stood the wooden statue on top. "Time for prayers," he said. They both stood in front of the figure.

Tobin placed his hands on his chest. "What do we offer if not our lives?" they said in rough unison. Then Tobin stood a moment longer, his lips barely moving, while Olei studied the carved figure and tried to be still.

The first of the bisonfolk walked up quietly. They clasped their hands in front of their hearts as Tobin had done and kneeled to kiss the cloth, careful not to unbalance the figure. Olei heard bits of murmured prayers. "Alera protect us… Alera make us grow strong."

"They know this is just a carving, right?" Olei whispered.

"They know this is not Alera herself, if that's what you mean," Tobin replied. "But it's more than a carving. They believe Alera hears their voices through the image. They respect it the way they would respect Alera if she were actually here before them."

"Friends!" Tobin called out as the crowd began to gather. "Alera hears your prayers. She sees your arms raised to the sky; she tastes your tears. Today she brings a small token of her bounty for the weakest among you. For the rest she brings protection and peace, and the blessing that your milkhouse and your herds will be stronger and more numerous than before!" A few murmurs rose from the group. "Friends, go and find whatever you saved for yourself this day. Uncover those hidden morsels and bring them here. If you have nothing, then go and fetch clear water from the well so that we can drink. Let us eat together in the warmth of the new Sun!"

The crowd was growing, their mood becoming brighter. Most of those who lived near the milkhouse were making their way toward Tobin and the wagon. A number had disfiguring burn scars on their arms and faces. Skins and furs appeared and were laid on the grass. Two middle-aged men approached Tobin and grasped his forearm in greeting. They set to work unloading the remaining items from the cart. Tobin was engaged in conversation with the men and didn't notice as Olei slipped away.

The bison village had undergone various stages of rebirth since the Ruhatsi raid. Several new small houses were finished and stood sturdily, their wood still the color of straw. Many more temporary shelters of branches and skins were clustered together. And there were a few structures that had not fully succumbed to the fire. Olei made his way to one hut of stacked stone and scorched wood.

Obo, the man who had lived with them after Olei's father disappeared, lay on a pile of straw heaped against one wall. The hut was dark, as the only window faced west, away from the morning Sun. The stench of putrid meat was overwhelming. Obo's right leg was cracked and swollen, with gray crusts oozing fluid. His hands were misshapen, his face almost unrecognizable due to its scars.

"Obo?"

"There's nothing to take, you whelp," Obo said.

"Obo, it's me. It's Olei."

Obo took several wheezing breaths. "All of this and you're still alive? How come it, boy?"

It was a conversation they had repeated several times since the raid, as Obo's burns had cracked and failed to heal, then festered, and now had deepened, taking the big man's strength and his mind. "I had a hiding place," Olei said.

"You're a smart one. And your mother? You hide her?"

"No," Olei said, as he had said many times before.

"No," Obo repeated. "Too much to hope. They were devils from inside the earth. I saw their horns and their faces. I don't understand it. They live just to kill."

Olei vividly recalled the man he had seen cut down in front of the Altarnary. "There was a horse," he said.

"Ruhatsi don't ride horses," Obo said. "They're silent. They move through the earth, then spring out and destroy everything."

"Your leg is getting worse," Olei noted.

Obo made a *humph* sound. "It turned poison inside, and that's running though my veins."

"I can find some frogperch," Olei offered. During a previous visit, Obo had instructed him in the healing properties of the orange, shelf-like mushrooms. Often, they could be found at the edge of the riverbank. When he had been stronger, Obo had steeped them to make a tea, which he poured over his bandages.

"Too late for that."

"Well, I've got the priest here." Olei, said, briefly imagining Tobin correcting him. "He can do something." *Tobin is better than a priest*, Olei thought. *He knows things the old priest didn't.*

"No being alive is going to fix this leg."

Olei felt his jaw quiver. He tried to blink away the tears blurring his vision. His breath came in short sniffs. He glanced around, trying to focus on inanimate things: a rough shelf affixed to one wall holding a pair of tin plates and cups; Obo's herding staff leaning against another, whittled smooth and twisted like a backbone worn down by a lifetime of work. The end of the staff was blackened from use tending the fire in the small stone hearthgrate. He listened. Obo's breaths were now deep and ragged.

"Fetch me a dipper of water. I'm finding it harder to reach it myself."

Olei welcomed the opportunity to focus on a task. A wooden pail and dipper were on the floor near Obo. The bottom of the pail was barely damp. Olei grabbed the pail and ran outside, heading for a well near the milkhouse. The river was closer, but as a young child Olei had learned to say "dirty downriver" almost as soon as he could speak—a reflex for village living his mother had built into him. Fortunately, the well was fresh. He pulled up a bucket of cool water that he transferred to Obo's pail before hurrying back toward the hut.

A massive bull bison had appeared out of nowhere, and now stood between Olei and the hut. He stopped. The animal stared at him. Its eyes were the size of a goose's eggs, and as dark as the bottom of the well, except for flecks of gold in their depths. Thick, black horns curled tightly against the side of its head. Tufts of white hair protruded prominently between the horns. The animal was the Korun, the chief of the herd. Its front shoulder stood higher than Olei's head. It examined Olei for a long moment, as if deciding whether he was worthy to serve the old herder inside the hut, then it slowly turned, and even more slowly stepped away. Feeling vaguely guilty, Olei walked the rest of the way back.

Obo's breathing was still ragged. Olei tried to hold a dipper full of water to the older man's lips, but he sipped only enough to moisten his mouth while the rest ran down his chin. Olei searched the small hut in vain for anything he could use to make his friend more comfortable. Outside again, he walked over to the newly rebuilt milkhouse. No one was around; Tobin had been successful in getting everyone's attention over in the field. Olei pilfered an armload of scrap wood and carried it back to the hut; he then returned with one of Obo's tin cups and filled it with sawdust. He filched as many pieces of firewood from the surrounding huts as he could carry and took everything back into the dim room.

Since he had started venturing out with Tobin, Olei had learned always to keep a few things in his pockets. He produced a pair of flints and soon had a small flame going amidst a cone of sawdust. He fed the flame chips and sticks until it was large enough to withstand some of the heavier kindling, and soon he had a decent fire popping and cracking in the hearth. The smell of burning resin began to win out over the smell of rotting flesh. Olei felt like he could breathe normally again.

He stacked the remaining firewood in a way he hoped would allow the fire to feed itself as it collapsed. He knew that at best it would keep the room warmer and brighter for only a while longer.

He lifted the long herding staff from the wall, thinking to use it to stir the fire. It was heavier than he expected, and warm, as if it had been setting next to the fire for hours. Using it for a stirring stick seemed wrong. He replaced it carefully.

Obo had not re-awakened. The same empty ache Olei had felt sitting next to his mother's body began to fill him again. His jaw quivered and tears rolled down his face. Wiping his cheeks with his hands, he strode purposefully out and headed toward the crowd without looking back.

Perhaps six dozen people had spread out on the grass near the wagon, some standing, others sitting. Happy chatter was punctuated with the laughter and shouts of children running around the periphery. Someone had brought a pair of sawbucks and boards, and the carving of Alera now sat higher and to one side, smiling benignly at her subjects. One wheel of cheese and half of the smoked meat had been set aside, but the rest had been eaten down to crumbs and bones. Olei was surprised that anything was left over. Then he noticed people had other things to eat as well. Almost everyone had flatbread, and he saw the remains of what once had been sweetened cakes. Crocks full of pungent, fermented vegetables had been brought out and were sitting to one side of the meat and cheese. People were sharing everything they had. Olei brightened as he wandered through the group, picking up and eating bits of cheese and bread and meat until he felt full himself. He returned to the wagon and leaned against it, letting the Sun warm him as it peaked in its daily arc.

By the time the Sun was well into the west, the bisonfolk were drifting back toward their work or their huts. The carving of Alera had been moved closer to the construction site. Under the guidance of a middle-aged woman, two of the bisonherders had already fashioned a much sturdier platform for the figure. They would no doubt have a hutch built to shelter Alera by nightfall.

Tobin had Olei walk through the flattened grass, picking up pieces of food that had not been consumed. By the time he had gleaned the area, there seemed to be as much left over from what people had brought with them as had been in the wagon to begin with. The scraps were soon tucked away in bundles and left next to Alera's figure, and he and Tobin were back on the path toward town.

Olei's warm mood faded as he walked. He had planned to check on Obo again, to take him a small bundle of food, but hadn't had a chance, or, he realized, hadn't really looked for one. Obo was right. He was already dead, save for the exact moment of his passing. Olei could not have done anything else to help. But then he thought of one other thing: his knife, tucked under his tunic. He could have slipped it under Obo's ribs and saved him from suffering the rats that would come when the fire faded and the Sun set.

"Tomorrow we continue the wood charring project," Tobin said.

"I don't know why people would buy half-burned wood," Olei replied.

"Not half-burned. Burned a special way."

The recovering village was on Olei's mind as they neared the outer huts of Halrin's Spur. The Ruhatsi were clever in their own evil way. They killed, looted, and destroyed, but left enough for the village to rebuild itself, like a tree that regrows from a stump if the roots are left undisturbed. Then they could return to kill and steal again. In a way, the people of Halrin's Spur were being harvested.

"Why do the Ruhatsi hate us so much?"

"Because Ruhax created them out of his own hateful heart."

Olei looked to the west, where the Red Eye burned high in the sky. "Why doesn't Malach just destroy Ruhax?" he said.

"I don't know. The gods do not share their thoughts with me."

"He should kill Ruhax. Then there would be no evil left in the world."

"Do you really think so?" Tobin replied.

They reached the entrance to the Altarnary kitchen. Olei maneuvered the wagon into a small corral before stepping inside. He looked at the half-empty shelves, but with less trepidation than he had felt that morning. "They brought as much food as we did," he said.

Tobin yawned and sat on one of the tall kitchen stools. His voice was softer than usual. "If everyone worries about getting their share, then there are never shares left over. But if everyone shares with others, then there is always more than enough to go around. That is Alera's blessing." He stood and stretched his back. "Put everything away before you go to bed. Tomorrow we work hard."

Olei thought about Obo, who had worked hard and might already be dead, and then about his mother, who worked hard raising him. People worked hard every day. As far as he could tell, they bore their pain alone. Why should their success belong to the gods? The blessings of Alera seemed highly selective.

"Every morning you ask me 'who do we serve?' Isn't there more than service?" he asked.

"Do you have something better in mind?"

Olei didn't know how to express it, but he was sure the answer was yes.

3

Two days after Alera's feast Olei had returned to check on Obo, but the old herdsman was dead. A small handful of his fellow herders helped Olei get the body out of the hut and place it on a small pyre of wood scraps. Olei imagined it would be over quickly, but one of the men told him no, that they would likely have to build another pyre and burn what was left on it. The life of a person could be extinguished as easily as a candle flame, but the body, it seemed, was more durable.

Visiting the hut for the last time, Olei hefted the herding staff. He decided to keep it, his one tangible memory of his friend. He worked on the staff when he had time, smoothing it with pumice stone and rubbing bits of animal tallow into it until the wood took on a deep, dark gleam. He scraped the char from the blackened end until he reached solid heartwood. Despite his work, this part remained as black as the char that had covered it.

He thought he would carry the staff around, using it like a walking stick. Tobin put an end to that quickly. "Why do you need it?" he asked. Olei wasn't sure how to explain its value as a way of remembering his friend. "Are you a herder? Or perhaps a sorcerer," Tobin griped. So Olei kept it hidden in his room and rarely brought it out.

By the following Summer Olei no longer looked up at Tobin when they talked, and the Summer after that he could see the top of Tobin's head. Though taller, he felt thinner, and even though Tobin continued to reassure him they would not starve, he felt hungry all the time. But though his stomach often felt empty, it was not hollowed out: his muscles had grown hard as wood below his ribs, and his arms were measurably thicker than they had been a year before.

New clothes had been necessary, and now Olei was dressed more like Tobin, with sturdy breeches and a one-piece hooded cloak he often wore outside of the Altarnary. Unlike Tobin's supple leather cloak, Olei's was stiff and rough, and somewhat oversize, but it would soften and come to fit better with time.

Tobin, it seemed, had the energy of ten men. He had ideas for everything, but instead of doing all the work himself, he skillfully organized and motivated others to work with him. Halrin's Spur had been transformed in the four years since the raid. Any sign of the night's destruction was gone. In fact, there was no trace of the rough houses and skewed shops that had once crowded up to the edge of the river. They had been torn down, and a broad expanse of land, at least three gross hands wide, now extended from the banks of the river to the first structures of the village. The Altarnary itself stood like an arms-captain in the middle of his men, daring anyone to cross the river and try to assault them again.

A dozen people from the village had been employed to work in the newly cleared space between the river and the Altarnary, planting and staking many gross of small cuttings in orderly patterns. It seemed an odd place to grow a garden, especially as it was within the flood plain of the river. Tobin had said the stakes weren't necessary, but not all people trusted him as Olei did, so they struggled on. The plants were remarkably hardy, Tobin said, and in any other place would be considered an enormous nuisance. They were cloudnettle, and within a few short years they would grow up and knit together into a soft, billowy, yet utterly impenetrable hedge of tiny stinging thorns. The branches themselves were pliable and hard to break, and they contained a substance that resisted fire. Attempting to hack one's way through would fill the air with minute stinging needles, which would drift into the marauder's eyes and lungs. After one touch, no person or animal alive would try to push through them to reach the village from the river.

Tobin had set out strengthening the village's defenses without being asked and without asking for permission, either. He had simply started working, and then directing, and soon the people of Halrin's Spur responded as if this had been their plan all along. But defenses were not his only preoccupation. Tobin had shown Olei the secret of changing firewood into a form that was better preserved and could generate a hotter fire than mere logs. Until then, Olei had not imagined that fire could be hotter than it already was. Tobin explained that hotter fire was the secret to many things that made a village advance. Charcoal-fed fires allowed smiths to melt and cast metals more easily, and even combine metals into stronger forms. The making of charcoal yielded pitch, useful for waterproofing. And, if made well enough, Tobin said, the charcoal could be sold to other communities, getting more needed goods from them in return.

Charcoal was on Olei's mind. Two years before, he had never heard of it, and now he was more familiar with it than any person in Halrin's Spur, save Tobin himself. Across the river a half-dozen charcoal kilns rose from the muddy banks like huge, misshapen tortoise shells. They were his handiwork.

Olei learned quickly through trial and error. And, like

Tobin, he soon had a small group of men and women doing most of the labor for him, as they cleared woodland on the far side of the river, built mounds out of the resulting logs, and covered them with mud. They learned to build fires deep in the middle of the log piles that heated the surrounding wood without allowing it to burn, until the pile was transformed into hard, black lumps. Tobin said he had uses for all that the charcoal. But over time, Olei and his team became so good at making it that Tobin began to have thoughts of selling it, too.

And then they found buyers. Caravan traders traveled the Great Road between Antola and the outlying cities, buying in one place and selling in another. Word of their uniquely well-made charcoal reached Bhinton, the largest town between Halrin's Spur and Antola itself. A small delegation had been dispatched to find out if it was worth their while. Craftsmen from the city of Madros, in particular, had use for hot-burning charcoal. They were famed for their glass, which they not only blew into vessels, but could fashion into flat discs. Windows in the Lord Governor's house in Bhinton were filled with pieces of flat glass. Olei had seen them. They looked black to him, but he was told they were as clear as water. Someone could stand at the window in the worst weather and not have to close the shutters. In Antola, not only did the Crown's palace have dozens and dozens of glass windows, but shops and homes had them, too, or so Tobin said. Antola was a city of riches.

Charcoal was not only used in glass furnaces. Madros was equally as famous for its tools, which required bronze, which required hot fires. Bronze knives and axes and plow blades were essentials even in Halrin's Spur. And though there was no war, there was always a drive to prepare for it, and that meant business remained brisk for makers of swords and spears and arrowheads.

For more than a passage Tobin had been preparing for the

arrival of their guests, which resulted in more work for Olei. Compared to the freedom he had been given to manage the charcoal kilns, he was once again under Tobin's thumb for the delegation visit, and he resented it. "We want to impress them," Tobin said, but did not explain why. One day Olei mentioned questions he was eager to ask about the wider world. "Don't engage them in idle talk," Tobin said. "And if they have questions, refer them to me, even if you think you know the answer."

"What if you don't know the answer either?" Olei asked.

Tobin paused, appearing irritated.

"You have little experience with people from the wider world. Traders can look at you and practically tell what you are thinking. They will use any advantage. The next thing you know, you feel as if you are doing them a favor to let them take your goods for free."

"They will not get my charcoal without a good price," Olei said. And in a way, it was his charcoal. He had taken what Tobin had taught him and had taught it to his crews, only at greater scale. He had multiplied the gifts, just as Tobin taught. He thought he deserved to be present for the negotiations, at the very least.

"This isn't about your pride, Olei. Pride will bring you more pain than praise."

Olei had his own assistant, Calus, one of the children who lived around the milkhouse, four years younger than himself. Since the last New Sojourner, he had been working Calus hard in preparation for the visit, having him scrub the floor of the altar room and the steps of the Altarnary. They pulled out long-stored cushions and beat them dust-free, then he set the boy to polishing bronze candle trees until they shone like gold. The day before their visitors arrived, they dragged two long tables from the back of the Altarnary and positioned them on the terrace in front of the great doors. Poles were fitted into sockets and cloth was affixed to create an awning over the tables. Tobin's intent was to serve their guests a midday meal where they could not help but look out and see the charcoal kilns.

Now, Olei stood just inside the Altarnary doors, waiting for the delegation. They had left Bhinton four days before, a stately pace even for walking, so there was plenty of advanced warning of their approach. The previous evening, they had camped within sight of the milkhouse and had even made some small purchases of milk and sorghum syrup. The delegation itself consisted of four caravan merchants, traveling within their own carriage, as well as three lancemen and an arms-captain from the Bhinton shield. Not only was the wagon pulled by horses, but the arms-captain rode his own horse. Horses were a rare sight; the bisonfolk gaped at the magnificent animals accompanying the delegation. It took a strong and skilled rider just to stay atop a massive warhorse. The arms-captain's presence was a show of strength not lost on those who gathered to peer at them from the fringes of their camp. By late morning the delegation had doused their cook fires, packed the tents, and hitched the carriage. Nonetheless, it was after mid-day before they rode abreast of Halrin's Spur, turned off the road, and started down the track toward the Altarnary and their welcoming party.

Tobin and several other men from the community waited on the stone terrace. In addition to the charcoal, they had brought and hoped to sell their best tanned bison hides, which were stacked at one corner of the terrace. Olei felt left out. He had assumed that he would be part of the welcoming party. Instead, Tobin had shooed him behind the doors, declaring the delegation would not be pleased to be greeted by a boy of sixteen years, no matter how talented. Olei was to act the part of servant and not speak unless necessary. Tobin had hired several other villagers to act as servants and servers as well. Olei was not even in charge of them.

The delegation rolled up the road at a snail's pace and stopped at the broad bottom steps. Four individuals stepped out and blinked in the bright sunlight. The first three were of average height, appeared very well-fed, and were dressed in the richest clothing Olei had ever seen: thick red and green fabrics shot through with golden threads. The three men all had a sheen on their faces. Their clothing was too heavy for the day; the closed carriage no doubt had only made them warmer.

The fourth occupant of the carriage was almost a hand taller than any of the other three and dressed differently as well, wearing a short black cloak covering an unadorned blue tunic and matching breeches. At first Olei could not tell if he was looking at a man or a woman, but then noticed the slightest hint of breasts beneath the tunic.

"She's even taller than you," Calus said softly, having appeared at Olei's shoulder. Olei dismissed the younger boy's grin with a wave. "Go see that the refreshments are brought up," he said.

Olei watched Tobin descend the steps and greet the three elaborately dressed travelers, while giving the tall woman barely a nod. They all ascended the steps toward the prepared tables. The arms-captain dismounted and handed his reins to one of the lancemen.

"Your men are welcome to join us, Captain," Tobin said to the man. "Of course, this is an Altarnary, so I would ask that they leave their weapons at the foot of the steps."

"My men disarm when I tell them," the captain growled. The three lancemen took up positions in front of the building, standing spread-legged in the warming Sun and staring menacingly at the unthreatening river. Olei took note that the captain kept his own sword at his side as he climbed the steps to the terrace. Tobin surely noticed as well but did not make any further comment.

"Welcome, friends and guests," Tobin said. "We are

honored by your presence." The merchants extended two fingers and each touched Tobin's outstretched palm. The tall woman did not acknowledge the greeting, and after a brief pause, Tobin seemed to ignore her in turn.

The parties took their seats, and Olei and his fellow villagers hurried to fill cups with ale and bring trays of cheese and early vegetables. Olei served the officer. He seemed to have relaxed and was enjoying the food and the breeze coming off the river, paying about as much attention to Olei as he would to a bird flitting around the table.

The tall woman, however, was watching him intently. Feeling uncomfortable, he tried to avoid her table as much as he could, but the moment came when the ale jug on her table needed replacing. Olei picked up a full jug in the kitchen and headed for the table, telling himself he was just imagining things.

But as he stepped onto the terrace, it was obvious the woman was still staring at him, and as he set the jug down, she reached out and grabbed his hand.

"Such long fingers for a herder's bastard," she said softly.

Olei tried to pull his hand back, but her grip was strong. "I am not a herder's bastard," he said.

"No? Where are your parents?"

Before Olei could answer she let go with her left hand, slapped him sharply across the cheek, and grabbed his hands again. He jerked backward, but her grip was strong, and his arms and wrists suddenly felt as if they were on fire. "Just a kitchen boy, is that it?" she said. She let go suddenly and he stumbled backward into the table behind him.

"Thanla, that is unseemly," said the oldest of the other merchants, a man named Rohul. He had been engaged in conversation with Tobin and appeared to be the one in charge. The woman merely smiled back.

Olei was about to protest that being struck in the face was

more than unseemly, but Tobin calmly said "Olei is an orphan. His mother was killed by raiders." He gazed steadily at the woman. "He is under my protection in the Altarnary."

"My apologies, your grace," said Rohul. "Our companion has proven to have rough edges. Thanla, leave the boy alone." He raised a cup in Olei's direction. "Fine work, young man."

Olei retreated to the pantry in the back of the Altarnary, his feelings hurt far more than his face. He found reasons not to come out again until the meal was finished.

Tobin had selected what he considered the best examples of the charcoal he meant to sell. After the tables were cleared, Olei began stacking trays with the samples. Calus suddenly appeared with a consternated look on his face. "Tobin said not yet. They have asked for the sacrifice."

Olei was sure Calus had not understood. "It's not SummerTop," he said.

"They have asked for Malach's Oblation. Tobin said to get the bird."

Olei shook his head. His distaste for their visitors was growing. "Then light the candles," he replied irritably.

He knew from experience that Tobin disliked the sacrificial ceremony as well. Olei had now watched him perform it three times, always at SummerTop as expected, an offering of gratitude for the beginning of a new year. Olei failed to understand how killing another creature was supposed to satisfy the gods. Unlike every other question, this one Tobin failed to answer. The choice of animal was not specified; Tobin seemed to prefer pigeons. In both instances he had spoken the words of the ceremony perfunctorily, then had sliced the pigeon through the breast, allowing the blood to flow down his bare arm and drip onto the altar, before tossing it on the altar and walking away. Olei came in later and cleaned up the blood, then took the carcass behind the Altarnary and burned it. "Is it still there?" Tobin had asked the first time, while Olei was still cleaning up the blood. He thought for a moment Tobin was being critical of his cleaning skills, but Tobin only patted him on the shoulder as he worked. "Apparently the gods have no use for a dead pigeon. Imagine that," he had added.

At the beginning of every Summer Tobin climbed to the roof to capture a new pigeon. He caged and fed the bird so it would be ready for the ceremony. Olei had seen him reach into the cage and pet the bird on the head, trying to calm it. Tobin was stern but never cruel. It was no wonder he had no taste for this particular function of his job.

Olei stepped into the small cupboard. A cage holding the pigeon sat next to the window. The pigeon flapped a bit when Olei lifted the cage, but then settled down as he carried it to the altar room. Calus had placed a table near the altar, covered with a thick white cloth and supporting a wide bowl of water. Olei set the cage next to the bowl and then retreated behind the columns. The woman had something to do with this, he was sure.

The lamps and candle trees were lit but were hardly necessary, as daylight streamed through the oculus and gradually crawled over the altar. The silver flakes in the black stone flicked tiny, bright reflections across the walls. The delegation filed inside the circle of columns and stood facing the altar. Tobin appeared from the back of the room and stepped in front of the altar, facing the delegation. His face was a mask, devoid of emotion.

"The gods have blessed us greatly. They have given us food and they have given us shelter. And they have given us the gift of knowledge, second only to their own. But life we only borrow," he intoned.

He stepped to the table and dipped his arms in the water. Then, arms dripping, he opened the cage and deftly grabbed the bird, wings pinned to its body. The bird bobbed its head nervously.

A silver dagger, all of one piece, with a narrow, leaf-shaped blade, sat in the center of the table. Tobin picked it up and held it above his head with one hand, the bird in the other.

"Mighty gods," he intoned, "we return to you what is yours." And as he said the next line, the members of the delegation repeated it with him. "May our enemies fear your wrath and feel our swords." Then, with a swift motion, he slashed into the bird's breast. Blood spurted across the altar. The motion was so swift that the bird itself seemed surprised: it cocked its head and stared at the blade. Tobin held the bird aloft while the surge of blood slowed. He then turned his back to the delegation and placed bird and dagger gently on the altar. Olei noticed a quick movement of Tobin's hand as he neatly broke the bird's neck, ending its suffering. He dipped his arms again, turning the water red, and then walked out the way he came, trailing pink drops.

The delegation stood around the altar, not sure what to do next. "That was quick," the woman called Thanla said, disappointment obvious in her tone. Olei looked at her through slitted eyes. He was sure now that she had been the one to insist on the ceremony.

Tobin reappeared, having donned his cloak. Once again, he seemed like his normal self. "Shall we get on with what we came here to do?" he asked, ushering the delegation outside.

Olei was torn between his desire to see and hear the reaction to his work and his wish to avoid the tall woman. He took the bird and cage out behind the building and had Calus clean up the blood. He then brought the trays of charcoal onto the terrace, covered as if they were delicacies at a feast, before retreating several steps behind Tobin.

Tobin removed the covers from each plate of charcoal with a flourish. The charcoal had a subtle gleam in the diffuse light under the awning. Rohul picked up a piece about one hand in length and grimaced as he squeezed it. He then threw it to the terrace floor, hard. It shattered into several pieces. Olei, startled, looked to Tobin to object. But Tobin looked pleased, as if he had expected the man to do this.

"How long did you say you have been producing charcoal?" Rohul asked.

"Since the Summer before last, honored Rohul."

"Less than two years?"

Tobin nodded in reply. Rohul picked up a similar size piece and tapped it against the edge of the table. He tapped it again, harder, and finally whacked the table with considerable force, shattering this piece as well. Olei forced himself not to speak out. The behavior seemed frankly offensive, and yet still Tobin did nothing.

"Where do you get your wood?"

"We have found stands of willow and birch in the forests beyond the river," Tobin said. "They will allow for easy coppicing."

"You don't import it from the Greensee?"

Tobin shook his head. Rohul picked up one of the shattered pieces and held it up to the light. "I have known charcoaleries that have been firing wood for years that cannot make this quality," Rohul said.

Olei was surprised and suddenly pleased. He recalled that the first charcoal he and his crews had produced was soft and dull, more like compressed ash than anything. Without being told, he had worked to refine his techniques. As if he had always known what to do, he began stacking wood in different ways, leaving just the right empty spaces deep within each pile, and he had quickly learned how strong and for how long the fires had to burn to produce a harder and darker finished product. This just seemed like what charcoal should be. Now he had verification that his intuition had been correct. He smiled slightly, thinking Tobin would mention him at any moment.

Thanla appeared and stepped toward the table. Olei crept

back, suddenly glad that he had not said anything. She picked up one of the subtly gleaming pieces of charcoal.

"The Polfre make charcoal like this. But they do not share," she said, and gave Olei a half-lidded look.

"You are welcome to inspect our kilns, which you can see just across the river," Tobin replied. "We have spent long days perfecting how to stack and cover our wood."

Rohul stepped in front of the woman, and Olei used the opportunity to slip back into the altar room. He wanted nothing more to do with her. Calus had already cleaned the altar. Olei returned things to their rightful places and busied himself with household tasks for the rest of the day. He thought Tobin would eventually come and apologize for the behavior of his guests, but that didn't happen, and his resentment settled into a sullen mood.

A much larger feast had been planned for the evening, with everyone in Halrin's Spur invited, to be held in the wide space between the Altarnary and the river. Olei had nothing he needed to do for the feast, as it was being handled by the owner of the Curly Top and other villagers. A pit had been dug right in the middle of the road to hold a large fire, over which they were roasting an entire wild boar.

Eventually Olei had no more chores, so he slipped quietly up to his cell. He thought about climbing to the roof and watching the festivities in secret, but the thought only made him feel sadder. He sat on his cot, fingering the herding staff, and feeling calmer with the heavy piece of wood in his hands.

The Sun fell low in the west. The light through his window gradually climbed the wall, while the rest of the room grew gloomier. He heard familiar boots scraping on the steps. A moment later Tobin entered the room.

"Our friends are here. Rohul has already been entertaining anyone who will listen with stories. He was just telling the story of Gol and the Raptor. Have you heard it before?"

Olei shook his head.

"It seems there are as many versions as there are storytellers," Tobin said. He reached over and took the herding staff from Olei's hands. Olei thought he might scold him again for having it out.

"The head of this thing looks like the head of a raptor. Had you noticed?" Tobin asked.

Olei shook his head again. "I didn't think raptors were real."

"Rohul's stories are so good you will find yourself wondering. Come down."

Olei remained silent. Tobin handed the staff back. "The woman is not there."

"Who is she?" Olei asked.

"She's not a trader. Rohul probably hired her for extra protection. He thinks he has more control over her than he does with the arms-captain."

"But why would she slap me?"

"I don't know. Best just to stay away from her."

"I don't understand," Olei said.

"I don't either, to be truthful. But she acts as if she knows you, and she resents it. There is something…unique…about you, Olei. You have a way of learning things that makes it seem like you know them already. The way you order the woodpiles in the kilns, for example. It's as if you can pick up a piece of wood and read it, like you read a book, and know where to put it."

"It just seems right. There's nothing special to it."

Tobin stared at the wall for a few moments. The golden light in the upper corners of the room was fading fast. "Come down for something to eat. Rohul wants to talk to you. The woman has returned to their carriage and will not be joining us tonight." He handed the staff back to Olei. "Soon," he added, and headed back down the stairs.

Olei knew that Tobin was trying to make him feel better.

But he had been humiliated by the slap, and that humiliation was beginning to burn as resentment. The staff, initially cold and heavy, seemed to warm in his hands.

4

When Olei stepped cautiously out onto the Altarnary terrace, the fire in the roasting pit had died down, but the heat from the red coals was intense, and the boar's carcass spit and sizzled. Torches had been planted all around the terrace and out in the road. Most of the villagers and a large handful of the bisonherders had come to participate. The crowd was cheerful; ale from the Curly Top was plentiful.

Rohul was seated at the center of the festivities, close enough to feel the fire's warmth without getting burned by the hot coals. He spied Olei almost immediately and waved him over grandly.

"Here he is!" he cried. "The master of charcoal! Sit with me and have something to eat and drink. I am going to make a lot of coin because of you!" Several people laughed and clapped. Olei took the steps to the street, feeling a bit better. As promised, the woman was nowhere to be seen.

"Olei, what shall I do? Your people ask for bedtime stories. I need a challenge, a story worth telling. So, I said, find me the young charcoaler. Clearly, he has great knowledge; he must be a scholar. Find me Adept Olei, I said. He will know what story to tell!" More clapping, and a few cheers, as Rohul seemed to skip the requirement of schooling and granted Olei a degree on the spot. "No," Rohul continued. "I said, find me Master Olei!" Rohul's words were straying close to mockery, but seeming to sense he had gone too far, he hurriedly pushed on. "We need a topic, young Olei. What shall we talk about? What great mystery must we explain tonight?"

The crowd seemed to quiet. Olei glanced up at the sky, as stars began to twinkle. He noticed the mean glow of the Red Eye high in the west. He had the unsettling feeling that it had been waiting for him.

"Tell us about the Ruhatsi."

Olei's voice spread like ripples on a pond. The villagers closest to the fire stopped their conversations to listen, which gained the attention of those a bit farther out, until the street was quiet, filled with people listening expectantly.

"The Ruhatsi," Rohul repeated, looking around. The village was still. "If that is the story you want, then we must start with another story first." He paused for a moment, then began.

Now, if you don't know this story, believe that what I'm telling is true. And if you do know the story, remember that truth comes in many forms.

Long ago, something terrible happened to our ancestors, the people we call the Eidos. Those who survived that time left their home and made their way to a new land. What they found was beautiful beyond anything they had ever experienced. They found forests filled with tall trees, perfect for building new homes, and tall mountains feeding streams of pure water, and things to eat everywhere. Fruit trees were covered with pink and orange blossoms at the start of Summer and were bending under the weight of fruit by Harvest. Onions and turnips grew in the ground; beans and gourds grew on vines. The sea was filled with fish. They were surrounded by plenty, with everything they needed. They were happy and at peace, and they showed their gratitude by building shrines to Malach, who had led them to this land, and to Alera, who made it bountiful. And they built two great cities, Faerith and Forought, which sat astride the mouth of a great sea. And for many years they were blessed with everything they needed.

If you don't know, the word "Eidos" means "first people." But, in fact, they were not the first to live on Lhosa. Far from their cities, across Lhosa's great length, and unknown to the Eidos, lived another group of people. Some say that the Polfre and the Eidos were once a single people. But if so, that was so long ago no record of it remains. What is true is that the Polfre were here long before the Eidos arrived.

How long before, you ask? I will tell you. If you lived a gross of Summers, then you would live as long a life as many Polfre, for they have long lives, longer than ours. And if you lived that life twice over, and then all of those lives a dozen times in turn, you still would not have lived as long as the Polfre have lived on Lhosa. And there is something you should know about the Polfre, if you don't know it already. Their way of living is very different than the practices of the Eidos. They practice the *Rha*, which means they take a careful accounting of every tree, plant, or animal needed to live their lives. They do not believe in using anything without replacing it. For example, they might cut a tall tree for its wood, but then they will plant another tree to replace it, and perhaps a second to make up for the loss to the birds and animals who might have made their home around the original tree.

Even though the Polfre live a long time, their numbers have grown slowly. Some Polfre women never have children, and those that do rarely have more than two. Again, this is what they call the Rha. Though the Polfre were here long before the Eidos, they have spread to live on just a small portion of Lhosa. Their most secret places have always been hidden in the Adamantine mountains, and to this day none but the Polfre know where they are.

As it happens, they were a more populous people when the Eidos first arrived than they are today, and they had spread beyond the mountains into the nearby woodlands. Most of you know of the Greensee, which is only a few days walk north from here. At one time more Polfre lived in the Greensee than lived in the mountains. And that is where our real story begins.

It is the nature of the Eidos to explore, and within a few generations of arriving they had explored the length and breadth of Lhosa, and they had discovered the Greensee, and thus the Polfre. The Eidos were surprised and a bit frightened when they first learned there were other people on Lhosa, but the Polfre had somehow known of the Eidos, and some might say were even expecting them. The Polfre sent emissaries out to greet the Eidos warmly, and brought many gifts, and soon found they could communicate well. "Let us be neighbors and friends," they said. "This land of Lhosa is great and bountiful, and there is plenty for all." The Eidos, who had suffered much hardship for so many years before arriving, were delighted. And for many years they lived comfortably, and comfortably distant from each other. The Eidos continued to expand their cities near the Crespe sea, and the Polfre remained far to the east. And they learned from each other. The Polfre tried to teach them to live in the way of the Rha, which was new to the Eidos, while the Eidos began to plant fields of emmer and barley, which the Polfre had never seen.

By the way, if you have ever grown fields of grain, then you have seen how a small amount can quickly grow into a large amount. A single stalk of barley bears twelve kernels, one for each finger on your hands. If you plant them at the start of Summer, and every kernel sprouts, then at the end of the season you will have twelve stalks with twelve kernels each. The next Summer, instead of twelve stalks, you can grow a gross. And the following Summer a gross gross, until by the sixth Summer you have enough grain to make bread for two families for an entire year, plus enough left over to plant an even larger field for the next Summer.

The Eidos' hunger for farmland was as great as their hunger for bread and ale, and before long they had plowed great swaths of land east of the Rhoctan mountains. Not only did their fields grow quickly, but their numbers did, too. Eidos women may not be quite as fertile as a field of barley, but it seems at times they are not far behind. Even though the Eidos do not live as long as the Polfre, within a few generations there were many, many more Eidos than there were Polfre. And the Eidos kept planting fields, and when the barley starved those fields they would till new ground and plant more.

Eventually the Polfre who had first greeted the Eidos grew old and died, and their children grew old and died, and their children's children had only heard stories of a time when the land was theirs alone. And they could see that the Eidos had spread far across Lhosa, yet had learned little about the Rha. "Why should we care about starving a patch of land," the Eidos said to the Polfre. "There is land as far as the eye can see. We will just plow more." So the Polfre became more guarded and less helpful toward the Eidos. They strengthened the borders of the Greensee and hid the passes into the mountains. Gradually, the neighbors became enemies.

By this time the Eidos covered much of northern Lhosa. You may want to stop me and say, "But that is impossible! The northern half of Lhosa is a great desert." That is true now, but it was not the case then. Then, the Tyros was a great inland sea, black as the night sky and full of fish. There were Eidos villages everywhere, and some were large enough to consider themselves proper towns, with taverns and shops. The Eidos began to think of themselves as the rightful owners of all Lhosa. Their village leaders got together and began to talk about how the Polfre had become distant and even hostile. The Polfre no longer shared their skills, even when it left Eidos villages at the mercy of disaster. They asked themselves what should be done about it.

You might say "they should have gone and talked with the Polfre and found ways to restore their friendship." But others might say, "They should have stood up for themselves. If the Polfre were going to treat them unfairly, then it was time to fight!" And, being Eidos, you can guess which approach most of them chose.

Now, if I asked you who was the greatest leader in the history of the Eidos people, I'm sure some of you would say Donal, and you would be entitled to that thought. But if you ask me, I would say Farus was the greatest. Where there are great deeds, and great disasters, you will usually find great people. Farus was one of the greatest. At that time, he was the chief of Faerith. But the Eidos called on him to be the chief of all arms men, and that made him the chief of all Eidos. Arms men were recruited into shields from every village. He gathered together the shields to form a great army, and they marched on the Greensee to make war.

No doubt you have heard stories about the great war between the Eidos and the Polfre, so we won't repeat all of them tonight. The Eidos had a dozen arms men for every Polfre. Despite that, nothing changed. The Eidos did not take any ground within the Greensee or get anywhere near the mountains, even as the Polfre seemed to disappear from the world. But if any Eidos were foolish enough to venture into the forest, their lifeless bodies were found beyond the trees the next morning. The Polfre had their secrets. They had acquired knowledge and abilities of which the Eidos had no understanding. The Eidos fought with spears and swords and arrows; the Polfre, it seemed, with magic. It was said that the Polfre could kill a man simply with their touch.

Farus saw that the war was unwinnable. If he kept losing ten men for every Polfre, soon there would be no arms men left. But instead of bargaining for peace with the Polfre, his anger grew, and he became obsessed with the idea that his people were being cheated of their due.

So Farus decided to seek out Malach and ask for his help. He searched far and wide. But he did not find him in the village, and he did not find him in the fields. He found him walking in a river valley far to the south.

"Great Malach, the Polfre do not treat us as neighbors ought to be treated," he said. "And when we fought back to defend our place and our honor, they used magic against us. Help us, mighty god, to claim what we have so long deserved. Our enemy should fear your wrath and feel our swords."

But when Malach answered, none of it was good news.

"There are powers older and stronger than me, my brother Farus. This land is under the domain of Ruhax, the Lord Sorceros. He has given the Polfre their magic power, and it is not possible for me to change this. If you want to change your situation with the Polfre, you must talk with Lord Ruhax."

Farus shook his head. "Lord Ruhax disdains all mortals. He brings only pain and suffering to our kind."

"Nonetheless, he is the one who controls the magic of Lhosa, so him you must see."

"Then I will go and speak with him at once," Farus said. "Where do I find him?"

Malach looked away. "You might search your entire life and never find him, or you might turn around and feel him all around you. You can only pray and hope that Lord Ruhax chooses to find you."

So Farus returned to Faerith, and he prayed and offered sacrifices to Ruhax for days on end, but there was no response. Eventually a wise old priest suggested that Ruhax could only be found in his temple, which was lost somewhere in the Rhoctan mountains. Farus had teams scour the mountains for many passages, looking for evidence of the temple, to no avail. Finally, he set out alone to discover it himself. For most of a year he trudged through deep valleys and climbed snow-swept peaks, calling to Ruhax and hearing nothing but the wind's response. Then one deep Winter day, at the brink of exhaustion, he stumbled upon four columns of black stone, reaching skyward until they curved in toward each other, forming a pair of arches high above a perfect circle of stone beneath. *This must be it*, he thought. He fell to his knees underneath the arches, and prayed non-stop for a day and a night, but did not receive the slightest response. So he hunted until he found and killed a young buck, which he dragged back to the stone floor and burned in sacrifice. But even then Ruhax did not come.

Feeling he could do no more, out of food, once again weak and exhausted, Farus admitted defeat. He had only enough strength to return home. But as he walked, the snow began falling in a great storm, until it reached his chest and he could no longer push forward. The snow itself defeated him. He had nothing to use to build even a tiny fire. He wrapped himself in his furs as well as he could and curled up either to wait for the storm to pass, or to die. Deep in the night the storm did pass, and then the clouds ripped and scattered, and he could look up and see countless stars. And in that frozen place he heard a voice call his name.

"Farus, do you not rule the world?" the voice said. And there, standing in the distance was a towering figure. A red cloak billowed about him. His hair was as white as the snow, and from his head sprouted a magnificent and menacing pair of curved horns.

"Lord Sorceros, the Polfre refuse to share with the rest of the world, and they use tricks to defend themselves," Farus replied. "As your humble servant, I beg you meet our needs. I need men of arms who can withstand their magic."

Ruhax stepped forward until he loomed over Farus. "Have you ever humbled yourself to me before now? Have you ever shown your appreciation to me in any way? I am feared by your people, reviled by your priests. Now, in desperation you ask for my help, but what do you offer? What can you give me, mighty Farus, that I cannot simply take for myself?"

Farus dared not look into the god's face. "I have nothing," he said. He feared that Lord Ruhax might kill him then, just for his impertinence. But Ruhax asked again. "One thing only you have, that I cannot take. What is it?" Long and hard Farus thought. And just as he feared Ruhax would tire of waiting, the answer came to him.

"You can take everything from me but my loyalty. That is something I must freely give."

"I will grant you a force like no other," Ruhax replied. "Go and enter the cracks at the feet of the Rhoctan mountains. Search until you find the great adamantine staff that holds the world together. Take the staff and call forth your arms men. Once you have called them, they will follow your command without question until the last of your enemies lies dead."

Farus felt the earth tremble beneath his feet. In the time it took him to look down and back up, the form of Ruhax had disappeared. But the terrible voice continued, coming from everywhere. "Your loyalty I will request in my own time."

He remained huddled in his skins until morning, when the Sun rose bright in the east, and with it he felt his spirits brighten as well, and he headed that direction.

The black, smoking fissures of the Rhoctan rifts have warned away all but the most fool-hardy explorers. Yet that is where Farus went. And that is where he found the Ruhatsi. They were little more than vicious animals when he first encountered them, killing anything entering the rifts, and killing themselves in the meantime. But Farus found the adamantine staff, driven deeply into the foundation stone of the world. He took the staff, and just as Ruhax had promised, the Ruhatsi responded to his call. For weeks he scouted the noxious underground, gradually building a force that responded to his command. When they finally came out of the ground, Farus commanded three times the men he had led before.

Word spread quickly of the horrible force that had emerged from the ground to march eastward once again. Villages ahead of them sent offerings and pleas that they would pass to one side. But Farus had no intention of pillaging local villages. He sent their emissaries back to tell the villagers they would be safe. And he sent emissaries ahead to contact the Polfre, challenging them to meet once again on the great plains south of the Tyros sea, or suffer the destruction of the Ruhatsi let loose in the Greensee.

The Polfre must have heard word of the terrible force advancing on them, for this time they came together as a force outside the Greensee, and they brought with them their machines of war. But they were still badly outnumbered as the battle began. The Polfre used all their magic and all their machines, but the Ruhatsi were fearless and unstoppable. They survived the Polfre machines and advanced until they were face-to-face with the Polfre defenders. Too late, the Polfre realized that whatever power they had over the Eidos in hand-to-hand combat did not exist against the Ruhatsi. It was sword against spear, and the Ruhatsi were ruthless.

As Sunset neared, the battle wound down, with the Ruhatsi forces close to triumph. Finally, the only surviving member of the Polfre force was their commander. Wounded but still able to walk, he was captured, stripped of his armor, and brought before Farus.

"You rejected us when we came to you as friends," Farus said. "Now you see what happens when you make us your enemy."

The Polfre commander looked up. "Mighty Farus," he

said, "you have killed our best warriors. Our homes are defenseless. We will not recover from losses this great for generations to come. Now, only I am left to protect my people, I, the last of your enemies."

And the Polfre commander pulled a knife from beneath his tunic and plunged it into his chest. He pitched forward, dead.

"Arms men!" Farus cried. "The Polfre forces have been utterly defeated! Tomorrow we march for the Greensee and take what should have been given us!"

But the Ruhatsi suddenly seemed to be paying little attention to Farus. He called for their attention again. Instead, a quarrel broke out between two Ruhatsi arms-commanders and spread like wildfire through their ranks. Within moments the war seemed to have broken out again, only this time between the Ruhatsi and each other. Farus was powerless to stop it. Worse, several groups broke free from the ranks and scattered in different directions. Farus screamed for attention and waved the staff over his head, to no avail. In fact, a spear soon whizzed by his head, and he had to run for cover, as several of the Ruhatsi appeared intent on attacking him, too.

By nightfall, Farus' Ruhatsi shields had either killed themselves or had disappeared in all directions. Alone, he made his way slowly west across the land. Along the way he passed small groups of people who seemed to be fleeing their villages. "Demons," they told him. "Demons attacked our village, and we were lucky to escape."

Farus' journey back to the mountains was long and lonely. But at last he stood under the black pillars again, and he cried out to Ruhax. "You used me to spread more destruction through the world!"

"I did everything I promised," came the voice from everywhere.

"Stop them, before they destroy the world," Farus said. But the voice did not respond.

Full of shame, Farus resolved never to return to his people. He would die alone in the mountains, the only fate he deserved. He wandered, refusing to find himself food or water, until he was weak and hoped the end was near. But then another figure came to him, walking over the ground.

"What have you done, Farus?" the figure said.

"I have unleashed demons into the world," Farus replied.

"You have removed the pin that holds them in their place." Farus still carried the adamantine staff. "Return it to its rightful place, and Lord Ruhax will be forced to restore the world to its proper order."

"Thank you, Lord Malach," Farus said. "My people shall forever worship you and you alone."

"No," Malach said. "You have made a bargain with Lord Ruhax, and he has not yet claimed his part of the deal. Until he does, you cannot swear complete loyalty to any other god."

So Farus returned to the cracks of the world, found the place where the adamantine staff belonged, and shoved it deep into the ground.

When Ruhax saw that the staff had been returned, he caused a great blast of light and heat to cover the land. The Ruhatsi were caught in it and burned from the world. The land itself was disfigured: the great grasslands of the north were burned into desert, and the Tyros Sea was mostly boiled away. The remnants are to this day full of salt; poisonous to fish.

But the burned land caused the Eidos to suffer as well. The light destroyed the twin cities of Faerith and Forought, and only those Eidos who lived far from there were spared. Their fields of emmer and barley were burned, and they were forced to return to hunting to survive. The remaining Polfre were forced out of the Greensee and retreated into the Adamantine mountains. And in the end, a few Ruhatsi survived as well, though they were terribly disfigured by the blast, and remain so to this day. And over the many, many years since, in small roaming bands, they have continued to exist, and they continue to terrorize Lhosa as they have since released from Farus' control. Used by Ruhax, and cursed by Malach, their assault continues, so many grosses of years since they first crawled from the fissures and set foot on the world. So it will continue until Farus' debt to Lord Ruhax is paid.

Ruhax withdrew, while Malach became god over all Lhosa. But to this day Lord Ruhax waits, and watches. And the day may yet come when he demands the debt of loyalty be repaid, or all Lhosa will again suffer his ruinous power.

The villagers were quiet for a moment, followed by a few desultory claps. Olei remained silent, thinking. If the Ruhatsi were not responsible for their fate, then perhaps they deserved pity. But that was too great a concession. They had killed his mother. He hated them and hoped they all would die. Then Tobin broke the mood.

"You are a spell-caster, honored Rohul! Quick, some wood for the fire, before the Ruhatsi creep into the streets around us!"

Tobin meant to sound light-hearted, but his comments deepened the disquiet in the minds of the townsfolk. He sensed the need for a different approach.

"Olei, take your crew and go get a couple of barrels of cider from the pantry. Surely that will brighten the night"

Olei found Calus and relayed Tobin's message. While the younger boy trotted off to find additional help, Olei re-entered the Altarnary. The candles, lit for the Oblation, had since burned away, leaving the altar room in deep gloom. But years of familiarity allowed him to move through the building in the dark. He returned to his room to grab his cloak, as the night air was turning cool.

The Sojourner was not yet up, and no light entered his small cell from its tiny window. He moved silently, barely discerning the cloak lying on the edge of his bed. As he prepared to slip it on, he was sure he heard a couple of footfalls outside his door.

"Tobin?" He grabbed his ember pot and flicked the lid.

Thanla stood in the doorway. She had removed her short cloak and was dressed only in the armless, skin-tight tunic emphasizing her muscular body. A scar had been branded into her right upper arm: a five-pointed star centered in an inverted triangle. In her left hand she held the silver dagger from the Oblation. "I found the creature, cornered in its hole," she said with a sneer.

Olei yelled as loud as he could, but he could not find words, and he knew it didn't matter. He was too far away, and the stone too thick for him to be heard. Thanla lunged forward, and Olei threw the ember pot. She flicked it away with the dagger. It clattered against the wall and fell to the floor, remarkably, staying lit. The blade flicked back, and Olei felt the tip slash into his right arm.

"Try for me," the woman said. "I know what you are. Try to touch me! I am much faster than you can ever imagine."

They both leapt at the same time. Thanla took a great cut with the knife, anticipating he would come straight for her, but missed as he leapt sideways instead. Olei lunged for his staff. He managed to grab it and swing as he fell onto the cot, and Thanla had to jump back to avoid being hit in the side. Olei knew he was at a great disadvantage, but his staff was much longer than the dagger. He pushed it forward with one hand while he struggled to stand up. Thanla leapt forward and slashed again. He attempted to parry the dagger with the staff, but his one-handed motion was slow and weak.

Nonetheless, the staff managed to contact the blade. The woman cried out as it fell from her hand and clattered through the doorway. She hurried after it, cutting off escape down the stairs. Now Olei's only choice was to take the steps to the roof. He ran up, tossed the staff onto the roof, then crawled after it, hoping to call to the crowd below for help.

But Thanla was indeed fast. He felt the blade slash at his breeches as he cleared the steps. He grabbed for the staff. Thanla was already standing behind him. As he turned to face her, holding the staff in front of him, she gradually circled, climbing the black stone of the dome so that she was standing over him. Her sneer returned.

"Why?" he gasped.

"I know what you are," she repeated.

"You're wrong," was all he could think to say. Then she lunged again. As she did, she expertly tossed the knife from her left hand to her right. Olei swung the staff at the same time, but her feint worked, and he missed her completely. He stumbled forward into the range of her knife. At the same time his staff struck the dome.

There was a crack and a shower of sparks. Thanla, preparing to strike, took a step back instead. The staff had gouged a chunk out of one of the stones. Olei sensed her hesitation and tried to swing the staff again. Again, he was slow. She took an easy step back to avoid the staff—and plunged through the central oculus of the dome. She managed a strangled scream before her body slammed into the altar below.

Olei stared through the Oculus as Tobin and Rohul rushed into the Alternary. Drops of blood fell lazily from his arm onto the body below. Tobin looked up.

"Olei!" he cried, and suddenly Olei felt dizzy.

"She attacked me," he said, then stepped back so he would not fall through the Oculus as well.

Tobin rushed to the roof and led Olei back to his room. "Stay here," he said, then left to get dressings. Olei's dizziness turned to nausea and cold sweats. Gradually, though, he was able to calm down. Tobin returned and dressed the cut on his arm, ordering him to stay in the room when he was finished.

But Olei heard voices gathering in the altar room below, so once he felt good enough to stand up, he made his way down the stairs.

"Oh, the boy!" Rohul cried. "What a horror! Tell us what happened."

"Not now," Tobin said, spying Olei at the bottom of the stairs. "Olei, you should be resting."

"Is she dead?" he asked. The room was lit with torches and lanterns, casting odd shadows. Black blood was splashed on the altar, and he could not remember if they had cleaned up after the sacrifice earlier. The woman was not there.

"Yes, she's dead," Tobin replied.

"Where is she?"

"Out back. You don't want to see her."

"Why?" he asked again. It seemed the simplest way to summarize the dozens of questions in his mind.

"She was Malacheb," the arms-captain said. Olei had not noticed him, standing toward the back of the room.

Tobin shook his head. "The Malacheb no longer exist."

"Oh, they exist," the captain replied. "She has their mark on her arm."

Rohul scowled. "But she was just a woman."

"Please!" Olei said, causing them to stop and look at him. "I don't understand."

"The Malacheb were the original tribe of Donal the Conqueror," Tobin said finally. "After he conquered Antola, some of them refused to civilize and continued their bloody behavior. They were eliminated by Serenity the First after the Council of Antola."

"Oh, they're still around," the captain said. "Only now they work in secret. They believe they are preserving Donal's original ways. I'm sure that's why she asked for the sacrifice ceremony earlier. But that wasn't enough for her. She was trying to sacrifice the boy, too. They think only human sacrifice preserves the true way."

Tobin shook his head. "If any Eidos tribes ever performed human sacrifice, it was far in the barbaric past. We are far too civilized for that now."

The captain made a noise somewhere between a cough and a laugh. "Have you ever killed anyone?"

"No," Tobin replied.

"That's why you think there's a distinction between one type of killing and another."

Rohul wrung his hands. "I had no idea," he said. "If I had known she was this Malacheb thing, I would have never allowed her to come with us."

He's lying. He knew what she could do, Olei thought. That was precisely why he hired her: to be his personal bodyguard. *He knew who she was.* But that failed to explain why she had singled Olei out for her attack.

Outside, the eastern sky was brightening. Everyone seemed to be lost in their own thoughts, until Tobin grasped Rohul's wrist. "The road will only get hotter and dustier, the longer you wait."

"What will you do with the body?"

"Our herders will build a pyre."

"More than she deserves."

"She is gone. The body is Alera's once again."

"You're from the west, I gather?"

"Dormond."

"How did you end up a Panthean priest?"

"I found myself in Antola as a child, not by choice. But I met someone who was kind to me. And I am not a priest; just a servant adept." Olei was surprised. This was more history than Tobin had divulged to him in three years.

By the time the air was beginning to feel warm, Rohul's wagon had been pulled around in front of the Altarnary and was hitched and ready to go. The arms-captain was already mounted; his horse toeing the ground restlessly.

"I cannot blame you for wanting us off, so that boredom

can once again return to your little village," Rohul said. Olei stood next to Tobin on the steps. "Take care, young Olei."

The wagon rumbled off. Finally, Olei turned to Tobin. "It wasn't just anybody. She was after me. It was like she was looking for me. How can that be?"

Tobin shook his head. "When I was young, I heard stories of the Malacheb and their heroic deeds. But those were just fireside stories, like Rohul's. When you get older, you don't take those stories seriously."

"What kind of heroic deeds?" Olei asked.

Tobin stared at the dusty trail left by Rohul's wagon. Olei wondered if he was going to ignore the question. "They were demon hunters," he said finally.

5

A year passed, and the cloudnettle sprigs grew together into a low but nasty tangle, as more than one bison man well into his mugs discovered after stumbling out of the Curly Top late at night. Another Summer passed, and Harvest was upon them again. Already there had been nights of light frost, and the tree line, which continued to recede farther into the distance as wood fueled the hungry charcoal kilns, was now a blaze of reds and yellows. Halrin's Spur was a quiet and healthy place, which only seemed to drive Tobin harder. Hedges of cloudnettle had been planted along the riverbank south toward the milkhouse, and a bridge had been built over the river south of the milkhouse fortified with a watchtower manned day and night. The huts and houses around the milkhouse were becoming a village in their own right, especially if a village was defined as any place with its own alehouse, as one had sprung up near the south bridge. The grassy fields between Halrin's Spur and the milkhouse had been turned and planted with squash and brown beans, now drying in their pods. There was plenty to eat and to trade. Halrin's Spur was easily the most productive village between Bhinton and the end of the North Road. That fact was evident in the frequency of visits it now received from representatives of the Crown. Except for their bison meat, which made its way to Bhinton and even Antola, the Crown had little interest in their goods available for trade but did not miss the opportunity to collect their due in coin. Tobin always made sure that some goods were traded for coin elsewhere, so that it would always be available.

Tobin and Olei were on the North Road, headed toward the northernmost scattering of dwellings that could be considered a village, named, oddly enough, Southwatch. It was less than a half day's walk south of the Greensee, which was easily seen from the hilltops surrounding the village. The Greensee itself was vast; it swept dozens of leagues beyond the northern horizon and abutted the Adamantines to the east. A herder traveled with them, tending the bison cow pulling their loaded wagon. The journey to Southwatch was a trip of almost thirty leagues, the farthest Olei had ever been from home. It was a hard four-days' walk, as the road became little more than a rutted track for the last ten leagues.

They slept beside the road each night, building a small fire. Two stayed awake at a time. Olei took first watch. He sat with his back to the fire, studying the darkness intently. He could still see the edges of nearby hills defined against the cloud-covered sky. As much as he was happy for the warmth, he thought the fire made them too conspicuous to anyone who might be creeping through the wilds. Tobin said there was more danger from animals than from people, and the fire would help keep them away. Nonetheless, Olei could not help but imagine Ruhatsi crawling over nearby hills and through the scrub, waiting for the perfect moment to jump out and slay them. Tobin relieved him in the middle of the night, and Olei crawled beneath bison hides and fell into a restless slumber of anxious dreams.

Southwatch appeared to be no larger than the village around the milkhouse, Olei thought, when on the fourth day they topped the final rise and saw it in front of them. It was already past mid-day. They had been forced to off-load the wagon and hand-carry everything across the last bridge due to its decrepit state. Even so, Olei was afraid the empty wagon alone would collapse the bridge as they rumbled over it. The tiny village hugged the side of a steep hill, and its few houses were scattered randomly, connected with meandering paths nearly over-run with asters and sundrops. Each house had a vegetable garden, and in many places the gardens seemed to be joined together. What little they grew had already been harvested; the gardens were empty save for rows of bean poles decorated with brown, rusting leaves. He saw several quail pop up and then disappear. Olei could not imagine what the people of Southwatch had to trade.

There was no alehouse (violating the first rule, he mused). Instead, they were shown to a low common-house in the center of the village. The interior was a single large room, with an enormous hearthgrate dominating one end. The fire itself burned low and red. There was no chimney; a hole in the roof allowed about half the smoke to escape, while the rest formed a perpetual indoor haze that caused Olei's eyes to water.

A huge blackened bowl stood on three legs at the edge of the fire. Olei wandered over and peeked inside. The contents had the earthy smell of bean soup. Tobin supplemented the soup with cheese and smoked bison from the wagon, and soon they had assembled a decent meal. Two small women from the village joined them, one considerably older than the other. At first, Olei thought they might be there to serve, but Tobin treated them with great deference, and suddenly Olei recognized the older one as the Polfre woman who had come to visit them a few years before. She bore herself in a way that marked her as the village's leader as clearly as any ring or cloak would.

"We thank you, honored Fasha, for your hospitality,"

Tobin said, bowing. "After three nights on the road, we look forward to the comforts of your village." Olei glanced around the room, devoid of furnishings. At least he could sleep with a wall between himself and the marauding Ruhatsi. Beyond that, the comforts eluded him.

"We are pleased to bring you gifts from our village," Tobin continued. Olei was mildly surprised. For years he had watched Tobin shrewdly trade one thing for another, gaining value along the way. He had come to accept this as the way to do business. He had never seen Tobin simply give things away. The people of Southwatch were poor, that was clear, but they did not appear to be starving. The woman motioned for all of them to sit on the floor. As they did, she looked straight at Olei, and held his gaze for several moments.

"Greetings again," she said finally. "I am Fasha."

"Olei," he said softly.

"Look at my eyes, Olei."

He stared, and she stared back. The center of her eyes glowed like tiny gold coins, just as they had when he had met her before. His hand unconsciously moved to the scar on his right arm. She reached forward and lightly grabbed his wrists. As before, he felt a tingling sensation travel up each arm. She then ran her hands gently over his forehead, across the slight ridge just above his hairline.

"I feel what I suspected before," she said finally. "You are especially welcome here, young Olei."

Olei felt pleased and flustered at the same time. The sensation in his arms was strangely comforting. He could not think of what to say in return. Fasha smiled at him, then turned her attention to Tobin.

"Little has changed for us in the past year, my friend. What prompts your visit?"

"I'm surprised your bridge has survived Summer's storms," Tobin said. "A team from my village can have it rebuilt by Winter. We can put a watch-tower on one side, as well."

"Where will the wood come from?"

"We have plenty of seasoned wood in Halrin's Spur. But we can plant saplings next Summer, if that is your concern."

She waved her hand. "Yours is the only wagon that has been here for some time. The bridge is fine for walking. And I know of nothing that requires watching."

Tobin sighed. "Security is a valuable thing, Fasha."

"The Seventh One has not managed to disrupt the peace," she replied.

"If you're referring to the Crown, then I agree. Serenity seems to have discovered that peace has its own rewards. But he does not control everything, despite what he may believe. We live many leagues from Antola. We must be ready to defend ourselves."

"You're looking in the wrong direction, Tobin. The riverflats south of Bhinton are a wound on the world. The people and beasts multiply and push the land to its limits. The Rha tilts too far out of balance. It cannot be allowed to continue."

Olei read the look of irritability that crossed Tobin's face. *So much for honored greetings*, he thought.

"What would the Polfre suggest?" Tobin asked. "Allow the people to starve? Would the Polfre sacrifice lives to restore leagues of useless heather and willow?"

"Some would argue that heather and willow have more value than untamed herders. But you know me better than that, Tobin. Those of us who venture into the world do so because the Rha is for all people, not just the Polfre. I do not want the people of the riverflats to suffer. But it is not just starvation that worries me. The people of the flats will soon outnumber the people of the city. That will only make Serenity more uneasy."

"My plan is to build to the south as well, Fasha. The bison-herders of the riverflats can learn to take care of the land.

They can learn to support themselves as well as support the Crown. If they can be self-sufficient, then it is good for the Rha and good for the Crown, too. Serenity will see that. Surely the Polfre can, as well."

Olei struggled to keep up with the conversation. For someone who lived at the end of the road, Fasha seemed to know a lot about the rest of the world. Though her voice was kind, talk about allowing people to starve, and the strange concept the Polfre called the Rha, made him uncomfortable. It was hard to process his feelings and follow the discussion at the same time.

"I've heard Madros now trades so heavily with Antola it's like they are one and the same," Fasha said.

"Trading has become more prosperous than conquering," Tobin replied.

"Does the Crown keep a shield of men in Madros?" Fasha asked.

Tobin nodded. "No doubt."

"Then they are one and the same. And when Antola needs more than Madros can give, will the Crown bargain at the tip of a sword with the next city on the Great Road? With Solanon? Then Dormond, and then Ismay? Does Serenity plan to rule all of Lhosa?"

"No man can rule all of Lhosa," Tobin said. "That is my point, honored Fasha. We must be free and healthy to govern our own lives. As long as one person is unable to feed himself, the world is not well."

Fasha smiled. "You have a big heart, adept Tobin. But you do not see how this ends, how it always ends. Antola will stretch, demanding more and more until the world is far out of balance, and then disaster will come. The Polfre will not allow that to happen."

"But really, what can you do? There are so few of you."

"We've done it before," Fasha replied.

"Done what?"

Done what? Olei echoed in his thoughts. *What could they do? Who were these people, and did they fear anything at all?*

"Ultimately, the land will decide what is right for itself. Then we could all be at peril."

"Still, a new bridge would be a good idea," Tobin said, trying to smile.

Fasha laughed, turning to Olei. "Your friend sounds like an adept of the Sophenary, rather than the School for Servants," she said.

"I don't know what that is," he said, his brow furrowed. Now he was feeling just plain ignorant.

She waved her hands as if molding her answer out of the air. "The Sophenary is a castle of learning, found in Antola. I'm surprised Tobin has not mentioned it. Surely he has talked about his own education at the School for Servants."

"Something I have been meaning to say more about," Tobin said hurriedly. Olei continued to scowl, but Fasha suddenly stood and placed herself between them, before he could ask anything else.

"You are a good teacher for your young apprentice, Tobin, but it is time for him to know more. Olei, there is someone I would like you to meet." As she said this, the young girl who had been sitting next to Fasha stood as if she had been waiting for this cue. She was no taller than a young child, yet Olei could tell from her face and her figure that she must be at least approaching adulthood, though he could not guess more than that. She held her eyes downcast but flicked him a quick glance, and in that moment, they glowed golden, reflecting the fire. "This is Pipit," Fasha said. "Please, my dear, show Olei around the village. Tobin and I have more things to discuss."

Their bisonman companion, finished with his meal, had begun to snore in the corner. Olei stood reluctantly. He thought he had done enough, and experienced enough, to prove to Tobin that he was no longer a child. He understood the politics of the wider world better than the average villager and was eager to learn more. He was on the verge of saying as much when Tobin shot him a raised eyebrow, meaning he was to comply and they would talk later. He thanked Fasha for the meal and followed the young woman out the door.

The Sun was reaching for the western horizon. Pipit seemed to have a destination in mind. He followed her as she climbed a meandering track around the gardens and up the side of the hillside. They reached the top and were bathed in golden light. The distant tree tops of the Greensee were not green but glowed with reds and yellows.

"This is my favorite time of the day," Pipit said. "Our work is done, but so many creatures are just beginning to start theirs. Then the Sun will set, the air will become cool and still, and the dew will form again on the grass and leaves."

"I've always wondered where the water for dew comes from," Olei said.

She cocked her head to look at him, like a bird. "From the air, of course."

"No," Olei said. "There are no clouds tonight, no rain will fall, and yet dew will be everywhere in the morning."

"Where does the water for the rain come from?" she asked.

"The clouds, of course."

"And where do the clouds come from?"

Olei realized he did not have a good answer for this.

"There is water in the air, like the steam rising from a cook pot or a still pond in the morning. Warm air carries more water than cold air. As the air cools at night, the water collects on anything it touches, creating the dew. The air is colder far above us, so the water forms clouds, and eventually there is so much it falls as rain."

"Why is the air colder above us, when it is closer to the Sun?" Olei said, hoping to pick apart her argument.

"Why is there snow on top of tall mountains, when there is none down below?"

Olei frowned again. He felt slightly foolish. "How old are you?" he asked irritably.

"Twenty-seven Summers," she said.

Olei stared, and she smiled sweetly at him. "But you…you look like a child," he blurted. He was immediately embarrassed.

"I am a child, at least as far as we're concerned. And I am small, even for the Polfre."

"I thought most Polfre lived far away in the Adamantine mountains. Are you and Fasha related?"

"All Polfre are related. Our home has been in the mountains for many gross dozens of years. But you can still find us many other places."

"Is your family here? In Southwatch?"

She took his hand, and when she did, he felt the same slight sensation he had felt from Fasha. She began walking, and once he began to follow, she let go. Olei found himself wishing she had not.

"Most Polfre choose never to leave the mountains. We have everything we need, and we live in harmony with our home. But there is a wider world. A few Polfre leave the mountains to explore that world, though we eventually go home again. I am an explorer, you might say. Like Fasha, I have chosen to live with the people of Southwatch so that I may understand our neighbors. But I always want to live in sight of the mountains, and one day, when I choose to have my own child, I will return there for good."

"Twenty-seven seems plenty old to have a family," Olei said.

"The Polfre live longer lives than the Eidos," Pipit replied. "I am too young for a child. I am only just becoming fertile." Olei blushed, but she was not looking at him, and he hoped she didn't notice. "To us, the Eidos rush headlong into each day's troubles without contemplation. When I have lived forty or fifty years, perhaps then I will consider finding a mate and having a child of my own. How old are you, Olei?"

"Eighteen Summers," he said, somewhat abashedly.

"And so tall. Tobin is not your father." She said it in a way that indicated she knew for certain. "Do you have family in your village?"

"My mother was killed by the Ruhatsi."

"The Ruhatsi? You are sure?"

Olei felt his defensiveness return. "I saw them myself."

"I don't mean to doubt you," she said. "Many think the Ruhatsi are just stories from long ago. I confess that is what I have always thought."

"It's hard to believe you've been so lucky. I don't think this little place would stand a chance if the they came through. Maybe they don't know Southwatch exists."

"We aren't defenseless," Pipit said. She pointed to the Greensee. "There is protection in the wood."

Olei gazed north. Two or three leagues separated them from the first shadowy eaves of the forest. The land rose and fell, and small copses of trees provided numerous locations for ambush along the way. "If the Ruhatsi came in the night, you would never get a message to the woods quickly enough."

"There are many ways of knowing that do not require words," she said. They had walked a short distance along the crest of the hill, and now Pipit led them down the slope to where a handful of slender willow trees stood; their trunks forming a rough circle. Between the trees, the stump from the original trunk was black and soft. Many years had passed since it had been harvested, and the current trees, arising from a central mass of roots, were nearing the age where they could be cut again. Pipit walked up to the nearest trunk and placed both of her hands on the bark.

"Tell me, how long ago did these trunks sprout from the ground?"

"About twenty to twenty-five Summers, I would guess," Olei said. Charcoaling had given him some knowledge of trees.

"Place your hands on this one, then tell me how old it is."

"How will that help?"

"Place your hands on it," she insisted. He did as she said, palming the rough bark. "Now, close your eyes, and try to feel inside the tree with your hands."

"What...?"

"Please do it," she said firmly. He closed his eyes and pretended he could feel beneath the bark. He knew that the age of a tree could be measured by counting the rings in the wood. He tried to estimate the number of rings based on the size of the trunk. He imagined her hands on the opposite side of the tree...and then, suddenly felt as if he could tell where her hands were, without opening his eyes. She shifted one of them.

"Did you move your left hand?"

"Good," she said. "Now continue concentrating."

Olei pushed his consciousness into his hands. It was as if he could see her hands opposite his, and in between...he could see the layers, could feel the rush and pause of each season. Seventeen layers lay between his hands and the central core of the tree, and then sixteen layers again until he reached Pipit's hands.

"It's eighteen Summers old," he said.

"Good! Just like you. When you were born, this tree was starting life as a tiny sapling, just a sprout from the old trunk. Now concentrate."

Not knowing what he was concentrating on, he focused on the sense of her hands opposite his. Suddenly he was aware of a much older existence. He thought he could see the trunk that had preceded these; a single tree growing in the wild. Just as suddenly, the image vanished. He opened his eyes to see that she no longer had her hands against the tree.

"How did you do that?"

"You did that," she said. "You could feel my hands, is all, and that helped you focus."

"Everybody can do that?"

"No, no. Not everybody. Listen, Olei. All living things speak, in their own way. Most can only hear the words of their own kind, but the Polfre hear more. We don't have to see raiders approaching to know if they are near. We are in tune with this part of the world." She stooped and picked up a rock, about the size of her own fist.

"This rock fell from that side of the hill," she said, pointing to a seam of exposed rock about two hands high. *Anyone would have figured that out*, Olei thought. She closed her eyes and gripped it tightly. "But it has been there for far, far longer than there have been people on Lhosa. Mostly sand, but melted together beneath the mountains long ago, and then shoved to the surface still red and soft, like the coals in a fire." She handed the rock to him. "Close your eyes and feel what you can feel."

He closed his hand around the rock, then closed his eyes. He tried to imagine the rock lying in the same place for year after year, its edges slowly wearing away. There were seams in the rock, he thought, creases and strains, where it had been forced together so long ago. Sand, forced to be a rock, and now trying to return to sand. With a soft crack, the rock split into several pieces. He opened his eyes. Pipit was staring at him.

"What did you do?" she asked.

"Nothing. I didn't do anything."

"Why would you want to break it?"

"I didn't. I barely squeezed it. It just…it just broke itself," he said, knowing the comment seemed foolish. Pipit cocked her head again but said nothing else.

The Sun had set, and the first stars were appearing. To Olei, the first stars of the evening played a game with him: one moment not visible at all, the next right there, where he had just been staring. The colors of the Greensee faded quickly until it was only a vast blackness. Behind them, scattered windows in the cottages were lit with lamplight: stars against the hillside.

"We should go in," Pipit said. They began to walk down the slope toward the nearest cottages.

Since meeting Fasha years before, a question had been worrying the edges of Olei's mind. Having the full attention of another Polfre seemed an ideal time to ask it. "The Book of Obligations tells us about the family of gods. But there aren't any stories about the Polfre. Do the Polfre have their own god?"

"If you mean, do we pray and to whom, the Polfre don't actually do that," she said.

"But you believe in the gods, right?"

Pipit stopped walking. "Why do you think the Eidos worship the gods?"

Olei frowned at her capacity for asking unanswerable questions. "Because they are the gods. People want to please them."

"Why do you seek to please them?"

"So they won't be angry."

"And yet there is pain and suffering everywhere. It seems they must be angry all the time," she replied. Olei had long thought the same thing, though he had never expressed it out loud, not even to Tobin. It was unsettling hearing it from someone else. "And what do the Eidos pray for, when they pray?" she continued. *"Alera protect us. Malach bring us strength and victory.* Things for themselves. You seek to please yourselves, not the gods."

"You think we are foolish," he said.

She took his hands into hers, and once again he felt the

warm, tingling sensation. A moment before he had felt defensive; now he only felt confused. "No, Olei. It is foolish to mock the beliefs of others. People can have the same experience and yet believe different things about it. I am only saying the Eidos say they serve the gods, when in truth they can't help but expect the gods to serve them. The Polfre do not seek anything from the gods. We only seek to find harmony within ourselves and the world we live in. We don't need gods for that. Whether they are real or not does not directly affect our lives."

"But what about Lord Ruhax? He is the one who gave the Polfre their abilities." Olei said.

"I believe there are powers greater than the individual, Olei, and maybe that's the same thing. If the gods teach us to reach for a higher purpose, that is a good thing. If they teach us selfishness and cruelty, then it is not. I believe, once in many dozens of generations, an individual may be born who lives out an extraordinary life. Perhaps Malach was one of those; perhaps even Ruhax, long ago. The Eidos have chosen to call them gods. Maybe I just have a different name for them than you do."

They opened the door into the common house. After having spent time in the crisp evening air, Olei was almost smothered by the smoke. Fasha and Tobin were head to head, talking quietly. The bisonman snored in the corner.

"It was a pleasure to meet you, Olei," Pipit said. "But I have to return to my cottage and rest." She turned to Fasha. "The frost will be heavy tonight, and there will be a skim of ice on the ponds by morning. I will be off for home at daybreak, but as I promised, I will be back before the last New Sojourner of Winter."

She bowed deeply before Olei, and he felt his face flush again. "I am sure we will meet again," she said.

After her departure, Olei unrolled his furs and sat, a bit of his irritation returning. Her argument seemed so simple, because, he finally decided, it was too simple. There was more to the gods than she allowed. Tobin would have known what to say. He needed to understand more. He sat listening to snatches of the conversation between Fasha and Tobin, trying to concentrate. But very quickly he found his head falling forward, so he stretched out to be more comfortable. He closed his eyes again and did not open them until dawn.

Pipit had been right. The morning air was very cold, even though the sky was blue and the Sun was bright. They set off for Halrin's Spur in silence. Tobin was uncharacteristically quiet, while the bisonman, who had said perhaps five words during their entire trip, did not seem inclined to add a sixth.

"It will be a cold Winter," Tobin finally said. Olei gave him a sidelong glance, anticipating a lecture on their need to prepare. But Tobin seemed to have nothing to add. Olei turned his attention again to the rutted road. He was almost lost again in his own thoughts when Tobin said, "Calus is turning out to be a useful assistant."

The truth was, he had been perfectly happy before Calus had come along. Now, it seemed, Tobin's attention was divided between the two of them. He liked to think of Calus as his own assistant, not Tobin's.

"He won't have your ability with the charcoal kilns," Tobin continued.

Olei snorted. "Calus doesn't know anything about charcoal."

"You may have to teach him."

"Why? I don't need his help. I already know who is best for each job. Maybe he can fetch mud from the riverbank, if he wants to help."

"Next Summer will be your nineteenth Summer. That is when most students start their training at the School for Servants."

Olei stopped. For years, he knew, he had gradually been craving more. He had read everything he could find in the

Altarnary twice. The only book outside the Altarnary was a thin volume of vaguely dirty poetry sitting on a mantle in the Curly Top, and he had read that so many times he could see each page in his mind. Yet he had never admitted to himself he could be more than Tobin's assistant. He had never actually thought it possible that he could somewhere, learn the same things that Tobin learned, and then return to Halrin's Spur as Tobin's equal. And if he had imagined it, he would have had no idea how to make it happen. Where would he stay? How would he eat? And most of all, how would he live among people he had never known?

"Are you coming?" Tobin said.

"But I don't know how," Olei replied.

"You put one foot in front..."

"No! How do I get to the School for Servants?"

"As a servant adept, I am allowed to nominate candidates for selection. I have explained your usefulness to me, and your intelligence, and I have received word back. They expect you next SummerTop. Interestingly, Fasha was not so sure. She thought you should wait a few years and then apply to the Sophenary.

"I don't want to wait a few years!"

"That's what I told her. Besides, the Sophenary is a strange place. I think you will do well at the School. They have enough books to fill an entire room."

"What...what do I take?"

"That's over a dozen passages from now. There's plenty of time to get ready."

They walked in silence, each caught up in his own thoughts. Just like that, Olei felt he had been invited to walk through the doorway into a wider world. "Next Summer, we should begin building on the far side of the river. Paddocks, storehouses, and even some dwellings."

"You're right. I've been thinking the same things."

"We need the space, and the forest edge is getting to be too far from the kilns."

"Good ideas, Ologrin. I'll let you know how things go."

"Good what?"

"I will write you at the School and let you know how things go."

Olei pondered the ground in front of his feet, replaying the conversation. "What did you just say?"

"The School for Servants."

"No. You said good ideas, and then something else. Some word."

Tobin reached over and touched Olei on the face. In their years together, he had rarely done something quite so tender. It surprised Olei almost as much as if he had been slapped.

"Many names have meaning," Tobin said. "My own name: I've heard that it means *the gods are good*. I like to imagine my own parents looking over me as a baby, naming me for that reason. It also means *mud dauber*, for the workers who used to build walls out of mud, before we baked brick. So maybe I'm that, too."

"What does Olei mean?"

"That's just it. It doesn't mean anything. But Olei is not your name."

"How can that not be my name?" Olei surprised himself with the agitation in his own voice.

"Your mother, I believe, called you Olei. Your father, I think, said something else. Olo, I'm guessing, but that is only a word fragment, so likely it was your nickname, a substitute for your real name."

"Olo," he said. "Olei." He tried to recall his mother calling his name, but the memory was too dim.

"Fasha and I talked about a great many things, including your name. She insists it is Polfre. Your mother, she thinks, called you Olei. It comes from *olo*, which means *small one*. But it's only ever used as part of larger words, and those words are not names for a child. It would be like naming a child 'worry' or 'brightness.' Nobody does that. Fasha is convinced, and now so am I, that it was just a shortened form of your real name.

"What's my real name?"

"Your real name is Ologrin. Literally translated, Fasha said, it means *small spark, new flame*. But she said that didn't capture it exactly. It had something to do with the hidden ember that starts an unexpected fire. Certainly not a name for a child, I said. Nonetheless, it is you."

"Ologrin," he said, trying it on. "Why do I need a new name?"

"It has always been your name. You just needed time to grow into it."

"But why do I have a Polfre name?"

"That's the real question, isn't it? Interestingly, on that one subject Fasha wouldn't tell me what she thought."

"Ologrin," he said again. "You know, I think my old name is fine. It's mine. No one else can tell me to change it."

Tobin smiled. "That's true. But you might find that new circumstances warrant a new name. Sometimes people change. Their names can change, too. Anyway, let's hurry. It's going to be cold again tonight."

SECOND PASSAGE

Gorval, who later became Serenity the First Incarnation, claimed to have one vision per night for twelve dozen nights in a row. Each vision became one passage in the Book of Obligations. *It is a rather slender book for having been the source of so many sleepless nights.*

After writing down the Book, Serenity realized he needed his own school for educating the many priests and servants he dreamed of spreading throughout Lhosa. He modelled his school after the Sophenary, even to the point of granting warrants adept to his graduates. But one of the biggest differences between the Sophenary and the School for Servants is that the Sophenary serves the needs of its students, while at the School for Servants, the students serve the needs of the School.

Scholars now debate whether, with the Book of Obligations, Serenity intended to create a historical document or a sacred one. All documents have errors. Histories by their very nature are incomplete. There is always room for new findings to correct or further illuminate the existing narrative. Sacred documents, on the other hand, assume an aura of authority, which makes them impervious to change, even when new information illustrates their errors.

Second Passage

Sacred documents are elevated above the realm of debate. As a result, they risk becoming objects of worship even more so than the gods whose stories they tell.

—From *The Invention of History* by Robin the Archivist

6

Apprentice servant fourth-year Ologrin stood at the low railing that defined one side of the fragrant Crown's Walk, feeling a bit like royalty himself. His stiff-collared grey cloak resisted the breeze that blew constantly from Gosper Bay up the steep slopes of the Purse. It was the beginning of Summer, and the dozens of flowering scarab trees planted down the middle of the Crown's Walk were perfuming the air and dropping yellow petals by the bucketful, gilding the walkway. Several other strollers were enjoying the fresh breeze and crisp blue sky. A couple, elegantly dressed in brocaded and bejeweled fabrics, strolled the Walk, delighted in each other's company. As they approached Ologrin they quieted, and both gave the slightest bow. "Your grace," the man murmured as he passed by.

Ologrin felt both thrilled by and a bit guilty over the title. It most certainly did not yet belong to him. Only the priests who had completed the rites were officially entitled to be called "your grace." Tobin had often been called that, but he, also, did not deserve the title, as he had never advanced into priestly studies. The public, however, rarely made the distinction, especially in a place where acknowledging social rank was important. Anyone in the gray or white cloaks of the clergy was likely to be called "your grace" several times a day, regardless of their actual rank. Even though Ologrin might never hope to own a fraction of that couple's wealth, he still gained their respect.

Antola. The Crown of Lhosa. Its biggest city. Without question, he thought, its most important. There were other cities arrayed along the southern half of the continent—Madros, Solanon, Dormond, Ismay—but they were not the jeweled city. The richest and most powerful people lived in Antola. Serenity the Seventh, the current Crown, lived here, in the palace not far from where Ologrin stood. The Lord Priest lived here, making it the administrative home of the Panthea. Antola's influence stretched to the far edges of Lhosa. Ologrin had been taught that the Panthea was vital to that influence. And he was a part of that, now in his last year before applying for the priesthood himself. He had come a long way from tiny Halrin's Spur.

He looked east and down, across the tight, twisting streets of the Purse as they peeked between the profusion of wood and stone houses, rooftop gardens, shops, looms, and forges, winding inexorably toward the docks. Ten ships were moored there, and another half-dozen stood out in the harbor, waiting their turn. A huge loading deck, a marvel of engineering known as the trestle lift, ascended and descended the steep slope, cutting a gash through the Purse. The deck rode on massive rails supported by an interlaced web of timbers and pilings, pulled up the rails with ropes as thick as a man's leg connected to capstans inside the winding house, itself just below the Crown's Walk. Ologrin could hear a musical hum coming from the winding house nearby, as some great mechanism inside worked to haul a load of daily provender up from the bay and into the open mouth of the city. Neither smoke nor steam escaped from the winding house, only music.

Beyond the docks was the vast expanse of Gosper's Bay.

Ologrin could not see the foundations of the mountains that formed the far shore; the peaks appeared to rise from the water itself. It was proof that, like the Sojourner, their world was yet another sphere. It was obvious to anyone who took the time to see, thought Ologrin, although several of his fellow students looked at him quizzically when he said such things. Once, several of them had made the difficult, two-day trek south of the city to the tumbled stones of the Salient, a collapsed tower on the bluffs that looked out over the Southern Sea itself. Ologrin had pointed out how both water and land disappeared when they looked west along the ragged coastline. "Do you really think the land itself falls off the edge?" he had asked them. Their pensive gazes told him they feared it might.

Ologrin turned in a slow circle. The northern end of the Crown's Walk terminated at the steps to the castle of the Sophenary, built against the first mountain in the Adamantine chain. Its heavy stone towers and lanterns seemed carved from the mountain itself. At the southern end, much closer to where he stood, the Crown's Walk ended at the unassuming palace of the Crown, a walled plaza with buildings of smooth-carved sandstone blocks. Compared to the soaring heights of the Sophenary's castle, the palace was a low and rambling collection of buildings. The Crown's personal apartments and court were no doubt splendidly appointed inside, but from without were indistinguishable from the carefully laid sandstone walls of the administrative buildings that comprised the rest of the palace.

Ologrin's destination was not the palace, but a wide set of steps descending from the Crown's Walk to the western half of Antola. This was the true city, the western residents liked to say. Homes and gardens for the wealthiest of Antola's merchants competed much more formally for his eye compared to the ragged, tumultuous architecture of the Purse. Twelve wide terraces stepped their way down to the ledge of the escarpment, which towered six gross hands above the river valley below. The escarpment was topped by an insurmountable defensive wall, interrupted by a pair of heavily defended granite arches: The Western Gate.

Two terraces below where Ologrin stood, the tenth terrace bulged outward at its center, forcing a distortion in the terraces below it. The broad bulge provided the foundation for two of the most important institutions in Antola. To the south was the merchant's market, fed by a tunnel from the Purse, where virtually all goods and foods brought up on the trestle lift flowed into the western city. Though officially existing for the city's re-sellers, the merchant's market attracted many Antolan shoppers, who enjoyed strolling amidst the noise and smells, looking for bargains or for rare spices and produce that tended to be snapped up by tavern owners and never made it to street-side shops. But Ologrin was not headed for the market, either, as much as he enjoyed it. In contrast to the market's disordered bustle; to its north lay the gardens of the School for Servants of the Panthea, engraved with straight, crisscrossing paths and crisp stone buildings. In the middle rose the High Altarnary itself, a massive black block and dome that could easily have housed four Altarnaries like the one in Halrin's Spur. From the valley floor, leagues to the west, approaching Sojourners would make out two structures above the escarpment long before any other buildings in the city became recognizable: the castle spires of the Sophenary, and the black bulk of the Altarnary.

At times, it was hard for Ologrin to believe he had already been here almost four full years. A few more passages and he would have the same education as Tobin. When he had first arrived, he had felt terribly out of place among the other students, most of whom were from important families in either either Antola or Madros. That feeling had not entirely disappeared, and there were always students intent on making sure he did not pretend to deserve their social status.

But social status was not his goal, education was. Much of the work of the students was indeed service: apprenticing to the Altarnary priests for their many duties and ceremonies. On occasion, one of the priests would hold a class that students from a particular year were expected to attend. Otherwise, formal classwork was uncommon. Ologrin discovered he was, by and large, responsible for his own education. In his first year, he read and re-read the Book of Obligations and the associated Commentaries, something few of his classmates seemed to do. During his second year, when he was no longer required to serve as an acolyte in the Altarnary, he spent whole days in the School's library, searching through the dusty shelves and bins. In addition to the books copied in standard Antolan, there were dozens and dozens of original, handwritten rolls. The library steward, an old adept named Linas, pointed out that the rolls were stored based on common themes, such as letters, commerce records, and Crown proclamations, but otherwise in no meaningful order. Ologrin worked his way through bin after bin. Initially, his reading was slow, as they had not all been written in standard Antolan. But with time he began to see the patterns, regardless of the writer, and found he could read them more easily.

Eventually Ologrin discovered an unusual collection of rolls, all written in the same neat, small hand. They were a different set of records describing Antola's past, and they did not always agree with what the Panthea taught. Ologrin was deeply fascinated, and many days he read until late in the evening, when Linas would finally shoo him out the door.

Ologrin understood that the Book of Obligations was meant to convey a specific message. He could therefore forgive the stories that seemed improbable and could even swallow some of its contradictions. But he had less patience with the Commentaries. Instead of explaining these difficult passages, they merely glossed over them. By contrast, the rolls he had discovered told a different story, one where the details seemed to be the point, but the message was elusive. At times, gazing upward in the evening at the timeless machinery of the skies, he could not help but think the workings of the Panthea had been hurriedly and not so neatly assembled.

Ologrin quickened his step, as he did not want to be late for class.

By design, the wide stone steps leading from one terrace down to the next were not aligned with each other. Ologrin had to walk a zig-zag pattern to work his way down. But he had long since determined the shortest routes from anywhere back to the School, and soon he was walking across the gardens between the buildings. Today's class was in the High Altarnary, but not in the Grand Altar room itself. He entered the building and headed for one of the small Winks surrounding the great hall. Inside, each Wink was laid out like a miniature Altar room: a round room with benches curving around a central altar. The ceiling was gently domed, and in the central oculus a plastered, painted sky stood in for the real one.

Ologrin unclasped his cloak and hung it on the hooks provided, then found his favorite bench. The benches themselves were cushioned and covered with supple leather. Everything about the room was soft and luxurious.

"Commentary Thirteen, and I believe we left off at Thesis Nine, is that correct?" Servant Priest Moran, their lecturer, stood in the center of the room. He was perhaps fifteen years older than Ologrin. He wore a gold band around his collar announcing he had achieved the priesthood. He was poised, well-groomed, and infinitely assured of himself. He was the embodiment of grace.

"The discussant suggests this passage in the Obligations gets to the heart of the relationship Malach has with the other gods. Malach kneels before them and speaks: *'You have manifested your sacrifice and become worthy to stand before me. I, in turn, kneel before you. Your leader is your servant.' Then Malach stood and bade each come before him, where he pressed his blade to their neck, marking them as his own.*

"Most commentators focus on Malach's act of kneeling before the other gods before he asserts his dominance. In this way, they say, Malach not only asserts that he is both servant and lord, but foreshadows the worldly rule of the Crown, which both serves and leads us all.

"But I would like you to comment on the first phrase. *You have manifested your sacrifice.* What do you suppose Malach meant by that? Anyone have an opinion?"

Every head was down, as if they all had suddenly become so absorbed in the wonders of the text that they didn't hear the question. Eventually one student glanced at Moran, and immediately regretted it.

"Xedus, you have an opinion?"

Ologrin had noticed Moran seemed to be calling on Xedus more, even as his responses contained less. Xedus was the younger son of a man who had once served as the arms-commander of Madros, and now controlled the market for many Madrosan imports. As the youngest of two, Xedus' path to power was not going to be as easy as his older brother's, but he had only to stay out of too much trouble and he could expect to be made a priest, after which higher positions would eventually be his. Moran, however, seemed intent on pushing Xedus to the point of humiliation. The result was that Xedus had begun to lash out at others, and Ologrin had been a frequent target of his anger.

"You have an opinion?" Moran repeated.

"Oh. Well, yes, your grace," Xedus replied.

"Would you mind sharing with the rest of us?"

"Yes. Well, we perform Malach's Oblation because it is what we must do. To show our loyalty."

"Very erudite, apprentice Xedus. Would you all agree?"

There was barely perceptible nodding. The class suspected

Xedus was being mocked but didn't want to ignore the possibility his answer was also miraculously correct.

"Anyone care to comment? Ologrin?"

Ologrin winced inside. Not only was Moran calling on Xedus more, he was calling on Ologrin afterward, pitting their intellects in front of the rest of the class. Regardless of his response, it only served to irritate Xedus. Increasingly, not only Xedus but those who surrounded him and benefitted from proximity to his family's wealth made it clear they did not think Ologrin belonged in the school.

For his part, Ologrin did not begrudge Xedus his wealth or his station. He had no illusion he was the young man's equal simply for sitting in the same class. He would be happy to avoid the attention of Xedus and his friends. Moran was making that impossible.

Ologrin knew that if he failed to answer Moran's question, Xedus and his friends would mock him for it later. But if he answered the question correctly, then he would appear to be making a fool of Xedus, and retribution was just as likely. There was no way to win. He spoke slowly. "To call something a *manifest sacrifice* is redundant, if you ask me."

"Indeed?" Moran said. "Are you suggesting that the sacred text is too wordy, perhaps? That it is in need of some skillful editing? Are you offering your services?"

Several students chuckled softly. Xedus cast him an evil, sidelong smile. "No, your grace," Ologrin said.

"Would you care to enlighten us more?"

Ologrin had made his choice. He would not be today's fool. "A sacrifice is hardly a sacrifice unless the recipient knows about it. Thus, it is already manifested to that individual. To refer to something as a manifest sacrifice suggests that the purpose is to make it obvious to everyone else. The gods' sacrifices were meant to impress each other with how much they were willing to do in service to Malach."

"Interesting. But why would the gods want to do that?"

Ologrin was warming to his subject. "It turns the sacrifice into a competition. Instead of just trying to please Malach, they are also trying to best one another."

"Are you suggesting the other gods were serving their own personal agendas at the same time they were honoring Malach? What kind of offering is that?"

"Malach is a god. What he wants he takes. He doesn't need anyone's offerings. He needs their loyalty, the only thing he cannot simply take for himself. The sacrifice is a test, to see how far they are willing to go to manifest their loyalty to him."

"Does anyone else agree with Ologrin?"

Moran let the silence hang in the room for a few moments. A few of the students followed Ologrin's argument and were inclined to agree, but feared it represented the too-radical position: the one to be dismissed. Of late, many of their classes had devolved into a one-on-one discussion between Moran and Ologrin. On some occasions Moran would correct Ologrin, but on others would praise him for his insight. In the meantime, they were beginning to feel like they were the ones being sacrificed so that Ologrin could show off.

"Understanding the true meaning of the Obligations requires each of us to think deeply about what we read," Moran said. "The authors had many moments from the gods' lives to choose from. That they chose these is more than simple storytelling, it indicates there are deeper meanings to be found. Truths within truths. I, for one, agree with apprentice Ologrin. Malach seeks to know if the gods will do just enough for him, or if they are willing to prove their loyalty by whatever means are necessary. Xedus, if I asked you for a sacrifice, what would you give me?"

Xedus had the look of someone stabbed from behind. "I... your grace?"

"Would you give me your cloak? Would you sacrifice your warmth?"

"Yes, your grace."

"Would you give me your meal?"

Xedus, who understood he was at least pretending to learn something about serving, answered more firmly. "Of course, your grace."

"If the Crown asked you to leave your family and live like a bisonherder, would you do that?"

Xedus snickered; the idea was so ridiculous as to not even be offensive. "That would never happen," he said.

"But what if it did? What if there was no good reason, except that the Crown commanded it."

"My father..." Xedus began.

"Forget your father. What if you had to give up everything most important to you, to live in filth, just to serve the wishes of the Crown, even though you didn't know why? Could you do it?" The tips of Xedus' ears had turned bright red. "*That* would be a manifest sacrifice," Moran said finally.

Xedus stared straight ahead. Ologrin doubted Xedus had ever had his privileged life challenged, even hypothetically. He imagined the young man was seething inside. The longer Moran's attention was on him, the more pain it would mean for someone else later.

"The Panthea purchases animals for use in the Oblation, is that correct?" Ologrin said, breaking the silence.

"Of course. We don't have the space to raise our own animals," Moran replied.

"Those who raise them get paid, and it costs the Panthea less than it would to raise the animals themselves."

"I imagine that's true," Moran said.

"Then there's not much sacrifice anymore, is there? Certainly not a manifest sacrifice."

Moran's attention was no longer on Xedus.

"It is symbolic of something larger. Sometimes the symbolism is sufficient."

"Symbolic of human sacrifice?" Ologrin asked.

The room fell silent.

"What did you say?" Moran asked coldly.

"You said a manifest sacrifice would include giving up something very important. Sacrificing a life would be much more manifest than losing a silver or two."

Moran stared at him. Ologrin was suddenly very uncomfortable. It had not been his intention, but he sensed he had crossed a line. It wasn't the first time. In his first week, when he failed to recognize the cloak of a young priest and did not address him as "your grace," he crossed a line. When he told the story of his experience with the people of the milkhouse and their response to the wooden statue of Alera, he crossed a line with the old priest Bromon, who found the story vulgar. The line was always invisible until after he crossed it. "That's how you learn," he was told, after he had suffered through the embarrassment. But no one else, it seemed, spent any time across the line.

"A symbol is a reminder," Moran said stiffly. "Malach could call on you for much more at any time."

Ologrin sat quietly until the lesson ended. He stared up at the image of the sky in the oculus, a ridiculous depiction of fat stars and blue sky made up of fragments of painted glass cemented to the inside of the dome. He thought of the real stars, impossibly tiny pricks in the curtain of the night sky. He could see fewer of them here in the city. He surmised it was because it was never truly dark in Antola. The uncountable house lanterns and candle-filled windows stained the night with leftover light.

Moran dismissed the class. Ologrin sat until the rest of the apprentices had departed, hoping to avoid running into Xedus or his friends. He finally stood to leave. He found his cloak lying on the floor beneath the pegs, with a dirty footprint on it. He tried to wipe it off. It was an accident, he told himself, one of many that seemed to befall him. As he left the Wink, he saw Moran standing in the gallery of the Grand

Altar room, waiting for him. The coldness in his eyes had thawed somewhat.

"I appreciate your enthusiasm, Ologrin, but sometimes you go too far."

"I didn't mean to be offensive."

"The celebration of the Oblation has deep meaning to many people. It connects them to their gods and to their past," Moran said, as they walked out into the gardens.

"In the past, though, the Oblation was much more, right?"

"What do you mean?"

"Doesn't it have its origins in Malacheb ritual sacrifices?"

Moran stopped and looked Ologrin in the eyes. "That is not a fit subject for discussion."

"I meant…"

"You meant to suggest there was a time when the ancestors of Antola might have used living persons in their rituals. You meant to draw a connection between the sacred Oblation and stories about savagery from the long ago past. Let me stop you. Those are nothing but offensive myths."

"But I thought…I thought it was practiced by the Malacheb before they…before the Eidos came to live in Antola."

"Where did you hear that?"

Ologrin had first heard it from the arms-captain, the night he had been attacked. But then he had read it again in the library and had assumed it was common knowledge. "It's something I read," he replied.

"What kind of something?"

"Rolls."

"You have been reading rolls? What were they called?"

"*The Chronicles of Grebe the Elder.*"

"I see. Those rolls. And adept Linas is aware of this?"

"I believe so. Well, most of the time he sleeps."

Moran looked at the walls and sighed. "They were written by the Polfre," he said. Seeing the ongoing look of confusion on Ologrin's face, he continued, "The Polfre cannot be trusted. They are a self-centered people, and they have a self-centered explanation for how Donal conquered Antola. Much of it is in direct contradiction to the Book of Obligations."

"I met someone once…" Ologrin trailed off. He thought often of his experience with Pipit at Southwatch, years before. *"People can have the same experience and yet believe different things about it,"* she had said. Self-centered seemed the wrong way to describe Pipit. What had he missed?

"Raw stories and simple customs may be the practice where you come from, but you must learn they can be offensive in civil society," Moran added. "You must have years of training to understand the true meaning of things. Talking about them without fully understanding them is disruptive, and, quite frankly, might be considered heretical. Talking about the Oblation in this way is as offensive to civilized ears as…as being referred to as a shit-swimmer."

Ologrin blushed. More than once, since arriving in Antola, he had heard the poor people who labored along the river-flats, tending the Crown's bison herds, referred to in that way. Before arriving in Antola he had never imagined someone might think he was one of them. Yet now he was careful not to talk about his previous life in Halrin's Spur, for fear no one would make the distinction between him and the people of the flats. They would think he was a shit-swimmer, too.

"What do we call this school?" Moran asked.

"The School for Servants."

"For most of the students who pass through here, that is exactly what they are destined to be. And what will they serve?"

"The Faith. The Panthea."

"What else?"

Ologrin paused a bit too long.

"The Crown, Ologrin. Never let that leave your head. Serenity brought together the Council of Antola not simply to anoint a new faith, but to bind people together politically. We are producing servants for the Crown. Look around. Do you think the treasury would spend this much on a place just so a handful of overly-serious priests could debate the finer points of the Commentaries?"

At times, lying on his bed in the evenings, Ologrin had imagined himself returning to Halrin's Spur and debating the Commentaries with Tobin over a mug of cider. He realized he had never actually seen Tobin reading them. Tobin probably did not care about the Commentaries. He cared about his neighbors and his village, and in that way he served the Crown. Ologrin felt his ears flush again.

"Your mind can be too sharp for your own good. Perhaps the time has come to limit our discussions to private meetings. Do you know where the Upturned Shield is? Seventh terrace?" Tobin asked. Ologrin nodded slowly. "Good. Tomorrow just before Sunset. Meet me there and we will talk. We can make it a regular event. Surely an apprentice servant won't turn down at least one free meal per passage."

They walked out into the slanting late afternoon light. The terraces gleamed. On the other side of the ridge Ologrin imagined the Purse was already in shadow, and lanterns had already been lit.

"From now on, in class, you just listen while I will tell the rest of them what they need to know. Then they can sit there hoping I don't call on them to repeat it," Moran said.

Ologrin tried to smile. "I am sorry, your grace."

"Don't worry about it. That's how you learn."

7

Though they were in the first passage of Summer, the next day was cool, and rain clouds hung low over Antola. Ologrin pulled his cloak close about him. Many of Antola's more prosperous merchants and arms officers lived on the seventh terrace. Fine stone houses of two and three floors stood side by side, some with glass in their first-floor windows instead of shutters. Shops displayed luxury fabrics and wares of bronze and silver. The Upturned Shield was nothing like what Ologrin would have considered a tavern prior to moving to the city. Tables were made of heavily carved wood, with ornate chairs instead of benches for seating. The walls were nearly hidden behind banners and displays of old weapons. Ologrin entered hesitantly. An older man in a red tunic and breeches approached. He expected to be challenged, but the man said "Welcome, your grace," and went about his business. Ologrin undid the clasp of his cloak and spied Moran sitting by himself at a large table near a great stone hearthgrate. The fire was banked low but radiated warmth across the room. Moran noticed him at the same time and waved him over.

Another red-dressed man set pewter plates and cups

before them, and food arrived unbidden. Ologrin was relieved to see it was familiar: fish, followed by bison stew, along with small loaves of light, airy rye bread. The stew was exceptionally delicious, prepared with a sauce he had never experienced. Fortunately, Moran's attention seemed to be taken up with the food as well, as Ologrin did not think he would have been able to concentrate on questions while eating. When he finally sat back, the shadows outside were long. Several glass-paned windows faced the street. The windows of nearby houses were filled with cheery candles. Ologrin sipped at a cup of dark wine. Moran seemed especially pleased with it, but Ologrin found it to be full of strange tastes, and not nearly as good, he thought, as the cider he drank back home. Moran seemed to be lining up questions in his head.

"What do you know about the Council of Antola?" he said finally.

"Well, I know it was called together by Serenity the First, about fifteen dozen years ago. It was meant to remind people that the gods are a family."

"Forget the gods," Moran said, to Ologrin's surprise. "It was meant to bring people together. Religion is politics, Ologrin. Why would the gods care if some mortal chief suddenly declares them to be part of this family or that? And if they did, do you think they would tell us by directing a bunch of scribes to write a book, when most of the people can't read? Most people still believe the gods talk to us through earthquakes and sorcery. Even those who can read would think it strange to look for answers in a book. Almost no one outside of the School for Servants reads the Obligations, much less the Commentaries."

Ologrin recalled he had read the Obligations twice before even getting to the school.

Moran opened a book he had been hiding in his lap and began to read. "*Malach, seeing that his people were just and faith-*

ful, brought them to a high place, where they looked down on a great city. Malach said, 'Behold the city of power and enchantment. By my might, you shall conquer this city, and throw down its people, and it shall be yours for as long as you remain true to me.'" He stopped and looked at Ologrin. "What is that from?"

"*The Obligations*, Second Vision."

Maron smiled thinly. "I knew you would know. Here's another question. When you were reading those Polfre rolls, I assume you found writings about Donal the Conqueror?"

"Yes," he said, hesitantly.

"Let me guess what you read. According to the Polfre, over four gross years ago Donal led his people, the Malacheb, through the mountains and onto the escarpment and found a complete city just waiting for them. The Polfre had already been living in Antola for more than a dozen gross years. Before Donal's father's grandfather's grandfather was born, they had cut the terraces out of solid rock, had built the Crown's Walk, had dug out the harbor and built the docks. By the time Donal arrived, Antola was a fortress like Lhosa had never seen. Yet the Polfre just invited them in. They simply stepped aside and let Donal and his tribe take over the city. Is that about right?"

"Yes," Ologrin replied.

"Doesn't that strike you as exceedingly strange? That after a dozen gross years they would just step away? Nothing about being conquered or cast down; they just gave it up. Which story more believable?" Moran asked. "The one told by the Polfre, where they just give a whole city away, or the one in the Book of Obligations, which shows Malach's might?"

"Maybe both?" Ologrin said.

"But which one matters?"

Ologrin was silent.

"Did Donal find the city, or did Malach find it for him? For those of us who serve, the real story is that Malach *ordained* it.

Donal was the first Crown, and every Crown since has been one of his descendants. Did Donal's tribe sacrifice living people, at some point in their far, far past? What if Polfre histories say they did? Would that be more important that the Panthea saying they didn't? Which history is more important? Which does service to the Crown?

"Serenity convened the Council because he wanted to bring the people of the Lhosan continent together. Donal worshipped Malach; he believed Malach was a warrior by his side, and so the Antolans have worshipped Malach ever since. But in the fertile lands of Dormond they have little use for a warrior god. They need a god of fertility, Alera, to protect their fields and orchards. Serenity realized he needed Alera, too, because he needed Dormond, because Antola had grown too large to feed itself."

Moran pointed at Ologrin with a crust from one of the loaves. "Have you ever seen a field of rye?"

Ologrin shook his head again. He wasn't sure he would know one if he saw one.

"That's because all the rye we use comes from Dormond, as well has half the fruit and vegetables. Serenity knew he needed Dormond, so he remade Alera into Malach's wife. He even tried to include the Ismayans, creating a god for them too: Bochlus, calling him the brother of Malach."

Moran's casual dismissal of the sacredness of the Panthea surprised Ologrin. This was not the collected wisdom of the ages. It was a hastily constructed scaffolding. Ologrin could not decide whether he felt a bit scandalized, or perhaps just foolish for having ever accepted anything about the gods at face value.

"You have not escaped attention, Ologrin. You are a candidate for the priesthood. But it is not enough to be smart or studious. You must fit the cloak. They are not going to alter it to fit you."

Ologrin's eyes were drawn to Moran's crisp, white cloak,

and the single gold band surrounding the tall collar. White was such an impractical color. It signified living a life requiring no physical exertion. A life spent thinking.

"Tobin and I were at the School together; did you know that?" Moran added.

Just the mention of his friend's name lifted Ologrin's spirits. "You know Tobin?"

"He was one year ahead of me. When he contacted me saying he had a good candidate for the School, I didn't hesitate. I'll admit, when I found out about your origins, I was concerned...I was concerned they might conflict with our more traditional students, but I thought it was nothing that couldn't be managed. And now I see how correct Tobin was. You are destined to be more than just a servant adept. But like I say, you need to fit the cloak. And that means you're going to need a better heritage."

"I can't change my heritage."

"Does anyone here really know your heritage? Have you talked to the other students about where you came from?"

Ologrin shook his head. "It didn't seem like a good idea."

"Good. We'll make something up. We'll invent your heritage."

"What if someone finds out?"

"No one will care, unless you do something to stir their interest."

Ologrin felt uncomfortable. He trusted that Moran knew exactly what was needed for him to move forward into the priesthood, but a lie was a lie. Or he used to think so. For Moran, the facts seemed to be secondary to the goal. As if he could read his mind, Moran spoke again.

"Don't forget, Ologrin, we are servants. We have chosen to serve the Crown and the people of Antola, and to defend the Panthea of the gods. Some do so by worshiping the gods. Others do it by protecting the Panthea from those who would undermine it. We need both. You have the intellect to hold two simultaneous, competing thoughts in your head. Two things can be true at the same time. It is not easy, nor is it comfortable to think that way. But we need that for the Panthea."

Ologrin appreciated the flattery, but it did not ease the knot in his chest.

"I don't want to ruin your eagerness to explore and to learn, apprentice Ologrin. I only want to remind you that you are here to serve, and that service to the greater good comes before satisfying your own curiosity. So, if I warn you to be careful of what you read in the library, it comes from my greater experience. And if I stop you in class, it is not necessarily because you are wrong, but because you are putting service behind your personal pursuits."

They sat quietly for a few moments. Ologrin suspected Moran was studying him, to see how he reacted. Ologrin was learning to keep his troubled emotions from showing on his face. "Thank you, your grace," he said quietly.

"It's late, and I have kept you out far too long," Moran said. "You are welcome to stay in the tavern tonight. I will pay for the room."

"No, but thank you," Ologrin said. "I will be fine getting home."

"Then surely a lantern. The tavern can lend us one, and I will have it returned later."

"It really is no problem," Ologrin replied. "I can see just fine in the dark."

Moran cocked his head ever so slightly, and Ologrin suddenly wished he had just accepted the lantern.

"I mean, there are still many lamps and candles on this level," Ologrin said. "I know my way up to the school grounds without needing a light."

"Well, good night, Ologrin. You are a talented student. Let's put that talent to the right use."

The clouds were breaking when Ologrin left the tavern.

He caught glimpses of an aging Sojourner settling toward the eastern horizon. When he reached his cell, Ologrin found a letter had been passed underneath his door. Controlling his excitement, he carefully reset the door latch, then lit a small oil lamp with his ember pot and sat down to read. The seal to the letter was broken, but this was always the case. Ologrin had learned there was official oversight of anything that passed to and from the School and was accordingly circumspect when writing his own letters. He smiled as he unfolded the pages and saw Tobin's familiar handwriting.

My good friend. When you read this, we will have finished the late Winter planting. The heather brake between the village and the milkhouse has been almost completely taken over by a garden full of vegetables and berries, which the community shares in equally. The cloudnettle is in full bloom along the riverbanks. Calus is working hard and considers himself my chief apprentice, though he is of course my only apprentice. He plans to try his hand at making an iron bloomery again this Summer. I do not believe he can make one large enough to work, and the quality of the charcoal has definitely declined since you left, though I suppose that was to be expected. Meanwhile, I have more work for the carpenter team, who have pulled together remarkably well in the past two years. I do believe they may become our first genuine...

...and here a word had been blacked out such that Ologrin could not read it...

Together they built an entirely new inn close to the road in Pebbley, and charged actual coin for it, instead of barter. <u>Of course, they paid the Crown's share</u>...

. . .

...underlined, which Ologrin suspected was because Tobin knew the letter was being read...

They will be heading to the north bridge this Harvest, which we will finally rebuild, with a guardhouse on our side including some clever ideas of my own. We have more bison than ever before. More bison means more milk, more cheese, more meat, more work! We miss your skillful hands and fearsome heart.
   Your servant, Tobin.

Ologrin re-read the letter several times. Tobin's letters were always the same: a few personal words, but mostly updates on the different projects he had going to fortify the town. And in all cases, the successful projects were community projects. The town was helping itself. He would occasionally mention plans taken on by a single individual, such as Calus and his attempts to smelt iron. In most cases the individual projects failed. In all cases the community projects succeeded.

Ologrin had no way of knowing what community failures Tobin was leaving out. It didn't matter. Ologrin knew that Tobin was painting a larger picture, and if someone other than his former apprentice was reading the letters and getting that picture, then so much the better. Tobin was building a community that believed in itself, and that was spreading that belief to the surrounding communities. He was building self-sufficiency. He was building independence.

He reviewed his little cell. His small window faced the west just as he preferred, which meant he had to stand and look down to see the descending terraces, but also meant he could lie in his bed and see the Sojourner when it rose to follow its contrary path. His servant cloak hung on a peg. He had an extra set of gray breeches and a tunic, as well as a bundle of personal things he had carefully assembled over the years: bisonhide breeches, a heavy shirt, boots, and the traveling cloak Tobin had given him years before, which he had grown into and which had only become softer and more comfortable over time. His stool was old but solid and fit neatly beneath the wide windowsill, which doubled as his writing desk. He had few other things, because he needed nothing else.

The knot in his chest had subsided. Moran painted a picture of a Panthea that seemed to exist just to meet the needs of the Crown. But he would not accept that. The gods, if they had any true meaning, were the gods of all people, not just the Crown. Anything else was overtly unfair, and thus not worthy of worship. And if the gods did not care about the suffering of the people, then there was little point in caring about them.

He unrolled his bedroll onto his bed, then sat against the back wall of his cell, legs crossed. He carefully removed the false cap he had made in one of the legs of the bed frame and removed his knife from its hiding place. He rarely wore it unless he was spending the day away from the school. He considered running the edge against a small stone he kept for that purpose, then decided against it. Since he had been a child, he had never managed to get the knife any sharper. Rubbing it against the stone only served to soothe his mind. He slipped the knife back into its hiding place. It was his one tangible connection with his home in Halrin's Spur. He positioned himself so he could see a few stars through his west window, but before he could imagine flying among them he was asleep, hidden in his cell deep within the School for Servants, deep within the gleaming city, deep beneath the star-spackled sky.

8

Service took up a modest portion of each passage. In his first and second years, Ologrin had spent most of his time assisting the priests with their ceremonies, learning by participating. Most of them had been small and private, arranged by wealthier families and held in the Winks surrounding the Grand Altar room. As a fourth-year, he had spent more time reading and tutoring, and his only official classes had been the one taught by Moran and a class taught by Servant Priest Bromon, which consisted of the old man reading the Commentaries out loud in his mumbling voice, without discussion. It was a painfully long morning, which Ologrin had to endure three days out of twelve. After the first few sessions, many of the other students stopped attending Bromon's class. Priest Bromon gave no indication that he either noticed or cared. Ologrin soon learned to tune out the priest's monotonous voice and spent the time reading books he had slipped out of the library in his pocket. Over the years he had come to think of the library as his library, and the contents his to use as he saw fit.

However, within two days of his dinner with Moran a chain had been erected across the section housing the bins full of rolls. The message was obvious. Ologrin felt hurt and saddened. He began several letters to Tobin describing his plight but sent none of them. He could hear Tobin telling him to stop fretting and to get busy figuring out an alternative. Fortunately, there was another small section in the library he had only glanced at before. Here he found four small books on the maths. He opened one, titled *Beginning Maths*, out of boredom, but quickly discovered a new way of thinking he had not previously experienced. The book was small, and Linas said he did not care if Ologrin took it with him. Over the next few days he consumed it, sitting in his cell and practicing the book's techniques on parchment. The book turned out to be one of a series. He moved on to the next one, entitled *Maths of Hidden Numbers*, and felt like he had discovered a new type of game. As he practiced the puzzles, he began to discover their everyday use, something he had never noticed before. In doing so, he discovered a flaw in the wheels and gears of the world he had not previously fully appreciated. A year was 273 days long: three seasons of 90 days each, plus one celebration day at the end of each season. Just as it should be. But each passage was twelve days long. Twelve did not fit into 273 very well. Each year was twenty-two passages, with nine days left over. That explained why every SummerTop rarely coincided with a New Sojourner. Twenty-four passages per year would have been perfect. But to miss it by three days was unforgivable sloppiness on the part of the god responsible.

Ologrin flipped through *Advanced Hidden Numbers*, the third volume in the series. This one was considerably more difficult, and had been for the author as well, as there were several places where incomplete problems on one page had been scratched through and restarted on the next. Ologrin had just started working through a difficult problem when Linas suddenly appeared at his side.

"You favor the Polfre, I see."

Ologrin was startled by the man's sudden presence. "I know what the chain means. I haven't been back to the rolls."

"The maths books. They were written by a Polfre, too."

"How was I to know?" Ologrin said defensively. "There's no author name."

If Linas sensed Ologrin's frustration, he did not acknowledge it. "There are a few other books by Polfre on the shelves. I know where each one of them is."

"And you're telling me to stay away from them?"

"Not too many," Linas said. Then he seemed to process Ologrin's response. "Oh no, no. You can read them, as far as I'm concerned. Just very few do. But you're a book person, like me.

"The Polfre, they concern themselves with plants and animals and numbers, and words. They have lots of words. Some of our words are their words; some aren't. *Oculus.* That's a Polfre word. What do you think it means?"

"Room? Round room?"

"Eye. Lhosa itself is a Polfre word," Linas added. "What do you think it means?"

"Great land? Continent?"

"It's their word for the shadow panther."

"Oh, of course." Ologrin recalled the outline of the Lhosan coastline. "Faerith and Forought…"

"The cat's ears. That's right."

"Bomlin?" Ologrin asked.

"Their word for a cat's paw. See it stretched out on a map? What do you think they call Antola?" Linas said conspiratorially, though there was no one else in the room with them.

"What?"

"The cat's ass!" Linas laughed at his own joke until he coughed.

Ologrin could not help but smile. *No one else I know would say that out loud,* he thought.

"If you want to know something about the bigger world,

you'll find it in Polfre books. They've got them at the Sophenary, of course. They have a room twice this big filled with Polfre books, and another room just for rolls. There's Polfre that do nothing but make new copies of books all day long."

"At the Sophenary?"

"Some are, and some aren't. There's Polfre who live in the Purse copying books too."

"Polfre in the Purse? I thought the only Polfre in Antola stayed at the Sophenary."

"Ah, no. The Purse is full of Polfre. Some people say they just moved over there when Donal took over Antola, and they've been running the whole place since. But they won't have anything to do with you unless it's their choice. They're small, you know, and quiet. You have to look for those glowing eyes."

Ologrin well remembered the golden reflection from Pipit's eyes. He imagined many dozens of flickering eyes moving through the Purse at night.

"Where could I find more Polfre books?"

Linas smiled. "I wondered if you'd ask the question. You got to find a copyist."

"What happens to the books that the Polfre copy?" he asked.

"They sell them, of course."

Up to that moment, Ologrin had never imagined people owning their own books. He had certainly never imagined owning a book of his own. He suddenly wanted one very badly.

"How much would a book cost?"

"Oh, maybe a silver. Some less. Depends on the time it takes to copy one."

"Do they have shops for books?"

Linas laughed. "A shop for nothing but books? No, you got to know where to find a copyist."

"Oh."

"You'd like to know where, I'm guessing. Have you spent much time in the Purse?"

"Not much." In fact, Ologrin had not found a reason to enter the Purse during his four years at the school. It required an education of a different sort not to get lost in its warren of alleys and structures. He had to admit he was a bit afraid of it. *How strange,* he thought, *to live so close to people for years and yet not know anything about them.*

The days of Summer grew long and warm, despite the breezes blowing up from Gosper Bay every afternoon. Ologrin met with Moran once per passage. Their conversations had turned from discussions of the Commentaries to discussions of priestly service. Moran suggested that Ologrin already knew more about the Obligations and the Commentaries than many priests, but still lacked an understanding of people in powerful places. Politics were an essential part of every priest's daily work, and Ologrin was far behind.

Like other students, Ologrin was able to earn a few extra durri providing tutoring sessions to children of the wealthier residents. For most people, education was little more than learning to read and do simple sums. He found that he enjoyed the sessions, and he figured Moran would consider it good political education as well.

In twelve days it would be SummerTop, the start of a new year. It would also be the day of New Sojourner. That was something that happened only once every six years. Due to his newfound understanding of the maths, he now understood why. It also aligned with the end of his apprentice servant education. He would be awarded a warrant adept, just like Tobin.

Ologrin assisted in two brief ceremonies in the Winks, then had the rest of the day to himself. As he had done many times before, he decided to walk down to the first terrace. Here, the buildings were lower and simpler. They reminded him, except for the paved streets, of Halrin's Spur. Ologrin felt at home on the first terrace. He had a favorite place where he could eat for cheap, and if he wore his traveling cloak instead of his student cloak, he could be comfortably anonymous.

A broad expanse of pavers separated the buildings of the first terrace from the city wall itself. Stone towers were spaced widely along the walkway. Each was topped with a massive bombard facing the lowlands beyond the escarpment, but they did not appear to have been fired for many years. The city wall was at least thirty hands high, but it was the escarpment, rising almost vertically many gross hands from the flats and running south from the foundations of the Adamantines until it disappeared into the sea, that provided Antola its true defense. From narrow breaks in the wall he could see the flatlands stretching west toward the river Bhin at the horizon. Herds of bison, small as ants, grazed across them. What few structures dotted the landscape were held together mostly by prayers. Four years before, walking to Antola to begin his education, he had passed through the flatlands on the journey from Halrin's Spur. He had been surprised by the poor conditions most flatland herders lived in. "Shit swimmers" was crude, but not far from the truth. Yet these people were responsible for the meat and the hides that provided Antolans with food, leather, tallow, and parchment. It was strange, he thought, how most Antolans seemed to have such disdain for the people who fed them.

With the Sun reaching farther into the northwest, he decided to climb back to the familiarity of the tenth terrace and wander through the merchant's market. Rough stone warehouses lined the terrace wall. Even though he had little in coin, he could walk through and peek at the bundles and sacks. The buildings were infused with sharp, peppery odors.

He bought a Dormond orange for two durri, then sat on a loading dock near the tunnel to the Purse to eat it. The tunnel was wide enough to allow two fully laden carts to pass each other. This afternoon it was empty, except for a steady breeze whistling through from the east to the west. He sat enjoying the peaceful view until the Sun touched the buildings of the lower terraces, then headed for home.

A great bronze kettle was suspended over the coals of a small fire near the entrance to Ologrin's cellhouse. Adept Herbin sat leaning against a wall. Herbin managed the long, low buildings that housed those apprentice servants who did not have homes in Antola, which included Ologrin. Herbin had, no doubt, sat there for most of the day, supervising the laundry servants.

"How did you manage to do that?" Herbin said.

Ologrin gave him a puzzled look.

"You've been in your cell all day. How did you manage to get out and me not see you?"

"I've been out most of the day," Ologrin said.

"Weren't you in there with your friends?"

"When have you seen me with friends?"

"I thought maybe you had found something to do other than read books."

Conversations with Herbin were odd, but this one seemed more so than most. He stepped through the door of the building only to have the old adept call him back.

"I have a message for you." The man waved a small, sealed parchment.

"Why didn't you slip it under my door?"

"Didn't want to bother you and your friends."

Ologrin shook his head while opening the seal. Inside he recognized the bold, sweeping slashes of Moran's hand.

· · ·

Meeting tomorrow at the Lord Priest's residence, Mid-day. Dress your best.
   SPM

Until that moment, the priesthood, for Ologrin, had been somewhere in the future. Even though Moran had advanced the idea, it had not seemed real. But now, as he reread the note several times, he began to imagine himself with a white cloak. In twelve days, if accepted, it would no longer be an abstraction. Being called *your grace* would be his due. He had spent four years absorbed in the details of his education, without ever having thought much about where it would take him. Now there was no more time to wonder or worry. He hurried to his cell, trying to envision what he might be asked, what he wanted to say.

He opened the door. The smell slapped him, making him step back. His first thought was that he had managed to enter someone else's cell, and that they were truly disgusting residents. But he was at the end of the long hall. The door was his. The room, and the awful stench coming from it, was his. He stepped inside slowly.

His bedroll had been ripped open; the soft fir needle stuffing flung all over the room. The bed frame itself had been turned on its side and the rushwork weaving had been torn apart. All his clothing had been piled in the center of the room and reeked of urine. His few remaining belongings had been tossed in the corners.

And on the wall opposite his window, someone had painted a large symbol in red-brown paint. It was crudely drawn, but unmistakable: a five-rayed star painted on top of an inverted triangle. He had seen it before, a moment he would never forget.

"I know what you are!" she had said. But she was dead. Yet here, in the heart of the most civilized place in the most civi-

lized city in the world, the same message confronted him from the wall of his cell. He felt a surge of panic. *Why me? What should I do?* His face felt hot, and he had to wipe away tears. But then he forced himself to take a deep breath. "Malacheb. I know what you are too," he whispered.

Herbin appeared genuinely distressed at the condition of Ologrin's cell. The washing tub was still outside. He sent a messenger to reassemble his servants, so they could help wash Ologrin's clothing and do what they could to clean up the room. Fortunately, whoever had fouled his clothes had not had the desire nor cunning to slash them as well. He might still have something to wear for his meeting the next day. Herbin brought out an old spare sleeping roll. Ologrin assured him he had spent many nights sleeping on a floor and wouldn't be bothered by a few more.

"Vandals from the Purse," Herbin said, shaking his head.

"Why do you think they were from the Purse?" Ologrin asked.

"Who else would do this? Antolans would not do this."

"The Malacheb did this! Do you see the wall?"

"No, no, there aren't any Malacheb at the school," Herbin said.

"Then where did that symbol come from?"

The adept looked at Ologrin with a puzzled expression, as if his question made no sense. But he promised to have the bed frame repaired and the cell's walls whitewashed soon.

At the north border of the gardens stood the School's second-largest building, built of sandstone blocks so pale as to appear white next to the black bulk of the High Altarnary. The Lord Priest both lived and worked there, along with his attendant priests and servants. Ologrin presented himself just before midday the next day. They had managed to wash the smell out of his cloak and tunic, but both were still damp and left him chilled, despite the mid-Summer Sun. The servant at the door eyed his rumpled cloak and reluctantly ushered him into a small room, where he waited briefly until another servant found him and led him down a short hall.

The room he entered was spacious, with a low ceiling of timbers and plaster. A large table dominated one end, set before a pair of glassed-in windows. Two ornate globes, each the size of a man's head and supported on bronze stands, flanked the table. Thick glass prisms were set between gilded banding on each globe, and a bluish-white light emanated from them, visible even though the room was brightly lit with windows. The stands were made to look like a trio of shadow panthers chasing one another nose to tail. Ologrin had seen only one other glowglobe before: less than half the size of these, displayed behind the front window of a luxury goods shop and priced for an astonishing amount of coin. Two of this size and brightness bespoke the wealth and status of the Lord Priest as much as anything else in the room.

The Lord Priest Jarvas himself stood behind the table, conferring with a younger man wearing a priestly collar with two gold bands. Moran stood deferentially to one side. Until that moment Moran's single gold band had seemed like the pinnacle of achievement. Ologrin immediately understood how far there was to go, and how close to the bottom he was. He dropped to one knee and lowered his eyes, as he had been taught to do for a formal greeting.

"Servant apprentice Ologrin, your grace," he said.

Moran stepped forward. "Your Lord Grace, Ologrin is one of my students. He is in his fourth year and will earn his servant adept this Summer. He is most accomplished in knowledge of both the Obligations and Commentaries. He has been recommended for advancement into priestly studies."

"Have we met?" the Lord Priest asked Ologrin.

"In my second year. I was an acolyte at the SummerTop celebration."

"How is it that we have not talked before?"

Moran spoke quickly. "Your Lord Grace, Ologrin was accepted at the School by specific invitation. His father was a member of the Crown's Guard."

Ologrin remembered Moran's admonition to remain silent. He could not help, though, but give his teacher a quizzical look. He wondered how such a fiction could succeed. He shivered, not sure if it was from the lie or the damp clothing.

"Was, you say?"

"He was taken by the drowning sickness about fifteen years ago."

"Oh. I didn't think many died here in Antola," Jarvas said.

"He died in Madros, your Lord Grace."

"I thought you said he was in the Crown's Guard."

"On an expedition for the Crown, I'm told."

"Mmm. And mother?"

Moran swayed a bit, as if for some reason he was more reluctant to tell this part of the lie. "She was an attendant to Serenity's own mother, your Lord Grace." For whatever reason, this seemed to pique the Lord Priest's attention.

"Oh? Was she related to the Crown?"

"A cousin, I believe," Moran said.

"I see! A scandalous affair and an unexpected child; no doubt the true reason the father was banished to Madros. Ologrin, step close." He waved toward his side of the table, where bright sunlight streamed into the room. He put his face uncomfortably close to Ologrin's and stared into his eyes for a long moment. Ologrin tried not to blink.

"Look at those eyes," Jarvas said. "Moran, have you seen these eyes?"

"Why yes, your Lord Grace. He is my student."

"Those gold flecks. Unmistakable."

"I have been told not all that rare, your Lord Grace."

"Nonsense! Most definitely Donal's bloodline."

Suddenly the Lord Priest grabbed both of Ologrin's wrists and held them firm. Ologrin felt an unusual warmth in his chest, vaguely reminiscent of the feeling when the old Polfre woman Fasha had grabbed his wrists in Southwatch years before. This time, though, it was only enough to stop him from shivering. Jarvas' voice was suddenly low and menacing.

"You have brought an orphan into the School, priest Moran."

"Yes, Lord Grace."

"You know my concerns?"

"Yes, Lord Grace."

"An Antolan arms man and a member of the Crown's house, though?"

"That is correct, Lord Grace."

Jarvas let go of Ologrin's arms, and the chill suddenly returned. "We must be ever vigilant of our heritage."

"An unusual candidate, Lord Grace. But his intellect will be of great value to the Panthea."

Ologrin happened to glance over at the other priest, who was gazing steadily back, an unreadable expression on his face. He continued to stare until Ologrin looked away, afraid that the man would somehow see something in his eyes that the Lord Priest had not.

"Heritage is our greatest gift," Jarvas continued. "You may not realize the gift you have been given, apprentice Ologrin, and how it compares to others."

"Your Lord Grace, I am...grateful," Ologrin said. He had no idea what the man was referring to but thought it would be bad to admit this at that moment.

"Malach's greatest gifts were reserved for Donal and his tribe. We live in Antola because Malach thought it was fitting for his most favored tribe to live in the greatest city in the world. There are others, other Eidos, as the physionomists call them, who are like us physically, but not with the same perfection as Donal's own. Malach has given them the other cities of Lhosa. Then there are those who toil in the fields and flats. They may look like us on the outside, but they lack the intellect and sophistication of even the most distant merchant from Dormond or Ismay. Do you understand?"

The comment was so matter-of-fact that it took Ologrin a moment to grasp its offensiveness. But he reminded himself that Jarvas knew nothing about his actual upbringing. And the man was continuing to talk.

"You are going to ask about the Polfre," Jarvas said. "Have you had much contact with them?"

In fact, it had been the furthest thing from his mind. "Only a little," Ologrin replied.

"Good. Do not trust them. They have their secrets and sorceries, and only grudgingly share them when it suits their interest. Let them stay in the mountains where they belong."

"Doesn't the Crown depend on the expertise of the Sophenary? I thought it was run by the Polfre."

"What the Crown needs from the Sophenary is none of our business. The Polfre are a strange people with even stranger beliefs. They may act friendly, but they are not your friends. They have no gods but themselves."

Ologrin felt deeply unsettled by Jarvas' remarks. In his four years at the school, he had become accustomed to the idea that some people thought they were better than others, but he had never seen it so openly embraced. To become a priest, he needed to impress the Lord Priest, but the man was saying nothing to impress Ologrin in turn. It was very different from his interactions with Moran. He felt something unpleasant stirring deep inside.

"Let me tell you a story," Jarvas continued. "Do you know about Lord Bemal and the Sorceress?"

Moran gave Ologrin a warning glance, but he could honestly shake his head no.

"The Sorceress was part Polfre, but it is said her father was a true demon of Ruhax. He raped her mother, stole the child, and left it with Ruhatsi witch-women, who suckled the child on blood. Later, she returned to the Polfre, lived with them, and eventually became more skilled in Polfre knowledge than anyone. But she was not true Polfre. She was a *maleugenate*: no pure blood and no pure loyalty, an abomination in the eyes of the gods. At first she seemed to do great things. But these things were based on her evil knowledge. Fortunately, Bemal, the Crown, saw into her wicked heart and how she planned to betray the Malacheb. And so, with Malach's help he banished her from the world. But she was a sorceress, don't forget. She vowed someday to return and destroy the Crown. To this day the Malacheb are on guard for signs of her return. And that's why we don't trust the Polfre. They could be hiding her or her descendants this very moment."

Ologrin looked again at Moran. His teacher was visibly uncomfortable. He was sure Moran was mentally pleading with him not to say anything. Not that he had any idea what to say. Meanwhile, Jarvas seemed to be looking through him at the wall beyond, apparently lost in thought.

"So, you have been an acolyte?" Jarvas said suddenly. "I think it is time for you to do more, if you are going to enter the priestly studies. You will join me on the altar for this Summer's-eve Oblation. You shall be the bowl-bearer."

Ologrin forced his mind back to the present. "Of—of course. I shall be honored," he managed to stammer.

"What have we offered to Malach these past Summers? Birds? Rodents? Last year a hawk and a white cavy. The hunter and its prey, how clever." The Lord Priest's face tightened. "Wait until they see what we have planned for this year. Malach will be honored, this I promise you, and you will share in the honor, apprentice Ologrin."

The meeting ended abruptly. Moran offered his thanks and well-wishes to the Lord Priest, while Ologrin knelt and bowed once again and followed his teacher out. They crossed the gardens in silence. The Sun had become quite warm and Ologrin's clothes were now dry, but he continued to feel chilled inside.

"The Lord Priest has a talent for the dramatic," Moran said. Ologrin looked at him, not sure what to say. "He has the luxury of saying things that might not work in the real world."

"He really thinks we should avoid the Polfre?" Ologrin asked.

Moran waved his hand. "There are many different beliefs in the Panthea, Ologrin. Hence the name, right? I know many Polfre. We do business often enough."

"Are they your friends?"

Moran did not answer. They reached the path that led to the apprentices' cells. Ologrin turned to walk away when Moran finally spoke.

"Everyone will be looking at you during the Oblation."

Ologrin stopped, suppressing a shudder. He had wanted to say something to Moran about the vandalism in his cell, but now he hesitated.

"Even though they will be watching the Lord Priest, they will see you," Moran added. "Bearing the bowl may seem simple enough, but it is an important, symbolic role. Nothing embodies service more. This is not the time to question tradition, understand? You want to be a priest? Do this well."

Ologrin looked at the ground.

"Meet me day after tomorrow following my class in the Winks. SummerTop is only eleven days away."

Ologrin nodded again, watched Moran walk away, and then slowly headed for his cell. Adept Herbin had replaced the door latch with one that required a key to work. The adept showed Ologrin how to lock the door and admonished him to keep the key with him always. "Put it on a string around your neck," he said. Ologrin suddenly remembered his knife. His torn bed frame still lay on its side. He righted it and carefully removed the cap from the one post. The knife remained hidden in a hollow of the post. He slipped it around his neck. The knife, he decided, would henceforth always be around his neck. He would find a pocket for the key.

Though he had not eaten since the previous day, he was not hungry, so he obtained only a small loaf of barley bread and some fresh water and returned to his cell late in the day. He lit a candle, borrowed from Herbin. His pen, ink bottle, and few small pieces of parchment had been tossed from the window-sill but otherwise had escaped the attention of his attackers. "Probably didn't recognize them," he said to himself, trying to cheer himself up. He placed a sheet of parchment on the broad sill and began a letter to Tobin.

To Tobin, teacher and friend,

Every year that passes I appreciate the lessons you labored to teach me. I have tried hard to remember that to work with others is honorable, even when you do not share their beliefs. Who do you serve, you would ask. But today I am not sure. Will becoming a priest cause me to sacrifice the most important things you taught me...

He looked at what he had written, then allowed the candle flame to burn the parchment until it was nothing but a few black curls. He blew out the candle and lay down on the bed roll. The shutters to his window were closed and barred. He stared into the darkness, aware of the lingering smell of urine.

9

The last day before SummerTop was supposed to be a day of contemplation, as was befitting the last day of the year. Ologrin wandered across the school grounds, where tents had been erected and were being stocked with goods for the following day's festivities. The official location for the celebration was the School, but it would spread throughout the city. Over the past few days taverns had refilled their cellars, homes had been cleaned and prepared for guests, and shop shelves were overloaded with delicacies from the far reaches of Lhosa.

Ologrin had carefully saved his coin from the tutoring sessions with a specific purchase in mind. Dormond was famous for its fruits, and as far as Ologrin was concerned, the most desirable was a fat red berry that grew on short little shrubs. They were delicious by themselves, but the Dormonders cooked them with honey and sold the resultant concoction in small jars. Twelve durri per jar: half a silver, which was a passage's worth of simple meals, but Ologrin had saved enough for two jars and had been looking forward to the purchase all year.

With no Oblation requirements before sundown, Ologrin

made his way to the library. It was empty as well, save for Linas in his usual place. In addition to the maths books, there were several other Polfre treatises on the plants and animals of Lhosa as well as on the history and geography of different cities. Ologrin was torn between his interest in them and his fear that reading anything by the Polfre would be a mark against his new career. He looked for something else to read, but several lengthy essays on the Commentaries turned out to be intolerably boring, so he ended up napping in a corner while the afternoon Sun slid across the floor at his feet.

He lingered in the library until late in the day. By the time he left, the School grounds were filling with students and faculty, chatting in small groups and slowly making their way toward the High Altarnary. Ologrin slipped through the doors in the rear, where Altarnary priests were assembling the acolytes. He was given a white cloak to wear—*the cloak of a priest*—he thought proudly, though one unadorned with any collar bands or other marks. The priests reminded the acolytes of their various responsibilities. Ologrin would be serving as the Lord Priest's assistant. He was to pick up and hold the bowl of water before the priest for him to dip his hands, then continue to hold the bowl, unmoving and without emotion, until the priest cleaned the blade and stepped away.

"Yours is an honor," one of the priests said. "You will be closest to the Lord Priest. Do not faint." Ologrin gave him a slight smile, wondering if the priest had seen half as much blood in his years as he.

The Sun approached the horizon. The Grand Altar room was filling fast. Ologrin and the other acolytes were positioned outside the gallery columns. The Lord Priest would arrive in a carriage surrounded by cheering Antolans, then enter the Altarnary in great splendor, while the acolytes slipped around and filed in behind him.

Horns sounded outside, signaling that the Sun had

reached the horizon. The school's priests entered single file and formed a circle between the crowd and the altar. Younger priests stepped up and read passages from the Obligations and the Commentaries. Ologrin could hear the crowds outside cheer as the horns sounded again. Then the Lord Priest Jarvas entered, resplendent in a pure white cloak thickly embroidered with gold. Those in the Altar room knelt as the acolytes followed the Lord Priest up to the altar. Several bore bundles of flowers and sheaves of barley, which they placed on the arms of the altar. Ologrin took his place beside a tall table holding a dagger the size of a short sword and an enormous silver bowl, half-filled with water. He had never paid much attention to the bowl when attending the Oblation in the past. Now, looking at it, he hoped he could manage it without sloshing water onto the altar. Jarvas sat on a silver-wrapped chair, glaring into the distance, until everyone was in their place and the crowd sat back on the benches. He then stood and circled the altar slowly, taking care to turn his gaze on every part of the room.

"Fellow servants," he began. "The gods have blessed us greatly. They have given us rain and warmth, and soon Antola will be blessed with another great Harvest. Now, at the top of the Summer, we take time to thank the gods for having taken favor with us in many ways. Many generations ago, Malach gave us charge of this great city. We have repaid him by spreading far..."

Ologrin glanced up at the circle of darkening sky in the oculus overhead. A black speck of a bird flashed by, and he wished he could be that bird, soaring through the sky, without worry and without the need to listen to a speech.

His thoughts turned to the jar of fruit...and then he remembered the small maths book still sitting in his cell. A small book like that might only cost half a silver. He might have enough for both a jar of fruit and a book of his own.

"But life we only borrow," the people around him intoned,

replying to the priest and bringing his attention back to the room.

"I remind you," the Lord Priest said. "We can only remain pure of heart if we remain pure as a people. Antolans engage in commerce in all parts of the world. We trade with others, we eat and drink with others, we may even call others our friends. But it is all too easy to think there is no difference between us. We must guard against this. If Antola is to remain powerful, then Antolans must remain pure."

Again, the people around him repeated, "But life we only borrow." Ologrin moved his mouth to join in. It was going to be that kind of speech, he realized. Antolans were proud of their purity. But what did that mean? Did that include people outside of the city? Did it include the people of the riverlands? The people of Halrin's Spur considered themselves Antolans, but did the people of the city see it the same way? Was he Antolan? He could guess Xedus' response to that question.

"Malach defeated Ruhax and banished him to the rifts. For many, many years we have enjoyed peace as a result. *But there have been signs!*" Jarvas cried, arms spread wide, and Ologrin noticed he had the crowd's full attention. "The servants of Ruhax are on the move. And the maleugenate may have arisen again, and even now may move among us!"

The maleugenate. Jarvas had used that word during their meeting, Ologrin thought. A sorceress, he'd said. Sorcery was something from old stories. Surely he didn't think it existed in Antola.

"Malach defend us!" everyone cried.

"Pure of heart!" Jarvas cried, and the room roared in return. "Pure of thought!" he cried, and they cried "Pure as a people!" They responded with a prolonged cheer, while Jarvas raised his hands over his head.

There was a commotion at the front entrance. Ologrin heard the unmistakable bleat of a bison calf. Everyone was on their feet, and he strained to see. The Lord Priest removed his cloak and handed it to another acolyte. Ologrin wrapped his arms around the bowl and lifted it from the table. Four acolytes dragged the calf to the edge of the altar, where they held it in place with ropes attached to its neck and back legs. The priest dipped his forearms into the bowl, then picked up the dagger and held it aloft. The calf bleated incessantly. Suddenly Jarvas grabbed Ologrin at the base of the neck, and for a horrified moment Ologrin imagined that he, not the calf, was to be sacrificed. But Jarvas only positioned Ologrin so that the bowl was pressed to the base of the calf's neck.

"Mighty gods!" the priest thundered. He stood beside the calf, with the knife poised above his head. "We vow never to forget. Life is but borrowed. We return to you what is yours!"

"May our enemies fear your wrath and feel your sword!" the crowd cried in unison, and the priest plunged the knife deep into one side of the calf's neck.

Blood fountained over the priest's arm and across Ologrin. Several members of the crowd suddenly turned away. Others stood transfixed, their faces a rictus of enthrallment. The fountain became a thick red stream pouring into the bowl. Ologrin had no choice but to stand there while the calf gave him a pleading look, then collapsed at his feet. The priest plunged his arm back in the bowl of blood and water, still holding the knife. He seemed to make a show of splashing water over the altar, and over the two acolytes at the front of the calf. He turned, dropped the blade in the center of the altar, and walked out of the room, signaling the end of the ceremony.

The room erupted with noise. Those privileged to be inside the Altar room were in equal measure thrilled or horrified, but excited either way. They began talking as if they were shouting across the streets at each other. There were bursts of laughter, and shouts, and people pounded each other on the backs and grasped arms as if they had not just witnessed but personally survived the Oblation.

The bison seemed for a moment forgotten, a great inanimate heap at the base of the altar. Then someone jumped onto the altar and grabbed it by the head, lifting it from the gelling blood. Those near the man shouted and squealed again. Emboldened, the man stepped to the other side of the animal and repeated his performance, eliciting a few more laughs. Already, the terror of watching an innocent animal suddenly be butchered was waning. It was becoming just another show; memorable, perhaps, as for the next few passages they could say they were there, but then the memory would be trimmed and filed away. The man dropped the head and skipped around the blood so as not to get any on his feet.

Ologrin looked down at his own sandals, which had been drenched in hot blood. His feet felt sticky. The front of his new cloak was soaked a dark red. He noticed the smell then: metallic and sour. Vivid, ragged memories of the butchery in Halrin's Spur flooded back into his head. He felt more of a kinship with the bison than with anything else in the room. The animal's last act had been to look him in the eye, then bleed all over him, as if saying *"If I must give my life, I give it to you, not to them."* Ologrin silently accepted the sacrifice for himself. What would the priests think if they knew his thoughts? What would Malach say? He imagined explaining to the god that no one had a right to do this unless they had lived with these animals, had cared for their caretakers, and truly knew the value of their lives. Perhaps Malach had herded bison himself, long, long ago. Then he would place his hand on Ologrin's shoulder and give him a look that said, *"I know. What a waste."*

At that same moment he felt a hand on his shoulder. He thought it might be Moran, but the hand pushed down and squeezed until Ologrin turned out of annoyance.

"Look at you. Apprentice priest Ologrin," Xedus said. He,

too, was wearing a white cloak, though spotless and made of some cloth with a much finer weave than what Ologrin wore. Ologrin took a step back. It did not appear that anyone else was with Xedus at that moment.

"Aren't you going to share greetings with a fellow apprentice priest?" he said, holding his arm out. Ologrin looked at the arm like it was a snake, then looked Xedus in the face. The man was smiling, but that could have meant anything. Slowly Ologrin reached out and touched two fingers to Xedus' palm.

"What an honor to have been next to the Lord Priest," Xedus said. There did not appear to be any hint of the young man's infamous anger or sarcasm in the statement. Xedus then laughed. "You seem a bit overcome by it," he said. "I think I would have been, too. Congratulations, Ologrin. Again, what an honor."

"Thank you," Ologrin said, warily.

"And my apologies. I will admit there have been times when I have treated you without respect. They are my own failings. But I was shocked at what happened to your cell. Such things are not done among people who consider themselves civilized. And when I heard that you, too, had been selected to be an apprentice priest, I thought I needed to let you know that. What happened to you is not fit treatment for someone honored to advance into the priesthood."

Ologrin could not think of what to say in return. He had assumed that Xedus had at least arranged the vandalism of his cell, if not directly participated. Now, here he was commiserating.

"Thank you," he said again, then "You are a natural leader, Xedus. If you stand up for something, many will follow."

Xedus grabbed Ologrin briefly on the forearm. "If we are not yet friends, then we are at least companions in the journey. We are now adepts of the School, and apprentice priests.

The few that finish priestly studies are a special group, and the world will know it."

"Congratulations to you as well," Ologrin said carefully. "How many new apprentice priests are there?"

"Seven," Xedus said, and noticed Ologrin wince slightly. "I know, such an awkward number. But I wanted you to know that my family and I are arranging a private celebration this evening for all the new apprentice priests at a place belonging to my father. Of course, you are welcome to join us. In fact, it's getting late. I should be heading that way. I guess you could say I am also one of the hosts."

Ologrin looked down at his cloak once again. The edges of the blood had dried, turning it from red to brown. "I'm a mess," he said.

Xedus laughed. "Yes, get yourself cleaned up. You may have been honored, but I'm not sure that will be appreciated at a fine dinner," he said, gesturing at the bloody cloak.

"I don't know where your home is."

"Oh, of course you don't. And it's not at my home. It's in the Purse." Xedus laughed again at the look that crossed Ologrin's face. "Don't worry. My father has a great storehouse near the docks. There'll be tables of food and casks of wine. Far too much to fit into a home!" Xedus slapped Ologrin lightly on the shoulder. "Have you been to the Purse much?"

Ologrin shook his head slowly.

"You do know where the tunnel is, don't you? Cross through the tunnel. Several of my servants will be standing on the other side, near the trestle lift, with lanterns. We have exclusive use of the lift all night long, if we wish. One of my servants will escort you down the lift and to the storehouse. You will come, won't you? All of the apprentice priests will be there, and most of the Panthea priests as well."

"Of course. And thank you for the invitation." Xedus turned to leave. Politics, Ologrin suddenly thought. Xedus might not be sincere about the offer of friendship, but he knew enough about politics not to alienate any of his fellow apprentice priests on their first day.

The Altar room had nearly emptied out. People had either joined the celebration on the gardens in front of the Altarnary or were spilling down the terraces to taverns and homes for the night's feast. Ologrin had planned to wander through the gardens, enjoying the tents, and then head for his cell. Instead, he had an invitation to what might be the best party of the season. Feeling both excited and anxious, he took a side exit from the Altarnary and walked quickly toward his cellhouse.

Linas was standing outside when he arrived. He almost didn't recognize the man, as he had never seen him outside of the library.

"Ologrin! Are you okay?"

"Of course. Why?" But then he saw Linas' expression, staring at the bloodstained cloak. "No, no. I am fine. The poor beast, though…" After his unexpected encounter with Xedus, he had forgotten the calf. "Everyone tells me that was an honor. It's one I can do without in the future."

"You are welcome to stay at my place, if you need," Linas said.

Ologrin laughed but found the comment puzzling. "I'm fine. What would I need?"

"Just offering." The older man moved to open the door for Ologrin. "Will I see you in the library tomorrow?"

"I doubt it," Ologrin called back. "I'm heading to a party in the Purse. I think it may be late before I get home!" He unlocked the latch and stepped into his room.

Happily, he discovered the bison's blood had not soaked through the cloak onto his skin. Other than his feet, he would not have to wash. Unhappily, he realized he had nothing that seemed appropriate to wear to Xedus' party. His choices were the gray apprentice servant cloak, or his well-worn traveling cloak. Under ordinary circumstances, he did not mind wearing the traveling cloak around Antola; he did not care if a stranger marked him as a lowlander. But now he feared being compared to the other apprentice priests and found wanting. Reluctantly, he chose the traveling cloak. He would feel somewhat embarrassed to be the only apprentice not wearing the white cloak of the priests, but he would hold his head high anyway.

He washed his feet and slipped on his sandals. The knife dangled from the leather thong around his neck; he barely thought about it as he pulled his only clean tunic over his bare shoulders, then donned the cloak. He stepped outside into a very dark and very fine night. The celebration in the school's gardens was hitting its stride. Ologrin slipped behind the High Altarnary and headed for the merchant's market. Far fewer people were here. The mouth of the tunnel was black, as the markets and lift were closed at night, and there was little need to light its interior. Passing underneath the eleventh and twelfth terraces, the tunnel was nearly a dozen gross hands long—almost a sixth of a league. Ologrin approached with some trepidation. He could just make out a difference in the light at the far end marking the other entrance, a tiny spot that was somewhat less black than the surrounding walls.

Ologrin did not have a lantern, but he had his ember pot, so he flicked it open as he entered the mouth of the tunnel. The weak yellow glow failed to reach the walls on the far side. He stayed to one side, against the curved wall.

After a short distance, he closed the ember pot to see if he could see better in the dark. He could just make out the wall on his right. He continued along slowly, allowing his fingers to stay in contact with the wall. Almost immediately he thought he could make out an even darker, irregular shape in the roadway ahead. He heard a rustling and moaning sound. He flicked the ember pot open again. The light revealed a couple in the roadway in the final moments of gritty ecstasy.

"Leave, or leave a coin," a voice panted. Ologrin closed the ember pot and hurried along, smiling. The spot at the far end seemed marginally larger, and he could see well enough without the extra light. His anxiety lessened. Reaching the end of the tunnel would be like completing a small trial.

The far opening grew larger, and he could see a few stars above a far distant blackness: the mountains on the far shore of Gosper Bay. As he reached the opening itself, he stopped short. The roadway and walkway disappeared abruptly. Another step and he would have stepped into empty space. A scaffold of heavy beams descended into the darkness. He could not see how far it was to the ground, but he was sure it was not a survivable fall.

Somewhere nearby, he heard the musical whine of the machinery in the winding house. It was much louder than what he could hear from the Crown's Walk, and there were additional whines and hums as if the machines inside were singing to themselves. At first he noticed nothing, but then he realized that one of the myriad tiny yellow lamps of the Purse was moving toward him, rising from the docks below.

The Platform materialized out of the gloom. It seemed surprisingly big; wider than one of the ships tied up below. He could also see that the smooth planked surface was supported by its own deep latticework of beams. The platform seemed to float in the air. A single figure stood in the middle, holding a lantern. The platform slowed and then nestled up against the roadway with a quiet thump. Ologrin stepped carefully onto the solid surface and approached the figure.

"Your grace," the man said, without emotion, then turned to face the bay, and with the slightest quiver the platform silently began to descend again. Ologrin felt like he was flying over the Purse. There were people below, in the houses and taverns and tangled streets, and he heard happy voices and laughter. He looked behind. The yellow windows and lanterns of the Purse were sprinkled thickly against the hillside.

Facing the bay and through gaps in the buildings, Ologrin caught glimpses of the ships tied to the docks. They were symmetrically curved, with raised bows and sterns. Each had a tall mast as thick as a tree, with a single spar tied alongside almost as long as the ship itself. The masts were barely visible against the darkness of the sky and distant shoreline.

The jumble of Purse structures came to a sudden end, giving way to a broad dockway a half-gross hands wide. The platform once again came to a soft stop. Two men holding lamps stood at the foot of a ramp.

"Good evening, your grace," the taller of the two said, bowing low. His companion laughed.

"My name is Ologrin."

"Good evening, your grace Ologrin."

"Are you going to take me…"

"We'll be leaving as soon as you come forward with a silver."

"I haven't got a silver," Ologrin said. "I'm a guest of apprentice priest Xedus. I was told you would be escorting me to his family's feast."

"Well, we will, but first we'll need your share of the escorting fee."

Ologrin suspected he was in the process of being robbed. He looked inside his small purse. He did, in fact, have the equivalent of one silver, in the form of the twenty four durri he had been saving for two jars of fruit. "I have eight durri," he lied. "Four apiece."

The man's companion snorted. Ologrin walked down the ramp, handing the coins to the taller man while fingering the knife beneath his tunic.

"Come on," the taller one said. "We got some ways to go."

They walked along the docks for a short way before heading up into the maze of streets and alleys. Almost immediately Ologrin felt lost, but he glanced overhead at the stars to regain his bearing. Dark streets were punctuated with local hubs of activity, where lamplight and people spilled happily from doorways. The Purse, Ologrin mused, was the real world, built by people living from day to day, without thought for long-term dreams. The west side terraces were neat and artificial; the school was neat and artificial. Order was artificial. Chaos was real. Bochlus, god of chaos, created by Serenity to fill a gap in his order, might be the most real god of all.

Ologrin's guides quickened their pace as they dived deeper into the city. The odor of rotting fish grew stronger. They stopped in front of a large two-story structure. The first floor had several windows facing the street, but they were shuttered, and very little light came through. The upper floor shutters were open, spilling dim lamplight into the street.

"This is it," the taller one said. "Upper floor."

Ologrin looked around for a sign or directions. "Am I early? Where is everybody?"

"Upstairs. They're probably just waiting," the taller one said, as they started to move back into the shadows.

"The apprentice priest Xedus. This is his place? His father is a big importer."

"Look, I brought you where you wanted to go," the taller guide said over his shoulder.

Ologrin entered carefully.

The first floor was large, and unoccupied. It appeared to be a storage warehouse. Several barrels were dimly visible in a far corner, along with dozens of stacked wooden crates. A stairway rose against a side wall. He worried that he was the first person to have arrived. But there was lamplight at the top of the stairs, and he thought he could hear voices.

"Is anyone here?" he called. There was no response. "I'm coming up the stairs," he added, not wanting to surprise anyone. He climbed the stairs carefully, as there was no railing to prevent someone from falling over the side.

He reached the top. The second floor appeared to be an open loft, like the first floor, with scattered posts supporting overhead beams. Another stack of crates just beyond the top of the stairs blocked his view beyond. Nothing he could see or hear suggested there was a party going on. Moreover, no one seemed to be here. He had a growing suspicion that he had just been pranked by Xedus, cheated out of eight durri, and left to fend for himself in the Purse at night. He walked to the front windows and peered into the street, guessing that his so-called guides would be long gone.

Something massive struck him at the base of his neck, causing light to explode in his eyes and sending him sprawling to the floor.

The flash of light was followed by the sensation that he was falling into a deep tunnel. He heard gleeful laughter behind him. He tried and failed to pull himself up, and the room spun. Then he felt someone grab his shoulders and legs. Fighting to stay conscious, he could not get his limbs to move. He felt himself being lifted in the air and then thrown backward. The fall was short: it felt like he landed on a table. The back of his head smacked it hard and he saw flashes again.

"Tie him down!" The voice was instantly recognizable, despite his dazed state. He squeezed his eyes and then opened them again, trying to focus. Xedus stood at his side, while two others pinned his legs and yanked his arms outward. Thick ropes were thrown over his arms and legs and pulled tight, holding him in place.

"What is that smell?" Xedus said. "Gods, does that shit-swimming smell follow you everywhere?" He laughed loudly, and the others joined in. "No. Not just any shit-swimmer, though. I think we may have caught the feared maleugenate. What should we do with it now?"

"Xedus, you'll be thrown out…" Ologrin started to say,

but Xedus backhanded him viciously with a gloved fist, leaving the taste of blood in his mouth. A raw red scar covered Xedus' bare right upper arm: the triangle and star of the Malacheb, recently seared into his skin.

"Beat his teeth out!" one of the others cried, as if Xedus' question demanded an answer.

"We'll get to the teeth, but that's not why we're here. Get his clothes off!"

Hands grabbed his cloak and flung it back, then grabbed his tunic and ripped it open. He felt other hands at his waist, and his breeches were roughly yanked to the rope around his ankles, leaving him naked from the waist down.

"Look at this," Xedus said. He jerked the knife from around Ologrin's neck. "He comes armed. He was going to attack us! All of you are lucky the maleugenate hasn't already snuck into your cells and slit your throats in the middle of the night." He held the knife up, trying to see it more clearly in the dim lamp light. "Even the knife is a piece of shit," he said. He stabbed it deep into Ologrin's right thigh.

Fire exploded through Ologrin's body. He felt the pain of the hole in his leg, but it seemed to be secondary to the heat blazing through his veins. Blood pounded in his head. He closed his eyes and breathed hard.

"Are we warriors of Malach?!" Xedus bellowed. The others cried out in assent.

"Are we pure to the way!?" They screamed louder.

"The priests have gone soft. The people have become afraid. Malach demands blood. He does not want a bird. He does not want a calf. For Malach, the sacrifice must be manifest!"

Ologrin opened his eyes again. Xedus was holding a long, narrow dagger. He held it above his head, like a priest at the Oblation.

"Xedus, maybe we should hit him again and go…"

"Are you cowards or are you Malacheb?!" Xedus snarled. "Blood is required!"

Ologrin could see his knife sticking out of his leg. He pulled against the ropes on his wrists, and suddenly was acutely aware of their structure. He closed his eyes. Fibers were twisted with other fibers, which were entwined in the opposite direction to make strands, then woven together to make thick cords. In his mind, at his command, he saw the fibers relaxing, letting go of their fellow fibers: strands dissolving, ropes coming apart.

"Your mothers were raped by dogs," Ologrin said, with as much disdain as he could muster.

Xedus paused, not sure what he had heard. One of his attackers laughed and leaned into Ologrin's line of sight, preparing a mouthful of spit.

Ologrin ripped his left arm free of the rope and grabbed the attacker by the throat. The man's eyes widened and his hands reached for Ologrin's, but his arms seemed to spasm instead. He slipped out of Ologrin's grasp and collapsed on the floor. The second attacker grabbed for Ologrin's upstretched arm. As he did so, Ologrin pulled his right arm free and grabbed the man's wrists. His arms, too, seemed to spasm, and he gave a constricted cry. Ologrin heaved himself to a sitting position, pulling the second attacker off-balance in the process. Xedus stepped back, staring.

"Do it!" Ologrin cried. Xedus sprang forward. Ologrin felt like an observer watching his arms spring out and grasp the arm with the dagger. Xedus gasped, and the dagger clattered to the floor.

"Come on, do it!" he cried again, and grabbed Xedus' other arm. In his mind he could see the muscles in the young man's arms, could see the fibers unraveling as the ropes had done; could see the damage reaching into his chest and toward his heart. Xedus' mouth opened wide in agony, but he could not breathe. Ologrin released his grip and Xedus bounced off the table and onto the floor.

Ologrin yanked the knife out of his thigh. As he did so, a wave of weakness overcame him, and he fell backward. With every ounce of strength, he willed himself to sit up again. He sawed at the rope around his feet until it separated. He swung his legs over but fell as soon as he tried to stand. The knife skidded across the floor. He dragged himself several hands from his attackers and rolled to where he could see them. Xedus' mouth gaped like a fish and his chest moved in spasms as he tried to take a breath. The other two remained curled on the floor, moaning.

Ologrin slowly rolled to his knees, then pulled himself to his feet. He pulled his breeches up. One of the attackers appeared to be trying to get to his knees as well. Ologrin grabbed his knife and stumbled forward, then half stepped, half fell down the stairs and out the front door.

The street was empty. He found an alley and lurched toward it, tripping almost immediately over something hidden in the dark. He fell, and the knife slipped out of his hand again. He scrabbled around in the blackness, but then a scream came from the building before he could find it. Xedus had found his breath. Ologrin tried to run. His right leg was in such pain he thought he might fall every time he put his weight on it. He took two more alleys as quickly as he stumbled across them. Without warning he staggered onto a broad expanse of wooden planks, extending straight in either direction. He was back at the docks. A couple of figures noticed him lurch forward. They pulled their own cloaks close and hurried past. One of them glanced as he passed, and Ologrin thought he caught a flicker of light in the eyes.

He limped along the docks, trying to put as much distance between himself and his attackers as possible. His wounded leg threatened to send him sprawling with each step. He saw a large mass of crates and barrels stacked loosely against a building. He managed to limp over and found a narrow gap between the barrels hiding a somewhat wider space beyond, an artificial cave in the stacks, appearing just when he needed it most. He squeezed through and eased himself to the ground. The space was not large enough for him to stretch his legs, but at least he could not be seen from the docks. Within a few moments the pain from the stab wound was replaced by cramping pain in both legs. He tried to stand again, but he didn't have the strength, and now he felt trapped behind the barrels. He fought down a wave of panic and forced himself to think. He wiggled his back and attempted to cross his legs and found enough space to allow his muscles to relax somewhat, then felt considerably better. He decided to rest for a few moments before attempting to make his next move.

He could not see the sky, but assumed it was still the earlier part of the night. He had to figure out how to get back to the terraces. And after that…he did not know. Who knew how many Malacheb had infiltrated the school? What he did know was that, for some reason, the Malacheb wanted him dead. He tried to think of anyone he truly trusted. Had Moran known Xedus' plan? Would he help? Should he leave the city? Even if he could, he was certain it would take him days upon days to limp to Bhinton, much less Halrin's Spur.

He closed his eyes. Almost immediately, it seemed, a rapping sound next to his head startled him awake.

"You can't stay in there," a voice said. Ologrin held his breath and didn't answer.

"Come on out. You're not safe in there, and you can't be seen just appearing in the morning."

Whoever was speaking clearly knew he was behind the barrels; there was little to be gained by remaining silent. "I can't move my legs," Ologrin said.

After a moment, he heard scraping as someone slowly began pushing the barrels along the boards of the docks. The gap widened and an arm reached in. He took hold, and immediately felt a slight tingling in his hands. The arm proved to be exceptionally strong and remained steady as he used it to leverage himself to his feet. He extracted himself from the barrels and found himself standing next to a man who was much shorter than his strength and leverage would have suggested. Ologrin saw a slight golden gleam in his eyes.

"Follow me," the man said. He stepped onto the dockway proper. Ologrin stumbled after him. It was clear they were angling for the edge of the docks and the gangway of a ship docked nearby.

"Can you make it up?" the man said. Ologrin nodded, though he was not at all sure. He mostly crawled up the gangway and fell onto the deck. "Scoot yourself up next to the rail," the man said. "You'll be hidden from the docks, anyway." Ologrin did as he was told, and the man disappeared through a hatch in the deck.

He stared up at the sky above the mountains beyond the bay and then at the stars themselves. Their unchanging patterns comforted him. The jewel box. The mountain fox. The bison's horns. Their position told him it was later than he had thought. He must have slept for more than a few moments behind the barrels. He shifted his gaze toward the black mass of the Purse, strewn with random flecks of light from lamps and torches. The Red Eye dominated the western sky, staring at him, exposing his hiding place. "I'm not afraid of you," he said quietly.

"Do you know the star pictures?" the man said, reappearing out of the dark. He held a cloak, which he helped Ologrin wrap around himself. Ologrin suddenly realized how cold he had become.

"I'm a fair navigator, myself," the man continued. "That's the master's cloak, though I think he won't miss it tonight."

"I didn't know the Polfre served aboard ships," Ologrin said.

"I'm the only one I know of. My choice; I wasn't pressed into it. Though I can't think they'd have much luck pressing any Polfre that didn't want to go to sea. And what brings you to the docks, I should ask?"

"I was tricked. Someone meant to kill me."

"That can happen around here. Looks like they weren't successful. Though that's a fair wound you got in your leg. You got some salt in you to walk any length with that. Is it bleeding?"

"No. I think it stopped."

"Then leave it, 'til someone who knows what they're doing can take a peek."

"I don't know anyone around here."

"Ah, but I do."

Ologrin realized he was desperately thirsty. "Do you by chance have a cup of water?" he asked.

"My pardon," the man said, and hurried off, returning in a moment with a large tin tankard full of water. Ologrin sipped. It was cool and sweet, no doubt from a rain barrel on board. He drank half the tankard without stopping.

"Slow, or you might just bring it back up."

"Thank you," Ologrin said.

"You just rest. I'm going nowhere. We'll figure out how to patch you up in the morning."

Ologrin nestled the cloak around him and leaned against the ship's rail. The ship rocked easily with the waves of the bay. He relaxed and was instantly asleep.

10

He awoke facing a sky full of orange clouds drifting in from the Southern Sea. He tried to move, but every muscle in his body had stiffened like those of the dead. He noticed his rescuer sitting on a low circular step surrounding the ship's mast. The man's head was on his chest, and he snored softly.

"Hello? Is anyone up there?" A woman's voice cut through the morning air. Ologrin tried to reach for the man, but his muscles continued to fail him, and he only managed to knock over the empty water tankard with a clank.

"Bochlus' balls," the man said with a start.

Ologrin heard steps on the gangway. A woman's head appeared over the rail, looking down at them.

"We're here," the man said.

"Can you stand?" the woman asked, looking directly at Ologrin.

"I don't know."

"Adept Scaup, are you able to help Ologrin to his feet?"

"Yes, of course," the man said hurriedly. He offered his arm for leverage again. Every muscle in Ologrin's body complained, but he noticed he could put some weight on his right leg.

Ologrin struggled to comprehend the woman standing before him. She had disks of blue glass perched on her nose and held to her face with wires that disappeared into snowy white hair, smooth and straight, cut neatly at the level of her neck. "How is it you know my name?" he said warily.

"Forgive me. I am Vireo. Now you know mine."

He nodded slightly, though his question remained unanswered.

"Scaup, you have done Ologrin an excellent service," she said. "I am grateful. We are going someplace warm to get something to eat. You are welcome to join us."

"No. Many thanks, Master." Scaup said. "But I have the ship's duty."

"You have an aversion to dry land, I think, but I thank you again. Please forgive us if we seem to be in haste. There might still be those about who want to harm our friend." She turned and headed back down the gangway. Ologrin shrugged off the cloak and handed it back to the smaller man.

"Thank you so much," he said.

Vireo gave him a backward glance, looking over her blue bottle rounds at him. He had strong misgivings about following a stranger. But then he looked over at Scaup, who nodded and motioned forward with his hand. Ologrin stepped stiffly onto the gangway and followed her down.

The woman's clothing was like nothing Ologrin had seen before. She wore a vivid blue vest, almost matching the color of the rounds in front of her eyes, over the top of long woven skirts. The vest was made of an exotic cloth Ologrin had never seen, thick and quilted, and yet as iridescent as silver. The skirts seemed to be a muted brownish-grey, but they were filled with hints of color as well, such that they seemed to harmonize with their surroundings. She carried a black walking stick surmounted by a silver cap, but kept it tucked under one arm. Standing tall, the top of her head came to the level of his chin.

"You've had an adventure, it seems," she said.

"I don't know you," he replied warily.

"No, you don't. But if you would care to join me for breakfast, I would be pleased to introduce myself."

She continued, and he followed, allowing his curiosity to overcome his wariness. She held herself in a way that made it clear she was accustomed to being called Master. Her clothing, her timely appearance, and her apparent familiarity with him seemed almost supernatural. "You're Polfre," he said at last.

"Indeed."

"I'm sorry. It's just that…that's a very nice vest."

"Nice enough for an Antolan, even?"

"I'm sorry. I didn't mean for that to sound rude."

"Have you known many Polfre?"

"Not many."

"I'm sure you have lots of questions, and there are nicer places than this for answers." She extended a hand, which Ologrin hesitantly grasped. Instantly he felt peaceful warmth flow through his body, melting away his caution. He was reminded of Pipit briefly holding his hand in Greensee years before. Yet, while Pipit's touch had been direct and surprising, this was subtle and complex. He found he could walk quicker holding her hand.

"Oh, before I forget, you lost something," she said. She pulled Ologrin's knife out of a pocket in her skirts.

"How did you find my knife?"

"Knife? Oh, yes, I guess it does look a little bit like a knife. And you've tried sharpening the edges, I see. That's interesting. I wouldn't have advised that." Vireo handed it over. Ologrin noticed the knife had been newly suspended from a leather loop threaded through one of the strange circles of the handle.

"Sorry I didn't get to you before those boys did. In my defense, I didn't get much warning," Vireo said.

"Wait. You...you knew I was being attacked?" Ologrin stopped walking. "Who are you?"

"We have a mutual friend. He thought you might be in danger. Turns out he was right."

"Tobin?"

"I don't know a Tobin."

"Moran?" he said. She shook her head slowly.

"Are you from the School?" he asked. "I've never seen you."

"At the School for Servants? No, I'm not from there."

They had been walking north along the docks, away from the trestle lift. Vireo turned and headed toward an alley rising steeply uphill. The tall walls and towers of the Sophenary loomed over this part of the Purse. They trudged up only a short distance, then made another turn onto a narrow alley with two and three-story structures on both sides seeming to lean toward each other, as if trying to shelter the alley below. They were protected from the breeze, making the air feel a bit warmer. Vireo headed toward a facade of polished wood, with lamps still lit on either side of a gleaming door. Ologrin had to duck his head to fit through.

Inside it was positively cozy, and Ologrin had the distinct feeling it had been built with shorter people in mind. Vireo moved toward a front corner where there was a larger table, apparently designed to accommodate someone of his stature along with Polfre diners at the same time. They sat, and Vireo removed the glass rounds. She had seemed determined and commanding during their walk from the ship. Now she looked at him intently, but with a slight smile, which softened her appearance.

He glanced outside. Even though the alley was largely shaded by the overhanging buildings, there were gaps in their eaves revealing the broken clouds. The Sun was high enough to send shafts of light streaming down to the stone pavement. "I'm going to miss my first day as an apprentice priest," he said. "That won't go well."

"Won't go well? How much worse do you expect it to get?"

He looked at her and frowned.

"Or what do you think just happened?"

"Xedus...someone I knew from the school lied to me. He tried to kill me."

"You think it was just this one person?"

"He had friends."

"But you believe you can go back to the School after this?"

"I'll tell Moran what happened. I'll tell the Lord Priest."

"You don't think perhaps the Lord Priest already knew?"

The question stung. Until that moment he had imagined the Lord Priest as powerful, even dangerous, but not clever. A man with selfish beliefs, but one he figured he could work around as he continued his studies. He suddenly felt foolish. The interview over his heritage, being selected for the Oblation ceremony: Jarvas might have known exactly what he was doing. Ologrin had been marked, singled out.

"Why would he want to hurt me?"

"Because of who you are."

"I don't understand. Who am I?"

Vireo tilted her head slightly. She studied him for a bit, her own forehead creased in concern. "You genuinely don't know, do you?"

Food arrived unbidden. Plates with cheese, mushrooms and onions in vinegar, sliced pumilas, and bread. Their server brought warm cups of mulled wine as well, and Ologrin felt his insides warm as he drank. He reviewed the fragments of his life. The death of his mother. The woman with the dagger. The Polfre girl. The Lord Priest. Xedus.

"In my life I've had two people try to kill me. That's more than my share, I think," he said.

"Did they have anything in common?"

Ologrin paused, but he knew the answer. "They both had scars branded onto their arms. They were both Malacheb."

"The Malacheb believe in the dominance of the tribe of Malach. They do not have respect for the lives of other Eidos. For some of them, even being Antolan is not enough, if someone isn't a descendent of the original tribe."

"Just last evening the Lord Priest called for purity," Ologrin said. "He used a word. Xedus used it, too. He called me a maleugenate."

Vireo furrowed her forehead. "That's an ugly word. It's meant to be demeaning."

"Well, if it's an insult, it misses the mark. I still don't know what it means."

"I have a better word, I think," Vireo said. "You are a mosaic." He scowled, still confused. "Most creatures are a blend of their parents. When pigments are blended together, you can no longer see the original colors. But in a mosaic, all the original pieces try to remain unique. From a distance they may seem blended, but up close they are separate bits, forced to work together. Mosaics are very rare. You are the first I have ever seen."

Ologrin's scowled deepened. "Then how do you know? My parents were ordinary people. What makes me different?"

"When did your father give you your tanj?"

Ologrin felt like the conversation kept tilting in unexpected directions, preventing him from gaining his balance.

"My what?"

"Your tanj. The thing you call your knife. When did you get it?"

"My mother gave it to me after my eleventh summer. She said it was from my father. He disappeared when I was younger."

"How young?"

"Three, I think. Why are you asking?" Ologrin said. His leg was throbbing, and he felt his irritability rising.

"The Polfre receive their tanj from their parents when they turn twelve. It marks the end of infancy."

"That doesn't prove anything. Twelve is an important birthday for everyone."

"How many other knives have you seen like yours?"

"Well, I haven't had the chance…"

"Forget knives. How many *things* have you seen that have been made from that substance?" Ologrin stared down, fingering the object around his neck, unable to answer. "You had to have noticed there was nothing else quite like it," she added.

He felt a wave of defensiveness welling up inside. "Well, thanks for returning it, but I think I should go," he said, and began to slide out from behind the table.

"You cannot return to the School. It is not safe."

"Then I'll go somewhere else."

"You cannot return home, either."

His defensiveness turned toward anger. "Why are you telling me this? People I barely know want to kill me. You say it is because I didn't…*blend* right? What makes you any more trustworthy than them?"

"Please," Vireo said, "sit and listen."

Ologrin stared out the window. His leg throbbed, and he felt sick and alone. He sat back down, not knowing what else to do. She fixed him with a slight smile that seemed as calming as her touch.

"Your father would have arranged for you to receive your tanj when you were twelve. He gave it to your mother, who saved it for you until the time was right."

Ologrin lifted the leather string from around his neck. The knife like object sat dull in his hand.

"That is your tanj," Vireo said. "It connects you to the world and connects the world to you in a way only the Polfre can experience."

"But I am not Polfre," he said.

"No one else has access to the material needed to make a tanj. That object is Polfre. Your real father was Polfre. You are half Polfre."

He stared at her, feeling defeated, not knowing what to say. From the time he had met Pipit, he had known something was different, but it was not something he had wanted. Over the years, he had tried to ignore the sensations he felt when touching, say, a wooden table or a tanned bisonhide. He had ignored them because they were not what he wanted to be.

"It is a very personal object," she continued. "Ordinarily we never reveal it in public. It is a gesture of great trust and intimacy simply to show it to another Polfre."

Ologrin's anger was draining away, leaving him feeling terribly sad. He started to hide the object under his tunic, but Vireo reached out and grasped his free hand. He felt the same comforting warmth he had felt before. With her other hand she reached beneath her vest and withdrew a fine silver chain bearing an object that looked somewhat like a seashell. It was made of the same dull, brownish metal. She held it for a moment for him to see, then slipped it back under her vest. He slumped back into the chair, and slowly replaced his knife —his tanj—beneath his tunic.

"We Polfre lived on Lhosa long before any other human race," Vireo said quietly. "Our lives are long, but we have few offspring, and so we are not many. Most of us live in our own land, where we are not much interested in the rest of the world. But the world moves furiously along, carrying us with it whether we wish it or not. Some of us spend at least a portion of our years in the larger world hoping to understand it better. And a few choose to stay for many years before returning home. They spend their lives attempting to nudge the affairs of history in favorable directions."

"A Polfre may find companionship with someone who is

not Polfre. Ordinarily, they cannot have offspring. Nonetheless, perhaps once in several generations, a child is born from such a union. We do not understand how it happens. That child will have characteristics of both their Polfre and non-Polfre parents. But those characteristics will not blend together, as they do for normal offspring. They live within that person as distinct parts, and not always in harmony. They produce a mosaic, patches of both in unpredictable combinations: black and white, oil and water, fire and ice, compassion and cruelty."

"And you think that is me?"

"The Polfre is obvious even to you, now. You feel it with my touch…"

"I don't have the eyes."

"No, but there are more subtle signs. Look at your fingers. For the Eidos, the middle four fingers are the same length. Their hands look square. Look how your third and fifth fingers are longer than two or six, and your fourth finger is longest of all. That's a Polfre trait. There are others, if you know what to look for. The double crease beside each eye. Your temporal ridges."

"My what?"

"Above your hairline. You can feel a distinct ridge under your scalp on either side."

Ologrin reflexively put his hands in his hair. "So?"

"The Eidos don't have those."

"What are they?"

Vireo looked thoughtful. "The residual of something from long ago, when perhaps we were a greater people."

"So why is being a mosaic a bad thing? Why do people want to kill me for it?"

"There are legends about mosaics, and not all of them good. To those few who might recognize one of your traits, you're the embodiment of legend. That makes you a potential threat. A disruptive force."

Ologrin laughed sourly. "How am I a disruptive force?"

"Most of the students and faculty of the School come from well-off families in the city. You don't; that made you an outsider from the start. Then you proved to be smarter than most of them, and that made you the competition. Finally, if I'm not mistaken, you had the audacity to challenge their beliefs, and that will always make you the enemy."

"I wasn't trying to challenge their beliefs. I was just trying to understand."

"But your job wasn't to understand. It was to serve, right?"

Moran warned me, Ologrin thought. *He tried to tell me to stop. He might even have known about Xedus' plans.* Vireo was right; he could not return to the School.

"Trying to understand things is what we do at the Sophenary. That is where you belong," she added.

The tall, ancient towers of the castle had always seemed so mysterious during his strolls along the Crown's Walk. Now, if he was not mistaken, he was being invited inside. Through his gloom he felt a ray of hope. And he felt an empathy from this woman he had not felt in a long time, perhaps not even from Tobin. Through everything she said, she continued to look at him with kindness. It was like cool water for a parched throat.

"Is that where you're from?" he asked. She nodded her head.

"But I thought the Sophenary was only for the Polfre. I can't just show up."

"The Sophenary accepts students who are not Polfre. Nonetheless, we have established that you are Polfre, at least in part."

"In parts," he muttered.

"Most applicants submit examples of their work and have recommendations from previous adepts of the Sophenary," she said. "But ultimately it all depends on an interview with the Dodecant, who has the final say."

"The Dodecant?"

"The faculty master and administrative director."

"If I can get those other things, how do I meet this person?"

Vireo smiled. "I'd say in this case she came looking for you."

THIRD PASSAGE

A time came when a group of Polfre chose to leave the Dha-Arenish, which to others they call the Lake of Skies. For many generations they labored to carve the city between the mountains and the sea. Antola, they called it, the heart of the mountain, and it could be seen from far away, glowing white in the Sun. From the remains of the mountain they began construction of the Great Road, stretching west into the lowlands.

In that same time a tribe rose up to become masters of the lowlands. Their skill in battle was great, but their hearts were cruel, and they put their conquests to the knife, man and child. In this way they became powerful like no other tribe, and all other people feared them. They were ruled by a mighty chief, Donal the Red Hand.

Donal raised his eyes and saw the city shining in the distance. "A great people must have a great city," he said. So he raised an army not seen since Farus of old, then sent word to the Polfre in the city. "Yield your city and depart, or none shall be left alive."

The Polfre considered their response. "We cannot yield to the bloody chief," some said. "The Eidos take what is not theirs, and do not respect the Rha." But then others spoke. "It is true that the Eidos do not own the mountain, but neither do we. What is the purpose of fighting until none are left alive on either side? The city is big enough for two peoples. Perhaps the tribe of Donal can be taught to live within the Rha and serve as an example for the Eidos everywhere."

Though these words were hard, many saw that they were wise. And so the road through the southern mountains was opened, and Donal's tribe was invited into the city

But there were many Polfre who were opposed to the decision. They returned to the Lake of Skies, counting the great city as a failure, and vowed not to venture into the wider world again.

—From *The Chronicles of Grebe the Elder*

Before the great voyage, I spent years in Antola without seeing a single one of my Polfre brethren. After we returned, the news of our voyage spread widely, and they began arriving, though at first only one or two each Summer. Many were well-learned in that deep and narrow Polfre way. For instance, one might have mastered the lore of the herbs with healing powers yet know nothing of the cultivation of simple crops. However, we had less need of deep knowledge and more of general capabilities: Polfre who could build as well as think.

With this in mind, I took upon myself the task of cataloging the sorts of knowledge available. It soon became clear that knowledge was of little use if not passed down in as broad a fashion as possible. So I found the greatest practitioners of the arts of physionomy, vitachemy, and astrolemy, and together we formed the Sophenary. This, in turn, began to attract a greater number of Polfre from the Dha-Arenish and Dha-Ghraensee. Within a few years, our small group numbered more than two dozen, and nothing less than a fortress of knowledge began to rise at the foot of Mount Arske.

—From *Wysel's Journals*, Volume Sixteen

11

Walking through the tall bronze doors of the Sophenary, Ologrin felt as if he were starting his life over yet again. To his surprise, Vireo disappeared almost immediately. He was shown to the initiates wing, where all new students lived until they were accepted into a specific knowledge curriculum. Unlike the School for Servants, students did not all start or advance at the beginning of the year. Some students had already been in the initiates hall for several passages when he arrived, while others trickled in every passage or two afterward. He struggled to make acquaintances over the next several passages, feeling awkward and out of place.

Students pursued warrants in three curricula: physionomy, vitachemy, and astrolemy. Classes met whenever masters decided to teach them and included only those they chose to invite. He would be invited to a class in a particular curriculum one passage, then receive no invitations for two or three passages in a row. He had no way to measure his progress compared to others, and he began to wonder if he was making any progress at all. Slowly and methodically, he finally realized, they were plumbing the depths of his knowledge before revealing theirs, which would lead to a recommendation regarding what curriculum he seemed best suited to study.

Vireo was not absent for long. He began meeting with her at least once or twice per passage: long conversations held in her rambling study on the second floor. Tall windows behind her table looked out across the vaults of the hall known as the Collegarum; the view beyond that was unencumbered to the western horizon. Slowly he felt more comfortable with their conversations, and as a result felt more comfortable within the Sophenary, though he never felt at home in the initiates wing. He decided Vireo was trying to explore who he was in the same way the faculty were interested in exploring what he knew. He asked several of his fellow initiates if they felt the same way about their meetings with the Dodecant. To his surprise, none of them were meeting with her regularly; most had not spoken with her since their entrance interview. He began to worry then that his place in the Sophenary was provisional, that his interview had not yet concluded.

Of the seven initiates in the wing when he arrived, six were Polfre and one was the son of an Eidos physionomist from the terraces. Over the next several passages, eleven more students arrived. Nine were Polfre; the other two were Eidos: one from Antola and one from the city of Madros. No one, as far as he could tell, was a mosaic like him. The Eidos students were oblivious to his differences. They likely thought he was just a river valley villager in far over his head. He assumed the Polfre were more sensitive to the characteristics that made him different from the other Eidos. Fortunately, the Polfre did not have customs that allowed for casual physical contact. Unlike the Eidos, who grab-handed and back-slapped friend and stranger alike, the Polfre were much more reserved. Thus far, he had not had reason to come into physical contact with any of the Polfre students. He knew the first touch would connect them, and then they would know he was not just another Eidos student. It was not a secret he could keep forever, he assumed, but it was not one he was ready to give up yet.

The faculty knew more about him, he figured, but as his only experiences with being recognized as a mosaic had been bad ones, he was careful with them as well. However, if they knew he was different they did not show it. Like most of the students, most of the faculty were Polfre, and they carried the same reserve. They were cordial in casual encounters, demanding but fair in academic situations, and uniformly supportive of all students. The only non-Polfre faculty member Ologrin was closely acquainted with was Albrect, a Madrosan, one of the vitachemy masters. Albrect had taken an immediate interest in him. Ologrin assumed the man's natural gregariousness was stifled around so many Polfre, and so welcomed a chance to serve as mentor for someone he assumed was one of his own.

As Ologrin's own seventeen-passage initiation neared an end, he understood that he would be encouraged to follow a single academic path. Of the three options, he at least knew it would not be physionomy. He felt overwhelmed by the material, and after the first few invitations, the physionomy faculty stopped seeking him out. So certain was he that it was not for him, he suggested that Master Vireo was mistaken when she told him he was expected in Master Heron's dissection chamber late one afternoon. With her smile reminding him he should never question her, she assured him he was, indeed, expected, and reminded him not to be late.

He was surprised when, later that day, only four other students arrived, all Polfre. Master Heron stood before them. She was an even smaller, short-legged Polfre woman, in complete defiance of her name. She appeared to be considerably older than Vireo.

The room was brightly lit with tall windows and several oil lamps hanging from the ceiling. Storage boards lined one long wall, and three rows of raised benches lined the other: seating for at least two dozen. The center of the room was dominated by two large bronze tables. On each table a body lay on its back, arms stretched outward as if receiving a blessing. Each body had been painstakingly flayed open, its insides glistening. Ologrin had, of course, seen dead bodies before. He had seen blood spilled indiscriminately, and insides violently turned outside. But he had never seen anything like this: the vital organs of another being so carefully displayed, as if he were looking at a form of art. He suddenly felt dizzy and broke out in a sweat, even though the room was quite cool.

"Everyone take a seat," Master Heron said. Ologrin glanced at his fellow students and noticed at least two others appeared just as queasy as he. He tried to focus on the Master, and not let his eyes stray to the tables.

"A rare and precious opportunity has befallen us," Master Heron said. "All of you have shown promise in physionomy, and so have been invited, at the Dodecant's request, to witness this lecture."

Ologrin was now sure there had been a mistake. He stood. "My respects, Master, but I'm terrible at physionomy. I'm afraid I'm not supposed to be here."

The master peered at him. "Oh, yes, Ologrin. Yes, you certainly have questionable aptitude. The Dodecant was quite insistent that you, in particular, be here. She has her reasons. You may sit." She positioned herself between the tables.

"Ordinarily, we perform our anatomy dissection on Eidos specimens. The Crown's prisons are quite willing to offer us specimens, so long as they have not been too damaged by whatever caused their deaths. One such specimen is on the table to my right."

"On my left, however, is a specimen of Polfre anatomy." She said it in a way that suggested great drama, and Ologrin noticed that his fellow students were appropriately awed. "As all of you know, the Polfre live to a great age, many times that of the Eidos. That, and the fact that virtually all Polfre choose to die in our homeland, means that it is quite rare to have a specimen for anatomical examination. But this individual made it clear that she wished her physical body to be used for just such an occasion, and so we are fortunate to be able to offer this experience for you."

"Be warned!" she said with sudden intensity, arms raised. "It is a great and rare privilege to be given access to the secrets of the body. Both of these individuals, regardless of their actions in life, must be given our utmost respect in death." Ologrin imagined himself spread open on a dissection table, and just as quickly tried to forget the image. He glanced at his fellow students. Each seemed to be pondering their own mortality.

Heron was speaking again, bringing them all back to the present. "Now that you have had sufficient time to re-gather your wits, I ask you to join me at the tables."

Ologrin noted that he was not nearly as weak-kneed as he had feared. He carefully got up and shuffled over to the tables, standing behind the Polfre students, as he was several hands taller.

"You will notice that, for the most part, these two individuals are the same. Two eyes, one mouth, two arms and two legs, two hands and two feet, twelve fingers and twelve toes. In fact, we have more in common than not with all bony creatures that walk the earth: two eyes, four limbs, and so forth. And yes, I know, winged raptors have a third eye, but there are always exceptions."

Winged raptors are a myth, Ologrin thought stubbornly.

"But there are subtle differences in the physionomy of the Eidos and the Polfre, which is why we say Eidos and Polfre are indeed two different species of human. The first, and perhaps most important, can be found up here." With that, Heron neatly removed the top of each specimen's head.

Ologrin could see that the scalp and skull of each had been carefully pre-cut and then replaced. One of the Polfre students promptly fainted into his arms.

"Thank you, Ologrin, and if you would kindly deposit Brant on one of the benches, we will proceed." Heron strode to the storage boards and returned with a tray bearing a pair of pinkish-gray, convoluted masses of tissue. "These are half-brain specimens. Most of the outer brain of Eidos and Polfre is similar, even to the shape of these folds. But you can see the differences deep inside. This structure is what we call the crown of the brainstem. You can see in this specimen, which is a Polfre brain, that it is twice as large as the one in the Eidos brain. It does not make us any more intelligent than the Eidos. But it allows us greater perception of ourselves and our environment, perceptions the Eidos lack. Oriole, would you be kind enough to return this tray to the boards?" she said, handing the tray to one of the students.

Master Heron positioned herself between the bodies again. "As you can see, I have carefully exposed the viscera, which required removing the anterior portion of the rib cage from each specimen. You may note that the Eidos have twelve ribs per side, compared to only ten for the Polfre. This accounts for their greater flexibility, and in part for their greater height. Nonetheless, it is a trivial difference. By far the most important difference between our two species is the organ right here." Ologrin noted Heron was pointing to a coppery colored tissue centered in the chest of the Polfre. Unlike the clearly defined lungs and heart, the tissue was an amorphous blob. Had he been doing the dissection, he realized, he would have cut it away as just so much extra glop.

"This, my young learners, is the tanjumus, and it is the central reason for today's lecture. This, more than any other thing, is what separates the Polfre from other humans. When you later study it with the magnifying lens you will find it is laced with several rare trace minerals, including tanjium, which imparts its unique color. Physionomists have learned to render samples of this tissue with great care, as it also contains small amounts of both amantadine and thorium, sufficient to yield unexpected results if the gland is allowed to dry. It is the tanjumus that reacts with your tanj to your benefit. It is the tanjumus that vitalizes the Polfre in a way that prolongs life. This thing"—and Heron pointed to the heart—"keeps you alive, and this part between your ears houses your thoughts. But it is the tanjumus that makes you unique. Brant, I trust you had a nice nap and are now ready to join us for the rest of the lecture?"

Ologrin stepped back to allow the abashed student to rejoin their group. As he did so, he placed his hand against his own chest, feeling the tanj beneath his tunic. Even with the knowledge that he was a mosaic, he still imagined himself to be Eidos, the thing he had always assumed he was for most of his life. He found himself wondering if Vireo might had been mistaken. As if reading his mind, Heron stepped over and gently poked him in the chest with her thumb. An immediate sense of warmth radiated from the point where the Master touched him. Heron smiled up at him. "Yes, my friend," she said softly, "it is in there."

Ologrin suddenly felt an overwhelming sense of gratitude. He stifled the urge to wrap his arms around her, and then hug each of his fellow students in turn. Suddenly, he knew he was home. The cold stone walls seemed to embrace him. He turned away to wipe his moist eyes.

Summer ran its course. Harvest came and went. Winter set in and lingered. But seventeen passages later it was time for Ologrin to specialize. By then he knew where he wanted to be, and it wasn't in the labs or dissection rooms. The sky beckoned him, like a friend. Here was the chance to finally understand the stars, and the slowly moving Red Eye, and most of all, the backward-racing orb that defined a passage, and thus provided framework for the passing of days.

When he told Master Vireo of his choice, she replied she had concerns, and his insides turned to stone. "The observations are only a small part of astrolemy," she said. "The real work is on paper, and you don't have sufficient knowledge of angular maths and hidden sums to do the work." So he threw himself into the study of numbers again, borrowing books from the library and working tirelessly, practicing the equations, and learning within eight passages the essentials he needed to proceed. Vireo later noted it wasn't so much that she granted him permission to study astrolemy as she stepped out of his way. She also gave him the key to a cell atop an observation tower located on the southwest side of the castle. "It's small, and at the top of thirteen dozen stairs," she told him apologetically. In fact, it was twice as large as the cell he had been given at the School for Servants, and it had its own small hearthgrate. Moreover, it was his alone, and more astonishingly in his mind, the tower's parapet was his alone as well. From there, he felt he could almost reach out and shake hands with the Sojourner. And it gave him one of the highest perches in the castle, allowing him to look down on all Antola. To the west he could see the High Altarnary, to the east he could see the docks, and the trestle lift laboring up and down the sloping sides of the Purse in the distance. And if he looked north he could see the wings of the castle pushing against the shoulders of the Adamantine mountains, then beyond that the snowy upper reaches of Arske, the first significant peak in the chain, rising in the near distance.

The great sphere they all inhabited circled the even greater fiery sphere of the Sun, so said his masters, which matched how Ologrin had come to understand things long before, growing up in Halrin's Spur. The Sojourner circled the Lhosan world in the same way that Lhosa circled the Sun—and in the same direction, he was told; it only appeared to fly backward around the world. Not quite believing, he set out to use his new skills in angular maths to calculate the Sojourner's movements and found that it made sense on paper. But it still did not make sense in his mind. Finally, he imagined himself perched on a star, looking down at Lhosa circling the Sun, with the Sojourner circling Lhosa, and suddenly he could see it was true. From this he learned something he suspected was even more fundamental: what appeared to be true depended upon one's point of view.

What Ologrin couldn't quite intuit was the size of one thing compared to another, and thus their distances from each other. At first, he was disappointed to discover that there was no consensus on the proper answers from astrolemers of the past. But then he realized this was an opportunity. In the process of understanding the orbits of the heavenly spheres, and of exhausting the existing knowledge on the size and nature of the heavenly wanderers, he fulfilled the requirements for his warrant adept in astrolemy and passed examination by the faculty without difficulty. Master Vireo declared that if he was successful in determining the sizes and distances of celestial objects as well, it would certainly be worthy of a warrant master. He just had to pull it off.

Vireo also reminded him that masters candidates were expected to obtain an adept in one other specialty. Once again eschewing physionomy, Ologrin began working with Master Albrect in his vitachemy labs. While the study of the skies was cerebral and esoteric, the work of the vitachemists was utterly practical. They were about the business of understanding how things were made or made better. From a political standpoint, it was the vitachemy work that was of interest to the Crown, and thus provided the coin and the support that allowed the Sophenary to exist. As an astrolemner, Ologrin found it easy to adopt the attitude of the academic: It was sufficient merely to pursue the joy of discovery. The vitachemists had no such pretensions. If the Crown wanted something, they were tasked with figuring out how to provide it.

• • •

Ologrin sat hunched over a table, filling the parchment before him with numbers, triangles, and circles. The table was awash with sheets bearing similar calculations, or carefully recorded columns of information representing dozens of nights spent on the small parapet above his room. One large volume sat opened next to him, while several more were stacked near his feet, having been discarded as, in his opinion, inaccurate or wholly nonsensical. Coals glowed red in the small hearth-grate, warding off the chill threatening to sink into the room from the parapet, as Ologrin had a bad habit of not closing the thick trapdoor between the two. In fact, he preferred the door to be open, except on the coldest of nights when it became intolerable. With the door open he felt connected to the night sky, which he had taken to thinking of as *his* night sky. At present the room was pleasantly warm. The late-Winter weather outside, though cloudy and damp, was not terribly cold, and the air was still. Eventually, though, the coals would dim, the room would chill, and his hands would stiffen. He would be forced to stand and stretch, then re-stoke the fire with fresh wood before getting back to work.

Focusing on his numbers and angles, Ologrin almost missed the soft knock on his door. He rarely received messages from the red collars, and certainly not after dark. He stepped away from his table and found he could barely walk, due to the ache from the old wound in his leg. He hobbled over, feeling a bit better with every step, and opened the door to find Master Vireo standing outside.

"May I come in?" she asked. The request surprised Ologrin. He was not sure he even had the authority to say no, were that his intention. "Please," he replied, and opened the door wider.

"Master Albrect is responsible for what may be a significant advancement. He is going to need help in enlarging the scope of his efforts," she said. Ologrin motioned for her to take the chair at his table, as it was the only chair in his room.

Instead, she sat carefully on the edge of his narrow bed, leaving the chair for him. "I know how deeply involved you are in your calculations. But I am asking you to help Master Albrect with this important new work."

Ologrin could not imagine refusing. He loved his new life, and he had her to thank for it. "You can tell me to do anything," he said.

"I am not telling, I am asking. You are an adept now, and nobody's servant. But I should add, Albrect has asked for you personally. And the rains do not appear to be letting up any time soon. You probably won't be doing much observing for a few passages," she said, smiling.

An odd statement, he thought, as she had been the one to tell him that observing was only a small part of astrolemy. Indeed, some of the most useful astrolemical publications had tables of observations better than those he had managed to make, and he spent most of his time calculating from them. Surely she knew that.

When she had pulled him from the docks, instructive yet comforting, she had been like a mother. Right after he began his initiation, coming face-to-face with her in front of other students and faculty, she had been cool and formal, his master in every sense. Then they began their meetings, and he felt like he was talking with Tobin again. Several passages before, he had attended a Sophenary-wide congress that featured, among others, the Crown's Minister of Affairs. Sitting on the dais in the Collegarum, Vireo had appeared magisterial, every bit the minister's equal. Now she sat primly on his bed, and she was someone different again, only this time Ologrin had no context for it. Her silver hair was carefully cut to frame her face. The vest she wore was so vividly and thickly embroidered he could not tell what the background color of the cloth might be. A short length of the chain holding her tanj peeked out of the vest before disappearing around her neck. Her knee-length cloak matched the style of cloaks favored by the faculty, but instead of being made of the sturdy leather most of them wore, hers appeared silky and supple, gleaming slightly. She gave him another small smile.

"I look forward to working with Master Albrect," he said. "The truth is, I need something to give me a bit of exercise. Astrolemy is going to make me into a bent old man."

She laughed lightly. "I think what he has planned will give you more than a bit of exercise. But if I judge you correctly, you will enjoy it. The excitement of something new. And Albrect speaks highly of you."

"He's Eidos. He can't see who I am."

She frowned. "He knows who you are. He doesn't care. There are a few people in the world who are not ignorant and prejudiced. Make them your allies."

Vireo stood, but Ologrin suddenly realized he did not want her to go. "I think I may have found a way to determine the actual size of the Sojourner," he said, motioning to the papers on his table. She leaned over, her shoulder pressed to his. "If we determine the geometrics of two objects with a known distance between them, and then the geometrics between ourselves and a distant object such as the Sun, we obtain a scale that we can use to determine the relative size of any object between the two." He waved at the drawings of circles and cones, and the scribbled equations surrounding them, as if the Sun and the Sojourner were sitting on his desk.

"If you can prove this, it will make you a master," Vireo said. "It's very exciting. The speed that you are progressing is remarkable."

"Thank you."

"Just be aware, the larger world requires politics, and they are often unpleasant. The more you change things, the more people will resist."

"I've never been good at politics."

"You have friends like me for that," she said. She patted

his shoulder and headed for the door. "See Master Albrect in the husbandry courtyard tomorrow at first light."

"Oh? Am I cleaning stables from now on?" he joked.

"You are indeed," she said, and let herself out.

Ologrin stared at the door after it closed, feeling out of sorts. Every encounter with Vireo seemed to be perplexing in one way or another. For a moment, he thought he felt that bond he had first felt when she fished him off the docks, but then it had vanished, and as she left it almost sounded as if he was being demoted. He turned back to his papers but could not concentrate. He replayed the brief visit over in his mind. Finally, he settled on one thing that seemed to bring him some comfort. She had said "friends like me."

12

The next day remained cloudy and damp, making it easier to convince himself he was not missing anything by working for Master Albrect. And as Vireo had promised, Albrect was waiting for him in the husbandry courtyard, standing next to an over-full wagon loaded with sweetly foul black manure, which Albrect explained had been slowly breaking down in a special pit for most of the Summer. The manure was thoroughly laced with a crusty white substance. It was Ologrin's job, he explained, to extract as much of that substance as he could and purify it.

Over the next couple of days, using buckets, trays, and fine strainers, he managed to boil a brown tea out of the piles of manure, then filtered the liquid through wood ash. As the solution cooled, a cloud of fragile crystals collected at the bottom. He poured off the remaining solution and let the crystals dry. From a wagon load of manure he managed to collect a bucket full of crystals. The Sophenary gardeners happily took what was left over.

At that point he re-consulted his notes, then set about refining the crystals. They dissolved quickly into a medium sized cauldron of boiling water and bison hide glue, which he skimmed, cooled, and allowed to settle. Down to a half-bucket of material, Ologrin washed it with cold water and let it dry. He now had a reasonably pure sample of niter, one part of the blast powder he was learning to make.

The Sophenary had a large set of milling wheels that could turn out enough blast powder each day to fill a single storage sack. They were in a thick-walled stone building about a half league north in the foothills. A much smaller set of milling wheels were housed in a heavy wooden box in Albrect's chambers, and these were the ones Ologrin used, measuring out a specific mixture of niter and ground charcoal and milling them for most of a day. He collected the powder, carefully cleaned the apparatus, and then milled another batch, this time adding a specified quantity of yellow sulfur. Master Albrect had given him only enough sulfur for the task at hand, as it was by far the rarest, and thus most expensive component of the blast powder.

Master Albrect's chambers were large, cold, and dungeon-like; the only natural light coming from a set of windows high along a northern wall. The walls themselves were stone blocks, while massive beams supported a ceiling at least four times Ologrin's height. The air was cool and musty, with the slightest acrid tang, and the irregular chips, gouges, and scorch marks on the floor and walls, up to about the level of Ologrin's head, testified to the occasional violent experiments in the room. He loved the place.

Before him stood a long table, equally as worn and scorched as the surroundings. The nearest wall was lined with storage boards full of urns and bottles and articulated apparatuses. Cases either held drawers full of other secrets or were filled with books covered in blackened leather with barely discernible titles. A dozen oil lamps hung from the ceiling on long chains, suspended about twelve hands above the tables and storage boards, brightening Ologrin's end of the room.

Ologrin stared at the two small vials he had set on the table. They represented the hard work Master Vireo had promised him when she had come to his room, almost two passages before. He had done the assigned work, found the relevant citations in the library, and had followed the instructions he gleaned carefully, never forgetting the dire warnings in each text that he could easily kill himself with a moment's carelessness. He was sure he had not missed a step. Now all he awaited was the arrival of the Master.

"When wood burns in a fire, what sustains the fire, and of what is the flame composed?" Albrect asked, striding into the chamber.

"There are compounds in the wood that burn in the presence of air, and the gas of this conflagration is the flame we see," Ologrin replied.

"How do you know air is necessary?"

"Because the flame dies if the wood is placed in a sealed vessel."

"Good. And what is charcoal?"

"Wood heated in a vessel where there is no air. The moisture is driven off, but the parts of the wood that will burn in air remain unburnt."

"So why must we add niter to the milled charcoal to make blast powder? Would not the surrounding air suffice to allow the charcoal to burn?"

"It makes it burn faster. There is something in the niter…" and here Ologrin faltered, because he had not fully understood, no matter how many times he re-read the texts "… Rather, the niter contains its own air within it…or some part of air…"

"And why the sulfur?"

This was the question he could not answer. He had looked in vain, finding many practical recipes for blast powder, all requiring the addition of sulfur, but none explaining why.

"That is what we are going to discover today," Albrect

said. He opened one of the wall cases and brought out a small apparatus holding a stone cup about one finger wide and two deep. The cup had a small hole near the bottom. Attached next to the hole was a striker mechanism comprised of a small strip of roughened metal and a spring-loaded arm tipped with a bit of flint. Albrect sat the device on the table. "I haven't just been using you for free labor. I wanted you to thoroughly understand the problem, and thus the answer." He pulled a small bag from his cloak, lit a candle on the workbench, then poured a small hill of black powder out of the bag directly onto the table.

"This is just milled charcoal," he said. He lit a long splinter of wood in the candle and set the flame on top of the little pile. With some effort and a puff of breath for coaxing, the powder itself caught the flame and burned weakly. They watched for several moments as the pile turned to gray ash, not even slightly scorching the heavy wood underneath.

"Not so impressive," Albrect said, then pointed to the vials Ologrin had brought. "Which one of these was made with sulfur?"

Ologrin pointed and Albrect un-stoppered the vial and tapped enough powder into the stone cup to half fill it. He cocked the flint. "Ready?" he said, then tripped the lever.

The powder burned with a loud *POOF!* and a flame over a hand high jetted briefly from the little cup, turning into a tail of grey smoke.

"Excellent! Very good blast powder, adept Ologrin. Now let's try your powder without the sulfur." He cleaned out the cup with his thumb and tapped in a similar amount of the second vial's contents. He cocked the flint and tripped the lever, and nothing happened.

"So, the sulfur imparts some property to the powder that allows it to burn instantly when lit with a spark, it would seem. Would you agree?"

Ologrin nodded.

"But now I am going to change the striking plate." He picked up the cup and eased the small bit of rough metal out of its clip. He then took a similar plate out of his pocket and fitted it in place. This one had a distinct brownish color that the first plate lacked. "On this one, the striking surface is made of tanjium with just a small amount of adamantine adherent to the surface."

"I didn't know you could do that," Ologrin said. "Why don't they react?"

"The amount of adamantine is quite small, and the glue holding it in place physically separates it from the underlying tanjium. That is, until we crush them together with the flint." Albrect set the pot on the table, cocked the flint and tripped the lever. A much brighter spark ensued, simultaneous with the bang and jet of flame from the exploding powder. Notably, there was less smoke.

"The hotter spark from the tanjium flint is sufficient to ignite the sulfur-free powder. Once ignited, it burns with the same power as the sulfurous powder. It turns out the sulfur doesn't make it ignite, it just makes it *easier* to ignite," Albrect said. Ologrin nodded, working though the argument in his head to be sure he understood.

"Sulfur is a mineral that occurs in limited deposits," he continued. "We have none that we know about anywhere near the Adamantine mountains. We have plenty of wood for charcoal. We can make plenty of niter from the waste of animals, ourselves included. Master Heron is, by the way, intent on finding out why our bodies make and then discard niter, since it seems to be such a useful and energetic compound. What we don't have is sulfur."

Albrect returned the stone pot to the wall cases and brought out a much heavier device mounted on a large base. It required both hands to carry it over to the table.

"Sulfur, as it happens, is plentiful in deposits near the Rhoctan mountains. But they are on the far side of a dangerous desert. We can only manage to buy sulfur in small quantities and at exorbitant prices. I have heard that they trade sulfur in Ismay, but they have never been willing to trade it with Antola. If the need came, we could not produce anything like the quantities of blast powder they could manufacture. That gives them a strategic advantage." He set the heavier object on the table. It was a miniature bombard about a hand in length, Ologrin saw, and a working one, judging by the striker and flint at the base of the bronze barrel. During his wanderings about the city Ologrin had frequently passed the half dozen full size bombards poking above the western wall of the city, pointed out across the escarpment. Ologrin had never seen stones stored near them, and now he realized why. They were just for show. Antola lacked the blast powder to make them into actual weapons.

Albrect took the vial of un-sulfured powder and tapped a small amount into the bore of the model bombard. He tamped it in place and then dropped a small ball into the bore, followed by a bit of cloth that he also tamped home. He then fitted the striker with the small plate bearing tanjium and amantadine. He aimed the cannon at the far wall, cocked the flint, and released it.

Ologrin jumped at the incredibly loud *BANG!* Simultaneously, a large chip flew off one of the stones in the far wall.

"The Ismayans have reportedly been fitting bombards to some of their ships," Albrect said. He let that sink in for a moment.

"Antola's bombards are facing the flats, not the docks. They're facing the wrong way," Ologrin replied.

"Very good," Albrect said, eyebrows raised. "So. We have the charcoal. Since the only sources of tanjium are hidden and managed by the Polfre, we have a secret and exclusive source of ignition. Our limiting factor to the large-scale manufacture of blast powder becomes the niter."

"Well, there are lots of animals," Ologrin said.

"Specifically, there are lots of bison out in the river flats. And it so happens, on my advice, the Crown has agreed to set up niter beds in the flats. You know this part of the world. This coming Summer, I want you to go to Bhinton and teach them how to extract the niter large scale. You will be our liaison."

Ologrin hadn't left the Antolan escarpment since arriving for the School for Servants. He hadn't been to Bhinton in six years. And beyond Bhinton was Halrin's Spur.

"But I already have my research," he protested, though he knew he wanted to go.

"The lament of the scholar. There is always something else that gets in the way," Albrect said, smiling.

13

The Sun at last set on Winter and rose on Summer. Ologrin stood near the Western Gate, looking down at the flats that spread into the distance from the foot of the escarpment. Though it was not yet mid-day, it was already warm, and the air was thick with haze, promising an uncomfortable day.

He studied the patchwork of fields nudging up against the foot of the escarpment. They held clusters of black dots, which he knew to be bison. A scattering of tiny, dilapidated milkhouses were spread in no meaningful pattern. Tracks were visible between some of the larger fields, flowing together into foot paths, then joining together as small roads, all leading toward the Great Road like a river picking up its tributaries and heading toward the sea.

The Great Road itself was separated from the fields by wide berms on either side, covered with swaths of grass. This was the Crown's grass, provided for the needs of arms men and their horses, where bison were forbidden to graze. This made the Great Road stand out like a green and white striped ribbon winding through the various browns of the flats. For a traveler on the Great Road, the berms elevated them from the squalor of the bison fields but could not elevate them above the smell. *If one good thing can be said for the heat and the haze,* Ologrin thought, *it is that it traps the smell in the flats below the city.* Unfortunately, the flats were his destination for the day.

The gate was already busy. A steady stream of people hurried past the guard-men at the near side of the gatehouse, while a half-dozen wagons waited to be searched before entering the city, their donkeys happy for the chance to rest after climbing the long, angled path cut in the side of the escarpment, known as the Repose Road. Ologrin heard the clop of heavier hooves approaching from behind. He turned to see an arms man mounted on a warhorse slowly approaching, leading a slightly smaller horse. The man's tunic collar sported a silver pin in the shape of a leaping panther, marking him as a member of the Crown's Guard. The arms man rode straight for him, bringing his charges to an easy stop when he came alongside.

"You must be Master Ologrin," he said. "Arms-Captain Aron," he added, and bowed slightly at the waist, while still sitting on his horse.

Ologrin had to shield his eyes to look up, as the man had positioned himself so the Sun was behind his shoulders. "You're going to be my, my...what do I call you?"

"Call me Captain Aron."

"I was expecting only a shield-man, or a lance-man," Ologrin said. The mounted officer squinted. Ologrin could not tell if it was a smile or a grimace.

"Do you ride?" Captain Aron asked.

"Never."

Captain Aron tugged on the bridle in his hand, and the second horse stepped forward. A smile crept over Ologrin's face. The horse was the same sand color of Aron's, but with a snowy white mane and tail, a vivid contrast to the dark rosewood-colored mane of Aron's horse. Standing on his toes put him eye-to eye with the horse, which returned his gaze and then snorted. He carefully ran his hand across the horse's rippling flank.

"How do I get up there?" Ologrin asked. The saddle was at chest level, and he was leery of simply trying to jump aboard.

Aron pulled a long wooden staff from loops on the side of the horse's saddle. The staff was almost as long as Ologrin was tall. "Hold this next to the saddle, then lock the reins around this and your hand. You can put your foot in one of those wedges at the bottom."

With some effort, Ologrin managed to haul himself up. The horse snorted again, but otherwise tolerated his clumsy efforts. Aron slipped the staff back into its loops. "In a pinch, this makes a decent club," he said.

"I never imagined riding a warhorse," Ologrin said.

"She hardly qualifies as a warhorse. She's the runt," Captain Aron said.

"This is the runt?"

"Keep your toes pointed in," Aron added, and then turned toward the gate. Ologrin's horse followed. The arms men at the gate cleared the wagons and throngs to either side. They rode through the larger entrance unimpeded, turned the corner, and started down the Repose Road toward the foot of the escarpment. The roadway itself was just wide enough for two carts to squeeze past each other. Ahead of them, the light traffic kept to the wall, leaving them an open path, albeit next to the edge. Captain Aron rode in front and Ologrin plodded behind. The steep drop-off to his right made him dizzy, so he focused on the rear of the officer's horse and tried to remember to keep his toes pointed in.

The escarpment was over eight gross hands high; the Repose Road stretched half a league from top to bottom. It hugged the contour of the escarpment so tightly that it was not possible to see the bottom from the top. The cut itself had been made a very long time ago by the Polfre when they still ruled Antola, or so Master Albrect believed. Exactly how they had done it remained a mystery, but Albrect surmised they had used a form of blasting powder, which meant that Ologrin's planned work was an effort to re-discover something that had long been lost. Ologrin wondered what other ingenuities once existed and were now lost, which gave him something to concentrate on besides the rhythmic rocking hindquarters of the horse in front of him.

It seemed half a day had passed when they finally curved away from the escarpment onto the incline of broken and packed stone connecting the Repose Road with the foot of the Great Road. Ologrin caught his first whiff of the bison fields.

"Where to from here, Master Ologrin?" Captain Aron said. Ologrin thought he detected a hint of a mocking tone in the question. "I'm not a master," he replied. "My actual title is Adept Ologrin."

"These people, all they know is you represent authority they don't have. It's best we reinforce that belief. To them, you're Master Ologrin. That's what they need to know. Insist they call you that. Don't get familiar."

"Master Ologrin," Ologrin repeated, trying it on for size.

"And I don't care what you call me in private, but around people, you refer to me as Captain Aron, or the Captain. Understand?"

"I understand."

"So where to?"

"Bhinton," Ologrin said.

Two leagues west of the escarpment, they came to a stacked stone column marking the intersection of the North Road with the Great Road. The crushed rock of the Great Road gave way to simple dirt, though packed hard as rock from the feet and hooves of countless travelers.

The bison were thin and widely scattered. They bore little resemblance to a managed herd. Ologrin noticed that the grass was patchy and brown. Large swaths of ground were nothing but cracked dirt. In addition to the smell of manure rotting in the hot Sun, there was the smell of rotting flesh. Lines of coarse vegetation indicated shallow irrigation ditches carrying no more than muddy rivulets of water.

Eventually Ologrin focused on the people working among the bison. They were so thin and dirty that they seemed to blend into their surroundings, which explained, he thought, why he hadn't seen them before. They moved as slowly and often as aimlessly as the bison.

They rode up to a milkhouse. It was just a thatched roof supported on poles, providing a modest amount of cover from the Sun or the rain. There were no associated huts, and Ologrin surmised that the milkhouse doubled as housing for the herders. Behind the milkhouse, a line of taller grass and thistles marked the edges of a tiny, festering creek. Ologrin tried to nudge his horse closer, but she shook her head and refused to take a step further. At the edge of the weeds the corpse of a child lay on its side, blackened and dried, its head bent backward as if in a last cry of anguish.

Ologrin shuddered as a wave of horror and guilt rose inside him. He suddenly felt very naïve. *Some would argue that heather and willow have more value than untamed herders*, Fasha had said. Jarvas had suggested the people of the riverflats were barely human. How could anyone believe such things? Yet before him was the body of a child, discarded as trash. *In truth*, he thought, *how could anyone believe anything else?* He remembered the resolve he had felt after his village had been raided. *Someone must bear witness.* Here, too, he resolved, witness was required.

They slowly continued north. Ologrin was appalled by the squalor he was seeing close-up. He counted at least a dozen bison carcasses allowed to rot in the fields where they had died. What he had not seen was anything resembling niter beds. Albrect had suggested the beds were already functioning. Ologrin had come to the flats to scale up extraction of niter, but there was nothing to extract. In his mind he could hear his Polfre teachers talking about the accounting of all things. To have niter, one needed composted manure. But that required healthy animals, and healthy bisonherders to tend them and build the pits. He found himself backing up his starting point and calculating what he was going to need to do. Initially, he had imagined the job of refining the niter would occupy him intermittently for the rest of the Summer. He was beginning to wonder if, working every day, he could even get his first pits functioning by then.

The Sun began falling in the northwestern sky. Ologrin and Aron rode toward another milkhouse, this one somewhat larger than the few they had passed before. A dozen people stood between the shed and the road, watching them approach. One stood slightly ahead of the rest, glaring at them. He had a long, slightly curved fieldman's knife at his side. Ologrin glanced over at Aron, who had a look of bemusement on his face. Ologrin brought his horse to a halt.

"Do you have anything to eat?" Ologrin asked softly. He saw a small child, perhaps two years old, standing untended at the edge of the group, her naked belly unnaturally swollen. He might be a poor physionomist, but Ologrin knew enough to understand just a small amount of bison's milk every few days would prevent that problem. These people were starving.

"I'm not asking for myself," Ologrin said more loudly. "Look at your people." He spied a couple of older boys who seemed to be modestly healthier than the rest. "You two, go find a couple of your biggest animals and bring them here. We need to get these people fed before we do anything else."

"Stay put." the man with the knife said to the boys before turning to Ologrin. "You can't come here and tell us what to do."

Captain Aron's mount came to life and took a step toward the man, but Ologrin raised his hand and the horse stopped.

Ologrin slid off his own horse and walked toward the man, who took a half step back but continued to grip his knife.

"We have a lot of work to do," Ologrin said steadily. "We need to get your people and your animals into shape. And you, my friend, are going to get fed. But only if you don't do something stupid with that knife."

The man hesitated, and Ologrin stepped to within an arm's reach. But then someone laughed, and Ologrin saw anger and shame return to the man's eyes. He raised the knife. Deftly, Ologrin stepped sideways and grabbed the man's forearm. The knife and the man's jaw dropped simultaneously. Ologrin continued to speak in the same steady voice.

"There is no need for anyone to get hurt. We are going to help each other, and things are going to get better. Does everybody hear me?" he finished, allowing his voice to rise. Heads nodded in the crowd. The man in Ologrin's grip sank to his knees. The two young boys looked at each other and hurried off. Ologrin let go and stepped toward the small crowd, which parted on front of him.

"I can't move my arm," the man said from his knees. "You froze it!"

"Nonsense," Ologrin replied. "In a day or two it will be as good as new."

By nightfall they had butchered two bison, dug a pit for a fire, and had started roasting meat. As a reward for their work, he allowed the two young men to take their pick of the meat. Ologrin pulled together a small platform that allowed him to stand a half-dozen hands higher than everyone else.

"These are the Crown's bison, don't forget," he said. "You are the Crown's bison-men. Be proud of who you are. And those who work the hardest will find themselves rewarded the most." Half of those assembled stared at him blankly, but the others smiled, and a few even raised a hand. Ologrin stepped down and searched in the gathering darkness until he found the two-year-old, still alone, sitting in the dirt and sucking a thumb. He picked up the little girl and held her for the rest of the evening. Later, when bones began to pile, he cracked one open against one of the milkhouse posts, scraped a bit of the marrow out and allowed her to suck it off his finger.

Captain Aron found him with the little girl sleeping in his arms. It was the first time he had seen the arms man off his horse. They were roughly the same age, Ologrin realized. Aron was just a bit shorter, but certainly more muscular. He seemed more at ease.

"A healthier man might've been a faster man. You should let me take care of threats."

"I'd rather not start our relationship with these people by shedding blood," Ologrin replied.

"The Polfre must teach more than making blast powder at that Sophenary. Any other sorcery I should know about?"

The comment was unsettling. Ologrin realized he had acted suddenly, without thinking about what rumors his actions might start. Had he given away his secret? Did Aron suspect he was a mosaic; a maleugenate? No one outside of the Sophenary seemed to take the news kindly.

Ologrin lay awake all night, thinking about his first day in the field. He was about to be these peoples' Tobin, but on a larger scale than anything Tobin had undertaken. The Sojourner rose in the west shortly before dawn, followed by the sky turning pink in the east.

A day turned into a passage, and a passage into a season. After the first few days, Captain Aron returned to Antola, though he checked on Ologrin from time to time. Ologrin worked from dawn until dark. He spent the first three passages just getting people into a condition that would allow them to work. He repeated the bison feast all around the flats and sequestered a quarter of the milk production for the children. There were four natural spring pools scattered across the flats; he had work gangs clear the banks to allow the bison to drink from them directly, and then he explained the need to herd the bison so they didn't foul the water afterward. It turned out that the one thing the bison flats had in abundance was young bodies, more than they needed to tend the herds and clear the waterways.

They had a mandate from the Crown, Albrect had said. So Ologrin spent heavily in those early passages. He estimated they consumed one out of thirty bison simply getting people fed. He traded half a dozen more for an equal number of cartloads of oak bark from Bhinton and had the bisonhides tanned and saved for later. The remaining bison had more grass to eat and became fatter as a result. If Captain Aron received word that Ologrin had arranged for select herds to be grazed on the Crown's grass in the middle of the night, he looked the other way. By late Summer the people and the animals of the bison flats looked transformed. Ologrin could finally turn his attention to plotting out the locations for the niter pits and having teams start to dig them. His incessant riding through the flats had given him a good sense of where to dig the beds to make them most efficient. People were amused when Ologrin told them they must urinate into the pits; that it was no longer acceptable to do so on the ground, but a collective mentality was taking hold, and soon the people were policing each other's pissing.

Ologrin finally decided his goal was to have eight niter pits functioning by the beginning of Harvest. It was about half of what he had hoped for, and the first usable niter likely wouldn't be available until the following Summer, but it was a start. More importantly, it was sustainable. The bisonherders were starting to take their job seriously. Older boys and girls were collecting manure, and even the younger children had been taught how to spread thin layers of chaff on top of the manure after it was a couple of hands thick.

Even as the days started to get shorter, the heat reached its peak and the stormy season began. Ologrin felt he had built as much as he could. The remainder of the year would be spent filling the pits and preparing for Winter. He sat on his horse, looking out across the flats from the slight rise afforded by the Great Road. The horse had been his constant companion; they had developed such an ease with each other that Ologrin wondered if there was some Polfre magic with animals he had unwittingly inherited. She was an unexpected pleasure, like the puff of cool air that precedes a Summer storm. He had named her Breeze.

He felt restless. Except for a couple of trips to Bhinton, he had not left the flats all Summer. He had not been back to Antola since the day he had ridden out with Captain Aron. He needed to get away. But it wasn't the Sophenary that was calling him. He noticed a small group of mounted warhorses on the Great Road about half a league distant. He set out for them, betting he would find Aron in their midst.

As he neared the group, he could make out Captain Aron's familiar form along with four additional arms men arrayed in a semi-circle around him. He caught the glint of gold at the neck of one of them, where he wore the gold panther marking him as an arms-commander, outranking an arms-captain. Aron half turned his horse in Ologrin's direction, then turned back. Even though it was hot, Ologrin was wearing his traveling cloak to give him some protection from the Sun. He had lost weight over the Summer, while the cloak itself had been bleached white. He looked like a gangly scarecrow, with the cloak flapping around him and the horse.

He was startled to see one of the men suddenly brandish his short sword. Aron did not back up, and after a moment the man put it away. After that, the arms men began to break up. They turned and set their horses into a slow trot in the other direction.

"I was hoping to find you," Ologrin said, riding up. "I'm heading north for a few days. Someone needed to know."

Aron continued to appear preoccupied with the retreating riders. "Friends of yours?"

"Hardly. They're mercenary from Madros," Aron said.

"What did they want?"

"They said they had come for the Crown's share."

"Crown's share? Surely they could see you're in the Crown's Guard."

"They said they were going to take it in hides."

"The people are going to need those hides this Winter. Did you tell them we are operating under the Crown's personal guarantee?"

"I don't think they were talking about bisonhides," Aron replied.

Ologrin thought about that for a moment. Two thirds of the bisonherders were young men and women who had witnessed fewer than twenty Summers. They had all looked old and half-starved at the beginning of the Summer, but now they appeared healthier and much more their age. They had begun acting like young people again as well, and Ologrin had no doubt there would be plenty of baby bisonherders come next spring. It did not take more thought to figure out what kind of skins the horsemen had been hunting for.

"Lucky for you they decided to honor the Crown's seal. They had you badly outnumbered," Ologrin said.

"I don't think that's what did it."

"What, then? They just came to their senses?"

Aron seemed suddenly interested in something in the distance. "I may have pointed out that you were headed their way."

Ologrin laughed. "Me? What possible influence could I be?"

"I may have told them you were more than you appeared to be."

"Well, I'd rather you not spread that around. Besides, it's

not like I could grab all of them at once. I would have been just as outnumbered as you."

"I may have mentioned something about you knowing sorcery."

Ologrin stared. "What?"

"Well, what would you call that thing you did to the man's arm? There are lots of rumors about what goes on in that Sophenary of yours. Some of them go back a long, long way. People outside of Antola are a superstitious lot."

Ologrin shook his head. "Listen, I'm going to be gone for a passage or so. I'm taking the horse and heading up the road north of Bhinton. I'm going to visit an old friend."

"I'm sure you'll be just fine."

The sorcery comment continued to trouble Ologrin. He had felt a growing friendship with the arms captain, and now that friendship seemed in peril. He felt compelled to pick at the splinter that had bothered him all Summer.

"Have you ever heard of the maleugenate?" he asked.

"Heard of it? Sure."

"I've been called that."

"I've heard that, too."

An alarm went off in Ologrin's head. "Is that what you said to them?"

"If I meant to call you that, I wouldn't feel the need to do it out of earshot. But, no, that's not what I said. I just said you were from the Sophenary, and that you folks knew how to do a lot of strange things. That's all."

Ologrin relaxed a bit. "It's just that other people have called me that, and then most have tried to kill me afterward."

Aron flicked his horse's reins, and it sidled up next to Ologrin, emphasizing the size difference between Ologrin and an arms man on a true warhorse. The tip of Aron's sword scabbard poked Ologrin gently in the chest. "I have real enemies to fight," he said. "If I see someone do good work, then I don't give my grandmother's good tit where they come from."

"My apologies for my suspicion and to your grandmother."

Aron watched the mercenary disappear in the distance. "You know there's a reason why people would want to kill a maleugenate, don't you?"

"Because they're a disruptive force?"

Aron barked out a laugh. "What? No. Because they're afraid of them."

"Why?"

"If there really are maleugenates, then who's to say there aren't sorcerers, too? Only a fool would not be afraid of that."

Ologrin looked out again across the flats. What once had been an unbroken stretch of dusty brown was now interrupted with large patches of green. Water in the distant spring pools reflected glints of sunlight. People were at work in the hot Sun, and from where he sat on his horse, he could hear occasional happy shouts, or even laughter. For some reason, it made him feel alone.

14

Three leagues from the Great Road, the North Road left the riverflats behind and began to climb into low rolling hills. Behind Ologrin, Antola was gradually disappearing. He rode until his backside ached, then walked. Breeze walked beside him without needing to be led.

By starting out before dawn he managed to come in sight of Bhinton's walls before the last light faded from the western sky. The southern gate was closed, but Ologrin produced a parchment bearing the ornate seal of the Crown and was let through. He found a stall for Breeze and an inn for himself, a luxury after having spent the Summer sleeping in the open of the bison flats. Nonetheless, he struggled to fall asleep, distracted by the belching, scuffling, farting and snoring that usually accompanied a night spent in a public tavern. The next day he explored Bhinton thoroughly. It had seemed like a marvelous place when he had lived in Halrin's Spur, but now seemed small and dusty. The city was built atop a hill, and the Altarnary occupied the summit. From its terrace he could see over the wall to the southeast, where a dark gray line marked the Antolan escarpment.

The western wall of the city bulged outward to accommodate the arms-commander's house, protected behind bronze gates. Ologrin toyed with the idea of seeing if the Crown's seal would get him inside. The house itself was as fine as any house in Antola's upper terraces. Two scarab trees grew in the large plaza in front of the house, the unofficial mark of Crown property.

Early the next day, Ologrin rode north again, his packs filled with provisions and a few gifts. The road was surprisingly busy. He rode until late at night, determined to make it to Halrin's Spur in two more days. There were campfires along the road, and he was welcomed by a small group of travelers who let him share their fire.

The next day was gray, with low clouds. In late Summer he was used to storms threatening for a day or two, then crashing down and flooding the ditches and creeks. But the rain stayed away and the clouds eventually broke. Just after mid-day he crested a final hill and spotted a familiar loop of river in the distance.

Ologrin immediately noticed that the track on the south side of the milkhouse, stretching from the road to the river, had been built up into a path almost as wide as the North Road itself. At its end a large stone and wooden bridge spanned the river, with a well-defined track beyond the bridge leading toward the western woods. There were now three milkhouses instead of one, and the shacks around them had been replaced with a proper small village. Green fields filled the land between the milkhouses and Halrin's Spur itself, and although his town did not look that much bigger, it was certainly built up, with several two and even three-story wood frame structures. The body of the Altarnary was no longer visible; only the black dome rising above the rooftops. Ologrin could not help but smile. "Come on, Breeze" he said. "We're almost home."

A dozen people stood in the middle of a field of grass reaching to their waists. A couple of them were wielding fieldman's knives, cutting the grass at ankle height. Several more were stooped, gathering the grass together or pulling it into larger bunches. One figure stood slightly apart, dressed in a brown cloak. Ologrin followed neat paths between the fields until he came close enough for the cloaked figure to spy him. The man stared for a moment, then began running his way. Ologrin laughed out loud. He could not remember seeing Tobin run for anything. He slid off the horse.

Tobin broke through the edge of the field and stopped, then walked up slowly. Ologrin grasped the man's outstretched wrist.

"Adept Ologrin," Tobin said, formally.

"Adept Tobin," Ologrin replied. Then Tobin suddenly hugged him, and he felt tears in the corners of his eyes. He was surprised to notice that he was looking at the top of the man's head. *Tobin has shrunk*, he thought.

Just as quickly Tobin pushed him back. "Come. I have things to show you." He waved toward the field where the others were cutting and gathering. "It's sweetgrass," Tobin said. "It grows naturally south of Dormond. We traded for a barrel of seed three years ago and found that it grows here just as well. We gather it and use it to help feed the bison during the Winter. We did not lose a single bison last Winter, and they all gave milk until Spring."

Tobin led Ologrin toward the milkhouses. Breeze, seeming to understand she had reached their destination, did not follow, but buried her head in the sweetgrass. Tobin talked as he walked, pointing out improvements everywhere. Ologrin noticed the shrine to Alera had been completely rebuilt, but the same wooden statue was nestled inside, brightly painted and with garlands of dried flowers resting around its neck.

"This section of the bridge can be raised like a tipping pole," Tobin said, as they reached the new roadway. "One person in the stone tower can release the weights and the section just pivots up. I'd show you, but then we'd need a bison to reset it, and they're in the fields on the far side."

Ologrin noticed the cloudnettle stretching in a thick band on the nearside riverbank. The river was wide enough and swift enough to form a formidable obstacle by itself to anyone who attempted to swim it. Ologrin had seen bison struggle to make the crossing, ending up far downstream from where they started. But he suspected warhorses could power across, and the cloudnettle extended only so far on either side of the bridge.

Tobin led him back to the North Road, where they could see all of Halrin's Spur. He continued to enthusiastically point out improvements they had made in and around the town in the years since Ologrin's departure. Not only had the structures improved, but the people as well. Several had become specialists in their trade, meaning they crafted enough to meet the needs of the village and have some to spare, which they sold to travelers for coin. Travelers, in turn, were beginning to make the trip to Halrin's spur just for the goods. The village had developed a particularly good reputation for cheese and leather pelts, in addition to charcoal. A new tavern had been built just beside the North Road on the main track into town, and the road itself had been raised on a gentle berm to allow it to dry more quickly after rains. As they entered the village proper, Ologrin noted locations where stonework had been started. It was just a stone fence here, or the back wall of a stone building there, but Ologrin noticed how they lined up with each other. Tobin had managed to get half a stone wall built around the town without it appearing to be a wall at all. There was purpose bordering on the obsessive here, he thought. As they approached the Altarnary, Ologrin could see the cloudnettle along the riverbank was almost as tall as he was. The narrow bridge leading across the river to the charcoaleries now sported a tilting section and a guard tower just like the bridge south of town.

Ologrin listened and nodded as Tobin explained their defenses and accomplishments, and he realized they no longer seemed like magic, springing fully formed from Tobin's head. He could even offer a couple of suggestions when it seemed Tobin might have missed a potential engineering flaw or behavioral consequence. The Curly Top had added a patio facing the river. Late in the evening, Tobin and Ologrin finally sat next to a patio hearthgrate and shared mugs of a slightly bitter ale.

"Tell me about your grand project," Tobin said. "We have more bison than ever before. Perhaps we want to be a part of it as well."

It was Ologrin's turn to be enthusiastic, as he explained his knowledge for making blast powder and how to enlarge it to a much greater scale. Tobin listened, but his mood seemed to darken. Ologrin sensed it would be easy to slip into their old relationship, with Tobin the master and him the dutiful assistant. But Tobin was no longer his master, Ologrin reminded himself. They were equals. He did not need Tobin's blessing for his current work.

"Even when your job was nothing more than sweeping out the Altarnary, I'd never seen anyone who so quickly figured out the best way to do something as you," Tobin said. "I have no doubt you have figured out how to gather niter in a way that will be more productive than ever before. But why, Ologrin? Why blast powder? Antola is not so defenseless."

"Our ships are. The Ismayans are carrying bombards on theirs, now. They could destroy our ships from a thousand hands distant, and we would be powerless to stop them."

"Why have bombards on a ship at all? Isn't there enough sea for everyone? What are you preparing for?"

"A ship with bombards can defend a city. It can defend other ships carrying much-needed goods. They will be more afraid to approach our ships if they know we can fire back," Ologrin said. He was irritated, and he knew it showed. He resented the fact that Tobin seemed to be twisting his work into something ignoble. Tobin failed to understand how the needs of the capital city might be different than the needs of a little town at the edge of the civilized world. Ologrin knew his work could potentially even the balance of power. Tobin was defending dozens. He was defending grosses of dozens.

"Blast powder also requires charcoal. Are you here for ours?" Tobin asked.

Ologrin thought there was an emphasis on the word "ours," that did nothing to settle his irritation. He had perfected the charcoal of Halrin's Spur and had turned it into their first true export. Tobin surely remembered that. Was he saying "ours" in a way that dismissed Ologrin's contribution, or in a way that said he was no longer one of them? Ologrin was worried that Tobin would start to inquire about their need for sulfur, and he would be forced to deflect his questions. The use of tanjium to ignite the blast powder was a Sophenary secret and was therefore an Antolan secret as well. Fortunately, Tobin seemed willing to drop the subject. The fact that he knew about blast powder did not mean he knew how it was made, Ologrin reminded himself.

"We have other sources for charcoal," he said flatly.

Tobin looked at Ologrin thoughtfully. "I think I have upset you."

"What are *you* preparing for?" Ologrin replied suddenly. "All this for Ruhatsi raiders? Or do you have a closer adversary in mind?" He stopped, afraid he would not be able to stem the flood of words that threatened to follow. *Yes*, he thought, *I'm good at figuring things out, and Tobin is playing a potentially dangerous game with the Crown*. Within the Sophenary, Ologrin had found both safety and community. The Sophenary survived by partnering with the Crown, not fighting it. If Tobin had dreams of an independent village, they were ultimately foolish and unnecessary. And if the Ruhatsi were still a problem in this part of the world, then perhaps what was needed was a company of arms men with Captain Aron as their head, rather than clever wooden bridges and stinging plants.

Tobin was silent for a long time. Ologrin, reviewing his own words, felt a bit abashed. At the beginning of Summer, the plight of the herders had given him purpose. Now, toward the end, he was defending the practices of the Crown. *What am I?* he thought. *A mosaic*, the voice of Vireo said in his head. *Bits of tile and glass that seem whole at a distance but are jagged and rough up close.* He wrapped his cloak more tightly around himself, as the night had become chilly.

"They hit Southwatch, you know," Tobin said finally.

"Who did?"

"Raiders. Whatever they are. At the beginning of the Summer. They swept down in the middle of the night and put the entire village to the torch. Most of the people there were killed. Fasha is dead. I sent you a letter."

Ologrin stared back at Tobin. "I haven't been home all Summer. I didn't know." He felt a shiver from deep inside roll over him. "What about Pipit?"

"She's missing."

"She made it back to the Greensee, then?"

"No. She never made it back. There are Polfre I deal with; that's how I know what happened to the village. She's missing."

"She said she wasn't afraid of the Ruhatsi."

Tobin rubbed his forehead. When he spoke again, it was quieter, as if he was trying not to be overheard. "I don't know if it was the Ruhatsi."

"Then who? Who else raids and destroys villages?" Ologrin looked around reflexively.

"No one ever actually sees them. No one knows anything about them except for these raids," Tobin replied. "Do you really believe demons come out of cracks in the ground and then disappear again?"

"I saw them," Ologrin said. "I saw what killed my mother. They were horrible creatures."

"People were trampled to death in Southwatch. Whoever did it did not come out of cracks in the ground; they rode horses." Tobin fingered the edge of his mug. "But I guess all sorts of people ride horses these days."

Ologrin felt his ears redden. After a moment, he stood to leave.

"I have a room for you in the Altarnary," Tobin said.

"No, thank you. I'll be fine here."

"I'm sorry," Tobin added. "That was not fair."

Ologrin could think of nothing to say. He briefly touched Tobin's arm, then turned to find Curly, the tavern's owner, and a bed for the night.

The next morning he wandered through the Altarnary, which was empty of people except for a broad, burly acolyte, who he realized with a start was Calus. The boy had turned into a young man. Calus revealed he had a woman and a baby on the way. Now he only worked for Tobin part-time. No one had taken his place, and it turned out there really wasn't any need, as Tobin rarely used the Altar room for any type of ceremony anymore. The building was kept clean and presentable but served little purpose other than to stand as a silent sentinel in the middle of town. Tobin had perfected the art of taking refuge to the people rather than waiting for them to come to him.

Ologrin climbed the narrow passage to his old room. The cot on its wooden frame was there, but otherwise the room was empty, except for Obo's old staff, still leaning in a corner. The blackness had spread to envelop half of the shaft. Ologrin picked it up and immediately felt a resonance he had not noticed before. He could not tell if he was feeding energy to the staff or it was feeding him, but it felt uncontrolled and brittle. He set it carefully back in the corner. He would take it back to the Sophenary, he decided. But rather than carrying it around and provoking Tobin, he would pick it up just before he left.

He spent the rest of the day exploring on his own. He did not see Tobin all day, and assumed he was back at work in the fields. He crossed the bridge to the charcoaleries and then walked farther west. The forest line had retreated almost half a league from the riverbank, but the stools of trees he had cut years before now sprouted growth already twice as tall has he was. Ologrin wandered into the forest alone. He would have been afraid to do so when he was younger, but today it seemed unthreatening, at least with the bright Sun overhead. He let his hand slide over a few of the biggest trees as he walked, just long enough to glimpse inside them. Some were more than six dozen years old. Destined to become nothing more than black lumps of fuel, he mused. He walked until the trees ran up against the bottom edge of a bluff perhaps thirty hands high. He scrambled up the bluff onto pastureland and saw the bisonmen with their animals in the distance. He had forgotten what truly healthy bison looked like. These were fat and tall, and just as intimidating, even at a distance, as he remembered from childhood.

He returned to the village and purchased a few provisions for the trip home, then ate in the inn and retired early. The next morning he was up at dawn. He had not seen Breeze since he had left her in the sweetgrass field and was beginning to wonder if he would ever see her again, but that morning she was standing behind the Curly Top, munching contentedly on tufts of grass growing next to the building as if she knew it was time to go. He had a few gifts to give out: a set of pewter utensils for Curly himself, and a fine braided leather belt for Calus. He thought he might have to search for Tobin in the fields as he passed to the south, but Tobin found him while he was still arranging his packs.

"You'll be back," Tobin said, as if it was not a question.

"Of course. I hope to finish some of my astrolemy work

this Winter, but I can come back again next Summer. I'll show you how to make the niter beds, and you can trade it for coin. And you can always come to Antola, you know."

"What for?" Tobin joked. "With so much coin, we will be the Antola of the north."

Ologrin reached into his cloak pocket, where he had stashed his gift for Tobin. He brought out a heavy pin, consisting of three twisted and interlocked rings of silver, designed to fasten to a cloak's collar. It was the symbol of the Sophenary. Each ring was set with a different colored jewel: white for astrolemy, green for vitachemy, and red for physionomy. It had been custom-made for Ologrin by metal smiths in the Sophenary, a one-of-a-kind gift for a one-of-a-kind mentor. He pinned it to Tobin's cloak.

"Until we meet again, Master Tobin," he said. He stepped away quickly and hauled himself onto Breeze's back. They trotted to the North Road before he gazed back at the fat little town. He let his eye wander over to the new village next to the milkhouses, then focused on the road until he and Breeze reached the hilltop where he had caught his first glimpse of Halrin's Spur two days before. He took one last look back, then plunged down the other side of the hill. Only then did he realize he had left the staff.

He had been gone for less than a passage, and the flats looked the same when he returned, but it was hard for Ologrin to shake the sense that he had been gone a long time. He fell back into his work easily, while his mind often wandered, climbing higher and higher as it had done when he was a young child. At night he would dream he was back in his tower, studying the sky. And in the dream, Vireo was by his side.

He found a young woman to oversee the niter beds for Harvest and Winter. "I'm Marle," she said when they met, as if she already knew he was looking for her. She was tall and square-shouldered, and though likely no older than himself, she had a daughter who was at least eight. He explained things once, and then she began working as if she had known how to do the work already, as if shoveling manure into a pit was no different than picking beans. Even though her official charge was just the niter beds, she seemed to have a natural authority, and none of the bisonmen argued with her.

The first frost came early. At the beginning of the Summer, Ologrin had hoped to be sending cartloads of finished niter up to Antola by Harvest. Instead, he hadn't even begun to arrange for the washing sheds he would need to purify the raw product. But he had done the best he could. He might have to come down to the flats once or twice to check on things, but the rest of the work could wait until next Summer.

His eagerness to return home was tempered by the anticipation of one sad parting. The Crown's Guard would want their horse back. He sat astride Breeze, watching the early frost melt into dew with the first touch of the morning Sun. "I promise I'll visit," he murmured to her, not sure if such a thing was possible.

Breeze raised her head, sniffed the air, then turned one eye to look at him and snorted. He patted her flank. "Time to go back," he said.

15

Harvest arrived. Scattered trees along the upper flanks of the Adamantines turned red and yellow first, licks of flame among the gray, impassive spruce. Then, like a fire burning the wrong direction, the trees below them turned, followed by the trees around Antola itself. The city blazed with color as the change swept north toward the Greensee.

Ologrin told Vireo about the destruction of Southwatch as soon as he returned. She immediately sent an emissary from the Sophenary deep into the mountains to the Polfre homeland.

Before long, days as well as nights turned cold. Leaves faded and curled, then dropped and scoured across the ground before stacking in corners. The Lord of the Crown's Affairs arrived at the Sophenary and disappeared into Vireo's chambers. Albrect came and went, but no one called for Ologrin. He caught word of the conversation later; the Lord Affairs had been full of complaints about the theft of Crown livestock. *I only did what needed to be done*, Ologrin thought resentfully. Who was this man to show up afterward, making accusations, when the riverflats were healthier than before?

Meanwhile, the emissary to the Polfre had yet to return.

Ologrin stood on the parapet above his cell, trying not to be distracted. *Why invent a world such as this?* he wondered. Just about the time everything and everyone shakes off the Winter, grows, and starts to produce, Harvest returns, heralding the doom of Winter again. The flaming colors were a warning: time to square away shelter and store enough food to survive until Winter itself passes away, hopefully with enough left over to start the next Summer just slightly ahead of where one was a year before. A wearying, endless struggle, and for what purpose?

Those thoughts, however, were the distraction, and he tried again to focus. The first stars were out. The only remains of the Sun's passage were a deep blue band on the western horizon. The Sojourner perched directly overhead, a half-circle bright in the sky. He had been trying to imagine how others in different places saw the Sojourner compared to what he saw at the same time. If Tobin were looking up at this very moment, he was seeing much the same thing as Ologrin. But what about people, say, far to the west? Ismay was three gross leagues west of Halrin's Spur. For them, at that moment the Sun was still visible, low in the western sky. And what did the Sojourner look like? It would not be directly overhead, but closer to the eastern horizon. By the time their sky was dark, the Sojourner would be setting. For locations differing north and south, objects in the sky rose and set at the same time. But for locations differing east and west, the same objects would appear to rise and set at different times. Hints of angles formed in his mind. There was something to it...

The sound of the door to his cell opening and closing captured his attention. He smiled, and the angles vanished. Only one person entered his cell without first knocking. He waited, then felt more than heard her presence ascend the stairs to the platform.

"Galah is back from the Lake of Skies. She arrived before Sunset. Heron insisted that she eat and rest before talking with anyone else." Vireo sat carefully on the parapet and looked out over the city. The trek to and from the Polfre homeland was intentionally arduous, she had once explained. No one other than the Polfre knew how to find it, and they would always keep it that way. Travelers often made the trip alone, making it more challenging, and toward either end they tended to become focused on their goal and might not eat or sleep for the last couple of days.

"There were two dozen and seven living in Southwatch when the raid happened," Vireo continued. "Nine were killed outright, five before the alarm could be sounded. Most escaped to the Greensee. Fasha refused to go. She was cut down outside the village longhouse. Four villagers continue to be unaccounted for."

"Pipit?" Ologrin asked.

"She is one of the missing. They say she is resourceful. She may yet appear."

Ologrin shook his head. "I have never heard of the Ruhatsi taking prisoners."

"Galah mentioned your conviction that this was the work of Ruhatsi raiders. The Polfre are not as convinced."

Ologrin knew he was incapable of remaining dispassionately logical when talking about the Ruhatsi. He struggled to keep the frustration out of his voice. "I don't understand these persistent doubts about the Ruhasti. I have seen them myself. Who else would it be?"

"Every human is capable of murder and destruction," Vireo said. "I have good news, too. Now that the bisonherders are healthier, Master Heron says far fewer will die this Winter. Perhaps one in forty, compared to one in ten. You have started a good thing."

"The Lord Affairs doesn't seem to think so," he replied, but he was distracted again, this time by the fact that he could feel the warmth of her presence. He felt his anger melting away.

"Lord Junger has no imagination. He doesn't understand how giving up something now will be better for the Crown later. The Sophenary paid coin for some of the bison you butchered over the Summer and has made promises to trade blast-powder for the rest." She slipped her arm through his. "It was a good thing. Any Polfre would have been pleased with your use of the Rha."

"I don't know how anyone could have ridden through the flats and not come to the same conclusion," he said. The image of a dead child's body, discarded in the dirt, came back to him again. The days and events of the past Summer were combining and simplifying in his mind, but that one image refused to be filed away. "How could anyone not care for their own people?"

"The Crown's Council don't see them as their own. Their people are only those at the top of the terraces or in the palace itself."

"But these are people. Doesn't that mean anything to them?"

"Truthfully, they were relieved by the Winter deaths in the flats every year. Their greatest fear is not punishment from the gods, but that their lesser will one day rise up and seek revenge. If repaying the Crown for the bison you butchered to feed the people is enough to distract them, then it is an inexpensive price to pay."

"Still, it doesn't seem fair that the Sophenary has to pay for something that benefits the Crown anyway."

"It will work out. We have plenty of time to square our ledgers."

"Am I still prohibited from returning to the flats?"

Vireo's brow furrowed. "I wouldn't say you are prohibited. Albrect thinks it's best if you just wait awhile. Next Summer, when Antola sees more meat and cheese than ever before, and when barrels of blast powder start stacking up, I doubt Lord Junger will care where you go. Besides, this gives you more time for your work here. That's what you said you wanted, correct?"

Vireo rested her head on his arm. "I'm glad you're back," she murmured. He stretched, and her warmth crept through him. How much of that was under her control, and how much was his imagination, he did not know. He slipped his arm out and placed it around her waist, and she did not resist.

Evenings were spent on the tower or in his cell, but days were filled with other tasks. Though Albrect had planned to spend the Harvest and Winter producing blast powder, the lack of niter made that impossible. However, he quickly found other things to do, and enlisted Ologrin to help do them.

The postern yard behind the castle took up as much ground as the castle itself. Stone walls extending from the castle framed the yard on either side. The only easy way into the yard was through the castle's cross halls. Outside of the walls the ground tumbled away, on one side toward the northernmost corners of the terraces, on the other side a sheer drop to the Purse rooftops sixty hands below. There was no wall at the back of the yard, as that was defined by a pleasant little copse of birch trees fronting a thick woodland, itself masking the steep rise of Mount Arske's southern flank. A broad path led through the woodlands, promising a pleasant, tree-shaded walk. This was true for a league or so, until one passed the thick-walled buildings Albrect had constructed for large-scale milling of blast powder. Beyond that the path split into a wye. To the left, it quickly became an irregular set of steps ascending the mountain. This, Ologrin knew, was the start of the path the Polfre took when heading home. An adventurous traveler could spend an entire day and night exploring the mountain on that path and not run into any serious obstacles. Beyond that, however, the path became much more treacherous. False turns and blind paths would trap an unwelcome traveler, leaving them hopelessly lost. This was the true starting point of the journey toward the Polfre homeland. It was a trip no one made without an invitation.

The right side of the path seemed easier to walk and headed down rather than up. It, too, became more difficult the farther one walked, but this was not due to Polfre design and was not intended to hide anything. As they took the downward path one morning, Albrect talked non-stop about plans he had to use some of the blast powder to widen and straighten the road.

"There was a time, long ago, when the ancestors of the Eidos practiced human sacrifice. I bet you didn't know that," Albrect said, somewhat out of breath. Though the slope was generally down, it required a lot of clambering over boulders.

"I did know that, actually," Ologrin replied.

"Well, those days are long past. Civilized people consider such things to be horrors."

Ologrin watched his feet and kept silent.

"Another thing civilized people avoid is the enslavement of others. Other people might consider slavery a necessary part of life. How else do you get those things done that require immense amounts of human labor? Cutting stone. Clearing forest. Or, to my point, breaking the side of a mountain down into a passable road? Since we do not use slaves, we could spend a lifetime getting it done with a hammer and wedge."

Ologrin thought about the bisonherders in the flats and wondered at Albrect's distinction. Still, he said nothing.

"That is why it is so important to discover and exploit the vitachemical principles that govern all things. In effect, we must enslave the principles themselves and force them to our needs."

"The Polfre would not agree with your choice of words," Ologrin said.

"Probably not. But so far, they haven't stopped me."

Before mid-day they came to a place where the path became smoother and more level, but also narrower. To his right, Ologrin suddenly noticed he was looking at the tops of trees. The mountainside plunged almost vertically away into a deep and narrow gorge, then rose again on the steep flanks of another set of peaks only a few gross hands away. If he had been alone, Ologrin could easily have convinced himself that he was the first person to discover this place. Looking high up, birds small as specks circled in a slice of blue sky.

"What holds the stones of the castle together?" Albrect asked.

"Mortar, of course."

"And what is mortar made of?"

"Sand, burned whitestone, and burned brownstone in equal measure."

"Correct. Wysel's mortar, we call it. And where do we get the whitestone and brownstone for burning?"

Ologrin was silent for a moment, then, "I guess you are about to show me."

"Very good."

The path jogged to the left. Ologrin found himself staring at a wall of white plunging into the gorge. The path widened and then seemed to disappear into the wall itself. A smooth vertical face rose forty hands high. At least two dozen wooden buckets covered in white powder were stacked neatly to one side. People had been carving into the side of the wall for years, he judged; probably for generations. And yet they had only taken a tiny portion of what was available.

"The treasure of a city is not just measured in its gold or silver," Albrect mused. "There is enough whitestone here to build Antola a dozen times over and still not exhaust it. And while there is plenty of whitestone around Lhosa, the brownstone streaks you see are rarer, only found in the tallest mountains. It is the burned brownstone, when mixed with water, that allows Wysel's mortar to set so quickly and become so strong. This wall of white, my friend, is priceless, and the Sophenary controls it." Albrect beamed, as if he had just divulged the secret to the Sun.

They began the trip back. Ologrin guessed that they had walked no more than two leagues to reach the whitestone cliffs, but it was a journey made much slower by the boulder-strewn path. He was a bit in awe of Albrect's confidence, imagining that blast powder could be used to carve a road. He could not imagine how he squared it with the Polfre concept of the Rha.

"Everything you use, you must replace. That is the Polfre way," Ologrin said. "How do you replace the side of a mountain?"

Albrect carefully worked his way over a stretch of loose stone. "You have to think beyond the obvious. We use the stone to build buildings that stand for many lifetimes and give people shelter from the cold and the rain. Why is that not an equal trade? In fact, why isn't that a great improvement over an otherwise unused wall of white rock?"

"So, you have the Dodecant's blessing?"

"She knows about it. I don't necessarily need her blessing."

"Why?"

"The Polfre may have started the Sophenary. They may still make up most of the faculty. But they gave up ownership long ago. I trust that Master Vireo understands what's best for the Sophenary is what's best for the Crown." Albrect paused in the middle of climbing over a boulder. "The Rha works very well for them, but it does not work for everyone."

"It's a worthy goal," Ologrin said. "What makes more sense than being careful to use no more than you can replace? In that way there is always enough for the next generation."

"Generations. That's the problem. Generation after generation, the Polfre population hardly changes. But put two Eidos in a place where they can eat and sleep, and a generation later you will have two dozen." Albrect stopped struggling over rocks and sat to catch his breath. "The Rha would have every Eidos family living in a little hut, planting just enough food for themselves, perhaps raising a bison calf every year. That leads nowhere. We need ways to allow a dozen Eidos herders to raise meat for a gross population. We can transform the wood and stone of this world into things that allow us to do more. There are hints, Ologrin, that our ancestors may have done much more than we can even dream of. I call that the Antolan Rha."

Albrect waved his arm in a wide arc. "I have plans to build a whole series of chimneys and forges in the postern yard. We will make charcoal, burn stone, forge metals, and help make Antola into more than it is today. And before you say anything, you should know that Master Vireo has agreed. She has seen my plans. She understands the Sophenary's need to continue to build and discover. You could say it's the Sophenary's Rha."

Ologrin could not help but smile at the man's enthusiasm. He helped the master to his feet, and they continued the climb. The path became narrow and steep as they approached the wye. Albrect stepped and puffed, and Ologrin chose not to burden him with questions requiring more of his breath. Once at the junction they rested again. The Sun was falling westward, its beams slanting through breaks in the trees.

"How did you end up at the Sophenary?" Ologrin asked.

"How did this Eidos end up among a bunch of Polfre? I grew up in Madros. My father was a bronze-wright, and his father before him. My older brother was destined to become one too. I thought that if I worked hard enough, and learned everything I could, that they would let me become part of the trade as well. But when I was twelve my father sent me to work with a mill owner who had no sons. I was facing a life of grinding grain and choking on the dust. So I ran away and came to Antola instead. I got work in the Crown's stable yards. When they saw what I could do repairing tack, they sent me to talk to one of the arms-captains, who got me work with one of the old vitachemists here. Then one day the Dodecant offered me a place as a student. And I haven't left."

"Master Vireo?"

"Oh, no. In fact, she became a student here about the time I earned my first adept."

"Did you want to become Dodecant at some point?"

"You mean me instead of her? No, thank you. She's the person for the job. She has a way of making all this work, you know. I've seen her take a member of the Crown's council to task such that I thought he might get on a knee and beg forgiveness. Yet most of the time she charms them. The ways she moves, and those clothes. They don't come from Antola, that I know. But you probably know that too. The two of you match up well, as the Antolans say."

Ologrin felt his face flush down to his neck. "She's the Dodecant."

"Don't tell me you're embarrassed by it?"

"She doesn't treat me any differently," he said, hoping Albrect believed it.

"Maybe you don't know as much about the Polfre as I thought," Albrect said. "They may have lots of rules about how they behave around others, but they are not shy about what they want. She has her mark on you. You're free to choose otherwise, of course, but as far as other Polfre are concerned, you're not available."

From the day he had entered the doors of the castle, Ologrin had nursed the fear that he wasn't there on his own merits. Being a mosaic was an abomination to the Malacheb, but not, it seemed, to the Polfre. But what was he, then? A curiosity? A collectable? If so, then he didn't really fit in at the

Sophenary any more than he had anywhere else. Without warning, the black pit had opened again before his feet.

"Everyone will think she is doing favors for me, that I can't do this myself. They'll think I don't belong here."

"That's not the Polfre way, and certainly not her way. If you weren't up to it, she wouldn't have time for you."

That did little to make Ologrin feel more at ease. "I still think you see more of a relationship that I do," he said, trying to convince himself at the same time.

"How often do you think about her when she's not around?" Albrect asked.

Ologrin blushed again.

"That's what I thought. I've seen her touch your arm, touch your shoulder. Anyone who's been around the Polfre for a while knows those aren't casual things. They don't touch unless they mean something by it. Let's get back."

But Ologrin did not move. "It feels...I don't know. I just don't understand. I feel like I know more about you than I do her. How can that be a relationship?"

"You have a lifetime to get to know her. You've noticed they are fond of bird names. The Polfre don't bond easily, but like many birds, when they do, it's forever."

Albrect glanced back, and Ologrin struggled to hide the raw, stricken look that had come over his face.

"Listen. Master Heron explained the mosaic thing to me," Albrect said patiently. "I remember stories from my childhood, of people so terrible they challenged the gods. I don't know if that's the same thing, and I don't care. What I do know is the difference between a children's story and the real world. You don't seem any different to me. This is where you belong, Ologrin, and there is no one here who disagrees with that. This is your home."

Ologrin tried to blink away the sudden tears, but they rolled down his face. This time it was Albrect who turned pink and quickly turned away. "Let's go," he said. "I need to show you my plans." Before Ologrin could say anything else, Albrect was walking the path again, talking as if he assumed Ologrin would stay at his side.

"The things we need require greater effort than simply pulling a turnip out of the ground and planting a seed for another. There are secrets in these stones and earths. Charcoal makes the fire hotter. Burning the limestone allows us to shape it and turn it back into stone again, in just the shape we want. The ashes from the fires have secrets: the potash not only fertilizes fields and makes soap, but is also used by the glass-makers. Which is better, bronze or iron?"

The randomness of the question helped bring Ologrin back to the present. "Bronze, of course. Iron is too brittle."

"Only because we don't make it right. I have read that, in the past, the Polfre were able to make iron that was both strong and malleable. We must learn these things for ourselves!"

Before long they hit the broader path leading back to the postern yard. Ologrin tried to imagine Albrect's forges and chimneys filling half of the yard. "You have a lot of work to do," he said.

"I can't do it by myself. I need your help. And you need to be a proper member of the faculty. So I need you to finish your astrolemy work too."

In the way that Tobin had simply ignored the yawning pit and had asked Ologrin to get back to work, he felt Albrect was doing the same thing. "Thank you," he said, finally.

"If I understand this mosaic thing, the different parts of you don't blend. Someday you may have to choose a side," Albrect added. "Just remember, there is nothing wrong with the Eidos side."

16

Brilliant late-Winter light shone down through the open shutters in the roof of the Collegarum, the most public space at the Sophenary. The three peaks forming the roof mimicked the Adamantine mountains in the distance. A cold breeze drifted through the space. Ologrin, standing just behind the raised dais, welcomed the air, as his new cloak was heavy and warm.

He was surprised at the number of people filling the Collegarum. All the faculty were there, as expected, along with most of the students. He saw at least a dozen arms men from the Crown's Guard. He had heard that two members of the Crown's Council would be in attendance. Most surprising was the number of Antolans with no connection to the Sophenary at all. They strolled about the hall, greeting each other enthusiastically, showing off their fine dress and fancy headgear. He continued to pick through the individuals in the crowd. Not a single cloak marked someone from the School for Servants. He was vaguely disappointed.

Someone placed a hand in the small of his back, and he turned to see Vireo slide up next to him. "The Lord Coronet is here," she said.

"Is that why there are so many of the Crown's Guard?"

"I invited him personally. I thought he would be very interested in what you had to say."

Ologrin's anxiety stepped up a notch. But it only made sense. If one of the purposes of the Sophenary was to provide for the needs of the Crown, then the Lord Coronet was the one person who needed to hear what Ologrin had to say. Still, it changed Ologrin from lecturer to salesman, a skill he feared he lacked.

"My, look at all the plumage!" Vireo said. "These are considered must-attend events for the well-to-do. They love to demonstrate their deep and abiding interest in the natural mysteries."

"So, it's not just me they've come to hear?"

"Oh, your presentation has garnered more than the average amount of interest. But many of them would come and listen to someone sputter nonsense, while they nodded their heads knowingly and planned how they would incorporate their newfound knowledge into conversation over their next meal."

Vireo glided onto the platform and down the steps to the front rows, where she greeted the faculty members. She was wearing one of her cloaks of pearlescent, supple fabric, cinched high at the waist. On one side her hair was pulled back with a clip made of silvery-black metal, adorned with a red stone. The metal flashed dazzlingly when touched by the Sun. For those who recognized adamantine and understood its precious rarity, and the Polfre's control of it, the clip was a statement hard to miss.

Vireo wore lightly tinted shades over her eyes. Ologrin had discovered she always wore tinted glass if she was meeting anyone who was not Polfre. He found it hard not to keep watching her. As far as he was concerned, she had an elegance that surpassed all the jewels worn by Antola's wealthy class. He had no difficulty understanding how she seemed to be equally successful dealing with the faculty and the Crown's representatives.

If she was testing his fit, he had decided, then he should do the same. He confronted her on their difference in years. She had lived through fifty-one Summers. His parents would not be that old, were they alive. Tobin was not that old. But she assured him age was not much of an issue in Polfre relationships, and many Polfre women did not seek a relationship until fifty. He insisted she not provide him with special academic favors. As if in reply, Master Crake spent a day testing him to his limits on his knowledge of maths, leaving him exhausted and humbled. Vireo said she had long ago learned how to separate her public life and her private life. Other Polfre would expect it, rather than be suspicious of it. For his part, he felt a sense of peace around her that he could not recall having felt before, to the point where that also had become a concern. He found himself daydreaming about how easy it would be just to disappear into her world and lose all his own ambition.

Vireo was making her way back onto the platform. From somewhere hidden several trumpets blew a short fanfare. Ologrin was so nervous it made him jump. The crowd took their seats. He wondered how such a small woman was going to be heard in such a great space. But Vireo began to speak, and something about the room picked up her voice and carried it over the continued chatting of guests.

"Lords, nobles, and honored guests, welcome to the Sophenary." Ologrin noticed she did not include "your graces" in her greeting, and he still could not see any of the cloaks from the School for Servants. The assembly became much quieter. "One to whom we have given shelter and the gift of knowledge, one who has already achieved adept status in not one, but two of our great schools of learning, has nonetheless seen fit to delve deeper into the knowledge of one of these schools, and after investigations wholly his own, has sought to challenge the faculty for the warrant of Master. The faculty have responded with days of examination and debate to determine if the challenge has been met, and I can tell you, as it always is, the debate was lively and not unanimous. In fact, our senior faculty in the very subject in question initially expressed his severe doubts, and without his consent, no warrant can be given. But after much reflection and discussion, he, too, has agreed. It is therefore my honor to announce to you that the Sophenary has granted the warrant Master in Astrolemy to Ologrin of the riverlands north."

There was a smattering of applause, and Ologrin stepped out onto the platform. He knelt on one knee before Vireo. She picked up a heavy silver neckpiece and placed it around his neck. He stood, and the applause was a bit stronger.

"And now, attend!" Vireo said. "Master Ologrin has consented to present a portion of his rare and valuable knowledge to us, his assembled guests."

It sounded so grand, and faintly ridiculous, he thought. He stepped in front of a tall table draped in a blue cloth. He checked to be sure his visual aids were still hidden behind the cloth, then looked out to the back of the crowd and began.

"As all of us know, the world we live on is round, like a ball." He suspected there would be some in the audience who didn't know this, but they would be reluctant to object, here in Antola's greatest hall of wisdom, when everyone else seem to be nodding their heads in agreement.

"It is quite a big ball, in fact. Even though we cannot see the curve from where we stand, if at mid-day I were to stand at the northern edge of Lhosa, and a colleague were to stand far to the south at the edge of the Southern Sea, I would find the Sun to be higher in the sky, and my shadow shorter, than my friend would find in the south, which proves our world is round. This was, in fact, demonstrated some years ago by Master Crake, our senior faculty in astrolemy." He was happy to see that Master Crake was nodding vigorously.

"By using the well-established principles of angular mathematics, we can use this information to find the distance round our world. Thus, we know if you were to start walking in any direction, and continue in that direction without varying, you would eventually end up back where you started, and would have traveled forty-eight and a half gross leagues to get there." He knew this would elicit gasps, and he wasn't disappointed.

He pulled a large ball with the image of Lhosa painted on its surface. "This shows the size of Lhosa in relationship to our entire world." He pointed to the small mass of land depicted on the lower half of the ball. "Considering Lhosa is about three and a half gross leagues at its greatest length, there is a lot of world left over." He had wanted to say this meant it was very likely there were other lands to explore, but had been strongly advised against it, as that was not a widely accepted conclusion. For some it was deeply disturbing, as other lands suggested other people—perhaps other kingdoms greater than Antola.

"As you can see, this world we live on is a big place. But there is reason to believe there are other things that are bigger still." He saw Master Crake begin to shake his head. This was what he had begun to research for his warrant master, and where he soon found himself at odds with Crake. Ologrin believed that applying angular mathematics to the Sun proved it was vastly larger, and consequently much farther away, than most people assumed. It was Master Albrect, practical as always, who had recommended an alternate research path, noting that information about the size of the Sun wasn't all that helpful in the day-to-day affairs of Antola.

"But that is not what I am here to talk about today. My presentation regards using the angles between ground and sky to determine where we are on this great ball we live on. If we can do that, then navigators aboard vessels at sea can do it, even when they are not in sight of land.

"The world, we know, spins around a central axis, which makes the Sun appear in the east and disappear in the west each day. One revolution is one day." He guessed about half his audience accepted this; those that did were his intended audience.

"The forty-eight and a half gross leagues I mentioned is the world at its widest. Imagine drawing a circle around the exact middle of the world, and then additional circles every eight dozen leagues north and south of the middle. Then imagine drawing circles around the world from top to bottom, making sections like an orange. A navigator with a map of the world containing such lines could figure out the distance between one point and another by using the lines as a reference." At this point, Ologrin figured he had lost most of his audience. *Just as long as the Lord Coronet is listening*, he thought.

"As I said, the height of the Sun appears different depending on where on the surface of the world the observation is made. The farther south one goes, the lower the Sun appears to be in the northern sky. Navigators already take advantage of this knowledge. They can calculate how far south they are without reference to land, by using a device to measure the height of the Sun at its highest point and compare that to a known height for a known location on that day of the year. Thus, navigators can tell where they are, north or south, by measuring the Sun, even if they cannot see the land.

"What navigators have not been able to do is determine where they are east versus west, if they cannot see land. They must stay near land or risk becoming lost. It is possible to look at the Sun and determine how far north or south one is, but not east or west.

"Remember the world is round. When the Sun rises in Antola, it is still dark in Solanon or Ismay. When the Sun sets in Antola, it is still visible in the western sky in Ismay."

Ologrin attempted to demonstrate, using one of the models, how the Sun would begin to shine on one portion while the other was in darkness. Fewer and fewer of those in the audience were following him. But sailors understood, and the Lord Coronet understood. "Unfortunately, when ships are days away form Antola, there is no way of knowing how the Sun above them compares to the Sun above Antola. Until now.

"The Sojourner has long been a mystery to us. The Sun goes from east to west. The stars go from east to west. The Red Eye goes from east to west. Why, then, does the Sojourner rise in the west and set in the east? The reason is because it also spins around the axis of the world, but it spins at a faster rate than the world itself. It completes almost two revolutions in the time it takes our world to complete one. Almost, but not quite, which results in it being one twelfth of a revolution shy of two revolutions when the world has completed one. It loses one revolution in twelve. So, for us, every twelve days starts a new passage of the Sojourner.

"For the navigator, this offers a second point of reference. For those of us in Antola, mid-passage is the day the Sojourner and the Sun are both overhead in the middle of the day. If a navigator found himself one quarter of the way around the world west of here, on mid-passage the Sojourner would already be setting in the east. At the same time, if the navigator were instead one quarter of the world east of here on the same day, the Sojourner would just be rising.

"I have calculated a set of tables. By comparing the position of the Sun and the Sojourner when it arises each day of the year, the navigator can use the tables to determine how far east or west of Antola they are. These tables are accurate enough, I believe, to allow the navigator to determine their position east or west within ten leagues. By using a Sun angle measurement, they can already determine their position north or south within ten leagues.

"Assembled guests, our ships no longer have to stay within sight of land to remain safe while at sea. This opens up exploration opportunities that have not existed before. In fact, anyone with these tables and the ability to measure the angle of the Sun can determine exactly where they are, not only on Lhosa, but anywhere on our side of the world, even if they have never been to that place before."

Ologrin stood there for a moment, until he realized his audience was for the most part so lost that they did not even realize he was done. "Thank you for your gracious attendance," he added.

Again, there was a smattering of applause that grew and then faded quickly. The audience stood, clearly relieved their responsibility was over. Ologrin recalled how excited he had been when he confirmed his calculations. It seemed momentous, and in his mind, he imagined others gaping in awe when he presented the finished product, recognizing it for the genius it was. He had practiced his presentation several times, looking for the right words, trying to be as clear as possible. Only after he had begun did he sense he was not capturing his audience, and he felt them slipping away even more as he progressed. *At least it's over*, he thought.

Vireo was smiling as she climbed the shallow steps to the platform, and Ologrin could not help but smile in return. She slid her right arm through his left. "You were brilliant," she beamed.

"I don't think anyone understood anything I said."

"If it were easy, they wouldn't require the Sophenary to figure things out." She tugged his arm gently and led him down the steps. Most of the faculty were standing near the front. Master Crake, tall by Polfre standards, gave Ologrin the slightest of smiles and held out two fingers. Ologrin held out two in return and felt a slight tingle in his hand when they touched. Crake was as reserved about touching as the most conservative Polfre; Ologrin realized this was a significant offering of friendship from the master. Master Heron, as diminutive as Crake was tall, also offered her hand briefly. By contrast, Master Albrect skipped the handshake and grabbed Ologrin in a bear-hug. "A proper Madros hello," he said with a wide smile. Ologrin greeted the remaining faculty in turn. Vireo kept her arm looped in his, and he was aware of the warmth of her presence, like the warmth of the Sun's rays on one side of his body. He glanced down at her, but she seemed busy greeting others, all the while gently guiding him through the remnants of the audience.

Ologrin noticed an elaborately dressed Antolan nearby, engaged in conversation with a small group of people clustered around him. He wore a short blue cloak fastened with gold buttons and elaborate braided loops, with identically colored breeches disappearing into glistening knee-high black boots. A leaping gold panther was affixed to each shoulder. Clearly, he wore the uniform of a high official. What was most striking about the man's appearance, though, was the circle of gold he wore on his head, as thick and round as Ologrin's middle finger.

"This is the one person you must meet," Vireo whispered. She let go of his arm and extended her hand toward the man. He took it in both of his, and Ologrin felt a brief pang of jealousy.

"My Lord, thank you for attending," she said. "Master Ologrin, may I introduce Lord Wesse, the Lord Coronet."

Ologrin, too, extended his hand, which the man shook perfunctorily. He was taller than Ologrin and had short-cropped graying hair and a neatly trimmed beard. He appeared old, perhaps forty years or more, but had a young man's penetrating gaze.

"Newest member of the faculty? And not Polfre, either? That's good. It's about time we got more of our own in here." He turned his attention back to Vireo. "He will do."

"Brilliant, as I told you," Vireo said.

"Yes, well, the presentation was interesting. Be sure to have extra copies of your calculations and your tables. I will have the Crown's navigators look at them as soon as they get a chance." Before Ologrin could reply he said, "Master Vireo, a delight to see you as always," and then turned back to his entourage. He did not give Ologrin a second glance.

Ologrin stood dumfounded. He had not expected the Lord Coronet to offer coin for his tables on the spot, but he had assumed they would first have a conversation about their value to the Crown. At the very least he had hoped for a word of admiration from the man, which would have been equally as validating. Instead he felt dismissed, and even more let down than before.

"That's it? That's all he has to say?" Ologrin asked, as they walked away.

"Your presentation was fine," Vireo replied. "He will have people who work for him get in touch with us. I have already arranged for copiers to begin making copies of your charts. You will even make some coin of your own from this. You deserve it."

Ologrin shook his head slightly. This was not how he expected to feel, after working so hard for so long. "What did he mean when he said that I will do?"

"I have offered your services. It's important, and it will do a great deal to continue the strong bonds between the Sophenary and the Crown. I have offered to have you serve as a tutor."

Ologrin stopped. "You offered me? I have to teach someone's child?"

"You are a master of the Sophenary," Vireo said. "You are a member of the faculty. As Dodecant, it is within my authority to decide who teaches what. This is your first assignment."

"But I have so much work. Albrect has me in his chambers all day, working on vitachemy projects. And there is the niter production. I have not been to the flats in almost a year. And I was hoping to continue my observations. I have some thoughts about the Red Eye."

"We are all busy." She grabbed his wrist. He felt the familiar warmth, but this time, felt he was being manipulated just a little. "This is an opportunity for you, Ologrin. These connections with the Crown are invaluable for you as well as for the Sophenary. Meanwhile, you shouldn't worry. We will be hearing from the Lord Coronet again."

"So, is it his child?" Ologrin asked.

"To be truthful, he didn't say. But you start in two days. We can both meet your lucky student then."

She let go and headed for another knot of people slow to leave the Collegarum. Ologrin returned to the platform and began collecting his things. He felt a bit of sweat drip from his neck and was momentarily surprised when he reached up and felt the heavy master's collar. He pulled it off to admire the elaborate engraving. He slipped the collar around his neck again. He wished Tobin could have been here. He tried to imagine the look of surprise on Tobin's face when he next saw him, wearing the collar around his neck. The student becomes the master. It would be worth the wait.

Vireo assigned new work chambers for Ologrin on the second floor of the castle, above the great doors. They were far larger than anything he could imagine needing, but they had high windows looking out to the east and south, giving him a view of the Purse to the left and the palace in the distance. The castle had a preponderance of dim hallways and dungeon-like rooms. It was, no doubt, with the goal of not frightening the child that Vireo chose this overly generous space. Ologrin had brought in sheets of parchment and charcoal pencils, as well as some of the most basic books on mathematics. His models from the presentation sat on a table against one wall. Still, he had no idea what he was expected to teach. For all he knew, he would spend his time telling made-up stories about the Sun and the stars.

With the space as prepared as he could make it, he stood next to the windows, wondering what kind of disruption below would announce the child's arrival. Soon enough he noticed three soldiers mounted on warhorses trotting toward the Sophenary. He assumed his student would follow in some form of elaborate wagon, and so he was surprised when only the horsemen appeared. He headed down to the great doors in hopes of finding out more.

Walking out, he saw that Vireo was already at the base of the stairs. The horsemen dismounted. The first two had leaping panthers on their collars. The third, somewhat younger, was dressed in the same blue cloak, but without devices of rank. *Perhaps the father,* he mused. *Perhaps today is an inspection day and the child will come later.*

Vireo turned and spied him at the top of the stairs. The uniformed soldiers made directly for Ologrin, but then passed him without comment and entered the castle. Vireo walked up with the other man at her side.

"Master Ologrin, how fortunate you are here," she said. "This is the Serene Lord Terval."

Ologrin bowed a little, though he was aware that Vireo had not.

"So, this is the genius," the plain-cloaked man said, smiling. "Lord Wesse said your lecture was brilliant. So brilliant, in fact, that most of the audience were blinded as to when it was over!" He laughed, and it did not seem to bother him that no one else laughed with him. "He also said you were not Polfre, but I did not expect you to be so tall! You are a head taller than me." He chuckled again. Ologrin noticed that the man was quick to show his teeth, which were as white as snow and perfectly formed.

"Serene Lord, I am honored to be a tutor for your child," Ologrin said.

This made the man laugh even harder. "How old do you think I am?" He looked at Vireo. "I don't think the genius understands what is happening here, do you?" He turned again to Ologrin. "Master Ologrin, forgive me for not introducing myself properly. I am to be your humble pupil." He bowed so low that Ologrin was afraid he might fall over.

"My...my apologies, Serene Lord," Ologrin said. His face began to burn.

"No, none of that," the man said. "Please refer to me as Terval, for that is who I am. And I will try to remember that I am in the presence of a master of the Sophenary and address you properly, but if I slip and simply say Ologrin, I hope you will forgive me."

Ologrin glanced at Vireo, expecting to see her laughing along with their guest, but he could see concern in her gaze. He felt her connection though she was still several steps away, and it made him feel stronger. "Terval, then," he said. "It is still my distinct pleasure to be able to work with you. If you will follow me, I will show you our work chambers."

Ologrin turned to the stairs, but one of the horsemen quickly stepped in his way. "I shall lead. The Serene Lord shall follow me, and you may follow him."

"Well, if you know where you're going..."

The horseman gave him an irritated look and started up the stairs. Terval flashed Ologrin another big smile and followed, and Ologrin took up the rear. The second horseman remained standing at attention in the entryway. "First door to the right," Ologrin called up, as they hurried up the stairs. The horseman entered and stationed himself just inside the door. Terval immediately headed for Ologrin's models.

"So, this is our world," he said, picking up Ologrin's model. "And these are the lines Lord Wesse mentioned, I see."

It is a map, is it not? We could peel the entire thing off and flatten it into a map of the entire world."

"Except it would not lie flat," Ologrin replied. "To make it flat, we would have to stretch the top and the bottom, making them look larger than they really are."

"Not so easy to use this at sea, then."

"Smaller sections can be made into maps that work well enough."

"Fascinating. Have you ever been to sea, Master Ologrin?"

"No."

"And yet you worked all of this out in your head, as if you had been. As if you had already been all the way around the world."

"When I was younger, I used to close my eyes and imagine myself flying over Lhosa, higher than a bird. I could see everything, from Antola to the Crespe Sea, all at one time." It was a fantasy he had never previously shared with anyone, and he was surprised to hear himself mentioning it now.

"Remarkable. And what lies beyond the shores of Lhosa? Can you see that?" Terval sat on the edge of the table. He seemed as relaxed as if they had known each other for years.

"I cannot. I can only see what others have depicted on maps."

"Then perhaps we need better maps."

"Perhaps."

"Or perhaps you need to go to sea and make them yourself."

Ologrin had never imagined sailing anywhere himself. The idea was intriguing.

"And I will go with you!" Terval said. "But before that, you must teach me this method of navigation. And I am mystified by this thing you call angular mathematics, so perhaps first we should start with that." Ologrin nodded happily.

Terval was indeed unfamiliar with the principles of angular mathematics, but he was well versed in the prerequisite knowledge, so over the next few passages they made rapid progress. Terval turned out to be a serious student and a quick study. He applied himself to the task with a level of intensity Ologrin was not expecting, thus he found himself devoting more time to preparing for his tutoring sessions. Terval was clearly reviewing the material between lessons as well. Within a half-dozen passages he was demonstrating sufficient grasp of angular mathematics that they were able to begin work on more complex subjects.

"Everything above the surface of the world falls toward the center of the world," Terval repeated one day.

"It is the only logical explanation."

"If I fire a bombard directly at a distant target, the stone falls down—excuse me, falls toward the center of the world—and so falls short of the target. But if I aim the bombard above my target, the stone at first rises above my target, but then falls into it."

"Yes, and angular maths allow you to calculate how high to aim the bombard."

"And we have imagined a very powerful bombard, one that could throw stones so far that we cannot even see the target from where we are, because the world curves and the target is below the horizon."

"True."

"So, it is conceivable that, if we had a powerful enough bombard, we could fire the stone in the air, and it would not strike the ground until it came all the way around the world, back to where we are."

"If the bombard were powerful enough."

"And if it were even more powerful, the stone might go around a second time, or a third, or forever."

"At least based on the mathematics."

"Which explains how the Sojourner continues to circle the world and not fall toward its center."

"Yes, exactly," Ologrin said.

"The gods must have a mighty bombard to fire something like the Sojourner, wouldn't you say?" He nudged Ologrin's shoulder.

Terval's movements were naturally graceful. He had been perfectly at ease from their first meeting. He was physically gregarious in the way that Antolans treated their best friends. He frequently touched Ologrin's back or shoulder as if it were a form of communication.

"If that's the way you want to think of it," Ologrin replied.

"How else can you think of it? Everything has to have a starting point, does it not?"

Ologrin was about to say something about not being drawn into logical arguments, when Terval laughed. "You know I'm right, Master!"

"The student is pleased when he thinks he has learned all there is to learn. The master is the one who understands there is always more to know."

"Ologrin, I cannot tell if you are a master or a priest." Terval wandered over the tall bank of windows looking out over the Crown's Walk. "Take a look, my friend." Ologrin joined him at the windows. "Look how small it really is. The greatest city in the world, and we can see almost all of it from your windows. Now look at the ships in the harbor. They are tiny by comparison. And yet they can make their way, league by league, to Ismay, or Bomlin, or just keep going, like your bombard stone, until they make it all the way around. All we have to do is climb aboard, and we can go and see everything there is to see. Like Runcel the Navigator, only we wouldn't simply sail all the way around Lhosa, we could sail all the way around the world! Your tables would get us there. Perhaps you will go yourself."

"Or you," Ologrin said.

Terval turned away from the windows. "No, it will not be me. I am afraid my life will never be that free."

Ologrin was hesitant to delve deeper. He realized he knew very little of his student, other than he was important enough to require a serious commitment from the Crown's Guard wherever he went, and that fact alone suggested caution. "Have you ever been to sea?" he asked finally.

Terval brightened suddenly. "Have I been to sea? Of course! Have you ever even been on a boat?"

Ologrin shook his head.

"Get ready, then. I think you're going to love it!"

17

Ologrin had not been to the docks since the day he had stepped into the Sophenary. He felt like a different person now, as he walked their length. He counted fifteen ships tied up alongside. Most were roughly the same size: eight dozen hands long at the waterline, and traditional in shape, with high, curving prows and sterns, and a single mast with one long spar. They came and went from Madros and Solanon, and even as far as Ismay, a journey of three gross leagues that could take five or six passages to complete there and back.

Ologrin knew the story of Runcel the Navigator, who long ago had sailed west out of Gosper's Bay, and one year later re-entered the bay from the east, having traveled completely around Lhosa in the interim. It was a feat that had not been repeated since, though there were stories of those who had tried. The Adamantine mountains marched off the northern end of the continent into the sea, creating a treacherous barrier of submerged obstacles blocking access to the northern coast from seas to the east. The southern coast of Lhosa was well-traveled, even as far as the city of Bomlin, on the far western tip of the continent. But few were willing to venture north beyond its peninsula. Sailors told stories of monstrous things that had come to live near the Crespe Sea. Thus, the western approach to the northern coast was considered impassable as well.

The docks bustled with ships being loaded and unloaded, merchants haggling over costs, and children darting about hawking food and ale from nearby shops. Ologrin had no doubt there were thieves everywhere, but his tanj was securely at his chest. Anyone who came into intimate contact, intentional or not, risked an unpleasant surprise.

The ship he was looking for was moored much closer to the palace, necessitating a walk south along the length of the dockway. Ologrin walked slowly, enjoying the sights and sounds. The sky was clear; the air was cool and breezy. He passed the base of the trestle lift, now half filled with goods bound for the other side of the city. The lift was more of a mystery to him now than it was when he had stepped onto it four years before. Now he understood the principles of capstans and counterweights and four-purchase pulleys—things that would have stayed a mystery had he remained at the School for Servants—but that only made the smooth, quiet functioning of the lift even more remarkable. It served to enhance his admiration for the Sophenary masters who had designed and built the lift long ago. *My colleagues,* he thought to himself, smiling.

Beyond the deck of the trestle lift he could clearly make out one vessel different than the rest. The hull was a dark, deep blue, yet it gleamed as if it were freshly painted. A broad band of gold topped the rail. The ship was somewhat smaller than most of the other merchant vessels, at about eight dozen hands. He walked the length of the ship, admiring its form.

Ologrin slowly walked up the gangway leading amidships. Several men were working on deck, but he did not see Terval. He could not help but feel out of place, even though he was sure this was the ship Terval had described. He stood at the top of the gangway for a moment and was promptly approached by a young man.

"You look like a man in the wrong place," the young man said.

Ologrin tried to suppress his anxiety. "No, I'm sure this is the ship. I'm here with Terval."

"With what?"

At that point an older Polfre man approached. "Can you not find something useful to do?" he said sharply to the younger one. Ologrin briefly thought he was the target of the comment, but the younger man hurried on.

"My apologies, master. What did you say you were looking for?"

Ologrin grinned broadly. "Adept Scaup, I believe? I'm here to meet Terval. And it's just Ologrin, if you don't mind."

Scaup cocked his head, and then a smile slowly began to curl across his face. But before he could say anything in return, a voice barked behind him.

"Ship Adept! Stand-to!" A third man approached, in the blue tunic and breeches of the Crown's Guard, only these were well-worn and lacking most of the finery. He squared up with Ologrin. He was not as tall, but when he placed his hands on his hips Ologrin could not help but understand who was in charge. He addressed Ologrin directly. "You're on the Crown's vessel, sir. State your business."

"My name is Master Ologrin. I may be early, but I was told to meet Terval here by mid-day."

The officer stood and blinked, as if processing an unexpected thought. Then light came into his eyes. "My apologies, sir, for my crew keeping you waiting on the rail. Ship Adept! This is the Serene Lordship's guest. Fetch his things to the Lordship's cabin!" Ologrin offered up the large leather satchel he had been carrying over one shoulder. "If you will point out the rest of your things on the docks, sir."

"This is it," Ologrin said. Scaup hurried off with the satchel.

"Again, my apologies," the officer said. "We don't usually refer to the Serene Lordship by his given name. I'd guess most of the crew don't even know it."

"To tell you the truth, I don't know what else to call him," Ologrin said. "Are you the ship's navigator?"

"I am the shipmaster," the man said. "Captain Weims."

"Is that the same as the navigator?"

"You're that Sophenary man with the ideas about finding your way with the Sojourner, aren't you? Never been on a ship before, I'm guessing."

"No. Never."

"Ordinarily we don't carry a navigator, a single ship like this going out and staying near shore. You're welcome to look around."

Ologrin wandered around the deck. He tried mentally untangling the lines leading everywhere and began to get a picture of how the sail was raised and long spar supported. The massive steering oar angled up through a slot in the stern. He slid his hands along the rail and against the spars. The ship whispered to him of great trees felled and transported over leagues, then slowly cut and fitted by dozens of craftsmen.

He heard hoofbeats on the docks and turned to see Terval's now-familiar three-horse entourage ride up. Someone whistled through their teeth loudly, and the crew stopped and assembled next to the rail. Terval dismounted and walked up the gangway. The ship's crew fell to one knee and bowed their heads, except for Captain Weims, who bowed his head but remained standing.

"Serene Lord," Weims said.

Terval touched the man lightly on the shoulder and spied Ologrin at the same time. Despite the passages that they had worked together, Ologrin was suddenly unsure if he, too, should sink to a knee. Instead, he bowed his head deeply.

"Oh, stop," Terval said, laughing. "Master Ologrin, welcome aboard the *Rayfish*. Captain Weims, is our good ship ready?"

"We are, Serene Lord."

"Then let's go sailing!"

Four crisscrossing ropes held the ship to the docks. They were soon released and hauled aboard. With a series of whistles and commands, Weims had his men untie and then slowly begin to haul a pair of heavy ropes. The long spar rode up the side of the mast and a large triangular sail slowly took shape above them. The leaping panther of the Crown towered over them, embroidered into the sail in gold thread. Ologrin was taken by surprise as the ship began to move, causing him to grab for the rail.

Terval settled himself on a small seat at the stern, behind the steersmen. "This is my favorite thing," he said, smiling broadly. "It feels like we are flying, doesn't it?"

Ologrin nodded, though he was uncomfortably aware of the ship's gentle fore-and-aft pitching. Terval closed his eyes and took a deep breath. Ologrin leaned against the aft rail, still feeling unsteady. The sound of the Purse faded quickly.

The wind was blowing steadily from the east, and the ship picked up speed. Ologrin had never seen his city from this vantage point. The Sun was high overhead, illuminating the Purse's intricate patchwork of brown and gray. The spires of the Sophenary seemed to grow out of the Adamantine foothills. The snowy peak of Arske glimmered in the Sun, dwarfing the city. To the south the land on both sides of Gosper Bay seemed to sink into the water several leagues distant, with a wide stretch of water in between. Weims had the ship pointed directly toward the middle of this expanse. The breeze freshened; the ship heeled modestly and leapt forward.

As the day progressed, Antola and the land to their right fell away, while to their left the opposite shores of the bay seemed to press against them until they passed the broad point made by the Ginney cliffs. Weims showed Ologrin a map of the bay. The cliffs were in fact almost directly south of Antola. They had slowly turned right until the setting Sun was in front of them, forcing Ologrin to mentally re-orient himself. Then the cliffs fell away, and they sailed into the broad lower half of the bay. They stayed just within sight of the coast to the right, while to the left there was nothing but water.

"We'll stay within sight of shore until morning," Weims said. "Then we'll head south and spend a couple of days out on the open sea. After that, we'll see if your charts can find us. This is storm season, so we'll see how it goes."

Ologrin ate an evening meal with Terval and Weims on the raised stern, then listened as they discussed the movement of ships along the southern coast. Most of the traffic was to-and-from Solanon, about eighteen dozen leagues to the west, though some was from as far away as Ismay.

Lamps were lit and raised to the top of the mast, and a sailor nestled in the overhead rigging kept an eye out for lights from other ships. Soon it was fully dark. The Red Eye glowered high above the western horizon.

"The Lord Sorceros is watching us tonight," Scaup said, passing by. "He doesn't want us to rest."

"Sharp eye, Ship Adept," Weims said. Scaup whistled up at the rigging and got a short whistle in return.

"I assume you masters of astrolemy have a different explanation for the Eye, right?" Terval said.

"There is no agreement," Ologrin replied. "The simplest explanation is that it is another physical body, like the Sojourner, only much farther away.

"How many leagues above us do you think the Sojourner sails?"

Ologrin felt uncomfortable sharing his conclusions. But he had made the observations more than once and had run the calculations several times more. It really wasn't a guess.

"It is about twenty-eight gross leagues above us," Ologrin said. Weims laughed.

"Our captain doesn't agree," Terval noted.

"We can't see land more than ten leagues from us at sea. How would we ever see something that far away?" Weims replied.

"It's very big," Ologrin said.

"Then the Sun is farther than that?" Weims asked.

"Much farther, and far bigger."

"How far?"

"About forty-eight gross times farther than the Sojourner. There really isn't any number to describe it."

Weims snorted derisively and stalked off.

"And the Red Eye?" Terval asked.

"It's very hard to determine. I have used different ways to calculate it. If there are rules that govern how all bodies move in the sky, then at least eighteen times farther than our world is from the Sun."

Terval shook his head. "But why? What's the use of things being that far away?"

"I can't answer that. They just are."

"And the stars? I have heard some astrolemers say they are Suns, just like our own. Do they have worlds around them?"

"I don't know. I suppose they could."

"Well, until you do know, you should not say. Limit yourself to this Sun. It appears strange enough."

Ologrin did not reply. They'd had conversations of this sort before, but they had never unsettled Terval like this.

"How do you even put order to something that big?" Terval added.

"It has its own order. That's the beauty," Ologrin said.

"No. You describe a sky that goes on and on, essentially forever. What order is in that? That makes us less than a grain of sand. I am more than a sand grain, I will tell you. The world must have meaning, and order, and purpose. You should not forget that."

"But they are two different things."

"You have made yourself into a great mind, Ologrin. You have ordered it in a way that very few have, even those at the Sophenary. Weims, here, has ordered his knowledge of ships and the sea, thus he is the shipmaster. We of Antola are ordering the world. Those of us who are able are creating order for the vast numbers who are not. We are their Sun, and they circle around us, depending on us for light and warmth. That is the way of the world, Ologrin. Why would the skies above us and around us be any different?"

Regardless of their specialty, the masters of the Sophenary had trained him to understand things using evidence, not intuition. Terval was making a fundamental error in thinking, but Ologrin sensed this was not the place to correct him. Perhaps in his chambers, but not here, where Terval was so clearly in charge, and he was just a passenger.

Terval put his arm around Ologrin's shoulder. "You will do great things for us, my friend. Don't forget that. You are the master of the skies, not its servant." Ologrin remained silent. The Red Eye cast one last baleful glance their way, then hid behind distant wisps of cloud.

The next day dawned clear. Weims had the crew spend the morning tacking the ship in different directions, and they soon left any sight of land behind them. By midmorning, though, clouds were building to the northeast, and by midday they had become an ominous wall of gray. When lightning flickered in the distance, Ologrin was nervous, but the oncoming storm seemed to energize the captain.

"We'll run with it, if it's okay with your Lordship!" Weims cried from the bow. Terval nodded. Ologrin began to be concerned that "run with it" meant head directly into it, but when curtains of rain appeared to be only a league or two north, Weims ordered the ship turned to the south. The incessant chopping motion of the ship settled into a rhythm with the swells, and the ship seemed to surge forward. A couple of men stationed themselves in the rigging and cried excitedly as the rain approached. There was a sudden cold gust, and then rain lashed them from the stern. Ologrin grabbed the rail. Lightning struck the water only a few dozen hands from the ship, stunning him with a massive clap of sound.

Ologrin suddenly felt as if every part of his body were overflowing with sensation. His first thought was that lightning had struck the ship. He felt the ship under him quiver with power. He sensed the strain in the mast as the sail pulled against its lines, then suddenly flapped and boomed with an errant gust of wind. The ship seemed as energized as its master. Mentally, Ologrin urged the ship forward. He imagined it could feel his hands on the rail and charged forward in response. It leapt defiantly from the wavetops and smashed into the sea: aggressive, angry, alive.

The storm relentlessly pursued and then outran them, and soon enough the rain lessened. Ologrin saw streaks from the Sun break out to their right. They continued charging forward to nowhere in particular, even as the clouds broke and the afternoon turned sunny and warm once again.

Weims let the ship run until the winds died down in the evening, then had them turn again toward the Sojourner, rising in the west. They set an evening watch and activity on the deck seemed to slow as they prepared to weather the night.

Most of the men were gathered mid-deck. Ologrin and Terval sat near the rail as the stories began to roll. The men agreed with the exotic nature of the port at Ismay. They decided the port of Solanon was a sorry affair by comparison, run by the insufferable Elders. They agreed that the barges that ran goods between Solanon and Dormond, far up the Sestern river, were crewed by dimwits and laggards who couldn't sail a stick across a puddle. Beyond that, their stories diverged. A couple of men talked about having been as far as Bomlin, which they claimed was even more exotic than Ismay. They were heard, but not altogether believed.

"There are treasures beyond belief in the forgotten cities," Scaup suddenly said, which forced a temporary silence.

"I've sailed everywhere there is to sail on the Southern Sea and never met anyone who's actually been to any forgotten cities," one of the older seamen said. "They're a myth."

"Just because you've never seen them, we have to say they're a myth?"

A younger man piped up. "Runcel sailed to the forgotten cities. You can't say Runcel was a myth." There was general agreement to this point, but also to the point that no one had been there since.

"Runcel wasn't the last to visit," Scaup said. "There was another voyage, but they were told not to go, and their trip was cursed. Only a few know the story."

"And you're one of the few?" the older man replied.

"I've heard lots of stories and seen lots of things in my time," Scaup said.

"Seen lots of empty ale casks," the man muttered, to general laughter.

"It was more than three gross years ago. There was nothing left of the cities but tumbled stones covered by forests of strange trees and vines. Two ships left on the voyage; only one returned. How'd I know the particulars if it wasn't true?"

"Just saying it doesn't make it true!"

"And there were sea monsters," said another. "Ate one ship, while the other escaped. We heard it, okay? Nobody believes it."

"They weren't sea monsters," Scaup said. "They were raptors." More snorts and chuckles.

"Hold on," Ologrin said. "You say there really were raptors?"

"Black as night, and almost as big as an entire ship."

"How many?"

"Two of them, from the mountains. Caught the ships unaware while still at anchor. They ripped the rigging from the first ship like it was kindling. Used their tails like whips to clear the decks of men. The captain of the other ship turned and made a run for the open sea as soon as the first ship was under attack. Tore the one ship to shreds, but never attacked the other."

"How do you know this story?" Ologrin asked.

"Don't encourage him!" the older man said.

"My grandfather's great-grandfather was the first of mine to leave home and go to sea. He was on the second ship."

"They tell stories about that ship," the younger seaman said darkly. He spat in the gloom. "Her master was that sorceress. She called those beasts onto the first ship so they couldn't bear witness."

"The stories you heard," Ologrin said. "Was there more about these raptors?"

Scaup frowned. "Wicked beak; wicked spikes along their necks. Long tail with a barb that could rip a man's lungs out."

"Eyes?"

"Yeah, orange as fire. Orange spot on the back of their head below the spike too."

"Did they breathe fire?" one of the other men said.

"No. At least not that I ever heard."

"See? Everybody knows that raptors breathe fire. I can't believe you would leave that out, if you're trying to get us to believe you."

Scaup looked down and said nothing, no doubt once again defeated in a debate he had started—and likely lost—many times before. *What motivated him?* Ologrin wondered.

"Just saying, you'd better hope Malach protects you if

those things ever decide to come all the way south," Scaup finally muttered, then was silent. He seemed to have taken the wind out of everyone's storytelling, and the boat was quiet for several moments.

"Well, that storm has run us to nowhere," Weims said loudly. "I guess we're as lost as we can be. Couldn't even tell which direction to turn, could we?"

That isn't altogether true, Ologrin thought. Ortak, the pole star, shone over their left shoulders. He knew that all they needed to do was turn right, head north, and they would reach land within a day or two. Where along the southern coastline was the question, one he meant to answer later when he pulled out his tables and made his calculations.

He was on deck with his instruments and a charcoal pencil well before dawn. He checked and re-checked the angle of Ortak above the horizon, as it was barely any different than seen from his parapet at the Sophenary. He calculated that, for all their sailing, they were no further south than the tip of the tail, the long peninsula that formed the southernmost point of Lhosa. He assumed they were west of the tip, but how far west?

The Sojourner dropped from high above toward the east. Ologrin waited. The eastern sky was already changing from purple to pink. Seabirds cruised nearby. If they had been in Antola, per his charts, the Sojourner would still be a fair angle above the horizon when the Sun rose. The Sojourner sank as the sky brightened, and then the first streak of orange fire appeared on the surface of the sea. Ologrin quickly measured the angle of both the lower and upper edges of the Sojourner. He could see that the Sun was now half risen. It seemed massive. An optical illusion, he knew, yet somehow evidence for how truly enormous it was, covering so much of the distant horizon. He retreated to the cabin below to make his calculations. When he returned, both Weims and Terval were standing at the stern, chatting.

"Well, master sky-spotter, where are we?" Weims said.

"Do you have your map?"

Weims unrolled a map showing Gosper Bay and the surrounding coastline in great detail. Ologrin calculated mentally for a moment, then stuck his finger down.

"We are here, exactly twenty leagues west of the tip of the tail, Captain. Have your oarsman steer directly east, three points off north by your oil needle. We will come in sight of the tip of the tail by the time the Sun reaches for the horizon later today."

Weims looked amused. "I judge us to be farther west than that," he said. "If we were to sail only one point off north, we are sure to spy the coastline by midday. But if we sail straight east, as you want, and yet I am right, then we will not reach the tip until after dark. We could run right into it, or worse, miss it to the south, sail right past it and be truly lost at sea."

"I suppose we're here to find out," Terval said. "Turn the ship."

The day remained bright and breezy, with only a few fluffs of cloud in the sky. The winds were lighter than the day before, but fortunately they were from the south, which meant the great triangular sail worked well, pulling them perpendicular to the wind. Nonetheless, their pace was far slower than when they had surfed in the storm. Ologrin worried that they might not cover the twenty leagues before dark. He knew Weims would abandon the experiment long before he risked running aground in the middle of the night.

The Sun arced across the sky and headed toward the western horizon. Suddenly a lookout cried from the rigging. Ologrin hurried to the bow and kept his eyes fixed to the east. Within a few moments he could just begin to make out a dark shape at the edge of the water. Very slowly it rose and became more distinct. The land rose from that point northward. South of the point was nothing but sea. The smile on Ologrin's face grew along with the land.

"I'll admit, he's done it," Weims said. Ologrin grinned as Terval slapped him on the back.

They sailed up the bay with the wind at their backs. It was nearly dark when they approached the black mass of the Ginney cliffs, but by then they could see the distant lights of Antola. Soon Ologrin could not tell the difference between the black water and the black land, yet Weims seemed to be able to navigate based on the lights of the Purse. The city gradually grew to loom over them. Ologrin thought they would crash into the docks at any moment, but Weims swung them around and brought them to a stop not two dozen hands away. Lines were heaved, and the ship was gently pulled into its berth.

"What did I tell you?" Terval said happily. "And now to the Swords to find something to drink!"

"I probably should return to the Sophenary," Ologrin said.

"Nonsense! You cannot go walking the length of the docks unarmed at night. You must stay with us."

Ologrin felt reasonably safe, but he admitted to himself he did not relish the journey back to the Sophenary all alone. He followed Terval down the gangway, and then he laughed when he reached the solid planks of the docks.

"It feels as if the entire world is rocking like the ship!"

"Nothing wine won't make worse," Terval laughed, and the horsemen who met him at the foot of the gangway chuckled as well. Ologrin happily followed them across the docks and up into the Purse.

18

The Twain Swords was the largest tavern Ologrin had ever seen. Built halfway between the docks and the top of the Purse, it appeared to have shoved aside the usual flotsam of buildings to make room for itself. Its east-facing windows were filled with squares of glass gleaming with golden lamplight. A pair of huge fish, with a spear protruding from each mouth and a spread sail on each spine, were mounted over the doorway as if they were engaged in battle. Ologrin noticed at least half of those already in the tavern were wearing the uniform of the Crown's Guard. Terval was immediately surrounded by friends and companions. Before Ologrin could decide where to sit, he was offered trays of food, jugs of wine, and mugs of ale.

Ologrin relaxed, ate, and drank. The trays were filled with bowls of clams, stacks of crabs, and large yellow fish with bulging white eyes. There were crispy bread-like things that were ignored by many, but were delicious, so he helped himself to handfuls.

He ate in contented anonymity until he was full, then sat back to watch the crowd. He had forgotten about Terval for a few moments and had now lost sight of him. He began to wonder where he might find a quiet place to nap for the evening when Terval appeared standing on a table in the middle of the room.

"Where is my navigator!" he cried. "Where is my astrolemer!" Ologrin stood slowly, once again feeling the waves. "Come up, come up!" Terval said. Ologrin started toward the table, but found his way blocked by a roomful of people standing between him and the center table. "Move!" Terval bellowed, and they suddenly parted to let him through. As he got closer his feet left the ground, as those nearest lifted him onto the table.

"My fellow Antolans," Terval began. "For as long as we have sailed the seas, only the most experienced shipmaster dared lose sight of land, for fear of becoming lost. Not anymore. Yesterday our master astrolemer, using his calculations and his incredible knowledge of the sea and sky, managed to pinpoint our exact position without sight of land, and was able to best the guess of one of my most able captains, who was sailing in waters he has sailed his entire life." There were cheers, as well as quite a bit of laughter.

"No, no," Terval said. "This was not the failing of my captain. This was the breaking of the chains that bind us to the land. No longer must we fear the open sea. We can go where we will, and when we will!" More cheers. "And our enemies will no longer be able to predict our arrival, as we pick our way step by step up the coast. Now we will strike them from any direction. They will fear the mists at their backs, knowing they could hide raiders from the sea!" The people surrounding the table roared. "And this man! This man made it happen. He has earned his rays!" Terval produced a large silver pin, matching the crossed fish over the entrance, and pinned it to the shoulder of Ologrin's cloak. The room cheered. "And those he meets forever after shall respect the rays…"

"Or fear the consequences!" the crowd yelled in unison.

Ologrin stepped from the table and was eased to the floor. He grasped wrists and endured a round of backslaps, then a voice spoke in his ear: "His Lordship asks that you join him in his private chambers." Ologrin followed one of the Crown's guards as he made a path through the crowd and led him through a wide door. It was immediately quiet on the other side. The guard opened a second door, and Ologrin stepped into a large, opulent room. A low platform filled with cushions and furs dominated one wall, and numerous wide, thickly padded chairs were scattered about. A fire burned in a hearthgrate on the opposite wall. Terval was sitting on one of the chairs next to a small round table. Lord Wesse, the Lord Coronet, stood over him. A young woman in the blue uniform of the Crown's Guard stood nearby. Ologrin was mildly surprised, then chided himself for assuming that only males would be in the guard. She had the silver panthers of an arms-captain on her collar.

"Wine for the navigator," Terval said.

"I'm already so dizzy I might fall..." Ologrin started, but then a crystal cup filled with a golden liquid was in his hand. He sipped, and it was cool and delightfully refreshing. Thousands of tiny bubbles grew on the inside of the cup.

"Sit, my friend, sit!" Terval said.

Ologrin murmured his greetings and sat down. The chair was covered in the finest bison leather he had ever felt. He seemed to sink into its embrace and felt drowsy almost immediately.

"I'm just saying, waiting is foolishness," the woman said. Ologrin, suddenly self-conscious, wondered if he had been invited into the middle of an argument.

"No one said anything about waiting." Wesse spoke slowly, with the assurance that no one would fail to listen. Ologrin noticed that the fabric of Lord Wesse's uniform was much finer than that of the young Captain. An arms man for whom coin is not a problem. "There is a difference between waiting and properly preparing," Wesse added.

"You won't keep it secret for long," the woman said. "It's not magic, it's maths. How long before someone sells the charts to Ismay? We have a year at best." She ran a hand through her short hair, revealing a triangle and five-pointed star burned on her right forearm.

Ologrin snapped awake. He tried to jump up from the chair, but his sea-legs betrayed him again, and he fell backward. He instinctively felt his chest to be sure his tanj was in place. They were all staring at him.

"Are you sick?" Terval asked easily.

"My…balance," Ologrin stammered. "I feel like I am still standing on the deck in the storm. I thought…I thought I was falling out of the chair." He tried to smile, and Lord Wesse chuckled. The woman, however, looked at him steadily, as if she were examining him for the first time. Terval stood and crossed to sit on the arm of Ologrin's chair.

"Captain Bana, this is Master Ologrin. He is our new navigator, and a valuable connection within the Sophenary." The woman bowed slightly at the waist.

Ologrin instinctively curled his fingers to hide them. He nodded then kept his head down, He hoped desperately she would not step over and offer to clasp wrists.

"Of course, Bana, the Ismay fleet will figure it out, eventually," Terval said. "It still gives us the tactical advantage. Meanwhile, our new Sophenary master may have more secrets to reveal. There are great works afoot. Is that not right, Ologrin?"

"Great works," Ologrin started to say, thinking about Albrect's plans.

Lord Wesse interjected. "Some of the projects shared between the Sophenary and the Crown are not Master Ologrin's specialty. I would not expect him to be informed enough to talk about them. Sometimes a little knowledge is worse than no knowledge at all."

A moment of irritation appeared on Terval's face. "Young men want to know everything, while old men want to hide it," he said. He leaned against Ologrin and wrapped an arm around his shoulders. "Ologrin is one of us. I have no secrets from him. But we are here to celebrate, not to talk. Another sip, my friend? It comes to us all the way from Bomlin. They say they have a secret technique to add the bubbles. Maybe you can figure that out for us too."

A servant appeared and poured more wine in Ologrin's cup. Terval returned to his chair. Captain Bana leaned on the edge of the table and stretched luxuriously. *She has a spectacular form*, Ologrin thought, and the tight tunic served to make sure it was at the forefront of everyone's mind. Against unwitting men, it gave her an overwhelming tactical advantage. Her prey would allow themselves to be captured, snared by their own fantasies. *Not me*, he thought. *I have my Vireo.* And seemingly not Terval, who barely glanced her direction.

"Ships can capture a harbor, but only arms men can hold a city," Lord Wesse said. Ologrin tried to concentrate. It was a question for hidden maths, he thought, so many numbers of ships versus numbers of men. But the wine seemed to be tugging him to sleep. The fire burned low, the room dimmed, and, despite the conversation, he was gone.

He awoke with a start, and his hand again went to his chest. The room was empty. Shutters opened onto a small courtyard garden, with the Sun striking the far side. He freshened up and let himself out of the suite. The main room of the tavern was half filled with late-morning breakfasters. No one looked at him and he recognized no one present. He noticed that the ground still seemed to be rising and falling, and for the first time he felt nauseated. He asked for a pitcher of water and drank half before setting out. A breeze was blowing up from the bay, which made him feel better.

He could see the *Rayfish* at the dock below him, sail furled and tied to the spar, no evidence that it had just spent three days at sea. The docks were bustling. He made his way slowly down and over to the trestle lift. It was filled with wooden barrels and crates bearing the brands of distant ports. He had an idea and talked to one of the loading supervisors. The man took one glance at the device pinned to his cloak and agreed, and shortly thereafter Ologrin was riding the platform up and over the maze of streets. The ride was as smooth as he remembered, once again causing him to wonder at how it could function day after day without any apparent source of fuel. The platform stopped with a gentle bump. He stepped off and made his way through the tunnel to the terraces on the western side of the city, then up to the Crown's Walk. He walked under the shade of the scarab trees, making his way slowly back toward the Sophenary. Halfway home, he stepped over to the east wall and scanned the line of ships at the docks, hoping to catch a glimpse of their ship, but it was hidden by the masts and rigging of the bigger ships around it.

The day was turning warm, and the Sophenary's great bronze doors were opened wide to allow a breeze through the cross halls. He met a red collar as he walked inside. "Master Vireo is looking for you," she said, then hurried away. He headed for the second floor, passing another red collar who relayed the same message. Feeling vaguely disquieted, he knocked and entered her chambers. Vireo looked small behind her large work-table. He stood at the door, not sure if this was an official or a private visit.

"As usual, when you choose to do something, you throw yourself into it, heart and all," she said. The tone of her voice disquieted him. He continued to stand, silent.

"I did not expect you to be gone three days," Vireo said, finally looking up.

"I didn't either. Is something wrong?"

Vireo paused for a moment. "No, of course not. You're a master. I don't have to know where you are every part of every day."

"But..."

"But I was worried. That's different."

Ologrin slowly walked into the room. He had thought she would be excited to see him, that she would be eager to hear about his trip. This was not at all what he had imagined.

"I'm sorry," he said.

"There was a storm," she replied.

Ologrin brightened. "It was remarkable. I've never felt anything like that. It was like the storm was feeding me its energy."

"I was worried that it might sink your ship."

"It will take more than a late Summer storm to sink the *Rayfish*."

"I didn't realize you had become an expert in ships."

Ologrin felt stung. "Something *is* wrong," he said. He looked at her steadily, but she would not meet his gaze. "This was the first real test of my work," he added. "Where else should I have been?" He stood planted in the middle of the room, not sure where to go next.

"I know. You're right."

"You said the work would lead to more opportunities. Wasn't this one of those opportunities?"

"It was," she admitted.

"The Crown must see that our work is valuable, so they will pay us and we can do more work. Isn't that what everyone has been teaching me since I arrived at the Sophenary?"

"He wants more than your knowledge," she interrupted, finally returning his gaze. "He wants you."

Ologrin blinked, trying to sort that through. "What?"

"Terval wants you. He is attracted to you. Did you not know that?"

"No…you can't…he is an honest, hard-working student. You can't say this has all been just because he is…attracted to me."

"Of course not. He is smart; he wants to learn. But he also wants you. I'm surprised you can feel the energy of the storm and yet cannot feel that."

The room still seemed to be gently swaying. Ologrin felt the need to steady himself by leaning against a nearby cabinet. "I don't…"

Vireo stood and came out from behind the table. The Sun had not yet spilled into the west-facing windows, so the room was dim. She was not wearing shades, and her eyes reflected flickers of flame from the hearthgrate. As often as he had seen it, it still took him by surprise. "The way he is quick to put his arm around you," she said. "The way he leans against you when you're sitting together. The way he smiles at every little thing you say. He wants you for his own." Instead of warmth from her, it felt as if a wall of air was pushing him over as she approached.

"I truly didn't think…" Leaning against the cabinet, he still towered over her physically. How, he wondered, did all that force emanate from someone so small?

"I'm not saying you have to choose me," she said. "He's offering you the world in a way that I cannot."

Ologrin imagined, briefly, Vireo with her arm laced through another man's arm, leaning her head on the other man's shoulder, and felt a twisting pain in his chest. But she was not in someone else's arms. She stood before him.

"My excitement may have blinded me to what he wanted, but not to what I want," he said.

She stepped within arm's reach, and he tentatively slipped his arm around her waist. "I know what I want," he added.

"I see you have a new adornment," she said, fingering the rayfish pin on his collar. "It looks official."

"Arms-navigator, I think," Ologrin replied.

"You are becoming a man of many titles."

"Some less deserved than others."

She slid her hand across his arm. "You were right to go. I'm acting jealous, and I apologize. It took so long to find you; I just don't want to lose you."

Nonetheless, the tightness in his chest did not ease. Ologrin briefly wondered if there was much difference between the pain of desire and the pain of jealousy.

After Sunset, Ologrin sat on the parapet of his small observation tower and watched the sky turn black. He easily picked out Ortak, the southern star, shining brightest in the jewel chest, identical to how it had appeared two nights before. The stars were ever constant. The air cooled quickly this close to the edge of the Adamantines, and he was soon shivering. He returned to his small room but left the door to the parapet open so he could glimpse a tiny square of sky from his bed. He blew out his ember pot and lay under his furs in darkness. Presently he heard the door to his room slowly open, admitting the glow from another ember pot. Vireo stepped through, blew out her own ember pot, and crossed the room. He sat up, and she sat next to him. She slid her hands across his temples.

"They're growing," she said.

"I know."

"Soon they'll be visible above your hair."

"Soon I'll have to cover my head."

"Why?"

"They make it obvious that I'm different."

"You are different. It's nothing to be ashamed of. Besides, I think they're remarkable." But he did not respond. She pulled her knees to her chest.

"Was it thrilling?" she asked at last.

"I was frightened. I had no idea how the ship would do in a storm. Then, in the midst of it, I could feel the wood whispering under my hands, as if it had come to life again. After that, there was no time to think or plan. We just had to react."

"And did your calculations work?"

"I was lucky. We were not more than a few gross hands from where I predicted we would be."

"You are too modest," she said. "I believe your tables will save many lives."

He sat quietly, thinking. Despite the cool air coming through the parapet door, he felt a rich warmth in his chest.

"The docks are filled with goods brought in from Ismay," he said finally. "But every time Terval talks about it, he speaks as if Ismay and Antola are enemies. I don't understand."

"Antola takes in more from Ismay than they send out in trade," Vireo noted.

"Why does that matter?"

"If Antola cannot trade equally for goods, then they have to trade for coin. That makes them feel as if Ismay has the upper hand."

"That doesn't sound like a good reason to prepare for war."

"Antola doesn't raise enough food by itself. They are dependent on trade to feed their people. That's a potentially unstable place to be. If Ismay or Dormond were to suddenly stop trading with Antola, there might not be enough to go around."

"Lord Wesse was there," Ologrin said suddenly.

"On the ship?"

"Afterward. In the tavern. And a woman. She was Malacheb. She had a brand on her arm." He could feel Vireo's body grow tense.

"What did she do?"

"Nothing. I don't think she knew what I am. So maybe Terval and Wesse don't know either."

"I don't think you can hide who you are forever," she said.

"I don't want to hide forever. But I want to be strong when the time comes."

Vireo seemed to give a little shudder. "Put your arms around me," she said. He tried to comply, without tipping them both to the floor. She was silent for a few moments; Ologrin noticed her breathing become slow and steady.

"He's very engaging," she said at last.

"Sweet Alera, you really are jealous!"

"Well, I'm sure he's used to getting what he wants. Just remember, you're the tutor, not the devotee."

"I told you, I know where my heart truly lies." He touched his lips to her hair.

"Don't go looking for storms," she whispered.

19

Late Summer storms turned to continuous rain. The clouds descended Arske's slopes and swallowed the parapet, making astrolemical observations impossible. Ologrin was forced down to his second-floor work chambers. Through the windows, the rest of the city appeared gray and colorless.

Sensing a lull in Ologrin's observations, Master Albrect lost no time enlisting him for his most recent project. He had found rolls in the library that tabulated the distance a bombard could throw a stone based on the stone's weight. He had asked Ologrin to verify the calculations. It had proved to be an exercise in guessing; there were critical hidden numbers that could only be found by experimentation. Ologrin had done the work as best he could, then went looking for Albrect to hand over his results.

He found him in the postern yard. Albrect's hired men had spent part of the Summer building a wooden platform off the back of the castle, jutting into the yard. With great effort, one of the old stone bombards had been moved from the top of the escarpment to the castle and now sat in a complicated sling of beams and ropes next to the platform. Six gross hands out, at the farthest end of the yard, Albrect and his team had assembled a target: a wall of sticks, stones, and mortar. The wood for the platform and the target appeared to have come from the small copse in front of the foothills. Only stumps remained, poking from the muddy ground, and efforts were underway to remove them as well. A machine of beams and pulleys, obviously of Albrect's design, was positioned over a large stump that had already been half-levered out of the ground. Master Albrect was directing the machine's operation when he spotted Ologrin on the platform and hurried over.

"You don't think the target is too small, do you?" Albrect said. He was covered in mud to his waist, as had been the case for the past many days. Ologrin had offered to help with the work, but Albrect had said it wasn't fit work for a master, while he happily spent as much time digging and hauling as any of his men.

"How big is it?" Ologrin asked, looking at the target.

"Twenty-four hands wide and tall. And two hands thick."

"Really? Doesn't look it from here."

"I thought you were the expert in angular mathematics."

Ologrin smiled. "That doesn't mean my eyes are fooled less than anyone else's."

"Have you double-checked your calculations?" Albrect asked.

"They aren't much more than guesses. We have no way to compare our blast powder to what they used in the past. If ours is less powerful, the stone won't even reach the target. Too powerful, and we'll blast it into the mountains."

Albrect slapped Ologrin on the shoulders. "I trust you, my friend. You won't be wrong." The gesture reminded him powerfully of Tobin. Once again, he hoped that Tobin would visit someday. He loved the image: Tobin wide-eyed as he walked up to the castle, Ologrin standing on the steps in his cloak and master's collar, waiting to greet him.

"That reminds me," Albrect said. He pointed to the field

of stumps. "I need you for a new project. You can see we've already started."

"You want me to dig stumps?"

"No, I've got hired men from the Purse to do all that."

Ologrin viewed Albrect's mud-encrusted breeches with suspicion. "I liked that little stand of trees. Wasn't there another way to get wood?"

Albrect laughed. "We're starting on the chimneys. I want you to check my plans; I'm not so confident of my own maths. And I thought you could lend me a hand with some of the design." But as he said it, a pained look crossed Ologrin's face. "What is it?"

"Master Vireo has been insisting that I get started on my physionomy warrant. I start working with Master Heron at the beginning of the next passage."

Albrect bit his upper lip. "Vireo said that herself?"

"She was insistent."

"What if you sweet-talked her?"

"Master Albrect…"

"I'm only suggesting! Besides, you're both Masters…"

"And she's the Dodecant."

"You're right, you're right. My apologies."

"I wouldn't if Serenity himself…"

"It was inappropriate for me to even suggest it. And she's right. You have no time for me. You must gain your warrant adept in physionomy. We need well-founded masters."

"You know I'd much rather do this."

"No, I understand."

Together, they looked out over the yard. Ologrin tried to imagine a new stoneworks rising from the field where the copse had been. He never felt more content than when he was building something, whether it was the charcoal kilns, the niter beds, or the navigation tables.

"You're going to have to extend the alley from the west courtyard around the back of the castle," Ologrin said.

"That's true," Albrect replied, nodding.

"There may be a way to avoid relying on massive roof beams for the furnace works."

"Buttressed arches," Albrect said, still nodding.

"I can probably find some time in the evenings."

"No, no. Well, if you insist, Master Ologrin."

The clouds began to break up that evening. Ologrin was in the yard early the next day, helping two students who had been tasked with assisting in the aiming and firing of the bombard. The bombard's weight rested on thick boards supported at an angle by notches, to allow for raising and lowering the angle of fire. Four freshly carved stone balls were neatly stacked in a pyramid next to the wagon. Well off to the side, underneath the viewing platform, a crate stored the blast powder, carefully folded into small parchment bags that could be loaded through the front of the bombard. Ologrin estimated each shot would require two bags, but there were too many unknowns to calculate the answer precisely.

Master Albrect took his firing team aside and rehearsed their steps one last time. One of the students would push the bags into the bombard with a short plunger, then the other would drop the ball on top. Albrect would poke a sharpened stick through the firing hole to open up one of the bags inside, fill the hole with a charge of blast powder, and then pull the rope that would release the tanjium striker. If necessary, they would adjust the bombard, re-load, and try again. Ologrin hoped they wouldn't need all four balls.

"Master Ologrin." A thin, nervous-looking student appeared on the platform, his face as red as his collar. "Master Vireo requests that you join her at the great doors to greet the viewing party."

Ologrin reluctantly left the final preparations to Albrect,

though he knew he wasn't really needed. He grabbed his cloak and followed the red collar toward the great doors.

Vireo stood in the doorway at attention, dressed in one of her shimmering cloaks and wearing her blue eye shades. Her hair was adorned with the adamantine clip and its red stone. She looked up and smiled as Ologrin stepped to her side. The Crown's delegation had arrived and were arranging themselves in the courtyard. Two arms-captains rode in front of a two-wheeled gig drawn by a single horse. Ologrin smiled in turn, pleased to see that one of the arms-captains was Captain Aron. Lord Wesse stepped down from the gig. Ologrin was vaguely disappointed not to see Terval. The two arms-captains lined up behind Lord Wesse and they ascended the stairs.

Wesse extended two fingers, palm up, and Vireo responded by touching his outstretched fingers with two of hers. "Any day that includes a visit with the Dodecant is a delightful day, indeed," he said.

"We are honored by your presence, Lord Wesse."

"I wondered if I would be afforded your presence, Master Ologrin. Should I assume that your genius has been applied to today's demonstration as well? If so, this should be a remarkable event." Wesse gave Ologrin half a smile that left him feeling uncomfortable, not knowing if the man was expressing admiration or sarcasm.

"The genius is Master Albrect's," Ologrin said. "He is caught up with final preparations and could not be persuaded to join us."

"Then let's find him."

The wide cross-halls of the main floor were meant to guide visitors from one side of the castle to the other, without betraying the maze of rooms and passages making up its working viscera. Doors were open at all ends, inviting a swirling breeze through the halls. Lord Wesse offered Vireo his arm, and they walked along, chatting as if they were good friends. Ologrin walked a couple of steps behind, feeling ignored. This casual interaction between people of power was a language all its own, he thought.

They stepped onto the viewing platform. No seats had been provided; the demonstration was expected to be relatively brief, with a midday meal inside the castle afterward. Albrect continued busily issuing orders and fiddling with ropes until Vireo called his name to get his attention. Albrect hurried up the stairs to the delegation, wiping his hands on his cloak. Ologrin loved the absolute lack of pretension in his mentor, but he worried how it would play for members of Court. He was surprised to see Albrect and Wesse reach out and grab each other's wrist.

"My Lord," Albrect said.

"It has been too long," Wesse said, grinning. "Always good to see you." Ologrin was left imagining what history the two men might have with each other.

"You are familiar with Antola's bombards?" Albrect asked.

"I will tell the truth; I had no idea what they were until I saw something like this fired from a distance, and that was during a visit to Ismay some years ago. A great noise and even greater smoke, I recall."

"Then let me quickly summarize. Over the past year, the Sophenary has built the means for large-scale harvesting of niter from the flats. We have developed our own formula for blast powder that does not require importing expensive ingredients. The powder is quite safe, unless it is exposed to a spark. At that point, it decomposes instantly into an enormous amount of hot gas and smoke, with the power to throw a heavy stone out of the front of the bombard."

Lord Wesse looked out toward the back of the yard. "That construction in the distance. You say the blast powder will be sufficient to hurl one of the stones that far?"

"Oh, without doubt."

"You are sure of yourself."

"Lord Wesse, once we figure out the ratio of powder to stone, we should be able to hurl one half a league."

Lord Wesse's brow furrowed for a moment. "Please proceed," he said. *He is not an easy man to convince,* Ologrin thought.

Captain Aron followed Albrect down to the bombard, while the other arms man stood next to Lord Wesse. Ologrin remained on the platform, nervous. He had settled on aiming the bombard at about a fifth of the angle between horizontal and vertical, but again, he had done little more than guess. The students assisting Albrect had to stand on a small platform to reach the front of the bombard. One carefully slid two small bags of blasting powder into the mouth of the weapon, and the other pushed them down with a short wooden pole. Working together, they lifted one of the stone balls and dropped it in. They then hurried to the rear while Master Albrect primed the firing hole and pulled the striking hammer back to its locked position. He stepped back as well. Captain Aron stood behind the bombard, hoping to judge how straight the ball flew.

"With your permission," Albrect called up.

"By all means," Wesse replied.

"It will be quite loud."

Albrect yanked the rope. Ologrin had prepared himself for a loud bang, but was surprised nonetheless, especially at how much he felt the blast in his chest. In the same instant, wood and dirt flew from a hole in the bottom of the target. Lord Wesse had fixed his face into a tight smile, so his flinch was barely noticeable. The other arms man jumped as if he had been smacked. It took Ologrin a moment to realize the ball had actually struck the ground in front of the target and then bounced into it, before disappearing in the woods beyond. An ominous roll of thunder resounded from the surrounding mountains, and then spread behind them over Antola's flanks. Vireo stood serenely; eyes closed.

"Raise by two notches," Ologrin called down.

Albrect hurried to the side of the cannon to loosen ropes, then enlisted Aron to help him leverage the bombard higher. The two Polfre students carried another ball to their loading platform, then returned to grab two more bags of powder.

"There is far less smoke than I recall," Wesse shouted.

"Yes," Albrect called back. "It will be an advantage not to have everything obscured by smoke."

"Is the ball on the other side of your construction?"

"I presume it is deep in those woods."

Lord Wesse appeared impressed. The trees marking the far edge of the yard began another thirteen dozen hands beyond the target, where they rose into Arske's massive flanks.

Ologrin noticed Aron grinning up at him, and he returned the smile. Aron raised his hands to his ears, suggesting that they were still ringing from the boom. Out of the corner of his eye, Ologrin could see one of the students drop the two bags of powder into the bombard's mouth and the other start to push it home.

The second blast caught everyone by surprise. Ologrin saw a flash of white flame erupt from the back of the bombard and envelop Albrect's head. A large chunk of stone smashed against the castle wall, missing Aron by a hand as he instinctively turned and threw himself to the ground. This time Ologrin felt dazed by the blast. He stared at the smoking bombard, trying to make sense of what he saw. One of the students was lying on her back at its side. The other seemed to have disappeared. Then he looked further out into the yard. The second student lay in a heap a good three dozen hands beyond. Two dozen hands further, the blackened push pole lay on the ground.

Ologrin leapt for the stairs. "The students!" Vireo yelled

behind him. As he reached the ground, the first student tried to sit up next to the small platform. He resisted the temptation to run back to Albrect and ran further out into the yard.

The second student, a young Polfre male, lay half on his left side, face down. His left arm was bent backward in an unnatural way beneath his body. Ologrin tried to roll the student onto his back, but his head did not properly follow. Cradling his head, Ologrin saw that something had smashed the boy's face. He was surprised at the blood that now covered his hands.

Ologrin felt his own head buzzing, and he could not focus his sight. He watched himself try to stand up, then sink back to his knees. Floating above his own body, he saw that Aron was up and at Albrect's side. Wesse and his delegation stood dumbfounded on the platform. Vireo was nowhere to be seen, but as Ologrin tried again to stand up she appeared with a half dozen others, running out of the castle and down the stairs. Aron hoisted Albrect up over his shoulder and headed for the foot of the stairs. The left side of the master's head and a good portion of his cloak were soaked a deep red. Aron carried the wounded man up the stairs as if he weighed nothing. Master Heron appeared in the doorway. "This way!" she cried, then disappeared back inside. The first Polfre student was now surrounded and appeared to be talking to her rescuers. Ologrin finally managed to stand.

Her rescuers supporting her, the first student reached the foot of the platform stairs, where Vireo met them. She leaned close and whispered something before the student continued up the stairs. Then she walked out into the yard. The adamantine clip in her hair caught the sun's light and reflected it into the red stone, which seemed to blaze with fire. For a moment, it seemed to Ologrin as if the Red Eye itself had come down to roost in her hair, fixing him with its accusing stare. He settled back into his body, filled with shame, no different than what he felt kneeling next to his mother years before. Vireo walked over and knelt by the student, then stood and placed a hand on his cheek.

"Oh, Ologrin. It's not your fault," she said, and then he burst into tears.

Master Albrect had been taken to his own chambers, where Master Heron labored over him wordlessly. Two of her physionomy students hurried between their labs and Albrect's room with supplies. Vireo had escorted the Crown's delegation to her public chambers. Ologrin was left alone, and his shame had morphed into a restless sense that he had left tasks unfinished. He returned to the yard. The body of the Polfre student had already been removed. Captain Aron was sitting on the wagon next to the ruined bombard.

Ologrin descended the stairs. "I thought you would have been with Lord Wesse," he said.

"I wanted to take another look at this thing. It's cracked into five pieces now, not including that chunk blown into the wall."

"That chunk almost took your head off."

"Yeah," Aron mused. "I've learned to dodge first and think later."

"Why did it go off?" Ologrin said.

"The striker had not been cocked," Aron noted.

"I know. I saw." He looked at Aron and could see genuine pain and sadness in the arms man's eyes.

"How is Master Albrect? Is he alive?" Aron asked.

"He's alive, at least when I left him with Master Heron. She's working on him now."

Aron stood and slid his hand along the broken stone. "These are fearsome things we have chosen to meddle with. When we start challenging the gods by making our own thunder, we should not be surprised if there are consequences."

Ologrin extended his arm in Aron's direction. The arms-captain looked, and then slowly extended his own. They grasped each other's wrist. "You are a good friend," Ologrin said.

One of Heron's students appeared above them on the platform. "Master Ologrin, Master Heron asks for you."

Trying to quell his sudden fear, Ologrin followed the student back into the castle and through familiar passages to Albrect's chambers. The door was open slightly. When he entered, he saw that Vireo was there as well. Albrect was propped up in his own bed, his eyes bright as beads. Ologrin was so relieved that he laughed.

"I think we missed a step," Albrect said.

"What step?"

"There must have been embers in the hole. We probably need to swab it out with water between firings."

"It's broken in several pieces. You won't be firing it again."

"Foolishness not to have practiced beforehand. That poor boy."

Albrect's left arm was bandaged against his chest. The left side of his neck and face were red, but otherwise he appeared to be intact.

"How badly are you hurt?" Ologrin asked.

Master Heron responded. "His clavicle is broken. And there was a shard of wood embedded in the muscles of his back. Part of his cloak was embedded with it."

"Is the break serious?" Ologrin asked.

"The break is of low concern. The wound is the more worrisome. This you would know if you were attending more of my classes."

"It felt like she was stabbing me with a poker from the fire," Albrect added.

"My student Junco will be tending the wound. You will follow her directions without question."

Albrect chuckled. "Master Vireo, I fear I may be hindered in my work."

"Your work is to attend to Master Heron as if you were her initiate," Vireo replied. She turned to Ologrin. "Did you return to the yard?"

"Yes."

"And Eider?"

"I'm sorry?"

"Student Eider. His body. Has it been attended to?"

"It has been taken to my chambers," Master Heron replied. "We will prepare it in the usual fashion, of course."

"I will be accompanying him home," Vireo said. "We must leave in the morning. Albrect, please forgive me, but I have preparations I must make." She slipped from the room.

Heron soon shooed Ologrin out of the room as well. At a loss for what to do, he returned to his new chambers with the intention of getting some work done. But he could not concentrate. He gazed out at a pretty blue sky. People strolled along the Crown's Walk, happy to be out now that the rain had finally stopped. Along the docks, a pair of ships unfurled their sails and began sliding slowly into the bay. He watched them recede and tried to imagine the excitement he would feel if he were preparing for a long voyage. He closed his eyes and pictured himself on deck. Once again, he was rising above the sea and earth, until he could see the horizon as a great curve in the distance. What was out there? Lhosa took up only a small part of the whole world, and he had seen only a small part of Lhosa. There had to be other lands, he thought. The real question was, were there other people? Did they have ships and sails, and bombards, or things even more amazing and terrifying. Or were they still trying to survive a day at a time, rarely looking up in wonder?

He opened his eyes again. The scarab trees of the Crown's Walk were starting to cast longer shadows to the east.

In truth, he felt useless. The Dodecant had yet another important responsibility added to her already important life. Ordinarily, he spent relatively little time in her official chambers, preferring to wait until she had time to come to him. He felt awkward there, as if his presence were a bit of a distraction. But he was afraid she might be too busy to find him later, and then she would be gone. He decided to enter.

Vireo was at her table. A Polfre male stood silently in the corner of the room, almost invisible in a dusty grey cloak. Ologrin was taken aback; he had never seen the man before. Behind Vireo, the afternoon Sun shone through the windows and made it hard to see her face clearly. Sheets of parchment were scattered in front of her.

"Yes," she said, as if she were continuing a conversation. "Master Crake will assume responsibility for the business affairs of the Sophenary while I am gone. Adept Hammei is going to take over most of Albrect's classes, but there may be a couple that are more appropriate for you to teach."

"You're heading into the mountains," he said, not sure if he was asking a question or not.

"I must return with the boy. His family will expect it."

"How long will you be gone?"

"No more than five passages, I would think."

Ologrin was surprised. He had assumed it would take less than a couple of passages to reach the Polfre homeland and return. He glanced over at the silent man in the corner. "How many are in your party?"

"Three." She stood and came out from behind the table. "Once we enter the mountains, we are safer than you are in your bed. The journey helps us let go of our outside lives and prepares us for the return to our people and for the ceremony that must follow. Eider's essential unity with our people must be preserved."

"Don't forget, you have people here too."

Vireo stepped close. "The journeys we take are never on the paths we expect. Some day you will make the journey to the Lake of Skies. We will take the passage, just the two of us. Meanwhile, you have become very important to the Sophenary. Your journey continues here, for now." She cupped his face, which surprised him, considering the stranger in the corner. "I will see you tonight," she whispered, and turned back to her table.

Returning to his tower cell to wait, Ologrin reviewed Albrect's initial sketches and writings for construction of the chimney works. Part of his mind kept looking for things to do, because to do things was to imply that life would continue. Albrect would heal; Vireo would return; and in the meantime, he would push the work forward.

He leafed through the large pages. Albrect was a master of understanding how one part of a structure supported another in the way Ologrin had become a master of understanding how objects moved through space. But instead of numbers, his drawings were filled with triangles and squares, and from these he seemed to make his calculations. Ologrin tried applying numbers to the shapes but found it hard to concentrate. Finally he retreated to his bed, meaning to only rest his tired eyes. He awoke to the sound of two finches sitting on the stairs to the parapet and twittering fiercely at each other, arguing over a twig, before flitting away into the Sun's light.

He descended the narrow stairway and hurried quickly to Vireo's chambers, but there was no one there. Sadness settled in his chest like a stone. He made his way down to Master Heron's labs, where Albrect sat propped up in bed, munching away at day old bread rolls soaked in ale. Just the sight of his friend raised Ologrin's spirits.

"Almost as good as new," Albrect said sloppily.

"How many cups of that have you had since I saw you last?" Ologrin asked.

"Medicinal."

Ologrin found a small stool and pulled it over. "Master Vireo is going to be gone for some time."

"She came by before Sunrise," Albrect noted. "Said it was best to go as soon as she could. Had a couple of tough looking guys with her.

"Who were they, anyway?"

"Not from the Sophenary," Albrect said. "But there's not any Polfre in Antola she doesn't know, I'd bet. And I wouldn't cross those two if I was an arms man twice their size. They can paralyze your arms just by grabbing you around the wrist. Don't know if you knew that."

Ologrin shook his head. He was still most comfortable when around someone of Eidos heritage, like Albrect. Being reminded of the ways he was different only made him feel more alone. "I should get a couple of students and start winching more of those tree stumps out."

"No," Albrect said. "I hired men from the Purse to do that work. Send out word that the Sophenary will be hiring wood cutters and stone cutters. There's too much to do. Your job is to find people who can get things done, then have them find people who can do the work."

"Should I talk to Master Crake?"

"Crake is perfectly capable of signing his name to any bills of trade you put before his nose. But if you're expecting him to actually make things happen, you're more apt to see your beard turn white." Albrect set down his breakfast and shook his head. "What was I thinking? Stone is brittle; you can break it with a hammer and chisel. Making a bombard out of stone is just foolishness. But bronze. That would work. Or iron, perhaps."

"Iron shatters like stone," Ologrin reminded him.

"I have been doing some work on iron alloys. It turns out iron may not be as useless as we thought. I have some papers in my chambers. Make yourself familiar with them, but do not share them, especially with anyone from the Crown."

"You think it could be valuable?"

"Imagine bombards light enough to be carried aboard ships."

"Oh…" Ologrin was quiet, as the implications unfolded in his mind. "Well, your papers will be safe with me."

"You already have my construction drawings?"

"Yes."

"Perhaps you are a little too resourceful. What do you think of them?"

"They are ingenious. I will have the chimneys built in no time."

"You…I'm not dead, you skinny stick! I'll be up and out-working you inside a passage. You just get things ordered. I'll still manage to get things built."

Grinning, Ologrin bowed low, then took the opportunity to snatch a roll from the table.

"Out, you Ruhasti thief!" Albrect yelled, as Ologrin darted for the door.

The shattered bombard had been removed, but otherwise the postern yard was unchanged. The push pole still lay where it had landed. Ologrin picked it up and headed for the path at the back of the yard, intending to drop it deep in the woods where it could rot. He walked the path to where it diverged at the wye. Not long before, Vireo and her party had headed up the steps to the left. At some point, he knew, that path became off-limits to anyone who was not Polfre. Impulsively choosing to go to that way, he began climbing. He didn't intend to follow her far. Nonetheless, he felt reckless enough to challenge anyone who tried to stop him.

The irregularity of the steps made it difficult to establish a rhythm. He climbed until he had to stop to catch his breath, then continued. Steps could be seen on an outcrop far above. He decided to reach the stony prominence before turning back. The path twisted around the mountain and then reversed itself, making for a much longer climb than he first imagined. He finally trudged up the last steps to the outcrop.

From there he could see the entire castle far below him, and could appreciate the way it had been built to blend with the flank of the mountain. Antola's terraces shone in the Sun, while the rooftops of the Purse reflected light away from its gloomy streets and alleys.

Turning around, the steps gave way to a path that soon split at another wye. The right-hand path continued north, while the left turned and descended the west flank of the mountain.

Ologrin followed the descending path. It quickly became little more than a suggestion, just a thinning of the undergrowth. Every now and then he found a place where the vegetation gave way to the underlying rock, and he could see evidence that the rock had been roughly carved. He continued down, until he guessed he had descended at least as far as he had climbed on the other side. The narrow path leveled out and hugged the side of the mountain.

The day was getting late; Ologrin knew he should return to the castle. But his curiosity triumphed, and he continued to follow the path. For several gross steps it was an easy walk, but then the path began to narrow even more. He rounded a bulge in the flank only to find that the path beyond narrowed to a point and then vanished into the side of the mountain. He looked around. There were no other connecting paths, no trails. He felt chastened. He assumed he had been following one of the deceptive dead ends. The climb back to the outcrop would take at least twice as long. No telling how many intentional diversions were along the road to the Polfre homeland. This one had been a gentle warning, he decided. The path could just as easily have lured him onto a ledge with no way back. He had been using the push pole as a climbing staff. He dropped it over the edge of the path and heard it crash through the trees and undergrowth below. Then he turned and began the slow journey home.

20

Not only was Hammei adept enough to handle Albrect's students, he seemed to have a comprehensive knowledge of the master's acquaintances and contacts. After only a single strategy discussion, Hammei had brought in experts from the Purse. These new chiefs had their own sources of skilled labor, and shortly thereafter stones were being set for the new alley that would connect the front of the castle with the new buildings behind.

Four days after Vireo's departure, a message arrived for Ologrin. Other than the occasional letter from Tobin, he never received messages from outside of the castle. Then he saw the wax seal imprinted with the figure of a rayfish. Inside was a brief note in familiar handwriting.

Master Navigator:
  We are planning our next sail—Solanon and back—and sorely need your expertise. You must try Dormond wine.
  Mid-Passage, dusk, at the Rayfish.
  Terval

. . .

Solanon was a major intersection for trade between Antola and Dormond. Barges filled with barrels of wheat and wine were navigated down the Sestern river to Solanon, where they were traded for Antolan meat, cheese, and hides. Ologrin had not yet developed a taste for the wine that came from the region, but increasingly Antola had, and it now arrived on the docks in the Purse by the ship full. Ologrin was excited by the invitation. With Vireo away and Hammei managing most tasks, it seemed an ideal time to go.

The next day, Albrect was out of his room. The day after that he was outside, trying to direct the stump-pulling. But the day after that he was in bed again, complaining of chills and meekly accepting Heron's admonishments for having done too much the day before. He was more careful after that, but the chills continued to bother him. On the ninth morning after the accident, Heron intercepted Ologrin on his way down for his morning visit.

"Albrect is as hot as fire," she said.

"Perhaps that's good. Before today he has been complaining of the chills."

"They are caused by the same thing. Really, Ologrin, we have to get your education started."

Fingering his master's collar, he felt a bit offended. She pulled him further aside. "I am sure I removed the fragment of embedded cloak. The wound was as clean as I could get it. And yet now it has a suppurative smell, and the redness spreads, rather than contracts."

"Can the wound be washed again?"

Heron shook her head. "What causes the suppuration is within the tissue."

Ologrin's irritation dissipated as he recognized the anxiety in Heron's voice. "What can we do?"

"Fortunately, I do have a treatment, but I am very low on the materials I need." She opened a small jar she had been carrying. Inside was a bright orange powder with a distinctive smell. "This is a shelf fungus you can find growing next to the river. I buy it from Bhinton, where they collect it and dry it."

"That's frogperch," Ologrin said. "When I was a child, we would boil it and make a tea to soak bandages in."

Heron scowled. "Well, it's more effective mixed with honey and applied directly to the wound. At any rate, I need more. They sell it in Bhinton. I need you to go."

"Why me?"

"Time is critical. And you have a horse."

"I don't have a horse. That horse belongs to the Crown's Guard."

"Then get it from them."

Ologrin appreciated Master Heron's directness, but at times she could be too simplistic in her search for the straight line. "I will figure out who we can send, perhaps even with an arms man escort. It will be just as fast." He did not mention that he was also thinking of Terval's invitation. He could not get to Bhinton and back in time.

Heron shook her head. "I am disappointed in you."

"Master Heron…"

"Some things we do not delegate. The life of a friend we do not hand to someone else. Things can go wrong. It is not just a simple messenger's journey when so much is at stake. I need you."

"Okay. I understand."

"Master Vireo changed all of her plans when she lost a student."

"I understand! I'll go."

It had been a year since Ologrin had been in the flats. But the strong suggestion that he stay out was not the same as absolutely being forbidden, he concluded. The Crown had not formally decreed it. Vireo might not want him to go, but she would not stop him, he thought, not when Albrect's life might depend on it.

It had also been a year since he had seen Breeze, and he had no real idea if the horse was still at the palace stables. He made his way to Vireo's chambers, where he hoped to find Master Crake. He was concerned that Crake would not approve his return to the flats, but after a short discussion, a sealed parchment was on its way to the Crown's Guard. Captain Aron, mounted on his warhorse, was at the foot of the castle stairs early the next morning, Breeze at his side.

"I seem to recall hearing you were banished from the flats," Aron said.

"That's nonsense," Ologrin replied, finding he had not forgotten how to swing himself into the saddle. "No one can be banned from the flats."

"You caused me more than enough grief last time," Aron said edgily. "I had to explain myself to the Lord Coronet before it was over. There and back, understand? We're not spending our time with the bisonherders."

"Fine. I don't have time for that anyway."

They rode like rulers down the terraces to the west gate, and then down the Repose Road to the Great Road. Harvest was approaching, and the thick green grasses of Summer were thinning out. Even so, the flats were a transformed place compared with the previous Summer. The overpowering smell was gone. Cracked, dried out ground had been replaced by broad stretches of pasture, divided by footpaths. Though it remained spare in some places, pasture closer to the irrigation ditches was thick with ankle-high grass.

Two leagues beyond the escarpment, they turned north at the rough stone column. Either there were more herders in the flats, or they were more visible, Ologrin thought. They all seemed to stop their work to watch the two horsemen. He raised his hand in a greeting. Several herders in a nearby pasture raised their hands in turn.

"You've become kind of a mythic being out here," Aron said.

"Me? I doubt anyone even remembers me."

"Palace delegations go back and forth to Madros on this road all the time. I'm on the Great Road as much as I'm home. I hear things. The herders talk about you."

"Right. *Whatever happened to good old Ologrin? We sure miss Ologrin!* Is that what you hear?"

"They say sometimes you come in the shape of a bison," Aron chuckled. "People will imagine any sort of thing, if it helps build a myth."

Ologrin let Aron's horse slip ahead, and then furtively reached up to feel his scalp. Something was definitely protruding, just inside the hairline at each temple. Thus far they were hidden, and as long as he did not cut his hair short they should remain hidden. A bizarre coincidence, he told himself. And if anyone were to take on some fabled importance to the people of the flats, it shouldn't be a surprise that they would conflate that person with the oversized animals they lived with and depended on every day.

They were being followed. What had started as a couple of individuals waving at them from the pastures had turned into a small stream of people trailing behind. Ologrin pulled his horse off the road onto a footpath leading to a milkhouse.

"Hey," Aron said. "I thought we agreed we wouldn't stop before Bhinton."

"Just to water the horses."

Soon a procession of people was walking beside Aron and Ologrin, chatting happily. The ones nearest seemed to take pleasure in touching his cloak, and then, unbidden, they assumed the role of a human wedge, parting the gathering crowd.

"Whatever you do, stay on your horse," Aron warned. "I don't know if they will let you back up if you get off."

Their horses navigated toward a nearby water trough. Ologrin doubted the water was meant for horses, but no one tried to shoo them away. A broad-shouldered man worked his way to the front of the crowd. Ologrin thought he couldn't be more than eighteen years, but the crowd clearly treated him with deference.

"Welcome," he said, and then stood awkwardly. Ologrin took that to be the entire welcoming speech.

"What is your name?" he asked.

"Temol," the young man replied.

"You and your people have worked hard and have much to be proud of."

The young man seemed to stand taller. He received a couple of pats on the shoulder from those closest. "You may have a woman if you wish," he said.

Aron snorted, and Ologrin felt his face become hot. "Oh, no," he said. "You are gracious, but no. We would prefer cups of fresh milk, if you have them."

"If you're thirsty, I have ale in my pouch," Aron muttered.

"They will have kept some in a cool place," Ologrin replied. "It's a treat, and they will be honored to share."

"If it's all the same, I'll just stick to my ale."

"You'll drink the damned milk," Ologrin said, smiling and nodding to the little crowd. But he heeded Aron's advice and remained on his horse, while Aron heeded Ologrin's and drank his milk. Eventually they were able to work their way back to the road and continue north. Their entourage gradually thinned, as they could make better time on horse than the people could walking through the fields. By the time the Sun reached the west, their horses needed water again, and Ologrin's legs were on fire from a day spent squeezing his horse's flanks. They stopped at another milkhouse. Here they were treated more like travelers than mythic beings, though again they both had to politely decline the offer of one of the local women for the night.

Ologrin awoke the next morning to the feel of a boot nudging him in the belly. The sky had only just started to turn blue.

"Get up," Aron said. "There's someone here to see you."

Another delegation of herders stood at the edge of the firelight. A tall woman, perhaps his age, stood just beyond the coals. She was surrounded by half a dozen other men and women who had not been there the night before.

"Marle?" Ologrin said.

"Why have you come?" the woman said. Her tone conveyed a matter-of-fact authority.

"Marle, you know me. I'm Master Ologrin, from the Sophenary. I selected you to oversee the niter beds."

"We know who you are. Why have you come?"

Ologrin was concerned something had changed their welcome overnight. "We are traveling to Bhinton. I thank you for your hospitality."

"Why does the Korun go to Bhinton?" the woman said.

"What?"

"They have been calling you the Korun, whatever that is," Aron replied.

"It's a name for a bison."

The woman waited patiently for an answer. Ologrin noted with concern that one of the nearby women had an infant on her hip, and that infant continued to have the bloated belly of malnourishment.

"We are going to buy orange frogperch," he said.

"If the Korun seeks frogperch, we have plenty and will share."

Ologrin wondered if he had missed something before he woke up. "What do you mean, you have frogperch?"

"We find it in next to the water ditches. It can be used for cooling a wound."

"When dried and powdered, yes," Ologrin said.

"It is better fresh."

He raised his eyebrows. Marle stood impassively before him. He turned to Aron. "Do you have any idea what is going on?"

"Supposedly they walked all night to find you," Aron said. "They arrived before dawn." If their arrival had surprised him as well, he did not say. That wouldn't look good for a member of the Crown's Guard.

Ologrin turned back to the woman. "Why has that child not been fed? I thought we fixed that problem."

This seemed to break the woman's demeanor. "They leave us very little meat or milk," she said, looking now at Aron. "The children do not do well with mudbeans only."

Aron appeared ready to speak, but Ologrin raised his hand.

"The Sophenary sends you coin for your work in the niter beds. That coin should be used to buy barley and sorghum from Bhinton. You're feeding children mudbeans?"

"Every time they sell us less and less for our coin. The last time, we sent the coin, but the barley never arrived."

Ologrin turned to Aron. "They're cheating them out of food."

"Hey, I don't know anything about it."

"They starve them, and then when the Sophenary sends them coin for food, they steal the coin! How foolish can they be? Does the Crown not know how much it depends on the people of the flats?"

Aron stood shaking his head, but Ologrin was now moving toward the horses nearby. "Find me as much frog-perch as you can find," he said. "I'll go get the barley. Captain, shall we ride?"

They reached the gentle hills north of the flats by midmorning. Ologrin could not decide whether walking or riding would be the greater torture on his legs, but he had to admit they were moving faster on horse. Shortly after midday, they spied the walls of Bhinton in the distance, and every hill they surmounted made the city appear larger and more detailed. Ologrin felt like he was getting used to Breeze's rhythm again, and she to him.

"I assume your backside gets thickened if you ride a horse long enough," he said.

"Saying a horseman has a wooden butt is a mark of respect," Aron replied.

In addition to his horsemanship lore, Aron turned out to know much about the taverns in Bhinton, and by Sundown Ologrin was settled with a plate of food and pitcher of ale. He felt relaxed in a way that he rarely felt in Antola. These were the people and the smells he recalled from Halrin's Spur. Later, the owner gave them a room to themselves. Whether it was due to the markings of the Crown's Guard or just the better character of the place, Ologrin didn't know, but he appreciated it nonetheless.

The next morning the tavern owner pointed them in the direction of the mill. Not having access to a stream, the miller had a pair of donkeys turning an oversized quern. Ologrin was fascinated by the simple and well-worn gears mounted on the stout millstone axle. Every lazy circle of the donkeys was converted into three turns of the upper millstone. If the deep, circular track in the earth was any indication, the miller had inherited the mill from his father, who likely had inherited it as well. A boy of about ten or twelve years fed barley into the center while keeping an eye on the four equally spaced buckets at the perimeter as they slowly filled with ground grain.

Two dozen sealed barrels stood at one side of the courtyard. Ologrin pulled out his bag of silvers and approached the miller. The man had been watching them carefully since they had walked into the courtyard, splitting his gaze between Ologrin and Aron. When he saw Ologrin pull out his purse, he shook his head and waved at them to leave.

"I have silver," Ologrin said. "I would like to buy your flour. Top price."

"No..." the miller said. "Don't need your coin. Not for sale today."

Ologrin stood perplexed. The miller continued to watch warily, with most of his attention on Captain Aron.

Aron suddenly spoke up, loudly. "I told you there was nothing to fear. You can find me if you ever decide what you're going to do. I'm going to get a drink." And he stomped out of the courtyard and noisily down the street.

Ologrin stood dumbfounded, not sure what had come over his partner. He looked back at the miller, who had now turned his attention to the bag of coin. He thought he would try again. "How much do you want for sixteen barrels of barley?"

But the miller shook his head again. "Won't take coin," he said.

"Well, what will you take?"

The miller looked Ologrin in the eye, and his tongue flicked out between his lips.

"I'd give four barrels of flour for one haunch of smoked bison," he said, quietly.

Ologrin remembered something from his long past. Trading was how things got done, Tobin had said. Coin was reserved for...and then he understood.

"You're afraid he's going to come back and steal the coin from you, aren't you?"

The miller did not answer, but Ologrin saw fear return to his eyes. "It's all right. You can trust him. I trust him." The miller's lips tightened. "If he was going to steal the coin, he would have stolen it from me, don't you think?" But even as he said it, Ologrin knew what he had to do. He sighed. "Where's the butcher's place?"

Aron was standing a few dozen hands outside the courtyard gate, grinning. Ologrin handed him two silvers. "Make yourself useful and see if you can trade this for some sorghum syrup."

Ologrin found the butcher, who had a similar fear of silver, but a considerable taste for ale. The brewer happily parted with four bull's heads of ale for a silver each, and the butcher traded for four smoked haunches. He agreed to deliver the meat to the miller for a few extra durri.

At the end of a tiring day, Ologrin had his sixteen barrels of barley flour and four of sorghum syrup, with some change left over. He invited the miller back to their tavern for an ale to seal the deal.

After downing the mug, the miller seemed more at ease. Ologrin sat next to him, sipping his mug more slowly. "Captain Aron has worked with me for a long time. I do trust him. He would not have come back to take your coin."

"If not him, then another," the miller said.

"You city type don't know what it's like out here," the tavern owner piped up, making no secret of overhearing their conversation. "We have to live with the mercenary, but we don't have to trust 'em."

"Captain Aron isn't a mercenary. He's a member of the Crown's Guard."

"Not any difference, if you ask me."

"And I'm not a city type. I grew up north of here."

"Oh, and where's that?"

"Halrin's Spur."

"Ah, now there's a place stirring 'em up."

"What do you mean?"

"They got some priest up there, thinks he's better than the mercenary. He's got everybody building things and doing for themselves. He's asking for big trouble, if you ask me."

Ologrin fought the urge to jump into the man's face. "He's trying to protect his people from the Ruhatsi. If he keeps them safe, it helps keep you safe. I would think you'd appreciate that."

The tavern owner sniffed a deep, liquid sniff. "He'd be better paying attention to this side of the river, too."

"Why would you say that?"

"Those Ruhatsi demons, they say they killed a man over near the river just two passages ago. But when the mercenary heard about it, they didn't send out any patrols or nothing. Instead, they just took that man's woman for themselves."

Ologrin closed his eyes, and for a moment he was back on the Altarnary roof, as the Ruhatsi above him made that unearthly call.

"Mercenary come in here once every three or four passages, push me around until I give 'em my stash of coin. Of course, I let them push me around just enough that they think they got me scared, and I don't give them my real stash. So, you see, I'm smart enough to live around them, but I got no reason to trust 'em. But sometimes I think it'd be better to get my throat slit by a screaming demon and get it over with than to be bled to death a little at a time."

A problem had been worrying the corners of Ologrin's brain, and a solution suddenly made itself known.

"You're not afraid of coin, I gather."

"Let's just say I'm smarter than the arms commander's men."

"And you must have a wagon for supplies."

"Wagon's not for sale."

Ologrin pulled a single silver out of his pouch and carefully set it on the table. It bore the profile of Donal, with the inscription *The Strong Survive* etched beneath. "I don't want to buy a wagon," Ologrin said. "But I've got to move several barrels back to the flats, and I've been trying to figure out how I was going to do that."

The tavern owner slid the coin into a pocket. "Happens I don't need it for a couple of days, though."

Early the next morning, the miller hitched a tired-looking donkey to his wagon, and then he and Ologrin maneuvered it through the streets to the miller's, where they loaded the barrels themselves. By the time they were on their way back to the tavern, the streets were already filled with people raising clouds of dust. Despite his time in Antola, Ologrin marveled at the number of people who could be in one place at one time, all seemingly in his way. Throughout the throng he saw countless tiny examples of friendship: a helping hand up, a pat on the back, shared laughter. He smelled baking bread and stopped to wave a woman and her two small children across the street toward the bakery.

Aron rode up, leading Breeze by her reins. Ologrin was already thinking about the hills between Bhinton and the flats. As gently rolling as they were, they were likely to be impossible for the donkey to manage with a full wagon.

They rounded a corner and saw the southern gate in the distance. The tavern owner grabbed Ologrin's wrist. "Not sure I understand what you're up to. If you feed those bisonmen one time, they'll only want more. But you're a good man." Then he hopped to the ground.

There seemed to be a mass of people, wagons, and carts all trying to get through the gate at the same time, bringing them to a stop.

"There's a pair of mercenaries up there checking everyone before they go through," Aron said.

"Is that going to be a problem?"

"Probably."

They crept forward in starts and stops. Ologrin had to jump down from the wagon and shove it from the rear every time they needed to move. When they finally got close to the gate, one of the mercenaries rode toward them.

"Crown's fee to cross the gate," the mercenary said.

"We're on the Crown's business," Aron replied, pointing to his collar.

"And that includes the gate fee."

Aron dropped Breeze's reins, then directed his horse around the wagon until he was shoulder to shoulder with the mercenary. Aron's horse was a hand taller at the shoulder, but the mercenary held his ground. His partner had noticed them and rode up on the opposite side. He held a lance at his horse's side.

"I see you have a spare horse," the mercenary said.

"That horse has the Crown's brand," Aron said. "Surely you aren't stupid enough to steal it."

"How do we know you didn't steal it? Long way from the palace, I'd say."

Ologrin jumped onto the back of the wagon, putting him at the same height as the mounted men. "Of course we'll pay the gate fee," he said loudly. "These fine men are doing their job, Captain, keeping us safe. They rely on the generosity of travelers to pay for their effort." Aron, he assumed, could draw his sword and cut down the first man before anyone else could move. But the lanceman almost certainly could throw as fast as Aron could draw. Aron would have to be lucky to avoid it. Ologrin produced his pouch and made a show of emptying the contents into his hand. "I have two silver left. I should think one each would more than pay the fee." He made a show of tossing one coin at each of the mercenary. The coins flew far over their heads and landed in the dirt behind them. Almost immediately, a man behind the lance-carrying mercenary stepped toward one of the coins.

"Back!" the mercenary said, swinging his lance around. Ologrin had already jumped down and gave the back of the wagon a mighty shove. The donkey obliged and began moving forward. "Pick it up and hand it to me!" the mercenary cried, but the man backed up instead, staring that the point of the lance. The first mercenary backed his horse to cover his coin. Ologrin jumped back onto the wagon. Breeze trotted dutifully next to them, and people spread out of the way as they passed through the gate.

"We'll get that horse later!" one of the mercenaries cried after them, but neither pursued, and soon enough Ologrin had his hands full controlling the wagon as they descended the hillside beneath Bhinton's wall.

"I didn't need your help," Aron said.

"There's two dozen more where those two came from," Ologrin replied. "How far do you think we could have gotten?"

"We could have outridden them."

"And leave the wagon? I would call that a failure all the way around."

Aron rode out ahead. Ologrin said nothing else, figuring the man needed a few moments to cool down. Breeze walked next to the wagon, staying with Ologrin, which he found comforting.

They reached the base of the hill, and soon the road started to rise again. The wagon came to a halt. Ologrin jumped down and started to pull barley barrels off the back. Each was at the limit of what he could manage, and he was winded after the first two. Aron rode back.

"What are you doing?"

"Unloading half," Ologrin replied.

"What happens if someone comes and takes it?"

"You're going to stay until I get back from the other side of this hill. Then we'll load this half and move it over the next hill."

"It's going to take us two days just to get back to the flats."

"I know," Ologrin said. "Hope those guys weren't serious."

The donkey struggled to make it up the hill, even with half of the load left behind. As they slowly climbed, Ologrin was fascinated to watch Breeze stay right with them. At the bottom of the next hill, he unloaded the rest of the barrels, unhooked the donkey's harness, and gently led Breeze in front of the wagon. The horse waited patiently while he worked to make the rig fit her larger body. Leaving the donkey to rest and graze, Ologrin turned the wagon around, and Breeze pulled them back the way they came.

Aron appeared to be unmolested, snoozing in his saddle as they rattled up. He took one look at the horse harnessed to the wagon and laughed.

"How did you ever manage that? A warhorse pulling a wagon. She'll kick the life out of you if she ever gets the chance."

"She volunteered," Ologrin said.

"Volunteered?" He shook his head, but he dismounted and helped Ologrin load the second half of the supplies onto the wagon, and then together they headed over the hill for the third time. Breeze trudged sturdily along, making better time than the donkey had managed. Still, after managing to get the load completely over the next hill, Ologrin was exhausted, and Breeze needed a break from the harness.

They managed two more hills before calling it a day. The Sun's rays were slanting from the west, and Aron wanted to secure some sort of camp before dark. There had been only scattered travelers on the road during the day, but they built a small fire and set watch, nonetheless.

Ologrin volunteered for first watch. The sky was clear. He easily picked out his favorite stars and watched as they slowly circled around Ortak, high in the south. The star shone about halfway between the horizon and the top of the sky. Thus, where he sat was about halfway to the southern axis of the world itself. Six gross leagues, more or less. There might be two dozen people in all of Antola who knew that, he thought. What mysteries must still exist in the wider world?

The Sojourner rose late and climbed rapidly out of the west. When it was almost overhead, he knew his watch was over. He woke the arms-captain and curled inside his cloak as best he could.

He woke to the Sun shining straight into his face. Aron was gone, but Breeze was grazing nearby, as was the donkey. Ologrin shook the soreness out of his muscles. The hills were more gradual as they approached the flats, so he figured they would make better time. Still, they would be lucky to reach their edge by nightfall.

He heard voices and snippets of laughter coming from the south. Travelers who had spent the night together for safety, he assumed. They sounded cheery, which alone helped his weariness. The first of the group topped the nearest hill. To his surprise, a full-grown bison lumbered up with them. There were at least a dozen men and women, tailed by an arms man on a warhorse.

Ologrin grinned as the first of the bisonmen walked up, a sturdy woman with a pregnancy just beginning to show. "We're here to help the Korun," she said, and then heaved one of the barley barrels back onto the wagon.

"They say the animal will pull the wagon," Aron said, riding up.

"The harness barely fits Breeze. How are we going to hook it up to that beast?"

But the bisonmen had brought ropes and seemed to know how to tie them together such that the bison was soon standing in front of the wagon, idly cuffing the ground with one leg. The women and men swarmed the wagon and had the remainder of the supplies loaded in no time. Soon they were rumbling south. The donkey watched them roll away, then gave a honk and trotted after them.

"I can't believe you left me alone in the night," Ologrin said, riding beside Captain Aron.

"How many times do I have to say, that's a warhorse. You were not alone."

The bison had no trouble with the fully loaded wagon. They were riding onto the flats by midday. The bisonmen took turns riding on the wagon, talking and laughing as if they were on an adventure. A few of them broke away and headed back into the pastures as soon as they reached the flats, but as they drove further south, others came to walk with them, and their entourage gradually grew. They reached the first milkhouse and stopped to offload some of the barley flour and syrup. By the time they were on their way again, the crowd was growing, and the laughing and chattering had been replaced by chanting, which was slowly being taken up by the entire crowd.

"They're chanting about you," Aron said.

"No, it's a song about the bison. *Horns high, shoulders wide...*"

Aron gave a short laugh. "It's also about you. *Full of courage, thick of hide.* Listen!"

Indeed, Ologrin could hear another chant, timed with their footsteps, underlying the first. "Korun, Korun," they were saying over and over.

"We're dumping the rest of this stuff at the next milkhouse and getting out of here," Aron said.

"You'll get no argument from me," Ologrin replied.

Marle was waiting for them at the milkhouse along with dozens more herders. She motioned and two of the herders each tied a fat leather pouch to loops on Breeze's shoulder harness. Ologrin could smell the musty odor of the fresh frog-perch inside. The woman pressed her hands together under her chin. Dozens of people began pulling barrels off the wagon. Everyone from the flats seemed to be converging on them. The chant of "*Korun, Korun*" began again.

"Time to go," Aron said. He used his horse as a ram to push the crowd aside, and Ologrin followed right behind until they were free of the crowd. The chant "*Korun, Korun,*" was getting louder. On a whim, Ologrin pulled out his coin pouch and tossed it into the crowd. There was a roar as the pouch disappeared into raised arms.

"What did you do that for?"

"There was only a handful of durri left."

"We need to go now," Aron said sharply. He kneed his horse and took off at a slow gallop. Breeze trotted after him without having to be told. After half a league Aron's horse slowed down, and Ologrin was able to catch up.

"You sound angry," he said.

"I don't think you know anything about crowds," Aron replied. "It doesn't matter if you think they are on your side or not. They're unpredictable. Anything can get them moving one way or another, and once they start, nothing can stop them."

"I don't know what I could have done differently."

"You could have not thrown them scraps like you were their ruler, or god, or whatever. That was foolish."

"It was only a few durri. They have better use for them than I do."

Aron maneuvered his horse in front of Ologrin's, pulling them both to a stop. "What are flats people going to do with a few durri? Come up to the terraces and buy a bowl of soup? Listen, Ologrin. I know you want to help these people. I admire that. But you can't let them think you are their leader. They have a leader. It's the Crown."

"I'm trying to help them lead themselves. That's what I was taught."

"Do you want to know why I came with you on this trip?" Aron asked.

"To provide protection. And to help, or so I thought."

"I was assigned to watch you, and to stop you if you tried to get these people to slaughter any more bison for their own use."

Ologrin scowled at Aron. "What do you mean, stop me?"

"I'm an arms man, Ologrin. I know where my loyalty lies.

And it's the same place that the Sophenary's loyalty lies, and where your loyalty should lie too."

They headed for the escarpment in silence. Ologrin could see several groups of people and a handful of wagons laboring up the ramp. It was another busy day in Antola.

"I thought you came because you were my friend," Ologrin said finally.

"You should grow up," Aron replied. "Why do you think I'm telling you this? Friendships have limits. There's always something bigger at stake."

Aron remained silent as they climbed the Repose Road. Ologrin felt weary. He thought of Albrect, and a deep anxiety settled in his chest that he had not felt since they'd left. That, in turn, made him feel guilty. He had been gone five days. Heron had expected him back in three. Was Albrect still alive?

They passed through the western gate onto the first terrace. It was filled with people, leaving or arriving, meeting others, or trying to sell to whoever would stop. The crowd seemed to move out of the way of the horses without looking, like flocking birds responding in unison.

"I'm sorry," Ologrin said finally. "I consider you a friend, whatever else you think."

Aron glanced over his shoulder, and his face looked as weary as Ologrin felt. "I have to report to my commander," he said. "Keep the horse for now. You can put her up in the Sophenary stable, I assume?"

"She'll be taken care of. I promise."

Aron paused, and Ologrin thought he saw sadness in his face as well. "Take care of yourself," Aron said, and then turned and rode away.

Ologrin let Breeze carry him up the northern steps. The Sophenary loomed over the terraces. He could see his own tiny tower far above and could hardly wait until he could wash the dirt from his body and sink into his small bed, peaceful and alone. He would deliver the frogperch to Master

Heron and then tell one of the red collars to leave him alone unless the world was ending. He patted Breeze's neck, and she turned her head slightly and gave him a friendly nicker. At the seventh terrace he turned Breeze to the left. There was a set of steps near the base of the mountain that led to the husbandry courtyard at the rear of the castle. They were steep steps, but he was confident that Breeze could handle them.

Soon they were walking behind the Collegarum. Ologrin recognized one of the stable boys, whose eyes went wide at the sight of a warhorse entering his domain.

"Master Ologrin! What a beauty!"

"Treat her well, okay?"

"The best!"

Ologrin dismounted and slipped through a side door into the castle, carrying the bags. He left them with an initiate in Heron's chambers and was about to climb to his tower room when a red collar spied him and came running.

"Master Ologrin! They're looking for you! They're looking for you everywhere!"

"Who's looking for me?"

"Everyone."

"I've been in the flats. Master Heron knows that."

"They're out front. They're waiting for you."

"*Who* is waiting for me?"

"The guards! From the palace. You have to come right now."

Ologrin followed her to the great doors, his sense of foreboding growing. They stepped out onto the steps. Two mounted arms-men from the Crown's Guard were on the plaza.

"Master Ologrin," one of them called out. "You have been summoned to the palace. You will come with us."

"I just got home…"

The arms man let the coils of a rope fall from his hand. He

held one end, while the other ended in a pair of leather manacles. "Will you ride, or would you prefer to walk?"

Without waiting for Ologrin to answer, the other arms man had already slipped from his horse. He sprinted up the stairs, grabbed Ologrin roughly by the shoulder and propelled him downward.

Ologrin turned and looked for the red collar. "Let Master Crake know," he said.

"He knows."

21

Ologrin studied the room around him. The floor was granite so smooth it gleamed as if wet. Square columns of the same material were spaced on the long walls, four to a side. The walls between the columns appeared to be made of blocks of exotic green-and-yellow marble. A third of the way up, the walls turned to smooth plaster, creamy white. The ceiling, over twenty-four hands high, was a grid of finely polished mahogany beams framing plaster panels, which were painted blue and adorned with patterns of swirling gold bands. There were no windows; light was provided by lamps along the walls. Tiny flecks of metal embedded in the granite reflected the light from the lamps. *Adamantine,* he thought. After several moments, when no one seemed to be coming to get him, he stepped over to the nearest wall. He pulled out his tanj and touched one of the metal flakes. A spark cracked and leapt between the two, sending a jolt up his fingers and leaving a small black pit in the wall where the metal flake had been. "Definitely adamantine," he said out loud. The message was clear. Here was wealth so great that the rarest materials were nothing more than wall coverings.

He looked around carefully. There was no place to sit. He

thought about sitting on the floor, propped up against the wall, but considering how grimy he was, he assumed that wouldn't be well received. There were only two doors into the room: the one he had been led through, and one in the opposite wall. Both were marked only by a thin outline; there were no latches or handles on his side. A most beautiful prison cell, he thought.

Still nobody came. After counting the ceiling panels again and re-examining the near-invisible seams between the stones on the wall, he thought he might pass out standing up. He was seriously considering simply lying on the floor when the door opposite opened, and an older man in a deep blue coat and leggings said, "This way."

He was ushered into another room as richly constructed as the last one, but this one was fully furnished. A thick weaving of intricate designs covered much of the floor. Storage boards lined one wall, with rolls and books carefully housed in them. A large table dominated the room, itself covered with rolls and a large glowglobe on a bronze stand. A soft-looking chair stood behind the desk, and a lounging bench covered in the same leather sat underneath a bank of windows. The window shutters were made of multiple panes of glass, allowing a full view outside even when closed. There still was nothing for Ologrin to sit on. Lord Wesse stood next to the desk and made no motion to offer Ologrin a seat.

"I sent arms men to bring you from the Sophenary at the first sight of Sun, and yet you are only now here," Wesse said. His voice was low and menacing.

"I was not at the Sophenary this morning. I was brought here the moment I returned."

"I had almost decided you were going to refuse this summons as well. In a way, that would have made things easier."

Ologrin was startled. "Lord Wesse, I have never been

summoned to the palace before. I would most certainly have come..."

"You were summoned to join Lord Terval on the *Rayfish* six days ago!"

"I...I sent word that I wouldn't be able to go."

"You sent word? You were sent a summons from the palace. You did not present yourself and request to be dismissed. You did not write a letter of apology, humbly begging forgiveness for not showing up. You *sent word*?! It's as if you are the master and we are the servants, and you can't be bothered with anything else."

"Lord Wesse, I did not intend to be offensive..."

"Are you the navigator of the *Rayfish*?"

"Yes...I suppose..."

"And you acknowledge that you received a summons from the palace, notifying you, as a member of the crew of one of the Crown's vessels, that you were expected for an upcoming voyage."

"Yes."

"And you ignored it. But you don't consider that an offense."

"I didn't realize I was being summoned."

"A message from Lord Terval, from the palace, and you didn't consider it a summons. Perhaps you thought it was an annoyance."

"No, Lord Wesse. Master Albrect remains ill after his injury. I went to the flats seeking botanicals for his treatment, following Master Heron's instruction."

"Ah yes, the flats." Wesse walked to the windows, as if he could look out and see everything in Antola. "Your people. *The Korun*. That's what they call you, right? What an honor, from the piss and dung collectors of the world."

Ologrin felt himself beginning to burn. *Aron must have wasted no time reporting once he returned to the palace,* he thought.

"But you have so many titles, don't you?" Wesse continued. "*Master astrolemer. Royal navigator. Your grace.* So many to choose from. And one, I think, so much more important than the others. I don't mean to be crude, but it is what they say, after all. *Maleugenate.* Am I correct?"

The word was like a knife slashing toward him. Ologrin felt a surge of both fear and anger. He looked around the room. If Wesse had weapons, they were well hidden. As if in response to his thought, Wesse walked over to another door into the room. Ologrin calculated he had a good chance of getting to the windows. If an arms man appeared when Wesse opened the door, he would run for the windows and jump.

Instead, a man with thinning hair and light skin stood on the other side. He walked in silently and headed toward them. Ologrin tensed, waiting to see what the man would do. The man had nothing in his hands, but he wore a long cloak that could contain any number of nasty surprises.

He walked up and began peering at Ologrin as if he were a specimen for sale. He looked closely at his eyes, then grabbed both of Ologrin's wrists and studied his hands. Without warning, he reached across and ripped open Ologrin's tunic, revealing the tanj hanging around his neck. Ologrin flushed again, feeling violated. The man reached into his cloak and brought out an unusual, intricate-looking device of a sort Ologrin had never seen before. Watching Ologrin's face intently, the man pushed the device against his left forearm. At first Ologrin felt only the cold tip. But then he felt a fiery jolt jump through his entire arm.

"Ow! What is that?!"

The man lifted the device, but then placed it back on his forearm. As if it were spring-loaded, Ologrin's right arm shot out and grabbed the man's wrist above where he was holding the device. The man gasped, and the device dropped to the floor. Ologrin held on for a moment, and the man's eyes widened. Ologrin imagined the ripping, paralyzing sensation reaching the man's shoulder and clawing into his chest for his heart. He released his grip, allowing the man to fall. Ologrin snatched the device from the floor and flung it at the wall behind him. He glared at Lord Wesse, who was still standing by the door.

"You should know," Wesse said, "that there are a half-dozen arms men surrounding the palace who have been told to kill you before you get away. The only way you leave here alive is if I signal them to let you leave." He turned his attention to the man on the floor. "Well?"

"No question. He's a mosaic. No Polfre could summon that much strength."

"Master Hinford here is a graduate of the Sophenary. The royal physionomist. A colleague of yours. You should treat him with care."

The man had backed up and was now picking himself up off the floor. "All in the name of knowledge, my Lord."

"If you're going to kill me, you'd better do it quick," Ologrin snarled.

"You mean because you are a maleugenate? If I wanted to kill you for that, you would have died on your way here. You would have died out on the flats. You would have been thrown overboard on your first sail. I've had my eye on you for a long time, Master Ologrin. If I was going to kill you, you would long ago have been dead. But you're not dead. You survived an assassin in your sixteenth summer. You survived an effort by your own classmates to have you killed. You're not so easily killed." Wesse helped the physionomist back to the far door. "Thank you, Master. You have courage I did not realize." He closed the door behind the man and walked back to his table in the center of the room. "The first true maleugenate spawned in forty-five dozen years."

"You've known all along, haven't you," Ologrin said.

"Suspected, but only just confirmed."

"What will you do now?"

"Do?" Wesse began pacing the room. "My talent, to the extent I have one, is my ability to see the world as it really is. My vision is unclouded. Though it may surprise you, I am not afflicted with bigotry and superstition. Those things have their use; they keep the people's loyalties focused. But I need to see things for how they really are. What I will *not* do is throw away the first mosaic in generations, unless I have to. I think the question, Master Ologrin, is what will you do? Will you continue to flounder about, trying to figure out if your loyalty is to the gods, or to the Sophenary, or to Master Vireo, or to those bisonherders out there? Or will you figure out where it truly must be?"

"To the Crown, right?"

"To the Crown!" Wesse slapped the table with both hands. "To the Crown! None of this exists without the Crown. Antola is nothing without it. The people out there, the ones you are so fond of, return to hunting for rabbits and killing each other without the Crown. Your Sophenary has no one to serve without the Crown. Everything must be given, every sacrifice made, if it supports the Crown." He walked up until he was inches from Ologrin. "You could kill me now, I don't doubt. If you do, then those arms-men out there will kill you, ridding us of a dangerous enemy, and the Crown wins. If you walk home alive, then it is because we understand each other, and the Crown gains a powerful force, and wins. Either way, Ologrin, either way works. The question is not what I will do, but what will you do?"

"I have spent most of my life learning how to serve people. Isn't that also serving the Crown?"

"It depends. Were you serving people so they could better serve the Crown, or serving people for their own ends?" Wesse walked toward the long windows. Ologrin felt his anger slowly being overtaken by an immense sense of weariness.

"Several years ago, the Crown's oldest son was involved in some terrible things," Wesse said. "He had taken to stealing young women from smaller villages, raping them repeatedly, and then disposing of them. One of the priests at the School found out. He began speaking out in the High Altarnary, saying the Crown's son was judged by laws of the gods, just like the rest of us. He called on the Crown to have his son punished just like anyone else, and said the Crown dishonored the gods by not doing so. Well, we took care of the son. He lives a long way from here and will never be Crown himself. But what do you think happened to the priest?"

Ologrin hated the man standing in front of him. He realized Wesse both knew it and was at ease with it. "You had him killed."

"Of course we did. He failed to understand his most important loyalty. The Book of Obligations, the laws of the gods, even the gods themselves. They exist to serve the Crown." Wesse released the hold backs on the embroidered hangings flanking the windows, which fell in place, plunging the room into gloom. He opened a small ember pot on the table and used it to light a nearby lamp.

"Lord Terval will return within the next passage. No doubt he will have tales to tell of their voyage to Solanon and back. You will not tell him we had this conversation. Doing so, in my opinion, would not be in the best interest of the Crown. Do you understand?" Ologrin stood as still as stone, but Wesse didn't bother to look for acknowledgment; it was obviously superfluous.

"Please check on my friend Albrect when you get back to the Sophenary," Wesse added. He crossed the room to the door Ologrin had initially entered from. "I hear his wounds were severe." He opened the door. "You will continue to find useful ways to use blast powder to serve the Crown. In his name, you will do great things for Antola. Some day you may stand next to the Crown yourself. You will be famous. But it will always be in the service of the Crown. Never forget that. I will be there, or someone who follows me will be there, and we will always be watching and waiting for the one time that your loyalty appears to waver from where it belongs." Wesse opened the door. "You can go."

"The arms men?" Ologrin asked.

"They were watching the window hangings. You'll be fine."

Ologrin walked slowly through the door. The anteroom was empty, and the opposite door was open to the entry hall.

Just as he was about to step through, Lord Wesse spoke again. His voice was low and ominous. "You will be tested, Master Ologrin. Your sacrifice may be great. Your loyalty must never waver."

Ologrin turned, but Wesse had already walked back into the room. Ologrin crossed to the entry hall, where he was met by the old man in the blue suit who guided him out to the courtyard. He left the palace unmolested and remained so for the long walk back to the Sophenary.

Walking into the shadows of the castle, he felt his weariness return, pulling him down as if his pockets were filled with stones. But then he remembered Albrect, and so hurried through the castle and down the stairs to Heron's chambers. The apothecary had been tidied up; no one answered his calls. He hurried on to Albrect's room. No one was in there either. The room had been cleaned and the bed clothes had been washed and folded. His throat felt tight. He returned to the cross-halls and stopped the first student he found.

"Where is Master Albrect's body?"

The student's left hand went to his chest and his right pointed to the rear doors. Ologrin was suddenly aware of the rhythmic sounds of a carpenter coming through the open doors. He passed through and into the bright sunlight bathing the north side of the castle.

The frame for the bombard had been torn apart. A bench had been made out of some of the wood, and a figure sat on the bench, watching the carpenter, who was shaping a beam. The figure was slightly hunched over in a way Ologrin had seen many times before. The lump in his throat evaporated as he ran down the steps and out into the yard. "Albrect!" he cried.

The older man turned slowly. His left arm remained splinted against his chest, but he was able to wave his right arm weakly.

"You're out of bed," Ologrin said, stating the obvious.

"I had to get away from that woman before she poisoned me."

Ologrin grinned. "Vireo says she is the best physionomist the school has ever had."

Albrect pointed to his shoulder. "Honey mixed with mushrooms, seaweed, boiled rags. She tried to push everything in there."

"That reminds me. You owe the Sophenary sixteen silvers." Ologrin found a bit of space on the bench.

"The palace is looking for you," Albrect said.

"They found me. Lord Wesse, at any rate."

Albrect looked carefully at Ologrin. "He's a very dangerous man."

The stumps were gone, and marks had been made for a lattice work of trenches that would support the foundations of the works.

"I thought you were building out of stone," Ologrin said, pointing out the single carpenter.

"That's for the tool shed," Albrect replied. "We'll dig these trenches to fifteen hands, then fill them with crushed stone and mortar for a foundation, then block for the piers, and finally backfill the dirt."

Ologrin tried to imagine the emerging structure. It seemed like days had passed since he had awoken stiff from a half-night's sleep on the ground outside of Bhinton. He felt as if Wesse had somehow beaten him to the ground again without touching him once.

"When I was young," he said, "I thought the gods were for the important people of the world. The gods didn't pay attention to the prayers of a bison village; they didn't care. Then I came to the School for Servants. Surely the gods listen to the prayers of their servants, I thought. I will become a priest and will come to know them that way. But they weren't there either. So I came to the Sophenary and thought the gods could be found in our big ideas. They would bless our great works. But Lord Wesse has cleared up that misconception. The gods, it seems, are here for just one person, and no one else. They serve the Crown. That's all it is. The rest of us? We're just the rubble that forms the foundation for them to stand upon. The gods have a god, Albrect, did you know that? Serenity the Seventh. The Crown. The ultimate god of all."

The carpenter had moved to another part of the yard. "You need to keep your voice down," Albrect said.

"Of course. I wouldn't want anything I said to get back to the only god who actually matters."

Albrect did not immediately respond. The carpenter returned and began whacking a portion of the platform stairs, loosening the individual pieces.

"Where is everyone?" Ologrin finally asked. "You're going to need six dozen people working on this to get anything done before Winter."

"Tomorrow is New Sojourner," Albrect said.

"So?"

"I gave them the day off. I thought they might want to spend it with their families."

"Oh."

"That seemed important."

They sat not looking at each other. The sounds of the city

were muffled by the great bulk of the castle. Ologrin closed his eyes, reaching out for the sounds of men shouting, or ship's bells ringing, but only heard the twitter of birds in the woodland and the sighing of the wind through long-needled pines.

"I've never spent much time worrying about the gods," Albrect said finally. "I just do my work. I like it, and I take pride in the fact that it helps the Sophenary, and maybe even other people. That's all I need. It sounds to me like what's bothering you most is not that the gods are only paying attention to Serenity, but that they're not paying any attention to you." He eased himself off the bench. "You need to get some rest, my friend. You'll be back to yourself by tomorrow."

Ologrin slowly climbed the steps to his cell. He tossed boots and cloak into one corner, then opened the door to the parapet to fill the room with fresh air. Wisps of white streaked the sky far, far above. He climbed the steps to the parapet. The palace buildings appeared distant and small from his perch. Smaller still were the ships tied up at the docks in the Purse, or, on the other side of the city, the tiny black arches that marked the western gate and the top of the Repose. The flats were unfocused fields of brown and green—greener with every passage, he thought with some satisfaction. He looked to the north. Beyond Arske's broad flanks the Adamantine mountains rose and fell. Somewhere deep within them was the Lake of Skies. Vireo was there. He had a sudden desire to put his boots and cloak back on, descend the steps and walk deep into the mountains again, where Lord Wesse would never find him. It was his birthright, just as much as it was anyone's with Polfre blood. He would find Vireo and convince her to stay with him, and together they would live a simple life: land and home, neighbor and starry sky.

He descended the steps from the parapet and sat on his

small bed, then stretched out and felt the bones of his spine settle gratefully into the softness of the mats and furs. He began to imagine a plan. Hammei would be a master soon; he would continue to be an able assistant for Albrect. Ologrin would explain the needs of the bisonherders to one of Master Heron's students. They would keep his efforts moving forward. He had more training, more study, more time spent in observation than most people alive. It was time to stop studying and start living.

He repeated this thought to himself several times, reshaping it and polishing it so that it mirrored his feelings exactly. Just as he thought it was perfect in his mind, a sudden pounding on his door shattered it. He sat up. The light in the room seemed to have shifted; the steps to the parapet were in shade, as they were in the mornings. His bladder told him that he had been asleep for a long time. The pounding continued. He sat up, feeling groggy and unsteady. He recalled telling one of the red collars not to disturb him and felt frustration for being so easily ignored. He lurched to the door and pulled it open.

"What?!" he said to the wide-eyed student before him.

"The smoke, Master. It's the flats!"

"What are you talking about?" But even as he said it, his nostrils picked up an acrid tang wafting in from the parapet.

"The flats. They're on fire!"

Ologrin's mind slowly came alive. He turned and fought the soreness in his back as he ran up the stairs to the parapet.

A heavy haze hung beyond the escarpment. He could not clearly see the broken green and brown of the pastures. But he could see scattered licks of orange flame. They were everywhere, stretching far to the south and west. It was if the entire flats had been struck by a single, vast bolt of lightning and were now a smoldering ruin.

Ologrin turned to the red collar. "Tell the stable boy to get my horse ready."

"Your horse?"

"He'll know! Go!"

Ologrin readied himself as quickly as he could, then ran down the stairs and to the husbandry yard. The stable boy had just fitted Breeze's tack and saddle; she stamped with impatience. Ologrin leapt onto the horse. He grabbed the reins, but before he could knee her Breeze took off at a gallop, and he found that he was holding on more than guiding.

Breeze flew across the terraces and down the steps. In moments they were galloping toward the western gates. "Make way!" Ologrin yelled, but the clatter of hooves was more than enough to make people look up and scatter. They flashed through the gates, and Ologrin had only a moment to see the surprised look on the faces of the guards before they were plunging down the Repose Road toward the valley floor.

Ologrin wrapped his arms around the horse's neck, fearing that at any moment Breeze would stumble and they would sail to their deaths hundreds of hands below. But the horse seemed magically possessed. They reached the foot of the escarpment in little more time than it had taken to reach the western gates.

As they rode out onto the Great Road, the smoke surrounded them, bitter and foul. Breeze slowed to a trot. Ologrin tried to shield his nose with his cloak, while the horse snorted and occasionally shook her thick neck. They came upon the body of a bisonherder lying face down on the edge of the road. Ologrin could not decide what seemed more shocking: the sight of a herder lying on the elevated roadway, or the maroon blood surrounding the herder's head, contrasting strongly with the crushed white rock. He noticed other bodies in the fields, both herders and bison themselves. Some of them were curled and smoldering, and the further they rode, the more the smell of burnt hair and hide permeated the air.

They rode to the crossroads. The nearest milkhouse was gone, nothing but blackened ashes in a circle. Bodies were scattered thickly, some burned, others bludgeoned. None moved. Even as Ologrin struggled to comprehend what he was seeing; a part of his mind began calculating. The work of raiders, without doubt, but in larger numbers than anything he had ever heard of. But it was mostly confined to the fields nearest the roads, he realized. The destruction wasn't total, and the marauders were not infinite. Dozens upon dozens of raiders, though, without a doubt.

The roadways, he thought again, and looked northwest along the road to Bhinton. How far, he wondered, and then kneed Breeze to leap forward again.

They galloped into the hills along the road to Bhinton. The air was clearer here, but the smell of smoke lingered. Any hut or paddock within sight of the road had been reduced to charred wood. He wondered at the speed of the destructive wave, which again spoke to this being many people, highly organized. If it was the work of the Ruhatsi, then it was by far the largest and most horrific thing they had ever done. It was more than a raid; it was the opening battle in a war.

Breeze seemed tireless, but Ologrin knew no horse could run forever, so they slowed, and both found fresh water some ways from the road at a tiny spring. He kept the horse at a trot as the Sun angled toward the western horizon. As they neared Bhinton, Ologrin did not notice any increase in the smoke, and he had some hope that the city had managed to defend itself. They topped a hill and saw the city's walls in the distance. Thankfully, no smoke rose from within.

Approaching the walls, Ologrin saw that the city gates were closed. Two arms men shouted at him from the rampart above the gates. He was too far away to understand them clearly, but as he trotted closer, a pair of arrows whistled overhead, making their intent perfectly clear. He pulled Breeze to a halt and cupped his hands to his face, hoping to be heard.

"I am unarmed!" he shouted. "I need a place for the night."

More shouting, and he picked out the words "Arms Commander's orders." He decided to approach much more slowly. Breeze moved forward at a slow walk. The two arms men watched him approach. But then one of them shouted again.

"No closer! We will shoot!"

"I am alone!" Ologrin yelled. "I need a place for the night. It is not safe!"

"The Arms Commander says the gates cannot be opened! We're to shoot anyone who approaches!"

Ologrin nudged Breeze to a stop again. "What's happening?! Why aren't there arms men on the road? Who is defending the people?"

The arms man shook his head. "No one in or out 'til it's over!" he shouted.

"Until what's over?"

But the arms man was now engaged in a heated conversation with his partner, which abruptly ended when the partner sent another arrow Ologrin's way. This one fell close to one side, and Ologrin thought it might have actually been intended to strike.

He turned Breeze and they headed back toward the nearest hill. Night was falling quickly. He spied a trail leading off into the scrub. The main road might lead through Bhinton, but a web of tracks and trails made their meandering way around the walled city, the product of countless individuals who over the years had reason to give the city a wide berth. He noticed a line of blackthorn growing at the base of a low, eroded hillside. There was just enough room to tuck himself and the horse between the shrubs and the hill's edge, making them essentially invisible.

Though Ologrin guessed the city walls were less than half a league away, he saw no city glow. The residents were hunkered down, too, he thought. Breeze folded herself onto the only clear patch of ground, and Ologrin sat with his back against her. His head nodded, but his sleep was light and fitful. He awoke several times, believing he had heard something, but the night remained quiet. He drifted into a dream filled with burned bodies crawling across the ground, staring at him with their opaque eyes. He awoke with a start as Breeze struggled to her feet. Something seemed different. He crawled out from behind the shrubs and clambered the rest of the way up the hill. Far to the north the horizon had taken on an orange glow.

"We have to go," Ologrin said. He grabbed the reins and led on foot. He could just make out the tiny paths as they continued to work their way around Bhinton. It was hard work, and Ologrin's knees and hips ached long before there was light in the eastern sky. Working their way along a dry stream bed, the ground rose suddenly. He struggled to the top of the rise and found himself on the roadway. Bhinton was at last behind them.

He managed to clamber up onto Breeze's back and they rode north. Ologrin was desperate to go faster, but he feared turning his horse's leg in the dark, so they proceeded at a walking pace. When the first light of morning made the roadway visible again, Breeze spontaneously broke out into a trot. Ologrin scrutinized the horizon at the top of every hill. The orange glow had remained distinct through the night, until it joined with the light from the coming dawn.

They met no one on the road; had met no one since leaving Antola. The road turned and crested a hill, and he could see the track leading off to the bridge south of Halrin's Spur. The bridge was in ruins. The posts that supported the near-side guard house had been hacked and burned, and the bridge itself had collapsed into the river. Ologrin kneed Breeze into a run. The smell of smoke was becoming stronger and was visible in the air.

The turns and rises in the road were at last very familiar. Another gentle rise, and then the river bent away to the west, yielding to the fertile pastureland around the milkhouse. As he feared, the milkhouse and everything around it had been burned to the ground. But now Ologrin had Breeze in a full gallop. For in front of them the entire village of Halrin's Spur was nothing but piles of smoking embers.

They rode in on the path between the pastures and the village. Just as he had seen in the flats, he now saw a scattering of bodies, some burned, some hacked or bludgeoned. Nothing moved. He rode into town and had to slow due to the bodies and smoldering timbers scattered between ruined structures.

The village had been destroyed. No one was alive, not even rats moved through the wreckage. The Altarnary stood like a great black cinder looming out of the smoke. He made his way in front of the building. The Curly Top was still burning, and as he watched, the remainder of the roof and two walls collapsed in a heap and a shower of sparks. Where the dirt itself was visible, innumerable hoof prints suggested the recent presence of dozens of horses.

He dismounted and walked up the steps of the Altarnary. The great wooden doors had been smashed, one held on by a single hinge, while the other lay flat on the stones. Filled with dread, he walked into the Altar room.

A body lay stretched on the altar, staring up at the oculus. The purpose of the five-armed altar was now painfully, hopelessly clear, as the body's limbs were stretched across the four longer arms, while the head rested on the shorter one. The body's torso had been flayed open and organs had been removed. The floor around the altar remained slippery with congealing blood. Dread crushed Ologrin's chest. He willed himself to look at the face, to verify once and for all what his heart feared so much.

It was Calus. The nose was smashed, and he had been

subjected to bruising blows before being sacrificed, but it was most definitely the young man who had taken Ologrin's place.

Ologrin fought down a wave of nausea. Every heartbeat filled his neck and head with rapid pounding. He stepped past the blood and made his way to the kitchen. It had been smashed, too. The floor was covered with trampled food and was awash with cider. Ologrin shook his head in astonishment. Whoever had done this had not bothered to steal anything; their intent was utter destruction. He walked carefully through the interior halls. Bloody boot prints were everywhere, heading to and from the Altar room. He methodically worked his way through the building, fearing he would turn the next corner and find Tobin's dead body, but the building seemed to be empty. He reached Tobin's chamber. A garish smear of fresh blood slanted across one wall, but the room itself was empty. He backtracked and worked toward the stairs to his old cell. He climbed the stairs to his old room, and then climbed the ladder to the roof.

From there, he could see there was nothing left in the entire village. Dozens and dozens of bodies were scattered everywhere, including on the banks of the river as well as across the river around the charcoaleries. The only moving thing was Breeze, who, spying him on the rooftop, neighed loudly and pawed at the ground. She was clearly as distressed as he was, and no doubt would not be willing to stand around indefinitely.

He climbed down and entered his old room. Amidst the destruction around him it was an island of peace, completely intact. The mats on his bed were neatly arranged, as if someone had expected him for the evening. Against a far corner, nearly hidden by the open door, Obo's old herding staff leaned against the wall.

He lifted it and ran his hands along its surfaces. The wood had turned nearly black, continuing whatever process had started when he had taken the staff from Obo's hut. It was warm in his hands. He stood for a moment, eyes closed, holding the staff in front of himself, willing himself to breathe. Then he descended the stairs and re-entered the Altar room.

A smear of red caught his eye, and he looked up at the collar of stone that supported the shallow dome, resting on the altar room's pillars. Whoever had done this had taken the time to figure out how to climb up there. Painted in blood—in Calus' blood, no doubt—was a large red triangle with five rays emanating from it. The rays were the arms of the altar, he now knew. It was the Malacheb.

The Ruhatsi were a ruse. It had always been the Malacheb.

Ologrin swung the staff blindly and savagely. It struck the altar beneath the body's left leg. An enormous flash and shower of sparks flew from the stone, and a huge bite was left missing from the altar itself. The staff resonated in his hands. It felt alive, eager. He stepped back and swung again at one of the candle stands. He cut through it as neatly as a scythe cutting stalks of cane. He swung again, striking one of the pillars surrounding the Altar room. The head of the staff seemed to explode through the center of the stone. The pillar slowly collapsed away from the collar, and the entire building groaned. Ologrin swung again, smashing a great gout out of the next pillar, then ran across the room as stones began to fall from the ceiling. He smashed another pillar, then dashed to the front, just inside the ruined great doors. More blocks rained from the collar, and now from the outer edges of the dome itself. Ologrin took aim and swung at one of the columns flanking the front entrance. The stone split as if struck by lightning. He turned and walked into the Sun's light. Breeze was waiting, but the pelt on her neck rippled in fear. Ologrin jumped from the terrace to the horse's back and urged her away from the building. Behind them, the sound of stones crashing to the ground continued, until with an enormous roar the entire dome collapsed, blasting dust and bits of rock from every open pore of the building.

They gained the road and turned south, toward Bhinton and Antola. Ologrin rode with the reins in one hand and the staff in the other and did not look back.

FOURTH PASSAGE

Then the Sorceress was brought bound before Malach. There were two warriors to hold the bonds of her arms, two for the bonds of her waist, and two more for the bonds of her feet. Her white hair flowed like a river of snow, and her brow was crested with the mark of Ruhax. In her eyes was flame from beneath the world.

"Kneel and profess your loyalty before your Chief," Malach said.

"I will not," she replied. "Not even if the Sojourner fell and the Sun rose cold in the sky."

"I cannot make you yield, but I can send you far from this world, to a place from where you will never return."

"I may not return in this body, but I will come again as the demon's child, and the Summer will become Winter, and your children shall turn into darkness."

"Darkness will always flee from the light," Malach said. And he waved his arm, and the Sorceress was banished from this world.

—from *The Book of Obligations,* Nine Dozen and Eleventh Vision

For the elite of Antolan society, the Endless Winter, in retrospect, created little more than inconvenience. Delicacies were few, and prices for staples were inflated. For those in the lower tiers, things were somewhat worse, but for most of them it meant only an occasional skipped meal. Those who suffered the greatest were the Eidos in small communities along and beyond the riverflats, and in the tiny villages scattered throughout Lhosa. But, if by and large the poor suffered more than the wealthy, they bore it more bravely. Those poor communities with a strong spirit survived with few deaths, as they were used to the endless search for food and knew where to find things to eat. Similarly, the small Polfre population in the Purse had a positive effect far beyond their neighbors, as their habit of cultivating innumerable small gardens allowed them to feed themselves as well as their neighbors.

The people of the flats went about their daily lives as if little had changed. The residents of the lower tiers responded to the Endless Winter with gossip and anxiety, but still managed to sleep well at night. It was the elite, those who suffered the least, who were consumed by their fear and distress, which they expressed loudly and vocally to the Crown's Council.

The risk of living at the very top of the tree of wealth is that it sways the most in a storm.

—from *The Invention of History* by Robin the Archivist

22

The sky above the castle was the vivid blue seen only on the coldest days of Winter, crisp and clear to the horizon. The steamy smoke from the chimney-works cast roiling shadows on the ground. Something was always burning. The air in the postern yard was thick with smells, mostly of wood smoke from the iron or whitestone chimneys, but also with the faint odor of rotting eggs, a remnant of the soda ash furnace. What had once been a quiet yard of grass and flowers, surrounded by stands of trees wandering into the mountains, had been transformed in the years since work had started on the chimneys. Stone paths led in many directions, but where there were no paths the ground was raw. A small mountain of crushed stone filled the far end of the yard. It was continually replenished by teams of donkeys making the trek back and forth from the whitestone quarry deep in the mountains. An equally large pile sat next to it, as black as the first pile was white: charcoal from the kilns in the western half of the yard, a pair of which were currently throwing off shimmering heat waves. Everywhere else were stacks of wood, cut and split. They varied from fresh, pinkish blond to ugly gray and brown: the wood most seasoned and ready for the furnaces. It took prodigious amounts of wood to keep the chimneys running.

A broad stone staircase spiraled from the rear doors of the cross-hall to the ground below. They were a permanent replacement for the wooden platform that had been built for Albrect's infamous and ill-fated demonstration. The stairs were finely crafted and beautiful, the opposite of the rough platform that had been there before. Each step was deeply etched with images of beasts and fish, which served to provide traction for the ice and snow of deepest Winter. The balustrades were finely carved marble, with a lattice of copper leaves and flowers forming the handholds. The copper was old enough now to be dark brown and would gradually turn lovely green in the years to come. The stairs were Vireo's price for Master Albrect's fires and forges and the pleasant meadow they had replaced.

Vireo stood for a moment at the top of the stairs, then descended and crossed one of the stone paths to the chimneys. It was difficult to say where the structures started. First, there were broad stone floors open to the sky, then the towering chimneys themselves, which also served as buttresses for stone arches. The arches, initially open to the sky, eventually supported wooden roofs. Then walls began to appear, finally rising to the tops of the arches and creating a maze of workspaces. She walked through it all, heading for a familiar space in the furthest corner.

The room she entered was cluttered with tables and shuttered storage board filled with all manner of things, many of which Vireo did not pretend to recognize. High window spaces made up the upper half of a far wall that supported a roof thirty hands high. Despite the time of year, the room was stuffy. A large hearth commanded the lower part of the same wall, as high as her crossed elbows, and contained a glowing, softly roaring fire. Smithworker's tools hung nearby or were sitting on the hearth, half in and half out of the fire. Two individuals worked at a large device next to the hearth. Both were covered in cloaks of heavy skins that also formed a peaked hood over their heads. The smaller of the two individuals worked a large crank on the side of the device, while the much taller one seemed to be guiding a glowing rope of fire out of the machine, allowing it to pass through a sluice of steaming water before feeding it into a large bucket of water to cool.

Vireo watched and waited. The fiery rope came to an end and was gently curled into the bucket, and then both figures stepped away and pulled back their hoods. The smaller of the two spied Vireo and bowed slightly, causing the taller one to turn around.

Ologrin wore a sweat-stained headwrap underneath his hood, which only served to give his head a lumpy, misshapen form. He smiled at Vireo and pulled off heavy, gauntleted gloves. He reached into a nearby bucket with a set of tongs and pulled out a coil of metal. It was a greenish-gold color, and not much to look at, had Vireo not known that only a while before it had been a molten mix of volatile and normally incompatible ingredients. Ologrin shook the coil lightly and it bounced open and closed.

"It is very malleable," he said. "I have drawn four coils through Albrect's forging rollers. It is now half as thick and four times as long as before, without any breaks."

"Then it is what you have wanted."

"Ouzel," Ologrin said, turning to the young Polfre nearby, "we are done for the day."

"I should put away the tools," Ouzel replied.

"I will get them. Thank you."

Ologrin handed Vireo the tongs. "It's still hot. I wouldn't touch it," he said.

The coil was heavy, not surprising considering it contained the equivalent of a dozen scarabs' worth of gold. Ologrin had obtained the gold himself, fifty scarabs in all. A gift from Terval, he had said. More than a lifetime's wages for the average skilled worker. Her own gift, if that was the right way to think of it, had been enough tanjium to form eight talismans for her own people. In its own way, it was far more valuable than the gold. Alloying tanjium with gold was a remarkable feat. Managing to include a small amount of adamantine, as Ologrin claimed, was astonishing, all the more so considering nothing had exploded and no one had been injured during Ologrin's experimentation. Well, a few small explosions, and a few cuts and burns suffered by Ologrin alone, but that was his price to pay.

"It is impressive, Ologrin. No doubt this would be sufficient to apply for a warrant master in vitachemy, if you had not already been admitted. Of course, then you would have to tell us what this is all about."

"In time," Ologrin said. He searched a nearby bench and came up with a small wooden box. "I have something for you."

"Thank you. It's beautifully made," she said.

"The gift is not the box."

She removed the lid and pulled out a long cord of vivid red, braided silk. A tiny intricate vine and flower dangled from the silk loop, made of the same greenish-gold metal of the coil. Vireo touched the charm lightly with her finger.

"It's made from your alloy. I can feel the tanjium," she said. She slipped the loop over her head. "It's a beautiful gift. Thank you."

"It's more like a trade," he replied.

"Oh? What am I expected to trade?"

"Take me to the Lake of Skies. Just the two of us."

Vireo laced her fingers through his and raised them to her chest. "You're really ready to go?"

"I'm ready."

"It's not just a trip. It's a commitment. To me."

"I know."

"Nothing would make me happier. If you're really ready."

"What if we went this Winter?"

She walked over to one of the worktables, fingering the tools. "What about your work here?"

"It can wait."

"And your work for Terval?"

A cloud passed over Ologrin's face. "Terval doesn't need me. The new ships are almost finished. Their captains know how to use the navigation tables. They don't need me either."

"Terval still looks at you the same way. Surely you know that."

"We have had this discussion. I don't want a physical relationship with Terval."

"He is a remarkable man. The two of you: that would be a pairing to change the world."

"I have no interest in a physical relationship with Terval," he repeated.

"You know why I have to be sure."

"I am not going anywhere," Ologrin replied emphatically. "This is where I want to live, work, and die."

She grabbed him around the waist. "You are a fire, Ologrin! Not a candle flame, not the steady glow from a lamp. You leap and burn and change everything around you. You know I find that exciting, but you cannot know how frightening it is. I have to know this is truly the choice you want to make." She released him and took a step back. "You have expressed your reluctance to move into my chambers."

"They are the Dodecant's chambers. I would feel like a servant. Or worse."

"But you can hardly expect me to move into that tiny, drafty tower of yours."

"Cozy," Ologrin corrected.

"Listen, I have had some designs completed for the chambers at the top of the great staircase. You know, the one you used when you first started tutoring Terval. The masons can add a nice balcony that peeks over the northern edge of the Purse. It would be a wonderful place to sit in the morning Sun and have breakfast. If I can convince you to come down from your tower, then perhaps I can leave the Dodecant's chambers for official business only."

Ologrin gave her a half-smile. "I think I could be persuaded."

"Good." She slipped her arm through his. "That's not the only reason I came down here, by the way. Heron wants you to accompany her tomorrow."

Ologrin's smile vanished, and he pulled away. "That's really why you came down here, isn't it?"

"Only one of the reasons."

"You know what my answer is."

"She needs you."

"She has five physionomy students, including one who is ready for her warrant adept. They are more than capable of assisting her. Does she think she is going to change my mind? That somehow everything will be fine again?"

"She says you know things."

"What do I know? I never even finished my physionomy warrant adept."

"You wouldn't stick with her curriculum, but that doesn't mean she doesn't see your talent."

"That's nonsense. I can't be manipulated that easily." He turned and began arranging tools around the fire.

"She has tried all of her herb inhalants, to no avail. She bandages his legs, yet they swell and weep."

"Has she tried hawthorn root?"

"She has. Only modest effect."

"Perhaps with drops of foxglove."

"Foxglove is a poison."

"Just drops. What is poisonous in great amounts can be very useful in tiny quantities."

"See? She needs your courage, Ologrin."

"Heron knows how I feel about the palace."

"Then don't think about it as the palace. Just think of it as someone who needs your help. Would you punish an innocent man for the sins of others?"

"I very much doubt he is an innocent man."

Vireo reached for his hands. He tried to resist the warmth, but it was as insistent as if he had plunged his arms into buckets of hot water. She looked steadily into his eyes. "We all failed you, Ologrin, in our own ways."

He leaned against a worktable. Even after five years, he could not shake the images of Calus on the altar. Lord Wesse, of course, had claimed no knowledge of the raids. He had been remarkably efficient at finding and executing those said to be responsible. Renegades. Mercenary Malacheb, he had said. Such a thing would never happen again, he said. Ologrin did not believe him. Wesse had made it happen. And though shortly thereafter he was named Crown Governor of Madros and rarely returned to the city, Ologrin felt his presence still hovered over the palace like the stench from a rotting carcass.

"You may be able to see Terval," Vireo said.

"I can see Terval at the Twain Swords whenever I want," he replied.

"He has asked for you to come."

Ologrin thought about the coils of alloy cooling in the buckets. He had not shared his thoughts about its usefulness with anyone, including Vireo. And he thought of his small cell, no doubt freezing now that the coals in the small hearthgrate had cooled, and he thought of the gleaming black staff he kept hidden in one corner. He walked over to the hearth and threw in several chunks of charcoal, releasing a flurry of sparks.

"Tell Heron I will meet her at the great doors tomorrow after breakfast. For now, I think I should get back to work." He pulled one of the coils out of its bucket and tossed it next to the coals on one side of the hearth, then watched Vireo leave.

It had been ten years since she had found him on the docks. By Polfre standards he had only been a child, with half-formed ideas and a lack of self-confidence. But she had impulsively shared her tanj with him, as if she needed to lay claim to him before anyone else could. Now he was undoubtedly a man, and he felt confident in his place at the Sophenary, if not entirely within the world. If he was a fire, would he burn her? Or would he burn out, leaving her alone for the long years ahead? Was he truly ready? He was irritated for even asking himself the question. Moving into the same quarters—wasn't that an answer?

After finishing in the chimneys for the day, he took advantage of a warm tub of water near the fires for a quick bath, then shared a bite with the stable boys. By the time Ologrin returned to his tower-top cell, the stars were already glowing sparks in the blue-black sky. A fire in the hearthgrate soon had the room warming, even though cold seeped through the doors to the observation platform and rolled down the stairs into the room. He sat cross-legged on the low platform bed and opened a large, leather-bound folio. Shortly thereafter, he heard a single knock, followed by the latch to the door being lifted. Vireo entered quietly. He hurried over to the hearth to throw on another wedge of wood.

"Oh, it's fine," she said. "I always think of your room as being so cold. But as you said, this is cozy." She walked over to the bed and picked up the folio. "*The Chronicles of Grebe the Elder*. That's interesting."

"Have you read it?"

"Of course. Grebe is considered one of the more important antiquarians. I didn't know you had an interest in Polfre history."

"Master Albrect says we are simply re-discovering things that were known and then lost a long time ago. I was looking for clues that might explain what they knew back then. For instance, the trestle lift. The more I know about things, the more I understand it should be an impossible machine. Where is the fuel, or the fire, or the steam? It hums and sings and goes up and down the Purse year after year as if by magic. How did they build it? We can't make anything close to that now. I thought there might be clues in the histories."

"If anyone recorded it, it would have been Grebe. But how did you know to look?"

"I read a couple of his rolls when I was at the School for Servants."

"They have copies of *Grebe the Elder*? I didn't know they were so enlightened."

"Once they discovered I was reading them, they put them off-limits."

"Of course."

Vireo curled herself on the bed with the folio in hand. Ologrin sat down next to her. "This Wysel person, though. He seemed to be the key to everything. Every major project, every discovery; he was involved in all of them."

"Wysel was a she."

"Oh? But it says 'he' in the book…"

"This copyist may have assumed the previous versions were wrong. But Wysel was definitely a she. She was, like you, a mosaic. The most famous mosaic of all, in fact, unless you count Farus himself, whom some people claim was also a mosaic, though I don't know how anyone would know after all these grosses of years."

"I had no idea."

"Is it a surprise that a woman could rise to such heights of fame and knowledge?"

"No, of course not."

"In the history of the Sophenary, the Dodecant has more often been a woman than a man."

"I'm not surprised," Ologrin said. "There haven't been

many women in my life. But all of them have been...formidable."

Vireo laughed. "Am I formidable?"

Ologrin picked up one of the hides cushioning the bed. This one was covered in a thick, black fur. "Vireo the Dodecant of the Sophenary? Of course she's formidable. Lords of the palace are nervous in her presence." He wrapped the fur around his and her shoulders at the same time. "Vireo who found me? Vireo who chooses me? I would say yes, still formidable."

She laughed louder, and then snuggled into his chest. "I am not the formidable one." He reached around her waist, and she pushed him backward until she was lying on top of him. She slid her tanj around until it was resting between her shoulder blades. "You know what they say," she teased. "Prolonged contact can lead to sparks."

A small part of Ologrin's mind tried to remain detached and observant. He was fascinated, for example, at how Vireo seemed to be able to manage the energy in her touch. At one point her hands were as warm as if they had been in a fire, and then moments later they would dazzle his skin with a tingling electricity. He could not tell if it was the most exquisite thing he had ever felt, or if he was actually in pain. He felt his movements were clumsy by comparison, but Vireo purred and bit her lip approvingly. He tried to catalogue those places, those moments that seemed most pleasurable to her, but the electricity kept building in him until it overwhelmed his faint attempts at remaining rational. Before he disappeared, though, he found himself falling wholly and completely in love with the small creature above him. He watched the tiny golden flower bob on its chain against her breasts until he could watch no more.

The fire burned down to glowing embers. Ologrin stared upward into the darkness. Vireo was curled into his right side, breathing slowly. He imagined the great wheel of stars outside and suddenly wanted to share them, as if they were his to share.

"Let's go to the platform," he whispered.

"It's freezing out there."

"We have lots of furs." Wrapping himself in an especially thick bison pelt, Ologrin rolled off the bed and headed up the steep steps. He pushed the wooden shutters outward and stepped onto the platform. It was indeed freezing; the cold bit at the inside of his nose. "Bring as many furs as you can carry," he called down. He was not sure she would follow, but after a moment he saw her head appear in the doorway.

"I think my feet are going to freeze!" she said, emerging through the shutters.

Ologrin spread a couple of the furs on the stones. "Quick. Lie on your back."

"If this is your idea of an amorous repeat…"

"Just lie down!" He quickly positioned himself next to her and enveloped them both in the remaining hides. By squeezing together and not moving, they were just able to create a tiny pocket of warmth.

"What do you see?" Ologrin said.

"Well, there's Ortak," she replied, pointing to the southern star, "and the jewel box, and that's the mountain fox, right?" She pointed to a group of stars straight overhead.

"That's right. Chasing the marmoset, which we can see if we crane our heads backward toward the west."

"It doesn't look like a fox to me."

"Look. Nose, ear, front leg, tail. It's kind of like a fox."

"Where's the back leg?"

"You have to use your imagination."

"My imagination tells me I'm looking at a one-legged fox."

"What else do you see?"

"Well, there's the Sojourner in front of us, about to go behind the mountains," she said.

"Yes. And its crescent edge will get thinner and thinner as it descends, until it is the merest slip just before it sets, as thin as a white hair." He smoothed her hair as she rested her head on his chest.

"Because the Sun is far below the horizon, that is the only part of the Sojourner we can see that is lit by the Sun, correct?"

"That's right," he replied.

"But in fact, much of the other side of the Sojourner is brilliantly lit right now. We just can't see it."

"Exactly!"

At that moment, a bright streak crossed the sky from east to west.

"A cast-off star!" Vireo said. "What do you make of those, master astrolemer?"

"I truly don't know. But as common as they are, they must be a part of the sky's natural order."

"They say Wysel was fascinated with the night skies too. Maybe that's a mosaic trait."

"How come I have never heard more about this person?" Ologrin asked.

"I don't know," Vireo replied, wiggling closer. "Every Polfre child learns who she was. Perhaps she is so well known to us, we forget that others might not know the stories as well."

"So, who was she?"

"As briefly as possible, it's fair to say Wysel created modern Antola. She knew things and built things that had never been seen before. She began work on the castle. She built the trestle lift. For a time, her ability to discover and build new things seemed unlimited."

Ologrin recalled many times that Albrect had suggested they were only now rediscovering the past. "Then something happened, didn't it?"

"Eventually she was opposed by the Polfre elders. They

saw her work as a fundamental violation of our belief in the Rha. They feared she was exploiting the world in ways that could never be repaid."

"You said she was a mosaic. Did the Antolans know that?"

"I don't know. Initially, the Antolans were very supportive of her, because they benefitted the most from her creations. But she saw how the rest of Eidos lived, with their short, ignorant lives filled with hunger and disease and brutal wars with their neighbors, and she began to imagine transforming their lives as well. Supposedly she tried capturing the power of the trestle lift on a much grander scale. Then something terrible happened. People died. And after that, she lost the support of the Antolans as well. They called it sorcery. Eventually, she left Antola and moved into the riverlands, where she began to teach the Eidos to care for themselves. But the Crown feared his own people then just as now, and so he had her imprisoned. And now, many years later, we are just beginning to recover some of her knowledge again, with our own mosaic, which I do not think is a coincidence."

Another streak crossed the sky, surprising Ologrin. Cast-off stars were common, but not such that one expected to see two in the same night.

"Beautiful," Vireo said.

"What finally became of Wysel?"

"Grebe's writings do not tell us. She escaped, some say. After that, no one heard from her again. No one knows what happened to her."

"How old was she, anyway?"

"A good question. My best guess, she was perhaps twelve dozen years old when she was imprisoned. No one knows how long she lived after that."

"Wait. You told me the Polfre rarely live beyond twelve dozen years. And you also said she was not a pure Polfre."

"That's right."

"So, mosaics live as long as the Polfre? Even longer?"

"The only one I know about is Wysel. But yes, it seems possible."

Ologrin felt as if the parapet were suddenly tilting to one side. For his entire life, he had imagined a life like that of the Eidos he so much resembled. Four, perhaps five dozen years to accomplish what he could manage to accomplish. But twelve dozen! Vireo's comments opened dizzying vistas in his mind. He felt like the tiny light of a star, surrounded by the vast blackness of the sky.

Another cast-off streaked across the sky, followed almost immediately by a fourth.

"I didn't realize they were so common," Vireo said. "I should have spent more time gazing at the stars."

"They aren't," Ologrin murmured, as another flashed overhead. They watched quietly, as the occasional streaks became more frequent, until there were two or three occurring simultaneously. Then, suddenly, the entire sky was lit by a huge fireball that seemed to arise from the west and split the sky. Its light was so bright that it cast fleeting shadows as it streaked overhead. Most cast-off stars left streaks like needles slashed across the blackness. This one looked like a flame, Ologrin thought, like a torch whipped overhead, and it left a distinct trail behind it. They watched silently as a flurry of cast-off stars followed, along with several more flaming stars, until they gradually became occasional, and then stopped completely.

"What was that?" Vireo said finally.

"I don't know."

"Well, it's a bad sign, for sure."

"You mean, like from the gods?" Ologrin asked, surprised. "You believe that?"

"No. But we can't have been the only ones who saw it. And many who did will wonder if it is a sign from the gods. And they're going to be asking the master astrolemer for an explanation."

"We can't explain everything. That doesn't automatically make it the work of the gods."

"How high were they?" Vireo asked.

"I was just wondering that," he replied. "Perhaps very high. There was no sound."

"Then perhaps they were seen everywhere," she said.

"Perhaps."

She was silent for several moments, and Ologrin sensed she was unsettled. "The Polfre will take it as a warning," she said finally.

"Of what?" he asked, but she did not reply.

Ologrin stood, wrapping himself in a hide as he did so. He looked out toward the far west. Fire from the sky. And yet there were no orange glows on the horizon. Nothing looked any different than it had before. "I think I want to go inside," he said.

Vireo stood up beside him. "I'm for that. My bottom feels like a block of meat in the cellar."

Ologrin snuck a quick feel and had to agree this was true.

They had not closed the shutters, so Ologrin's cell was hardly warmer than the platform above. He arranged more wood in his hearth, then coaxed the barely glowing embers until he got a lick of flame going once again.

"I have to say, I will be happy when our chambers are ready," Vireo noted. "This solitary life you lead up here is not my idea of comfort." She slid back into her tunic and slippers. "Tomorrow, my love," she said, giving him a quick kiss, and then she was gone down the stairs.

Ologrin sat on his bed, waiting for the room to warm again. He tried to make sense of the streaks in the sky. People would ask, and if he didn't have an explanation, they would invent one for themselves.

"I haven't lived long enough to see everything," he said out loud. How was that for an explanation?

Then he thought of Wysel's story, and the fullness in his

heart was replaced by pangs of loneliness and doubt. He had imagined Vireo living years past his own. But with a single story she had granted him two additional lifetimes, perhaps more. It was anything but comforting. What would the world be like then, far in the gloom of the future, when he finally let it go?

23

"Let's walk," Ologrin said. He and Master Heron stood at the top of the castle steps. The Sun was bright, the sky was clear, and every breath was a lungful of ice. The bare scarab trees cast tangled shadows across the Crown's Walk, and frost still filled the intersecting designs. They descended the steps and headed across the carefully fitted stones. Heron looked like a small blue bear, bundled in her furs. Ologrin towered over her, dressed in a green cloak with a vivid red headwrap. He carried a small satchel filled with things from Heron's chambers. Only a few hardy individuals braved the cold to enjoy the first rays of the Sun warming the Crown's Walk. Ologrin could remember a time, not that many years before, when those he passed glanced at his gray servant's cloak and referred to him as "your grace." Now they just stared.

Fewer than a dozen ships lined the docks. Despite the cold, the water of the bay rarely froze; nonetheless, trade by ship dropped off significantly during the Winter. Sitting in frames atop the docks, two large ships under construction caught their eye immediately. One of them was almost complete. The hull had been waterproofed and painted, and two great masts rose up through a lattice of ropes. The other ship was little more than a completed hull, with its two masts lying alongside in low cradles. Several tiny men could be seen working around both vessels. Weims had pushed the shipwrights hard for the twin masts, arguing that two masts, each with a narrower sail, would be easier to handle and sail faster than the traditional single mast with its huge triangle of cloth. But it was an untested idea. What was clear was that each ship would be large enough and stable enough to carry more than one of Master Albrect's newly cast bronze bombards. For defense, everyone said, but Ologrin had no illusions. They were building weapons of war.

"What do you think of our new ships?" he asked Heron.

She peered across the expanse of the Purse. "Which one is your ship?"

"The *Rayfish*. It's the one at the far end with the blue hull. And it's the Crown's ship, not mine."

"Looks small," she said.

"Like how you look standing next to me?" he asked, but her thoughts were already elsewhere.

"Next Summer, when the ribbon weed grows under the docks again, be sure to tell them to gather it to dry. We can use it all."

"I know," Ologrin replied.

"It's not just the purple dye, you know. The ash from the burned weed is also very useful."

"You have said many times."

"When added to bison tallow..."

"Master Heron, I know how to make soap." Ologrin smiled at the tiny woman. "I think the entire Sophenary has become one great vitachemy experiment."

"My masters would not recognize the place, that I know," she said. "It is hard, sometimes, to see the harmony in what we do."

"It's hard to see the harmony in the dead husks of a mid-Winter field. Yet balance returns."

"That's Vireo speaking through you," she said.

"I consider that a compliment."

The palace gradually rose up before them. Heron stopped to stamp her feet, saying she could hardly wait to get inside and warm them up again. Ologrin, on the other hand, felt his good humor fade and a sense of unease grow as they approached. They passed through the outer gate: little more than an architectural feature, manned by a pair of arms men tasked for the day with looking formal and freezing half to death. The Crown's Walk spread into a broad courtyard, where brown brittle scarab leaves were swirled by the wind. Beyond was another arched gate. Here the arms men were less for show and more serious about their jobs. Heron produced a bronze seal dangling from a broad ribbon. One of the guards took his time examining the seal, then allowed them into a smaller courtyard. Instead of the smooth granite slabs paving the outer courtyard, here they were made of translucent green and pink marble. The stone fascinated Ologrin. It reminded him of staring down into the green, foamy waves as they broke against the side of the *Rayfish*. Temporarily, he forgot his distaste for where he was.

The doors before them were filled with panels of glass, like the tall, multi paned shutters he had seen in Lord Wesse's chambers. Footmen in waist-length cloaks opened them as they approached. Warmth washed over them from an ornate firebox in the far wall. They were led by more footmen down a broad hall filled with light from additional glass set in the ceiling itself. Thick fabrics and accents of silver and gold competed for space on the walls, as if there wasn't enough space for the riches in need of display.

They came to another set of doors, flanked by attendants. A short man stood nearby. Ologrin recognized him immediately and froze. The man took an automatic step back, trying hard not to show his own fear.

"Master Hinford," Heron said. She looked back at Ologrin, then at the man again. "Do you know each other?"

"We've come in contact," Ologrin slowly replied.

"Well. Hinford, I am happy to assist a fellow physionomist. Is the patient inside?"

"He is."

"Thank you, and we won't be requiring your attendance."

The attendants opened the doors, revealing the most remarkable room Ologrin had ever seen. The floor was covered with a thick weaving, white as snow except for a wide gold band that encircled the room, itself embroidered with figures of fish and seashells worked in every color imaginable. Twin hearthgrates with cheery fires occupied the inside corners of the room. The far wall was a series of knee-to-ceiling, glass-filled windows in a great half circle. Ologrin looked out across a grassy patio to a sheer cliff edge. Beyond that was an unimpeded view of the entire lower bay.

Light streamed through the windows. In addition, the room was lit with more glowglobes than Ologrin had ever seen in a single place, all of different sizes. Some, he noticed, were so small he could have held them in his hand. That tiny, they served no purpose other than to show that their owner could afford to own glowglobes simply as toys.

An older man sat propped in a large bed where he could see both the room's entrance and the view from its arc of windows. In comparison to the opulence of the room and the ornate clothing worn by the ubiquitous footmen, he was dressed simply, in a tunic and breeches that reminded Ologrin of his own, except they were made of a soft, supple fabric.

"Ah, Heron...my dear friend! I have been looking... forward to your visit," the man said. He smiled but made no effort to swing himself out of the bed. "It must be...worse than I thought," he continued. "You had to bring...to bring an assistant."

"Supreme Grace, this is Master Ologrin," Heron replied. Ologrin bowed deeply.

"Oh, I know...who this is. Your reputation, sir...had reached me...even if your presence...has not."

"I am deeply honored, Supreme Grace."

"I would prefer...to be called...by my chosen name. Master Ologrin...I am Serenity. Pleased to finally meet you." He held out a hand adorned with a ring the size of a large coin, and despite the humility in his words, Ologrin knew what this meant. He approached, took the hand and kissed the ring. "I am your servant," he said softly.

Ologrin noticed the wheeze in the man's breaths. He watched him purse his lips slightly with every short exhalation. Bare legs poked out below the knee-length breeches. They were swollen and shiny, and a profusion of tiny red spots under the skin coalesced into solid discoloration halfway up his shins. A small open sore on his left shin glistened with beads of fluid. It was in ugly contrast to the pristine sheets of the bed.

"What have you got...for me," Serenity wheezed.

"If I may," Heron said. She motioned for one of the footmen to help Serenity lean forward in the bed. Quickly she stooped behind him and pressed the side of her head to his back. Then, unceremoniously, she pulled the tunic up and stuck her head against his bare skin. She motioned for Ologrin to come over. "Listen," she said.

With some hesitation Ologrin took her place and pressed his ear to the man's mid back. Each time Serenity took a breath he could hear faint crackles, like those from a distant fire.

Heron motioned for Serenity to recline again, which he did gratefully. Heron took Ologrin's hand and together they pressed lightly on the man's chest. She moved their hands further to the left until Ologrin could feel the tap of each heartbeat.

"Your heart is huge," she said.

"Ah, the great heart...of a great leader."

"In this case, bigger isn't better."

"What noxious elixirs...have you made for me today...my dear friend?"

Heron stood and fixed Serenity with her serious look. "Master Ologrin has proposed a new treatment. It has some risk. He proposes that a poison to the heart, if used in a sufficiently tiny dose, may prove to be of benefit. I confess, it speaks to harmony. And we will need a decanter of wine."

Serenity gazed at Ologrin. "You propose...to poison me? Is this...to heal the Crown...or to take it from me?"

Ologrin felt a pang of misgiving. "In truth, sir, I tried a couple of drops on myself. It made my heart pound, but caused no pain..."

But Serenity waved at him to stop. "I trust you...Master. Do as you wish. In the end...we are all nothing...but flesh awaiting the worm."

A footman produced a small table. Ologrin took his supplies out of the satchel. He lit a small candle and set it on the table. He crushed a small amount of hawthorn root in his mortar bowl along with a single leaf of fresh origum, then warmed the bowl over the flame. The smell of herbs filled the room. He unstopped the decanter of wine and added enough to the mortar to dissolve the botanical oils. He poured the wine back into the decanter, withdrew a vial from his satchel, and carefully counted two dozen drops of a dark liquid into the decanter.

"One small cup of wine twice in the daylight and twice at night," Ologrin said, swirling the decanter. "There is enough here for two full days and nights. Then we shall see. And whatever you do, don't drink this entire bottle at once."

Ologrin poured a small amount into a crystal cup, and

Serenity swallowed it in three quick gulps. "It is not an unpleasant taste," he said. "Something you…should aspire to…with your concoctions, Master Heron."

"We shall be back in two days," she replied.

"And then…I should really like…to talk more with your…infamous assistant, Master Heron. But I think…more rest is appropriate…this fine day."

Both Heron and Ologrin bowed. Ologrin collected his things, and one of the footmen showed them out of the room.

"So now you've met him," Heron said. "It wasn't too bad, was it?"

They walked slowly back toward the courtyard entrance. Ologrin admitted to himself he was feeling more at ease.

"He is shorter than I thought," Ologrin said.

"The physionomist must not be intimidated by rank or power. The true rulers of this world are those things we cannot see. Powers of the earth that cause a wound to be infected, or the essences that can either heal or destroy our frail bodies. Those are the real masters."

"Ologrin! Thank you for coming!"

Ologrin turned and saw Terval hurrying down the hall toward them. He grabbed Ologrin quickly around the waist, then slipped his right arm through Ologrin's left.

"Please tell me you are working your magic."

"This is Master Heron," Ologrin said, pointing out his diminutive colleague. "She is the master of physionomy at the Sophenary. I am just here to assist her."

"And did you assist well? How is he?"

"Time will tell us," Heron interrupted. "But his mood was good. He has a strong spirit."

"Why have you been avoiding me?" Terval looked at Ologrin and smiled, but his gaze was unyielding.

"I haven't been avoiding you," Ologrin said. "Darkest Day was barely two passages ago. I was at the Swords for the entire feast." He pointed to his stomach. "I am fatter than ever before."

"But I haven't seen you since then."

"Winter is my time to catch up."

"Join me for evening meals, then. I am just across the Crown's Walk from you. Take a gig. You still have one of the Crown's horses, I believe."

"Breeze is not a carriage horse."

"Beside the point. You know what I mean."

Terval guided them to the far end of the hall, which opened onto a small platform with much the same view that Serenity had in his chambers. The Sun was bright and filled the space, but the air remained cold.

"I'm not avoiding you," Ologrin repeated. "I'm avoiding the palace."

"He's gone," Terval said. "Lord Gerun is now the Lord Coronet. Wesse has not set foot in Antola for over two years."

"But he could. Nothing keeps him from it."

"He is forty leagues from here. That keeps him from it."

"But he could. As long as he is alive, he could walk through those gates."

Terval's voice dropped. "You are free to express your anger, Ologrin. That is more than most people get. But you are not free to choose who the Crown admits into his own house."

"Right. That is why I'm avoiding the palace," Ologrin said sharply. Terval released his arm and turned away.

From where they stood, the two new ships were just visible in the distance, beyond the jumbled rooftops of the Purse. Smoke rose from countless chimneys, forming a thin band of brown air far above them.

"Did you see our ships on the docks on your walk over, Master Heron?" Terval said, walking over to where she stood next to a low marble railing.

"I'm still amazed how something that heavy doesn't sink," she replied.

"Then you should come watch us slide the first one into the water. It's something to see. You think it's about to roll over and head straight for the bottom, but then it bobs up like a fishing float. You will never doubt that they float after seeing that. The first one should be going into the water within the next couple of passages. Ologrin, you are planning to come, correct?"

"So I am told."

"Ologrin only pretends to be uninformed, Master Heron. And if you wait for him to invite you to the launch, it will be a long wait. So, please be my guest. I will send for you. It will be a celebration."

"I look forward to it," Heron said.

"Both will be in the water by the beginning of Summer, and the first one ready to sail. Antola cannot stay hidden in its corner of the world. Every other place awaits. The past cannot hold the future hostage," Terval said, looking directly at Ologrin.

"Master Heron, would you excuse Ologrin and me for a few moments. I need the counsel of the Crown's navigator." He held the door, allowing Heron back into the hall.

"Did you see the lights in the sky?" Terval asked, with sudden urgency.

"I did, as a matter of fact."

"Oh, thank the gods. What were they? What do they mean?"

"I'm not sure they mean anything."

"People are saying that fires filled the sky from one end to the other. How can that not mean anything?"

"That's an exaggeration. It may not have been anything more than very bright cast-off stars."

Terval paced the platform. "Then people will make up their own reasons, and that will be worse. They know that

Serenity is not well. We all know he will be lucky to see next Winter. People will fear the worst."

"I don't know how I can change that."

"Make something up! Reassure people that it is a good sign, not a bad one."

"It's probably not a sign of anything. It is just something that happened," Ologrin said.

"The people will not ignore signs from the sky. They will not wait to see what happens. You are a master astrolemer. You must say something! For me."

"Then…I'll think of something," Ologrin managed.

"But are they a good thing? Say they're good news, and in half a year people won't care. Fail to do so, and it will only grow in their minds until they are convinced the gods have turned against them."

"I don't know," Ologrin insisted, feeling his own anger building. "The reputation of the Sophenary depends on our reliability. I can't just make something up. Vireo wouldn't let me."

"Why are you doing this to me?" Terval said angrily. Ologrin was taken aback by the anguish in the young man's face. "You treat me as if I were responsible for those killings. I was not! I have only championed you and loved you…aren't we friends? This thing I need from you." He suddenly grabbed Ologrin by the wrists. Surprised, Ologrin could not stop the sudden surge he felt through his body. Terval jumped back.

"What was that?" he said.

"I'm sorry," Ologrin said. "You surprised me, that's all."

"Was that some kind of warning?"

"No. Just…a reflex."

Terval crossed his arms and became very quiet. "If you think I'm a fool…"

"Of course not."

"You were my friend, once. I don't know what you are

now." Terval turned toward the door. "It doesn't matter. You still work for the Crown." He pulled the door open and stalked away, leaving Ologrin to find Heron and let himself out.

The morning of the launching dawned gray, but the northeastern winds brought a touch of warmth as well. The hull of the new ship loomed over Ologrin as he walked along the docks, admiring the launching rig. Thirteen woven cables as thick as his forearm led from fittings on the ship's deck to a row of capstans along the docks. Each cable ran through a pair of blocks and was coiled on the ground, enough length for eighteen men per cable when the time came.

Ologrin climbed onto the deck to examine the rigging for the masts. The ship would drop sideways into the water, causing the masts first to bend sideways and then whip back. Some amount of flexibility was expected of a good mast, but a broken mast would be a disaster. He bounced his fist against the newly braided lines, trying to guess how much tension would protect both masts and rig.

By design, the ship had been constructed on one of the widest spans of the docks, right in front of the trestle lift. Ologrin watched the platform, at the top of the Purse, fill with people and then begin to descend. He squinted to see if he could make out the small figure of Vireo. The trestle lift had been transformed into a viewing platform for guests of the Crown. In the middle, sitting in an elaborate chair, splendid in a crimson cloak, was Serenity himself. Their doctored wine had worked better than Ologrin had expected. Serenity's initial complaint of finding himself filling chamber pot after chamber pot with urine had been replaced by the simple joy of being able to walk across the room without gasping for air. He claimed to feel better than he had in a year and wanted to prove it by being seen at the ship's launch.

Chapter 23

No one could remember when Serenity had last been in the Purse. Arms-men lined the route from the palace to the market, then reassembled to line the tunnel between the market and the Purse. Serenity mostly rode, of course, but proudly stepped from his carriage and climbed to his perch on the trestle lift without assistance.

At least three dozen people were on the lift with him. A third of them, Ologrin guessed, were arms men. Terval was among them. Most of the rest were Lords of the Council. He caught a glint of pink and knew it came from the rose-colored, iridescent cloak that Vireo had chosen for the occasion. He smiled. Next to the pink figure was a little ball of blue fur that ensconced Master Heron.

The trestle lift floated down the hill and came to rest at the foot of the docks with a gentle bump. Ologrin could see Terval now, standing near the front of the platform. He was dressed in the blue tunic of the Crown's Guard. Ologrin hurried back down the ladder. His own cloak and headwrap were grimy from days of work, which made him reluctant to approach the trestle lift and its assembly of finely dressed dignitaries.

"Are they ready?"

Ologrin turned. The master shipwright stood with his legs splayed, as sturdy as one of the cradles that supported the ship.

"I suppose," he replied.

"Then I need to get these cables payed out."

The shipwright managed to emit the loudest whistling shriek Ologrin had ever heard. Men assembled and unfurled the ropes. Ologrin found a place behind the central capstan while the shipwright ran up and down the lengths of men, making sure they were in position. From where he stood, Ologrin could just see the front edge of the lift platform. Terval leaned back, made eye contact, and smiled. Ologrin acknowledged him by touching his forehead.

The shipwright returned, swinging a short length of wood like a club. "All set to go," he said. He waved at the trestle lift.

"Supreme Grace; honored guests," Terval began. Ologrin could just make out his voice. "Before you are the greatest ships to ever sail the seas. With them we will sail far from home, go wherever we wish, then return safely again. They will take us anywhere, without fear. With these ships we shall no longer be second to anyone else in establishing trade across all of Lhosa…"

Ologrin marveled at how the ship towered over the docks. Once in the water, a third of it would be hidden beneath. Even so, its bulbous shape and high bow and stern would dwarf other ships along the docks. A simple ramp would no longer do for loading and unloading. Ologrin imagined platforms being built next to the water's edge to match the deck height for a fleet of similar ships. The ships meant more goods, but also more men to move the goods, and more mouths to feed. He wondered how Vireo and Heron would calculate the harmony of what they were observing.

Terval was wrapping up. "With these ships, there is nowhere we cannot go. Long ago, Donal conquered the mountains. Now we conquer the seas!" He reached above his head with hands clasped, waited a moment, and threw his arms apart.

The master shipwright emitted another whistling shriek. "Haul the cables!" he yelled.

The cables leading to the ship grew taught. There was a moment when nothing seemed to happen, then a great creaking groan rumbled along the docks. The men shouted and hauled in unison, and, very gradually, the ship began to tilt slightly toward the docks.

The shipwright ran to the central capstan and shoved the wooden club into a slot made just for it. A nearby dock worker gave it a couple of whacks with a sledge to seat it. At the same time, men along the water side pulled ropes to dislodge support struts on the support cradle. They collapsed, leaving nothing between one side of the ship and the water of the bay.

"Release!" the shipwright yelled. Each team of men eased off and dropped their ropes. The ship moved a fraction toward the water, then stopped. Its entire weight was now being held by the central capstan, which was effectively jammed by the single piece of wood. The ship groaned again, and the club emitted several ominous snaps. The shipwright waved everyone back. Ologrin watched, fascinated, as the club began to bend as it tried, and failed, to support the weight of an entire ship. With a sudden loud CRACK the club burst into splinters. The ship tilted until Ologrin though it might simply tip beyond horizontal and shove the masts into the water. But then it gave way and slid into the bay with an enormous splash that buried half the hull. It bobbed back surprisingly quickly and launched an entire deck's worth of water toward everyone onshore. Ologrin ducked instinctively, but to little avail. An avalanche of ice-cold water fell on him and took his breath away.

There was a moment of silence, except for the sound of water sluicing off the docks and back into the bay. Then a great cheer went up from the dock workers. Ologrin walked toward the trestle lift, fearful of what he might see. Everyone on the platform was cheering as well, and none as enthusiastically as Serenity, who was standing in front of his chair, grinning and with his fist in the air, clearly soaked to the skin.

Terval spread his arms wide. "That completes the launching! There are roaring fires and warm drinks at the Twain Swords. You are all invited." He spied Ologrin walking toward the front of the platform. "And you!" he cried. "You have done enough here. These men know what to do. I expect to see you in warm clothes right away!"

Ologrin stepped onto the platform. "Yes, Serene Lord," he said, smiling.

"Did you plan that last bit?"

Ologrin laughed. "No. I was as surprised as anyone. I think the shipwright may have known. He seemed drier than everyone else, at least."

"You will be at the tavern, right?"

Ologrin bowed. "As ordered, of course. As soon as I find Master Vireo."

Terval slapped him on the back, but Ologrin saw a flicker of disappointment in the young man's face. He scanned the platform and saw the pink of Vireo's cloak partially hidden behind the cluster of guards who had now crowded around Serenity. He walked toward the nearest arms man, who stepped aside without comment.

"Spectacular, Master Ologrin!" Serenity said. "You seem to have endless talents. Healing the sick, building ships. Is there anything you cannot do?" Serenity's teeth were chattering, even though the arms men had produced furs from somewhere and had them mounded over the man.

"I think the master shipwright would take exception if I claimed credit for any of it," Ologrin replied. Vireo made her way around the guards to stand next to him. He touched her lightly on the elbow, not sure what the protocol was for a situation like this.

"Dodecant, do you know Master Ologrin?" Serenity said.

"Yes I do, Supreme Grace."

"He is a very clever man. He treats me with poison, and thus makes me feel better than I have felt since last Summer." The man said this loud enough for all the guards to hear. Ologrin winced inside. "Keep him close, I would say."

"I shall," Vireo said.

"And I think I had better return to the palace, before I chatter my teeth out of my jaws!"

"Off the platform unless you're returning to the city!" one of the arms men bellowed.

Ologrin looked at Vireo. "Are you coming with me to the

Twain Swords? It is the fanciest tavern you will ever set foot in."

"I think Master Heron is returning with Serenity to the palace. Perhaps I ought to stay with her."

"Master Heron needs no help." Ologrin gently guided Vireo to the edge of the platform. "And both of us will freeze if we don't get someplace warm, and soon."

They stepped down and joined the group gathering around Terval in front of the ship, that now sat impressively tall in the water. Before long a gentle rumble informed them that the trestle lift was on its way to the top of the Purse. Terval waved for the group to follow him, and he headed up into the jumble of buildings. The tavern was not far, and Ologrin eagerly anticipated its warm embrace.

They turned a familiar corner to see the windows of the tavern in front of them, bright and cheery in contrast to the cloudy skies. The Twain Swords was the place where Ologrin had found acclaim all on his own. He was proud of that and wanted Vireo to experience it. Fires blazed in hearthgrates at opposite sides of the long room. He claimed a table close enough to one of the fires to allow them to remove their shoes and warm their feet directly on the toasty hearth stones.

Fortunately for both, their cloaks had provided some protection from being completely drenched. They removed them and sat where they could see the rest of the room. Mugs of mulled wine and bowls of soup were brought to their table unbidden. Other than an itchiness under his headwrap, Ologrin felt as comfortable and as at peace as he had in a long time.

"You should remove that. Let your hair dry out," Vireo said.

"No. Not here."

"You can't keep them hidden forever, Ologrin."

"Now is not the time."

"Embrace who you are, regardless of the opinions of others."

"I know. I will. But not yet."

Before long, the tavern was filled with happy voices and laughter. The light, singing sound of a pair of bow-harps mingled with the voices. The players were experts. Terval had everything at hand for every occasion, it seemed. If food, warmth, and music were suddenly needed, he had only to wave his arm and they appeared. On a couple of occasions, Terval glanced their direction, but never came over to talk. Pairs were evident throughout the room, mostly man and woman, but not all.

Growing up in Halrin's Spur, the closest Ologrin could recall to a full-blown attraction had been the feeling he had for Pipit from Southwatch. But she was gone; a victim, he suspected, of the same marauders who had killed Tobin and Calus and wiped out Halrin's Spur. There had been plenty of sexual pairing at the School for Servants, but not for him. Too busy studying, he had told himself at the time, but now recognized it as more evidence he had been in the wrong place.

Now, it seemed, he had two choices. Terval's interest was more than friendship, that was clear. If he accepted, it came with nothing less than a key to the palace. He enjoyed Terval's company; the man was smart and skillful, and genuinely kind, an uncommon palace trait. But Ologrin could only pretend to have an intimate interest. How unsatisfying would that ultimately be? How long would it last?

He glanced at Vireo. She had her eyes closed, and one foot moved slightly in time with the music. She had laid claim to him as soon as she had seen him. He was now ready to turn that claim into a commitment. She was the only woman who had ever shared his bed. There never had been any question of who he would choose. The Sophenary was his home. If he spent the rest of a long life there, at Vireo's side, then he would be happy. He had managed to taste gods and kingdoms and had concluded they were for others.

He felt Vireo slip her arm through his. "Terval told me to thank you for your announcement regarding the cast-off stars," she said.

"I meant it when I announced they don't represent any ill-will from the gods. I was afraid he would want me to say more, though."

"The people of the city seem calm. He said that's all he wanted."

"Good," he said, and she snuggled against him. "Good," he said again, at peace in the world.

There were several members of the Crown's Guard in the tavern, and many of them appeared to be enjoying themselves as much as anyone else. So Ologrin initially thought nothing of the appearance of four more entering together, scanning the room, and then moving in Terval's general direction. But then he looked outside and noticed a half-dozen arms men with weapons drawn. A carriage pulled up, flanked by a pair of lance men on warhorses. He sat up, fully alert.

"Something is happening," he said quietly to Vireo.

The guards clustered around Terval and seemed to have a quick conversation with him. He turned and hurried toward door. Ologrin could see a deeply troubled look on Terval's face, but he did not seem to be going by force. All except one of the arms men followed him out. Ologrin watched Terval climb into the carriage. The remaining arms man was watching, too, and then turned to address the room.

"The Crown speaks!" he cried. He had to say it two more times to bring the room to silence. "His Supreme Grace Serenity the Seventh has passed this life and joined his ancestors at the table of the gods. His Supreme Grace Terval, son of Serenity, accepts your oaths of loyalty and service. Heed the word of the Crown!"

The arms man walked out quickly as the carriage horses bolted up the street.

There was a moment of stunned silence, followed by an explosion of voices. One of the Crown's guards positioned himself at the front door and appeared to be planning on blocking it.

"Do you know a back way out of this place?" Vireo whispered urgently. Ologrin nodded and slowly slid from his chair. Vireo immediately went a different direction. He heard her loudly ask a stranger to explain what was going on. He moved to the back of the room, where he spied a servant he knew well from previous visits. "I'm going back where it's quiet," he mouthed to the servant, who smiled and nodded. He slipped through the door into Terval's private chambers. The room was empty. Vireo appeared only a few moments behind him.

"Did you have trouble?" he asked.

"No one saw me," she said. "Where do we go?"

Ologrin led them to a servant's entrance. They popped out into a small alley. Vireo immediately took over and they zigzagged back down to the docks, only a few gross hands north of the trestle lift. Vireo stopped at a small shop, after which they had two stocky Polfre bodyguards moving loosely with them as they continued to hurry for the castle. As far as Ologrin could tell, it was business as usual in the Purse. But news would flow like a river overrunning its banks, slipping around and possibly ahead of them. By nightfall, Ologrin imagined most of the city would know that something momentous had happened, even if no one knew what. That, of course, would be the most dangerous time.

"We are leaving Heron back at the palace," Ologrin said.

"I know. But I have to tell the Sophenary. If Heron is in trouble, we certainly aren't going to storm the palace to save her."

Until that moment, Ologrin had not imagined Heron

being at risk. But, of course, they had no idea what had happened. Perhaps there had been an attack in the tunnel or at the palace. Perhaps Serenity had fallen suddenly and gravely ill, and for whatever reason, Heron was assigned the blame. He was painfully aware of how they had continued to refer to Serenity's medicated wine as "poison." Too many ears had heard what they did not understand, he thought, and smiled grimly. Moments of crisis taught the best lessons.

For the most part, their bodyguards slipped them through the Purse unseen. If anyone got a second glance, it was Ologrin. He attributed that to his height until he noticed, as they were climbing Purse stairs to the back of the castle, that he had lost his headwrap.

Vireo sent a red collar to assemble the faculty. Ologrin hurried through the castle to set whatever limited defenses they had. Doors were barred; windows near the ground were shuttered. He checked on the husbandry yard. Breeze stamped and snorted upon seeing him; the horse seemed to sense something was afoot. He returned to Vireo's chambers, where she was telling the rest of the faculty what little they knew. Then they positioned themselves where they could see the length of Crown's Walk and waited.

The cloud cover broke up in time to admit late-day, slanting rays onto the city. The terraces seemed to glow with patches of golden light. Just before Sunset, a one-horse gig, accompanied by an arms man on a warhorse, slowly traversed the length of the Crown's Walk and stopped in front of the castle steps. A small figure, clad in blue furs, climbed out of the gig and ascended the stairs.

"It was a classic apoplexy of the heart," Heron said, as soon as she came through the doors. "He suddenly began complaining that his chest was being crushed and that he could not breathe. Even the guards knew what it was. He lost consciousness in the tunnel. They hurried him to the palace, but by that time there was no way to revive him. I confess I'm glad the cause was obvious. I feared someone might blame us for our use of foxglove."

"We worried about the same thing," Vireo replied.

"I was a bit afraid there might be fighting. A shift of power, you know. But before I left, young Terval asked me to see him. He was in the Crown's council chamber. I told him his father did not suffer much. It's what you always should say, of course."

Several of the faculty seemed to relax. Ologrin, however, did not. He slipped out and then up the stairs to his parapet. The clouds had fully cleared, and early evening stars dotted the sky. The cast-off stars had been coincidental, he knew, but coincidences were the lifeblood of myths. He feared Terval would never trust him again. He half-expected another blaze of stars to fly overhead, simply to mock him.

"There are no gods," he said out loud, willing them to prove him wrong. He turned slowly from the west to the south, and then to the east, looking out across the still blackness of Gosper Bay. A flickering red reflection caused him to look up. There, high in the eastern sky, the Red Eye of Ruhax was rising, calling his bluff.

24

Antola seemed to take a big breath, hold it, and then, as nothing else happened, exhale slowly with relief. Serenity the Seventh's death was officially announced from the palace the next day. The day following that dawned clear and cold, another Winter day. Shops remained open, goods moved up from the docks, and people talked quietly to those they trusted the most. Albrect's workers arrived for work at the chimneys the same as they had the day before. The Crown's Guard were everywhere—in the shops, on the streets—but seemed to go about their normal business. However, they wore the hoods of their cloaks up, signifying respect for Serenity's death. Terval was in mourning, as everyone could plainly see, with his blue cloak and hood drawn about his face. He was spotted everywhere up and down the terraces, making official visits, accompanied by many members of the guard. The message was clear: Terval was now the Crown and had the full support of the Crown's Guard. The people were expected to get in line.

For the next four days, a superficial sense of normalcy filled the Sophenary. Ologrin went back to his own forges in the chimneys. Then a message arrived from the palace. The Lord Coronet would be visiting the Sophenary with an announcement. All faculty were expected to attend. Not asked; "expected." That message was clear as well: The Crown was asserting its authority over the Sophenary as much as any other part of the city.

The entire faculty were too large a group to easily fit in Vireo's chambers. By contrast, standing around in the great space of the Collegarum, they looked like straggling wayfarers who had wandered in and lost their way. There were no hearths in the room, so despite the bright day and many windows, it was cold, and they were dressed accordingly. An arms-captain arrived late morning to inform them that the Lord Coronet would be arriving shortly thereafter. Nonetheless, midday came and went before a larger procession was spied making its way slowly across the Crown's Walk. Four horsemen rode next to a large carriage, itself pulled by two additional horses, while two lance men trotted alongside. A smallish man stepped delicately from the carriage and was quickly surrounded by the arms men as he walked up the steps of the castle, then disappeared from view.

"Everyone take a seat. They will be here momentarily." Master Crake stood on the dais and tapped his walking stick on the platform, gaining their attention. Ologrin, along with the rest of the faculty, found seats near the front. Vireo was meeting with the Lord Coronet in her chambers, after which she would escort him to the Collegarum to meet with the rest of the faculty. Ologrin thought it was a lot of fuss to deliver a message of continuity. The Sophenary supported the Crown, while the Crown appreciated its service. Such formalities kept the axles greased, he supposed.

The doors behind the dais opened, and Lord Gerun appeared, trailed by the pair of lance-men. Ologrin was relieved to see that Gerun was still Lord Coronet. He had been worried that Lord Wesse might somehow re-appear, despite Terval's repeated assurances that Wesse was a long way away and far from having any direct influence. Perhaps, in time, Terval would find his own Lord Coronet. In the meantime, asking his father's Coronet to remain in the office was a comforting sign of stability.

Vireo entered the room last. Ologrin immediately felt she was troubled. His sense of comfort vanished. She stepped to one side. Gerun stood in the middle of the dais and looked out over their relatively small numbers. To an outsider, Ologrin imagined they looked like a surprisingly small group to oversee such an imposing structure. The Lord Coronet stood for a moment, then gave a sideward glance toward Vireo and coughed. She shook her head a bit and stepped forward. Ordinarily she was a master of protocol. Something was definitely amiss.

"Fellow faculty, thank you for your attention," she said. "It is our distinct honor to host a distinguished representative of the Crown today. May I present to you the Lord Coronet of the Crown and Commander of the Crown's Council, Lord Gerun."

This seemed to satisfy the man, who took a step forward himself and made an elaborate display of unfurling a roll he had been carrying under one arm.

"Distinguished faculty of the Sophenary," he began. "Though preoccupied with mourning over the death of his father, and busy with the many details of the domain, His Supreme Grace Terval sends his greetings and a message of good will. The gods have smiled upon him and given their blessings. His Supreme Grace is confident of your loyalty as well, to him personally and to all representatives of the Crown. He assures you that the affairs of the domain continue to be in order, and he is confident of the loyalty of all subjects of the Crown."

Gerun took another step forward, as if to signify that the

most important part of his message had arrived. "His Supreme Grace wishes to announce those who will serve with him on the Crown's council. I, Lord Gerun, will remain Lord Coronet, and those on the Council will answer to me. Lord Coltes will remain Lord Commander of the Guard. Lord Geldes will remain Lord Judge. Lord Austerian of Madros has been summoned and will assume duties as Lord Mercantile. Lord Vrenchew has accepted the summons to become Lord Affairs. Servant Priest Moran will become Lord Priest of the Panthea…"

Ologrin snapped his head up. His former teacher had certainly been a rising star in the School for Servants, but he had to be leaping over many individuals with greater seniority to be named Lord Priest. Ologrin wondered at the connections that existed without his knowledge. Was this a major shake-up of the School for Servants? Did Terval know Moran personally? His head was distracted with so many questions that he almost missed Gerun's next announcement.

"His Supreme Grace has determined that the future not only includes our domain over land, but of the sea as well. A new position shall be added to the Crown's Council. Master Ologrin of the Sophenary has been named Lord Commander of the Fleet."

Ologrin could not figure out what disoriented him more, the announcement or the cheer that was raised by the rest of the faculty. He looked up to see Lord Gerun staring at the room with an impatient look on his face. Sensing the same thing, Master Crake tapped his stick on the dais again.

"And finally," Gerun said, waiting for the group to quiet down. "And finally! His Supreme Grace is pleased to announce that Master Albrect has been appointed to the position of Dodecant of the Sophenary."

The room fell silent. Ologrin looked at Vireo, who seemed to be shaking slightly. "No," he said. He scanned the room until he saw Albrect, who seemed just as surprised as everyone else.

"The Dodecant is elected by the faculty!" It was Heron, whose voice rose loud and clear. But Gerun appeared to be prepared for this.

"His Supreme Grace appreciates the faculty's role in advising him on this position, but of course he has the right to appoint the members to his own council."

"Then the Dodecant won't be on the council!" Heron shot back.

Ologrin began to move toward Vireo on the dais. "No," he said more loudly. He reached the first step, but as he did, both lance men stepped forward and lowered their lances, pointing in Ologrin's direction. Ologrin continued to move forward. One of the lance men flipped his lance around and aimed the butt end in Ologrin's direction. As Ologrin stepped onto the dais, he jabbed it forward into Ologrin's chest.

There was a spectacular flash and crack, and brilliant light seemed to jump the length of the lance. The flash caused Ologrin to stagger backward, but threw the lance man to the floor. The lance clattered away. The second lance man leveled his weapon at Ologrin.

"No!" Ologrin repeated, raising his hands.

"Stop! That's enough!" Vireo cried. Gerun had already retreated several steps.

Master Crake stepped forward quickly. "Lord Gerun, thank you for your gracious visit. Please convey our condolences to his Supreme Grace." He waved toward the back door, but Gerun was already most of the way there. Crake leaned over the fallen lance man and offered him a hand up. The man wore a bewildered look that was rapidly turning to anger.

"You stabbed him, remember?" Crake said to the man, pointing him toward the door.

. . .

Without having to be told, most of the faculty made their way to Vireo's chambers. Ologrin stood near one of the tall windows, arms folded tightly across his chest. Vireo and Albrect entered last, together.

"He did not know!" Vireo said, as the assembled group moved toward Albrect. "No one knew. I did not know until Lord Gerun told me, just before we walked over to the Collegarum."

"They have no right!" Heron cried, and she was joined by a chorus of agreement.

"Listen," Vireo said. "Listen to me! I agreed to step down. The Crown's relationship to the Sophenary is changing. I am no longer the person for that change."

Heron's voice remained strong and clear. "The faculty have always chosen their Dodecant. If Terval doesn't want the Dodecant on the Crown's Council, that's his business, but that doesn't give him the right to choose who the Dodecant is."

"Then who would you elect?"

"You are our Dodecant."

"No," Vireo said. "I am done. I am resigning, and I mean it. So, who are your choices? Heron? Do you wish to be Dodecant?"

"Don't be ridiculous," Heron said.

"Why not? Physionomist to the Crown; what better credential is there than that? Master Crake, you have served in my place. Do you wish to be Dodecant?"

Crake slowly cleared his throat. "To be honest, I found the job tedious in the extreme."

"Master Albrect..." Vireo began.

"I knew nothing about this! I am perfectly happy in my work, and I'm perfectly happy with you as our Dodecant."

"Your work has brought new importance to the relationship between the Crown and the Sophenary. Your work has the potential to improve the lives of people throughout the realm. So, who better? And I call the vote now. All who would see Albrect serve as their new Dodecant, please kneel in respect."

Slowly, everyone except Albrect sank to one knee. He gazed about the room.

"I never wished…" he began, then was choked by emotion.

Vireo held both of her hands out, palms up. Everyone in the room did the same. "Be one with the world," she said.

Crake stepped forward and grabbed Albrect's wrists in the Eidos way. That seemed to break the mood, and the room was suddenly loud with the voices of those who felt they had just sidestepped a disaster. Vireo slipped around the room to where Ologrin stood next to the window.

"No one has congratulated you yet," she said.

"Me? For what?"

"Lord Commander of the Fleet."

Ologrin made a dismissive wave. "I won't do it."

"Of course you will do it. It's a wonderful opportunity."

"He's trying to punish me! Can't you see that? What good reason does he have for trying to get rid of you as Dodecant now, other than to make the point that he is in charge? And now he plans to force me to be at sea, away from you for weeks at a time. He is using his power to soothe his jealousy. Isn't that what they all do, once they get in power: use it for their own personal gain?"

"But you cannot deny he has the power. There has been no sign that the Crown's Guard will move against him. He is the next ruler of Antola. That's a lot of power to resist."

"The gods have smiled on him," Ologrin said, sarcastically. "He presumes to tell the stars what they should do for him."

"I had already been thinking about when I would step down as Dodecant," she said.

"But not like this. He's making the decision for you."

Vireo studied Ologrin. Like all Polfre, she found comfort in the genuinely luminous pupils of her people. He knew it was harder for her to read him through his dark eyes.

"I think you are less concerned with the decision for me to step down than with the fact that it is Terval making it," she said.

"I don't trust his purpose."

"He is the Crown. His purpose is whatever he chooses it to be."

"And why is that? Surely you don't agree that one man should have all that power. Where is the Rha in that?"

Vireo stepped closer and spoke more softly. "Part of understanding the world is knowing what you cannot change and doing your best with what you can. I will still be here. I can start teaching physionomy again. Heron needs an assistant, and you keep finding ways to avoid it. You could do much with this opportunity. Don't refuse it just because you question the motives behind the offer. Besides, Albrect won't want to serve long. In a few years, you will be the obvious choice for Dodecant." She slid her arm around his waist. "We will still have our life together. And what is this under your tunic?"

Ologrin felt himself redden. He turned so no one in the room could easily see, then pulled up the tunic to reveal a tight-fitting leather corset next to his skin. Ribs of a stiff material had been sewn into long, curving pockets along each side, making it appear as if the corset was wrapped around the bones in his chest.

"So, this is what you've been working on. And I'm guessing this explains the lightning show in the Collegarum, too. How many of these…ribs are there?"

"Six on each side."

She inhaled quickly. "Ologrin, do you know what you're

doing? You have ten times more tanjium next to your body than any Polfre would allow. The energy in that lightning bolt didn't just come from the air, it came from you too."

"Believe me, I can feel where it came from."

"If he had stabbed you with the blade instead of the handle, he might have ended up on the ground, but you would still have a hole in your chest. You're not invincible."

"I don't pretend that I am."

"You have no idea what the long-term effects of this might be. No Polfre would subject themselves to this risk."

"But I am not just Polfre, am I? People have made that clear. You say I am something special; they say I am something terrible. I'm the only one who can ultimately know who or what I am."

"Why would you hide this from me?"

Ologrin had asked himself the same question. For many passages, as he had crafted the corset, he had delayed telling her, first telling himself it was to be a surprise, then admitting to himself he feared her response: that she would tell him no; that she would tell him to put it away, like Tobin telling him to hide the herding staff. In the end, he knew it was simply because he could, because he could wear it and no one else could. If he was going to be unique, then it would be on his terms, not the terms of others.

Vireo ran her hand lightly along one of the ribs. "I can feel it. Remember when I said you were a fire, Ologrin? Now I can feel it as well." She pressed both hands against his chest, and he immediately felt the heat, as if her hands had been stones heating in the hearthgrate. The heat grew quickly into a pain filling his chest. He gasped, and she pulled her hands away. "I can use your fire against you. Near the right Polfre, this thing is not only a danger to them, but to you as well."

"It is not a weapon. It's for protection," he said, knowing it wasn't the full truth.

"Then I only ask you not wear it when we are together. You don't need protection from me."

He looked at her hands. Her fingertips were fiery red. "You're going to have blisters."

"Let's find Albrect. I'm sure he still feels terrible. The two of you have a lot to celebrate, and a lot to discuss."

25

The skies clouded over again, and days continued to grow colder. For the first time in memory, ice began to surround the ships at the docks and stretch out into the bay. At the Sophenary, less wood was being sent to the charcoaleries, while more was being used simply to keep the many hearthgrates warm.

At first, little seemed to change. But then Vireo began meeting more often with Albrect, meetings Ologrin was not invited to attend. And she was spending more time in the library but had not confided her interests to him. He became restless. The clouds prevented any meaningful observations, he needed new projects for his metal works, and there was nothing to be done with his inherited fleet until the days warmed and the ice broke.

"I am going to the flats," he announced one day to Vireo. "No one will know."

"Everyone will know," she said, as she packed away things from the table in her chambers. "The Crown's Council has repeatedly said they will consider it a provocation if you go down there. The guards at the gate will report it before you are halfway down the Repose Road."

"I'm on the Crown's Council now. I give myself permission."

"Ologrin…"

"I'm a prisoner in the city! This isn't right. I'm not the one who slaughtered grosses of innocent people; they are. Why should I be the one punished?"

"Why are we having this conversation?" Vireo said, and there was genuine irritation in her voice. "Tell me, Ologrin, are you the god of the bisonherders?"

"No, of course not."

"Then why would you do anything to strengthen that belief? Every time they see you, the myth around you grows. And what good will come of it?" She picked up a glowglobe and gave it a shake; it flickered into a warm white light.

Ologrin was temporarily distracted. The workings of glowglobes remained one of the secrets the Polfre refused to share. Dissecting one was high on his project list, but he would have to obtain one first, preferably without Vireo or any of the other Polfre finding out. He had already decided that, among the payments he planned to extract from Terval for naming him Lord of the Fleet, a glowglobe was on the list.

"And you're not a prisoner," she continued. "You can take a ship anywhere you want, anytime you choose. That makes you freer than most of us."

"When are you heading for the Lake of Skies?" he asked.

"I haven't said I'm going."

"We both know you're going. Ever since we saw those cast-off stars, you've fretted about how the Polfre in your homeland are going to respond. You're afraid of what they might do." He leaned on the table. "I told you, I want to go with you. I want us to go together. But I have these two new ships to think of. It will likely be Harvest before I can get away. Next Winter. I'm asking you, can you wait until next Winter?"

Vireo busied herself with the contents of a set of storage boards and did not answer.

"No answer is sometimes answer enough," he said, leaving for his tower cell. And despite having given himself permission, Ologrin stayed out of the flats.

The palace announced that the time of mourning would conclude with the end of Winter. Terval's incarnation as Serenity the Eighth would occur on the first day of Summer. Passages came and went, but the weather did not improve, and the bay remained frozen. Snow fell in Antola for the first time in a generation, and people could not decide if they were delighted or disturbed. There were days where the cloud cover was so thick that lamps had to remain lit day and night. Merchants grumbled about their excessive use of oil.

With barely three passages remaining until the end of Winter, the weather warmed enough for the ice around the docks to break up. But tree branches remained bare. Neither the Sojourner nor the Sun had been seen for many days in a row. Every previous year, as far back as people could imagine, the scarab trees along the Crown's Walk bloomed near the first day of Summer. As that day approached, the flowers still showed no sign of emerging from their tight buds.

Otherwise, the business of Antola and the Sophenary seemed to go on as before. Albrect was a poor student for the affairs of the Sophenary, Vireo discovered, as his mind was preoccupied with the chimney works. Master Crake resigned himself to an enlarged administrative role. Ologrin prowled the Castle, looking in on everyone and getting very little done himself. He had not fired up his own forges for days. Finally, with the incarnation only three days away, he sent word to the castle, requesting a meeting with the new Crown. The affirmative reply came back almost immediately.

He was admitted to the palace without difficulty and was

ushered to a location he had not seen before. The room he entered was large but low-ceilinged. Terval sat at a table covered with parchments and rolls. Lord Gerun stood at his shoulder. The room included several other small tables, each with a single chair, arranged in a semicircle in front of the larger table. Terval stood and smiled as Ologrin entered, which made Ologrin smile as well.

"You look well, Terval…"

"You may address the Crown as his Supreme Grace," Lord Gerun intoned. "It is appropriate to uncover your head in his private presence."

"Supreme Grace," Ologrin said. He pulled back his hood, revealing a carefully applied headwrap. "Thank you for seeing me."

"Master Ologrin," Terval said. "It seems almost every day you have a new surprise for me. Now I hear you are besting arms men with bolts of lightning."

"That was not my intent. The man struck me without warning."

"Should I be concerned for myself?"

Ologrin was taken aback. "Are you worried that I am a threat to you?"

"No, of course not," Terval said, stepping closer. "Though I can't help but wonder what would have happened to that man had you actually intended to harm him. But I am glad you came. I have questions for you. This lingering cold weather: it is one more thing that seems to accompany my father's death. You're convinced that the fiery stars had nothing to do with it?"

"Supreme Grace, I don't know."

"And yet you are completely convinced they are not an omen from the gods."

"Those are two different things. The latter gives them agency, makes them the conscious work of the gods. The former does not require intent, any more than a storm has the intent to blow over trees."

Terval paused. "That seems intentionally difficult to understand."

"Not at all…"

Terval shook his head. "It doesn't matter. You had something to see me about?"

"Supreme Grace, I respectfully ask you to consider someone more qualified to be Lord Commander of the Fleet."

"More qualified? You invented the navigation tables. That would seem to qualify you very well. Who else would you recommend?"

"Captain Weims, for one. He has far, far greater knowledge of the sea that I will ever have."

"But I could not care less what Captain Weims thinks or does. You, however, are someone whose thoughts are continuously surprising and whose actions bear close observation, as we have recently seen. I want you where I can see you, my friend Ologrin."

"I had great respect for your father. I have great respect for you. I only want to serve you through my work at the Sophenary. My desire is simple."

Terval waved toward the cloth on Ologrin's head. "Oh, I believe you intend that, but you can't even uncover your head as a show of respect without complicating it in your own unique way. None of your desires are simple, Master Ologrin."

Gerun stepped forward, clearing his throat loudly. "The incarnation will be held in the High Altarnary of the School for Servants. Please be prepared. And you are now dismissed, as his Supreme Grace has many other matters to attend to."

Ologrin felt bewildered. He had not had a chance to make his best argument, he thought. He looked at Terval, who looked back, and for a moment Ologrin saw Terval's face, full of hope and emotion. But then the face of the Crown returned. Ologrin turned and left the room, followed out by Lord Gerun.

Rain fell steadily for the next two days and seemed certain to fall on the day of the incarnation as well, but the clouds began to lift that morning.

"The people love a coincidence," Ologrin said to Albrect as they walked toward the High Altarnary. None of the remaining Sophenary faculty had chosen to attend. "And when his chronicle is written, a cloudy day will be transformed into one where the Sun broke through the clouds and shone on Serenity alone, right at the moment of his incarnation."

"But the ceremony is inside the Altarnary. The Sun can't reach him there," Albrect said.

"It could through the oculus. Antiquarians will move the Sun into the other half of the sky if it suits their story."

They walked down a broad set of steps to the ninth terrace. Arms men were present in groups of two or three. Many of them were mercenary from outside the city walls. As they reached the steps to the eighth terrace, they could see the number of arms men increased near the School for Servants. Several horsemen were also present. The school's carefully tended gardens and paths were being trampled into mud. Ologrin had not been on the grounds of the school in over ten years. He was glad for the hoods they wore in mourning; he did not care to meet anyone from his past life.

Closer to the building, they encountered members of the Crown's Guard, who recognized Ologrin and directed them both toward a familiar back entrance to the Altarnary. Ologrin thought the building was not quite as grand as he had imagined when he had been a student. He noticed the wear, the grime, and for the first time the unrepaired chips in the great columns holding up the collar and dome. What he had thought was marble was in fact only painted plaster hiding rough stonework underneath.

Lord Gerun intercepted them. "Members of the Crown's Council will file in from behind and sit in front, facing the altar. After his Supreme Grace receives the Crown, he will call out the names of each member of the Council. You are to step forward and kneel at his feet, and only at that moment lower your hood, signifying that the time of mourning is over and you recognize his Supreme Grace in his new incarnation. After that, you will return to your seat. And after he leaves by the grand entrance, you will follow. It's very simple."

Ologrin and the remaining members of the Council waited in one of the Winks while the Altar room filled. Ologrin had been imagining the events to follow, and the thoughts filled him with disquiet. When their time came and they filed out, he noticed the building was jammed with people. Considering the number of priests and members of the palace household present, there were only limited spaces remaining for the most wealthy and important members of Antolan society. The gardens had been filled with arms men. That left little room for ordinary Antolans, whom Ologrin imagined were watching from higher terraces or rooftops of the terrace below.

They stood before their seats, facing the altar. A platform had been built around it, level with the altar top, bearing a single seat embellished in gold. He heard orders barked outside, followed by a massive noise from the crowd that seemed to start in the distance and grow into a continuous cheer. From behind him the Crown's Guard came to attention, and then the altar room itself erupted into a deafening cheer as Terval strode into the building. He continued to wear the blue cloak signifying his membership in the Crown's Guard; he would trade it for the crimson cloak of the Crown during the ceremony itself.

Terval ascended the steps and sat on the seat, and then the

members of the Council sat as well. Aside from Terval, the eight members of the Council were the only ones with seats. A ninth seat remained empty, reserved for the Lord Governor of Madros. Ologrin was happy to see the chair remained empty. He did not have to worry about how he might have behaved had he been seated next to Lord Wesse.

Moran rose from his seat and ascended the platform. As he did so, Terval knelt in front of the golden seat.

"In the beginning of time, Malach stood where we stand now," Moran said. "He looked across the land and decided this was the place for his people. Many years later, yet still long ago, he brought Donal and his children out of the wilderness to this place, which was ours, and has been ours ever since. Fifteen dozen and eight years ago, Donal's descendant Gorval reaffirmed the family of the gods, and Malach renamed him Serenity. Today, the eighth incarnation of Serenity receives the Crown, and continues unbroken our rightful inheritance from Donal, and from the gods."

Moran turned to one side. An acolyte from the school ascended the platform bearing a glittering gold crown resting on a pillow. Moran raised the crown for everyone to see. In addition to a thick gold circle, silver and gold branches swept back from the center to either side, crafted to look like Scarab trees in full bloom.

Moran stood in front of Terval. "Terval, son of Vemal, the gods have chosen you as the incarnation of Serenity, to maintain the nobility of Donal, and to rule all the land in their name. Will you accept their grace?"

Terval's voice was clear. "I will."

Moran placed the crown on Terval's head. "Serenity you have become. Arise, our lord and servant. May you bring us strength and prosperity."

The room erupted in cheers. Moran stepped to one side again. With dread fascination, Ologrin watched two more acolytes ascend the platform. One held the bowl he himself had held his last time in the building, while the other held the silver dagger of the Oblation. Moran dipped his hands in the bowl. Ologrin wondered for a moment if they would come out covered in blood. Moran removed his hands, shook off the water, and took the blade. He stepped in front of Terval once again, then offered the dagger hilt-first. Serenity stood while Moran knelt on one knee. Terval touched the point of the dagger to the hollow between his neck and his sternum.

"Moran, Priest of the Panthea, you are named Lord Priest. Will you provide true counsel to the Crown, on threat of banishment or death?"

At last Moran pulled the hood back from his head. "I will," he replied.

Ologrin closed his eyes and concentrated, while Moran stepped to one side and Lord Gerun stepped onto the platform to go through the same brief ceremony. For three days, Ologrin had pondered the fact that his own moment of revelation was about to occur, but he had not expected it to occur at the point of a blade. He breathed deeply and worked to calm his heart. Lord Vrenchew, the new Lord Affairs, and Lord Geldes, who was continuing as the Lord Judge, were called and named. Ologrin tried to focus his mind elsewhere. He tried to rise above the crowd and watch the ceremony from overhead; perhaps find greater interest in the passing of a bird or movement of the clouds. Lord Austerian, the Lord Mercantile, and Lord Coltes, the Lord Commander of the Guard, were called up. Then Albrect. Try as he might, Ologrin could not separate himself from the moment. It was his turn. He ascended the platform and knelt on his left knee, looking up at the face of his former student.

"Ologrin, master of astrolemy and vitachemy, you are named Lord Commander of the Fleet." He felt the point of the dagger press lightly against the base of his neck. Ologrin's corset began to tingle. "Will you provide true counsel to the Crown, on threat of banishment or death?" Then Terval pushed the blade harder, and Ologrin was afraid it would draw blood. The tingling in the corset turned to fire. Ologrin desperately willed the energy to stay within his body, but it seemed eager to betray him and surge through the dagger.

"I will," Ologrin said. He paused, one last moment of obscurity, then pulled back his hood.

The gasp started with the members of the Council themselves before spreading quickly to the back of the Altar room. As ordered, he had done away with the headwrap. Erupting from each side of his forehead, a pair of golden, gleaming horns swept back to the tips of his ears, mocking the artificial glitter of Serenity's own headpiece. Terval let the dagger drop to his side. Ologrin kept his head down, refusing to make eye contact with anyone in the room as he returned to his seat. That, of course, only made his horns easier for everyone to see.

He turned and looked up at Terval. Scarlet colored the man's cheeks, but he gazed straight ahead, past the crowd and out through the open doors. At that moment, Ologrin knew, Serenity was truly born while at the same time his friendship with Terval passed away.

26

After the first passage of Summer, the air warmed enough to melt the rest of the ice in the bay, but thick clouds continued to obscure the sky. Serenity called the first meeting of his Crown's Council. The Lord Affairs reported that the lingering Winter had not seemed to affect the barley harvest, but sorghum plantings were off to a very slow start. Ologrin sat quietly through the meeting, while Serenity ignored him completely.

The chill persisted. Sailing traffic was down, and those ships that had been out and back were returning half empty, reporting that Solanon and Ismay were also being affected by the cold and the clouds. Costs for all goods were higher than ever. Merchants stocked their storehouses, hoping for a burst of spending to make up for the dismal Winter. Each fretted over and refined their inventory, trying to divine if Antolans would show their usual taste for delicacies, or would save their coin for more necessary goods. For some shopkeepers, the space between profit and ruin was going to be uncomfortably narrow.

Then the Sun broke through. For most of the next passage it shone through a high haze, and the air started to warm. The mood in the city seemed to lift. People began to talk about the power and the blessings brought by their new Crown.

Mid-passage, Ologrin helped Vireo onto the back of Breeze. Together they rode down to the first terrace to eat at the old tavern he had often escaped to while a student at the School for Servants. They ate and watched the sun set into fiery clouds.

"You've decided to go," Ologrin said as Vireo nestled against him.

Vireo continued to gaze at the Sunset. "You were right. I have to go. I want to get there and back before the real Winter sets in again."

He thought about her solo visits to the Sophenary library, her unshared writings, and her nights spent brooding in the darkness. "There's something you're not telling me," he said finally.

"The Polfre elders will know about the cast-off stars. They will know, of course, of this unending Winter. I'm afraid, Ologrin." She huddled closer. "I'm afraid they will say we have violated the Rha for too long and now must pay."

"Then they're just as superstitious as everyone else. Let them say it. What can they do?"

"You don't understand. The Polfre may have withdrawn from the world, but they are not powerless. They have abilities the Eidos know nothing of."

"You make it sound like we should be concerned."

Finally she turned to look at him. "The Polfre don't simply live by the Rha. They are masters of it. That the Eidos survive at all is in part due to their tolerance. We should all be concerned."

"The sea trials for the new ship are coming up. I have to be onboard for them. At least wait until I get back."

"That may be too late."

"You can't even wait for me to return before you go?"

"I've waited for you for ten years," she replied sadly.

Ologrin felt stung, even though he knew she was stating a simple fact. He ate in silence. But then he turned to look at her, and there was anguish on her face he had not seen before.

"Do you know what it is to offer yourself wholly to someone else?" she said. "You've known a lot of pain, Ologrin, but do you know the pain of having to wait, to wait for years and not know if the one thing you want will ever be yours? That is a unique kind of pain, and it has to be endured in silence, because you can't confide in the one person you hope to lean on."

"You can tell me…"

"Can I? Are we entwined, Ologrin? I hear you say we are, but I feel you always have one more thing to do. We Polfre are good at waiting, but not forever."

Ologrin wanted to object, but everything he thought to say sounded like an excuse. She was right. As much as he professed to dislike it, every delay was a delay for the Crown. "You insisted I take the job of commander of the Fleet," he said finally.

"You wanted it."

"I told you I didn't!" he replied hotly.

"You didn't want to just be a tool of the Crown. But you want the access. You want the power. To do good things, you tell yourself. To change the world."

"Why is changing the world a bad thing?"

"It isn't. But it doesn't leave room for me."

Ologrin finished his meal in silence. Afterward, Breeze flicked her tail and nuzzled Vireo as she clambered up for the ride home. He had competition for Vireo's affection, Ologrin thought ruefully. They rode back up the terraces without speaking, and while Ologrin stabled the horse, Vireo disappeared into their chambers.

The clouds returned. Often enough, midday on the terraces was as gloomy as the deepest alleys of the Purse.

Ologrin was alarmed one morning to find frost on his shutters, with SummerTop only a few passages away.

The first of the new ships had been sailed across the bay and back, but a real voyage was waiting until Master Albrect could deliver the first of three bronze bombards destined to grace the ship. At last the first one was cooled, finished, and polished. Master Albrect spent two days working hand in hand with the master shipwright to mount the bombard on the bow of the ship. They fashioned an ingenious design. The bombard rested on a short platform raised above the main deck, to allow it to clear the bow. It was mounted to curved tracks thickly coated with tallow. With limited effort, two men could swing the barrel across a full quarter circle. Lashed in place and poking out over the bow of the ship, the bombard appeared small compared to the tall masts and thick rigging. Serenity visited the docks to examine the ship as it was being prepared for its first extended sea trial. He likened the bombard to the stinger on an insect: barely visible, but terribly effective. At that moment, he decided the name of his new ship would be the *Wasp*.

Departure day was again cold and wet. A stiff breeze blew down the length of the bay from the mountains to the north. Ologrin stood on the afterdeck with Captain Weims, huddled in his traveling cloak. "It's a good wind," the captain said. "It will get us past the cliffs with no difficulty."

They eased away from the docks and raised both sails. The ship surged forward, surprising them all. The crew shouted at each other as they trimmed the huge triangles. Dozens upon dozens of people were lined up along the docks and the Crown's Walk to watch them depart, but Vireo was not among them. She had promised to watch from their chambers. Her last touch had been warm and lingering but was lost to the chill as soon as she stepped away. Ologrin supervised charging the bombard with a light load of blast powder and no stone, and they fired a single salute. The report boomed across the waterfront and rumbled across the bay like thunder.

By midafternoon, the Ginney cliffs were off their left and Weims had the oarsman ease them to the right, heading down the middle of the bay toward open water. The wind was shifting around to their left. With the booms eased over the right rail, the big ship accelerated. Ologrin knew that their apparent speed was deceiving. Sailing as fast as it could go, the ship could be outrun by a horse in an easy trot. But it felt faster than a horse, and the spray coming over the bow added to the feeling of speed. And, of course, the ship could sail on day and night, unconstrained by road or path, relentlessly pursuing its goal. Over a league, a man on a horse could beat them thrice. From Antola to Solanon, a distance of eighteen dozen leagues, it was a dead head, provided one could find a dozen riders and twice as many horses for the race. For distances further than that, the ship would always win.

The wind continued to shift, and by early evening it was coming from the south, bringing with it stinging pellets of sleet that rattled off the sails. Their speed slowed, and the excitement of their departure gave way to miserable cold. Without Sun or stars, Ologrin could not calculate their position, so Weims resorted to old-fashioned navigation by memory. They had agreed to round the tip of the cat's tail and then head east and north, a route few of them had sailed, as all commerce was found in the opposite direction. As darkness fell, they were essentially blind, so for safety Weims calculated a wide swing around the point.

Their first night was endlessly long. Ologrin sat curled on the top deck until his furs were soaked, then tried curling up on the underdeck, where it was so dark he guessed even a Polfre would not be able to see, but from below deck the ship had a pronounced waddling roll, and soon he was nauseated and struggling with a severe headache. Morning was forever arriving; the darkness reluctantly gave way to a colorless gray. But the sleet had stopped, and the air finally seemed to warm a bit. Weims abandoned plans to explore Lhosa's southeastern coast. Relying only on the oil needle for guidance, he turned the ship south. They had no way of knowing how close to the coast they were, or how dangerous that shoreline might be.

They spent two more days swimming around in the endless gray, until Ologrin felt thoroughly lost. The clouds never broke, rendering his navigation system worthless. At one point, ice began to form on the rails and the rigging. On the fourth day, Weims began to ease his way north, hoping to find the coastline without crashing the ship into it in the process. They dropped sails after dark and wallowed all night, thankful that the wind stayed from the northeast so that it did not blow them onto an unexpected shore, then found land to their north the next morning. Weims kept it off their left shoulder all day, until someone spotted the familiar profile of the gorge forming the outlet of the river Bhin. By his own reckoning, Ologrin would have guessed they were farther east than they were, and so he felt even more disappointed in himself. By evening they were back inside the boundaries of the bay and sailed up to the docks the following morning, the sixth after their departure. Ologrin was happy to have a carriage take him and his mound of wet furs back to the castle. He built a roaring fire in the broad hearthgrate of his room, threw the furs on the stone floor to dry, and disappeared into the large bed.

He awoke from a dreamless sleep, finally feeling as if warmth had returned to the tips of his toes. The fire was still crackling cheerily. He also noticed the slight scratching of a pen against parchment. Vireo was sitting at a small table illuminated by a glow globe, writing steadily. She was wearing a cloak of iridescent green, with a stiff, upright collar. He wondered at the seeming boundlessness of her wardrobe. He stretched his limbs while nestled under the bed's furs, causing her to turn his direction.

"It didn't sink, did it?" she asked.

"No. Why do you say that?"

"Your clothes are soaked."

"There was as much water above the surface as beneath, I think."

"It was a success, then?"

"I felt useless. I had no chance to use the navigation tables. Once again, we were relying completely on the experience and intuition of a single man. This title, Lord Commander of the Fleet, is ridiculous. I doubt I could have navigated a fleet of ships across the bay. Without Weims, we would still be lost at sea."

"No one expects you to be master of everything, you know."

A familiar sense of unease began deep inside as he considered the tone of her voice. "There isn't much to do out there," he said finally. "I had a lot of time to think about what you've said. Who am I supposed to be? I thought it was hard enough when my time was torn between astrolemical observations and working for Albrect. Now this title? Weims never once needed me for anything." He sat up in the bed, listening to the scratch of the nib. "What are you writing?"

"Heron asked me to leave information about my contacts in the Purse," Vireo said.

Ologrin sat silently, while a sense of dread and sadness grew. "You're going today, aren't you?"

Vireo scratched away for a few more moments, then stopped, staring at the wall. "Something bad has happened within the Rha. We both know it. The more I wait, the greater my fear. I need to know what the Polfre elders have to say."

"They will say it is the fault of the Eidos, and if we all starve, so much the better."

"That's not fair. You have no idea what power for change the Polfre possess. Used injudiciously, it could cause far more damage than a single Summer turned to Winter. The Eidos think we have abandoned the world. In fact, we protect the world from forces it cannot handle." She replaced the pen but continued to stare at the parchment. "I feel the need to go home. It calls me."

"You are home," he said, but he knew what she meant, and his dread solidified into ice.

"Every day I wait makes me feel like I'm being torn inside."

Ologrin gave a single laugh. "That's funny. Every day you talk about leaving without me, I feel the same thing."

She turned to look at him. Light from the glowglobe shone within her eyes.

"I still want you to go," she said.

"I feel like I'm losing you."

She crossed to the bed and sat next to him, placing her hand on his shoulder. He could tell she was intentionally focusing her emanation. Warmth bloomed there and spread into his chest, causing him to shudder.

"We will go when that is the only thing we have to think about. When you are not torn by too many expectations. When we can go together and come back as one. I promise this will not be a long trip," she added. "I will be back by the end of Harvest. You will be so busy, you'll hardly notice."

"Don't diminish my feelings," he said. "You can tell me what you have to do, but you cannot tell me how I am going to feel about it."

"You're right," she said, looking down. "I'm sorry."

Ologrin dressed and then stood at the expansive windows of their chambers. The small balcony overlooking the Purse was in deep shadows. He turned toward the windows that looked out over the castle's steps and the Crown's Walk. Lanterns seemed to be lit day and night now. Vireo returned to the small table and resumed her writing. He tried to memorize every detail of her. She was so small, he thought. A blast of wind, a crashing wave, and she would be gone.

It was too late to go to the chimneys for the day. He decided to climb the stairs to his tower cell. He had barely used it all Summer. The room was dark, the small hearthgrate cold and black. It seemed dead, as if whatever part of his life it had once held had moved elsewhere. Obo's staff leaned against a far corner where it had remained hidden for years. He picked it up, surprised again at how warm it seemed to be. Never having been happy with the ugly, beak-like upper end, he had fashioned a cap made of his gold and tanjium alloy: a pair of serpent-like horns fighting to emerge from the staff's top.

He climbed up to the parapet. He could barely see the first terrace below. The flats beyond were hidden in mists. Far away, shrouded by the fog, lay the cold bones of Halrin's Spur. He was gripped by a sense of profound loneliness. The fleet, the chimneys, even the stars: They were not life. Nothing, he decided, mattered more than his need for Vireo, and his desire to be her need as well.

SummerTop arrived. Tents were erected in the gardens around the High Altarnary as always, lit with a profusion of torches. Despite the dank weather, the people of the city turned out in full force, looking for something to brighten their day. Ologrin could hear the faint sounds of celebration from the front steps to the castle. One of the great doors opened behind him, and he recognized Albrect's heavy footfalls as the man joined him.

"Serenity has called another Council meeting for tomorrow," Ologrin said.

"Won't be there," Albrect replied. "I've been looking for you. I think we've found something that alloys well with iron."

"What would that be?"

"The air itself! We fill the bloomery with iron, charcoal, and whitestone, then blast as much air through the charcoal as we can. And then we must pound it. We heat and pound the impurity out of it. The result is wonderful stuff, lighter than bronze, and can be worked instead of cast."

"Sounds like a lot of extra work," Ologrin said.

"For every cart of copper or tin ore we pull out of the mountains, we can pull three dozen of iron. It's worth the extra work. Anyway, I'll be busy in the chimneys tomorrow."

"I would much rather join you than go to the Council."

"Still no word from Serenity?"

Ologrin shook his head.

"You took away his glorious moment, you know. You embarrassed him."

"I didn't really have a choice," Ologrin replied. "Lord Gerun made it clear I could not wear my headwrap."

"Still, you had to know it was going to cause a fuss. You couldn't maybe have cut those things off?"

"Feel them," Ologrin said irritably, lowering his head.

Albrect ran his hand over one of the horns. "Oh. They're hard as bone."

"Would you, say, cut off a finger just to please the Crown?"

"No, no, probably not."

"Well, it's done. Vireo said I shouldn't have been hiding them, anyway. So now the whole world knows what I am."

"And what's that?" Albrect asked, but Ologrin didn't answer. Both men stared out across the Crown's Walk. "If it was me, I would make sure that the world knew me for what I wanted to be," Albrect added, then turned and re-entered the castle.

The next day, though he could have commanded a carriage for the trip, Ologrin chose to walk to the palace. He wore the green cloak of the Sophenary rather than the blue of the guard. He wondered if this would irritate the Coronet, and only accentuate his sense of being separate from the rest of the group, but he did it anyway. He kept the hood up. A light mist filled the air, and cold drops fell from the leaves of the scarab trees. Many of them had already turned yellow. This by itself was concerning. They were only halfway through Summer, far too soon to be seeing color change in the trees. And in the Harvest, scarab leaves turned golden orange, not sickly yellow.

At the palace, Ologrin was escorted to the council room. He sat at one of the small tables facing the high table of the Crown. Food was served. Ologrin knew he ought to consider being a member of the Council a great privilege if only for the spectacular food, easily the best meal he had eaten in days. This day's menu was typical: small, tender rounds of bison; turnip tops cooked with vinegar, cheese and bread; and a small sponge cake dipped in sorghum syrup and topped with bits of real scarab nuts. And a dark wine, which Ologrin still found distasteful, but judged must be good based on the quantity consumed by the others.

"This is the best meal of the day," the Lord Coronet said at last. Until then, Ologrin had not imagined someone might have a meal like this every day.

Serenity sat at the high table dressed in a blue tunic and elegant black breeches. Gold panthers were fixed to either shoulder, but otherwise he was unadorned. "Let's get to work," he said. "The Lord Affairs. Your report would seem to be the most important."

Lord Vrenchew cleared his throat. He had the flat accent of someone who had grown up in Madros. If the native Antolans on the council secretly thought of Lord Vrenchew as uncultured, they kept it to themselves. To Ologrin, he projected an air of complete confidence, and he was a walking roll of knowledge. Ologrin found himself wondering again how he had any business on the Council with men such as this.

"Supreme Grace, the barley harvest is stored, and yields were not far off the mark. However, a blight has been reported in more than one storehouse. The vitachemists have suggested the grain should have been allowed to dry on the winnowing floor longer before being put up."

"The sorghum, however, will come off poorly. Entire fields have not produced any grain, and leaves are already yellowing. Ordinarily, the leaves do not yellow until the second passage of Harvest."

"Well," Serenity said, "I suppose we won't have as many of these cakes next year."

"Supreme Grace, the sorghum does provide molasses, true, but the stalks themselves are a valuable food for the bison over the Winter, and many people depend upon the grain itself for food."

"And of the rest?"

"It is mixed, at best. Some of the garden foods, such as gourds and root vegetables, don't appear to have suffered. But brown beans have done as poorly as sorghum. In many of the small villages, brown beans are most of their diet."

"Forgive me, Supreme Grace, but we have been counting numbers all Summer," Lord Austerian interrupted. "None of this gets us closer to the real questions." He looked around the room. His family owned much of the warehouse space on the docks closest to the trestle lift. That made the Crown his unofficial partner. His repayment was a seat on the Council as Lord Mercantile, the same seat his father had occupied before him. He brought to the table a comprehensive understanding of the trade that flowed in and out of Antola. In the previous meeting, Ologrin had noticed Lord Austerian's impatience with recitations of mere numbers.

"What are the real questions?" Serenity asked. Ologrin thought he knew the answer already.

"What has happened to us? And will it happen again next year? One year and the villagers don't eat well. Two years and you have a famine, and that's a much more dangerous thing."

Lord Coltes, the Lord Guard Commander, spoke up. He was by far the oldest member of the Council, older than Albrect, Ologrin assumed, and had also served in his post for many years. "Surely we all agree on what has happened. Something has angered Malach. The question is what?"

"You have no doubt?" Serenity asked.

"Fire from the sky, followed by Winter in Summer? How can anyone explain that without invoking the gods?"

Serenity turned his gaze to his new Lord Priest. Ologrin sat across the room from Moran. If Moran addressed Serenity directly, he could not also see Ologrin, who took the opportunity to scrutinize his former teacher carefully.

"Help me out, Moran," Serenity said quietly.

The familiarity was surprising. Ologrin studied both men carefully, but Serenity was looking down at the table in front of him, a picture of inscrutability.

"The intention of the gods is hard to measure over days or passages," Moran said smoothly.

"In other words, you'll wait and see how it comes out, and then decide what it means," said Coltes. The Lord Guard Commander was not a fan of the Lord Priest, Ologrin decided.

"If you're asking whether or not the gods have spoken to me directly, the answer is no," replied Moran. "I have not been so blessed. I have never been so blessed."

"A pity," Lord Coltes muttered.

"If you are looking for a mouthpiece for Malach, then I am not the right person for this job."

For years, Ologrin had wondered how Moran had reacted when he disappeared so suddenly from the School. Had he been concerned? Did he try to mount a search? Or had he known what was going to happen that night? As a result, was he surprised to see the maleugenate now sitting on the same Council with him?

Lord Austerian and Lord Vrenchew had much in common. They were in the tribe of wealth-makers and so had little time for Malach and his affairs. Ologrin dismissed them as potential members of the Malacheb. At first, Ologrin suspected Lord Coltes might be Malacheb, but from the start the Guard Commander expressed disdain for the priests, and that gave Ologrin hope. Albrect, of course, was someone Ologrin could trust completely, if he were only here. As for the Lord Coronet, Ologrin was fairly sure the man was terrified of him. That left only the Lord Judge Geldes and the Lord Priest Moran. Could either be Malacheb?

Serenity spoke up. "Lord Priest, no one expects you to talk directly to the gods. You are here for your unique knowledge of their history." He leaned forward and smiled in a way that Ologrin found very familiar, only this time it was clearly directed toward someone else. "Is there a development you have seen in the city, perhaps something you have seen in me, something which might cause the gods to show their displeasure?"

"Thank you, Supreme Grace," Moran replied, smiling back. "In you, of course, nothing at all. I can only imagine the gods would be pleased that you, an accomplished man and a true heir to the line of Donal, have become the Crown. Perhaps this has nothing to do with the gods. They have their world and we have ours. But if it does, then it may represent their response to something we have failed to deal with ourselves, some…blight, if I may borrow the word, on our people." Moran turned and looked in Ologrin's direction.

Ologrin tilted his head down, as if avoiding Moran's gaze. But in truth, he wanted Moran to get a good look at the horns on his head. When he looked up, Maron was still staring at him. *I have my answer*, Ologrin thought.

"We have a warrant master in astrolemy on the council," the Lord Coronet said. "I, for one, would like to hear what he has to say about this. Lord Ologrin, tell us. Do you think the flaming stars from last Winter, which heralded the death of Serenity the Seventh, have had anything to do with our disastrous weather?"

"I would accept one, but not the other," Ologrin replied.

Gerun appeared exasperated. "Explain, if you don't mind."

"The flaming stars were accompanied by a number of cast-off stars. Astrolemers have long observed cast-off stars and have carefully noted no correlation between their appearance and our affairs. They are thought to be part of the natural world, though we don't understand how. It seems most likely that the flaming stars were larger and more powerful cast-off stars. Even though they were frightening, they had nothing to do with Serenity's death."

Lord Austerian spoke up. "If you accept one but not the other, then you must believe that these flaming stars, though not sent by the gods, have still affected our weather. A blight from the unfeeling, unknowing sky, perhaps?"

"Perhaps," Ologrin replied. "Maybe there was something in the smoky trails left behind; perhaps some poison there, which has lingered in our skies and caused the rain and clouds."

"A poison that causes rain?" It was Lord Coltes, someone to whom the only things that mattered were the things he could understand and guard against. It was an eminently fair question, Ologrin thought, and one that he knew he could not answer.

"We have heard that locations as far as Solanon and Ismay have also been affected," Austerian said. "Why would something that happened over the skies of Antola affect them so far away?"

"The flaming streaks from the stars crossed leagues and

leagues, is my guess, perhaps farther than Lhosa is wide," Ologrin said.

"But that's impossible to believe! How big were these things?"

"Very big," Ologrin answered. "We know…astrolemers have shown that objects in the sky are massively big, some much bigger than our own world."

"If very big, then also far away, and yet you claim their poisons have reached us."

"The Sun is even farther away, and its warmth reaches the whole land."

"Not lately…" Coltes muttered.

"I want to move the conversation," Serenity said. "Lord Affairs, whatever the reason, we are facing the potential for shortages, and Winter will be on us again far sooner than we wish. We must start planning for it."

"I hear that ships full of emmer and millet continue to sail from Solanon to Ismay," Lord Vrenchew replied.

"And not here?"

"Supreme Grace, as you know, Solanon claims no oath of loyalty to the Crown. They say they are free to trade with everyone.

"Have we received grains from them this Summer?"

"Only a little, Supreme Grace."

"Perhaps they claim no loyalty, but what about simple fairness? Why are they not trading more with us?"

"Because, Supreme Grace, we have never agreed to open trade with them." Lord Vrenchew looked steadily at Serenity.

"Then what are my ships for? Why have we built those two new monsters in the bay?"

"Of course, we have some business with Solanon, and even with Ismay. But for generations Antola has been unwilling to trade much, and so has not received much in return. They would trade for our sorghum syrup, or our barley flour, and especially for our bison meat, but we are not willing to trade those things."

"I thought we traded with coin."

"Yes, of course. We send coin, and we get modest amounts of goods in return, mostly delicacies for the shops."

"I thought they wanted our coin."

"They want it for the silver and gold in it, which we won't trade them directly."

Serenity looked around the table. Most refused to look back, as if they had finally divulged a dirty secret, one they knew would come out someday. Ologrin suspected Serenity felt foolish, and distinctly un-leader-like.

"How many shiploads of grain does Solanon sent to Ismay each year?" Serenity asked.

"Three dozen, more or less," Vrenchew replied.

"And we get?

"This Summer? Two."

"Dozen?"

"Two shiploads."

Ologrin spoke up. "Supreme Grace, our capacity at the Sophenary has increased greatly in the past few years. We are producing materials that are ready for trade."

"What would you trade?"

"We are producing blast powder at a prodigious rate..."

"Not the blast powder," Lord Coltes said. "We cannot give away such an advantage."

"Then our charcoal, perhaps. Or burned whitestone. We are making it by the barrelful."

"Again, the advantage," Lord Coltes said.

"What advantage are we looking for?" Ologrin countered. "Trading is a partnership. There are benefits that come from making friends, instead of treating everyone as a potential enemy."

"Supreme Grace, I submit, despite the poor yields, this is not yet a crisis," Lord Coltes said. "The people of the city may not get everything they want this Winter, but they will not starve."

"And the people of the flats? Will they get what they need? Who will raise the bison if the people of the flats starve?" Ologrin asked.

"I have thought of that. My arms men can do it," Coltes said.

Ologrin was taken aback. "What? Is that a plan?"

"They are disciplined, and they can easily learn to manage the herds. We need not worry about starvation beyond the city's walls."

"Need not worry? We are talking about people starving to death!"

"It is my duty to offer solutions to this Council and to the Crown," Coltes replied.

Ologrin felt the tingling heat beneath his corset, hidden beneath his cloak. He noticed his hands were gripping the table. He let go. A slight discoloration marked where his fingers had been. "What is our duty to other people?"

"Lord Fleet Commander," Serenity interrupted. "Prepare your ships. I want as many as possible ready before Harvest. We will send a trading delegation to Solanon. And inform the Dodecant, who seems unwilling to attend these meetings. We will send whatever goods he has to spare that will allow those ships to return full of food." He stood, indicating the end of the meeting, and the rest of the Council stood as well.

Lord Coltes approached Ologrin immediately. "Whatever assistance you need, my Lord, my men will be able to provide."

Ologrin tried to hide his surprise. There was no sense of irritation in the man's voice, no sense that they had just been at odds. Everything was a calculation. Given an order, he was ready to carry it out.

"Those are people down there," Ologrin said again.

Discomfort flashed briefly across Lord Coltes' face. "Yes, but they aren't our people."

Ologrin tried to formulate a reply, but then heard Moran's voice behind him.

"Lord Commander of the Fleet." Ologrin turned to see Moran approaching. "I had no idea that you were a sailor." As the man drew close, Ologrin realized he was now a good hand taller than his former teacher. "I'd like to think I had a small part to play in your success," Moran added, smiling.

"Of that we can both be certain."

"Hopefully, I can be at least as helpful in the future." Moran held out his wrist. Ologrin looked at it carefully, aware of the fire still simmering beneath his corset.

"You don't want to do that…"

"Lord Ologrin. I wonder if I could have a private word?" Serenity was now approaching. Moran dropped his arm and backed up a step. Serenity smiled at the priest and touched Ologrin lightly on the elbow, turning him and leading him toward the wall of windows.

"Do you have some history with the Lord Priest?" Serenity asked.

"I spent four years at the School for Servants," Ologrin said, while wanting to ask the same question. "He was one of my teachers."

"Servant Priest Ologrin. That's hard for me to imagine."

"I wonder if he had a hand in their decision to—to terminate my enrollment early, let's say."

"Ah."

"I think he may be Malacheb, Supreme Grace."

"You have a tendency to think that about a number of people."

"When you're hunted, you tend to be on guard for hunters."

"And because you are a mosaic, that makes you hunted?"

"Forgive me, Supreme Grace, but Wesse explained that to me himself." They reached the bank of windows.

"Listen, Ologrin, even if the clouds go away tomorrow, this terrible weather is going to have long-lasting repercussions. Something like this unsettles everyone's view of the world. When that happens, long standing traditions, customs, partnerships, what have you—they all end up for review. You think being a mosaic makes you a target? You should try being the Crown. My survival depends on no one seriously entertaining the idea that there might be a better way."

Ologrin glanced across the room. The Coronet and Moran stood facing each other, attempting to engage in conversation, but he knew their focus was on where he stood, talking to the Crown, while they did not. *Politics*, thought Ologrin with distaste. Every interaction was colored by ambition, every conversation a carefully framed part of a larger plan.

"The Sophenary already has a comprehensive plan to manage limited Winter supplies," Ologrin said. "It is the Polfre way, you know. They sense these things in their bones, and respond to it the way a flower turns its head toward the Sun. Let the Sophenary take care of the flats."

"Antolans have their own natural way of responding too. It's stamped into every silver coin."

"The Strong Survive," Ologrin recited.

"And the weak do not."

"This is not a tribe in the wilds; it's a civilized city," Ologrin said, feeling the tingling under the corset again. "People can be expected to manage their selfish desires and still show compassion for others. We can't be talking about letting people die because that's the easiest thing to do."

"That is why I want to send the fleet to Solanon as soon as possible."

"With a ship bearing a bombard?"

"It will send a powerful message. I can't afford to look like a beggar, can I?"

Ologrin tuned to gaze out the windows. The glass was the best available, of course, without a hint of color, and with only a few scattered bubbles. The Purse disappeared below him into the heavy mist before it reached the docks. The bay itself was completely obscured. He tried to imagine navigating through the bay without being able to see, much less making his way many gross leagues down the Lhosan coast.

"I need you on my side," Serenity said.

"Supreme Grace, I have always been on your side."

"But not by it. Who is going to command the *Wasp*?" he added, before Ologrin had a chance to respond.

"Captain Weims."

Serenity nodded. "I figured you would offer it to him. And who's going to take over on the *Rayfish*?"

"I think I may keep that job for myself," Ologrin said.

Serenity tapped him lightly on the back. "A good choice." He turned and headed for the men at the other end of the room. Moran smiled as Serenity approached, then leaned in to whisper something in obvious intimacy. They both turned to leave. Serenity briefly placed his arm around the other man's waist, guiding him through the door. *A gesture stronger than words*, Ologrin thought.

He imagined the bisonherders out on the flats, and in the small villages dotting the Bhin. For them, subtle gestures were meaningless; surviving another Winter was the only thing that mattered. *Only the strong survive.* Stamped into coins, it was meant as an admonition, but could just as easily be taken as a challenge.

27

A casualty of the weather, the second ship would not be finished in time for the voyage to Solanon. Ologrin assembled a fleet of nine other ships, which, along with the *Wasp* and with the *Rayfish* as the lead, gave them a fleet of eleven. Ologrin had to remind himself there was no such thing as an unlucky number. He turned his attention to loading them with goods.

He stood with Master Albrect and Master Crake in what had been Vireo's official chambers. He was not sure who they belonged to now. Albrect was Dodecant in name only, as Crake took care of the day-to-day affairs. He needed both to agree on what the Sophenary could offer for the delegation.

"We have plenty of charcoal, and plenty of burned whitestone," Albrect said. "If I had more time, we could offer iron swords and lances. We are just beginning to make them efficiently."

"What about blast powder?" Ologrin asked.

Albrect was hesitant. "Trading our best powder means giving them the means to ignite it. I am very reluctant to trade away even the slightest amount of tanjium. The Polfre would not agree if they knew." He seemed to forget for a moment that Crake was Polfre.

"Don't we have a small store of sulfur? We could make and sell them traditional blast powder."

"That sulfur was expensive and hard to obtain," Albrect said. "We would never get its fair value back in trade."

"Yet it might motivate a trade when simply exchanging fair value would not."

"There has been less niter delivered this year," Crake said. "Be sure you are not trading away something we may eventually need."

"What has happened to the niter?" Ologrin asked.

"The people of the riverflats are struggling," Crake said, matter-of-factly.

"I thought we had been using some of our resources to make sure they had access to food," Ologrin said, alarmed. "Vireo assured me that we were not going to let them starve."

"They are not starving," Crake replied. "They have had troubles of…a different sort."

"What? What is happening?"

Crake seemed increasingly uncomfortable. Ologrin turned to Albrect. "Tell me."

"Things have gone well in the flats without your presence these past years. There have been some recent difficulties, but nothing you won't make worse by going down there."

"What difficulties?"

"Ologrin, you are forbidden to go down there."

"By you?" Ologrin asked. "By the Crown? I haven't been down there because I was assured that the people were taken care of, that there was nothing more I needed to do. You're implying that's not true."

The two older men stared at him. Ologrin turned to leave.

"Ologrin!" Albrect said. "Where are you going?"

"I have ships to get ready," he said without looking back.

• • •

"Alera protect us. Alera, make me grow strong," Ologrin said out loud, surprising himself. He no longer believed in the gods, but if there was one he could choose to make real, it would be her: a god who brought safety and comfort. If a god could not provide that, then what good were they?

He stood on his tower parapet, looking out at the blackness surrounding the riverflats. No doubt the bisonherders had suffered through the unending Winter. Meanwhile, the Crown's Council dismissed them as little more than a liability. For most of Antola, they lived and died unknown. But not to Alera. She would take care of them. He fingered Obo's staff. He would help her. He dressed in his warmest clothing, hefted the staff, and headed for the husbandry yard, where he had stopped earlier to make sure Breeze was harnessed and ready to go.

As he rode silently down the steps toward the first terrace, wisps of fog gradually coalesced into a solid cloud. The hood of his traveling cloak hid his face in shadow. A lone sentry stood sleepily inside the guardhouse of the western gate. He spied the silver devices on Ologrin's shoulders and sprang to the gate to open it. Ologrin and the horse passed through without a word.

Within moments they had left the gate behind and were swallowed in a thick blanket that completely obscured the terraces above and the flats far below. Ologrin thought he could sense the nervousness in Breeze as she carefully picked her footing. They descended in silence, Ologrin lost in thought. By the time they reached the foot of the Great Road, light was beginning to fill the air. Now he could hear things out in the fog: the moan of a bison, then the sharp voice of a herder. The mist was scented with the musk of large animals and the sharp tang of manure from a nearby niter bed. It was not entirely unpleasant. They were the smells of Ologrin's childhood, and they brought with them a comfortable familiarity.

He had not been on the flats for six years. At first, his grief had been too great; in his mind he could not separate the bisonherders of the flats from the people of Halrin's Spur. Later, staying off the flats seemed a reasonable trade. In exchange for the Crown's willingness to crack down on the cult of the Malacheb, he agreed to avoid doing anything that would further the illusion that he was any sort of symbolic leader. The Sophenary had continued to rely on the bisonherders for niter and had continued to teach them how to improve their use of the land. The result had been a healthier workforce and greater yields of meat and hides for the Crown. Everyone seemed to benefit; no one was interested in disrupting the balance. He had focused on helping Albrect build the chimneys and on completing his warrant master in vitachemy. His life in the riverlands, he had decided, was long behind him.

The road itself did not appear to have changed. But intersections with herding paths had been improved, with some built up as ramps on either side of the road. He came upon just such a ramp as a young herder materialized out of the fog, leading a half-dozen bison across the road. The herder spied Ologrin and began whipping his charges to cross the road faster. Ologrin pulled Breeze to a halt and waved to show he was in no hurry.

"Fine animals you have," he called out. The herder stared at him as he got the last of the animals across the road.

Ologrin and Breeze continued plodding forward. The fog seemed to be thinning. In addition, it seemed warmer here in the flats that up on the escarpment. He pulled his hood back. He did not have much of a plan. He had imagined himself sitting at a milkhouse, speaking with leaders from the flats, but had not thought of how he would arrange such a meeting. He decided to take the north road, as there had always been milkhouses close by.

Almost as soon as he turned off the Great Road, he heard

the steps of someone running. A young woman appeared out of the fog. She ran toward him, but instead of stopping, ran past him on the track and continued down the road. He proceeded a short distance further before hearing a series of short whistles, followed by the same pattern of whistles further in the distance. Breeze snorted and shook her head, no less aware than Ologrin that the whistles were a signal. They continued slowly.

The fog continued to thin. Ologrin could make out a small group of people standing in the roadway a few gross hands ahead. He brought Breeze to a halt. There were short whistles to his left, and then to his right. He could not see anyone in those directions, but assumed he was surrounded. He carefully slipped the staff out of its saddle loops, then waited while the group moved toward him.

"I am from the Sophenary," he said, when they were about thirty hands away.

"We know who you are," the man in the center replied.

"I wish to speak to your herdleads."

"Runners are already passing the word."

"For what?"

"We knew you would come."

Ologrin began to feel uneasy. "How did you know that?"

"We knew the Korun would come."

Six years, and the myth had not faded. But he did not correct them.

"Follow," the man said, and turned off the path. Ologrin obeyed.

They travelled further from the path than Ologrin expected. They approached a milkhouse, its low thatched roof dripping moisture.

He dismounted and let Breeze wander. He would have expected the ground to be little more than mud, this close to a large milkhouse, but the grass was surprisingly thick. They entered the house, and Ologrin was surprised to see that it was warm, neat, and dry.

"I'm surprised your house is so far from the path," Ologrin said.

"No one would build a milkhouse next to the road. Everyone knows it is not proper," his guide replied.

Six years, and a novel idea was being described as if it had always been common wisdom.

Several individuals wandered into the milkhouse, curious about their visitor, but stayed along the periphery. Before long, though, he was offered a mug and a warm bowl of thick soup. To his surprise, the mug contained ale. He took a careful bite of the soup and was even more surprised. It was delicious, made of some roughly ground vegetable with a nutty, slightly earthy flavor, further enhanced with bits of smoked bison meat.

"This is good. What is it?"

"Mudbean stew."

Ologrin kept himself from spitting. He swallowed hard. "Mudbeans?"

"They must be ground, then washed many times to remove the bitterness. But if the bison can eat them, we can too."

He carefully took another bite. With effort, he could imagine the faintest hint of bitterness. But it was still good. He finished the bowl, not realizing how hungry he had been.

"You find the mudbeans down by the river?"

"We plant them and grow them on the banks," the guide said.

"You plant them? Have they been affected by the cold and the rain?"

"Mudbeans do not need hot Summer to grow."

"You have plenty of them?"

"Enough for us and some for the bison as well."

He glanced around at those slowly filling the room. None

of the herders looked malnourished. Some had chests as broad as a warhorse and would have been a match for any arms man.

Ten herdleads eventually filled the room, some with their own assistants. After quietly conferring among themselves, a lean woman stepped forward. Her muscles twisted like ropes beneath her skin. After years among the pale-tan city dwellers, he had forgotten how deep brown the skin of bison-herds became. He looked at his own faded skin.

"I remember you, Marle. I am Ologrin, from the Sophenary…"

"I know who you are," she said, with the same, somewhat challenging tone of the man he had met on the path. "Why have you come?"

He was taken aback. "I was worried…we have been concerned about your welfare, especially with this strange and unwelcome weather."

"Malach's poison," someone said.

"Well," he began, but then stopped to reconsider her comment. "Why do you say that?"

"Malach is the god of the city. He hates the bison people. He poisoned the Summer to punish us, but we were ready. He has failed."

"Why have you come?" Marle repeated.

This was not what he had expected to find. Her words were a challenge, not a request.

"Tell me how you have defeated Malach," he said, hoping this would provide him answers he needed.

"Malach poisoned the Summer to kill the food of the bison people, and so kill us as well. He poisoned the barley, and the sorghum, and the brown beans. But that is the food of Malach's tribe. Bison people have their own food."

"Mudbeans," Ologrin said.

"Malach's tribe throws away food from the bison, which the bison people eat. It makes them stronger."

"The only things they discard are the entrails and gonads. You eat them?"

"A boy becomes a man by eating the bison's balls. It has always been," Marle said, with a conviction that had Ologrin imagining a custom passed down for centuries, until he forced himself to remember they had done no such thing when he was a child. These people were not only surviving, they were inventing their own culture.

"Malach's tribe comes in the night, but we fight back," she said. "We do not fear them. Soon we will be stronger than them."

Ologrin felt the hair on his scalp raise. "Wait," he said. "Who comes in the night?"

"Malach's tribe. They no longer scare us."

"Horses?" he asked.

Marle nodded. "Not many," she said.

"Where do they come from? From the city?"

She shook her head slowly. "From the Great Road," she said. "From the west."

Ologrin was finding it hard to concentrate. The fire beneath his corset burned like a forge beneath the chimneys. They came from the west. Madros was in the west. Wesse was in Madros. He gripped his staff tightly while imagining Wesse standing in front of him. The man would be defiant. *And then he will burn*, Ologrin thought, *until he is nothing but a greasy lump of charcoal himself*. That was his promise to himself.

"How often do they come?" Ologrin asked. "Every night?"

"Only when the Sojourner sets at Sundown," the woman said.

"Every time?" he asked. Marle nodded. He marveled at the careless arrogance of their attackers.

"New Sojourner is three nights from now," Ologrin said. Marle nodded again. "We will be ready."

. . .

Just as the Adamantine peaks gave way to the flats, the flats eventually gave way to a vast stretch of low-lying swampland formed by long ages of sediment dragged from the mountains and deposited by the river Bhin. The Great Road ran west along the edge of this boundary for twenty leagues from the North Road intersection to the river. Through most of its journey through the flats, the Bhin remained constrained in its meandering channel, but south of the road it spread into a wide, slow-moving panorama of muddy water a half-league wide. The transition point was a series of narrow gorges cut through the sandstone as the river stepped down to the swamps beyond. The Great Road met the banks of the river at one of these gorges, the last point where it was possible to construct a crossing. Four massive pillars of granite blocks had been built into the riverbed and surrounding banks, supporting five stone arches with a total span of three gross hands. Beyond the bridge, the road turned southwest and ran another fifteen leagues to the city of Madros.

Like any bridge, the bridge to Madros offered both defensive opportunities and challenges. It was a natural choke point for the movement of arms men, putting them at risk of ambush. For that reason, each end of the bridge was defended by an arched stone rampart straddling the road itself.

Over the next two days, an unusually large number of bison wandered close to the bridge on the eastern side of the river, followed, naturally, by their herders. Bisonherders this far from the escarpment were an especially uncivilized and unruly group, or so thought the arms men who stood guard on the eastern rampart. They gave the herders half a glance now and then, until a large group of bison were driven onto the slopes of the Great Road to graze on the Crown's grass. The arms men knew to ignore the odd animal or two that grazed near the road, as the unending Winter had been tough for everyone. But this seemed an intentional provocation. Finally, when several of the animals were herded onto the road itself and then stopped to take mountainous shits, it was too much. When threats and curses from the rampart did nothing to dislodge the animals or their herders, both arms men belted on their short swords, grabbed pikes, and headed down to the roadway to restore order.

A few pokes in the hide got the animals back onto the flats. One of the arms men rounded up a couple of bisonherders and ordered them to remove the dung piles. The herders protested, the arms men put hands to their sword hilts, and slowly the work was done. The bisonherders complained about their filth-covered arms; the arms men reminded them it was nothing a little scrubbing wouldn't remove.

"Not that they've ever dipped their bodies in a bath their entire lives," one of the arms men said, and they laughed as they returned to the rampart, unaware that a dozen herders had already slipped past the unguarded rampart and were now hidden underneath the bridge, settling down to wait for the following evening.

Ologrin had ridden Breeze hard to get to the bridge north of Bhinton by that evening. It was mostly in ruins; no one had tended it for years. He resisted the urge to continue north to the graveyard that had been Halrin's Spur. It was clear that no one had returned. What once had been grazing fields next to the river were already overgrown with saplings. He camped on the far side of the river, then early the next morning headed south into the western forests. Though there was no real road, there were trails cut by charcoalers venturing out from Bhinton. All day, the Sun was nothing more than a brighter spot in the thick clouds, and darkness was descending fast when he finally caught sight of the Great Road and the western rampart in the distance.

Barely half a league west of the rampart, where the road turned south toward Madros, smoke rose from a camp. He rode closer in the gathering darkness, until he could hear voices and laughter, along with occasional snorts and nickers from horses. One by one, two dozen torches were lit. The conversations grew quieter. From where he stood with Breeze, just inside the gloom of the trees, Ologrin could barely make out men and horses assembling on the roadway. The torches illuminated one man well enough for Ologrin to see him lift a bizarre tangle of branches to his head, which he belted in place with a strap under his chin. Ologrin felt the warmth start to build in his chest, but along with it there was a sense of calm. If he were a shadow panther, he thought, this is the way he would feel before surprising his prey.

Darkness was soon complete. The clouds shrouded the stars. The Sojourner would not rise until just before morning, though with the thick clouds, it could have been directly overhead and still be invisible. The raiding party began to move toward the bridge. Ologrin and Breeze carefully picked their way toward the roadway, intent on positioning themselves far enough behind the party that they could not be heard. It went without saying they would not be seen.

Fog began to curl up from the banks of the river in the distance. Though Ologrin could not see it, he could sense it, as it dampened the sounds from the party. Torches on the western rampart were visible from the roadway: twin pinpricks of yellow in the distance. Ologrin hoped the fog would not thicken too much. His plan depended upon still being able to see the raiding party's torches when they reached the far side of the bridge.

The raiding party stopped talking as they reached the bridge. They rested for a few moments, no doubt conferring with the arms men Ologrin assumed were manning the western rampart. Then they moved forward, stretching out to cross the bridge itself, which was only wide enough for two wagons to pass. Ologrin stopped short of the glow from the rampart's torches. He could not see the arms men above. Though he figured they were watching the party cross the bridge, he had to assume they might glance backward toward where he and Breeze waited on the roadway, and he did not want to be visible.

Slowly, the lead torches approached the opposite side of the bridge and the eastern rampart. He felt his heart beating faster, and the warmth in his chest began to build again. He slipped onto Breeze's back and held his staff across the saddle.

The far side rampart was instantly thrown into relief by a massive orange flash, and a ball of fire rolled into view before disappearing into a giant smudge of smoke. A moment later the air boomed as if the gods themselves had struck a drum. Shouts rose from the far side. Ologrin waited just a moment more and was rewarded with the sight of the two torches on his side descending and bobbing away across the bridge, as the two near-side arms men ran toward the chaos. He nudged Breeze forward into a trot. As he crossed under the western rampart, he saw the shadows of the dozen hidden herders join him on the bridge.

The shouts from the far side were overtaken by a human roar. The far-side rampart was once again illuminated, this time by dozens of torches. Ologrin knew that many more herders were massed behind those torches, rushing through the arch toward the raiding party. Regardless of what advantage they might have in hand-to-hand combat, the raiders were now trapped on the bridge, unable to fan out. A man might survive jumping to the rocky banks of the river, but a horse would not. Those at the back of the raider column broke and turned toward Ologrin.

"Light them!" he yelled. A dozen torches sprang to life around him. The herdsmen immediately threw the torches forward onto the bridge. The retreating raiders hesitated for a moment, but they saw only men on foot and a single horse. The torches burning on the bridge were little more than a nuisance.

Ologrin leaned in and a spark leapt from his hand to his horse's shoulder. Breeze sprang forward. With a cry Ologrin lowered the staff in front of him and charged toward the closest horse-mounted raider.

The head of the staff struck the raider in the chest as he was raising his own sword to parry. A much brighter flash filled the space between them, throwing the raider backward. He struck the edge of the bridge and fell into the darkness below.

The raiders' horses drew up. The blast powder explosion had unnerved them; now lightning from a mounted rider was too much. The herdsmen behind Ologrin yelled and ran forward, armed with scythes.

Ologrin charged into two more raiders, unhorsing them with back and forth swings of his staff, flashes lighting the sky. He could see the herders on the far side overwhelming raiders trying to find a way to retreat. Frightened horses reared and tossed their own riders overboard.

A piercing wail split the air. An icy spike seemed to drive through Ologrin, extinguishing the heat in his chest. He was transported instantly to a black night atop a distant Altarnary, a twelve-year-old cowering against the stones as a monster above him emitted the same heart-freezing scream. But then he forced himself back. A mounted raider turned toward him and leapt forward. Breeze seemed to snarl as she returned the charge. Ologrin aimed his staff again and saw the raider lower a long, barbed lance, longer than his staff. As the horses converged, the lance caught Ologrin square in the chest. He felt himself flying backward. At the same time, the lance burst into a shower of splinters and molten metal.

Ologrin hit the bridge hard, losing his breath. From the corner of his eye he glimpsed Breeze tumbling on her side toward the bridge's edge. For a moment he couldn't move. Then he managed to roll to one side. His muscles tried to fail him as he slowly pulled himself to his knees. He had dropped his staff; in the darkness he could not see it and feared it had fallen into the river.

The raider had managed to stay on his horse. He turned and drew a sword, then kneed his horse toward Ologrin again. Ologrin tried to stand and stumbled forward, and in doing so, he felt his hand sweep across the warm shaft of the staff. He grabbed it and felt himself forced upward by a surge of fire. He swung the staff at the bridge in front of him. Chips of stone exploded around him as the head of the staff blasted a crater in the bridge deck. The oncoming horse stumbled. Ologrin raised the staff and swung again, this time catching the raider in the chest as he fell forward from his horse. Through the shaft, Ologrin felt the man's chest crumple.

The herdsmen surged past Ologrin. Terrified horses bolted toward both ends of the bridge, heedless of their riders. Ologrin stood his ground like a pier in the middle of the river, as men and horses flowed around him. He paid them no mind, searching through the darkness and chaos for Breeze. At the edge of the bridge, he saw a shadowy shape pull its front legs under, then heave itself to standing.

Screams and the sound of fighting could still be heard from the eastern side, but they were fading. Ologrin reached Breeze and rubbed his hand across her neck. He walked toward the eastern side. Nearby, a single individual cried out in agony. Ologrin stepped toward the noise, and in the dim light cast by the few remaining torches, he saw a raider curled on his back, trying to stabilize the lower part of his leg, which was bent at a bizarre angle. Ologrin stood over him with the staff in his hand. He saw bone sticking out of the man's leg. He raised the staff and poised it over the man's chest. The man looked up in terror, the terror he knew had been in the eyes of everyone in Halrin's Spur. Then Breeze nickered darkly next to him. He stepped past the man and moved on.

Marle stood on the eastern edge of the bridge. The hair on the left side of her head was plastered in place with blood from a gash on her scalp, but the gash had already stopped bleeding. She carried a scythe at her side, black with someone else's blood.

"We are not afraid of Malach's tribe," she said again.

Ologrin saw the faintest twinkle over her head. He looked up and noticed the clouds were broken in places, and he could see stars. The clouds made the stars seem even farther away, like grains of adamantine scattered at the bottom of a deep lake.

"They were mercenary from Madros," Ologrin said. "They were Malacheb."

"You are the Korun," she replied, and said nothing else.

Seventeen of the twenty-four raiders lay dead or injured on the bridge. Three more lay unmoving on the rocks at the edge of the river below. Two herdsmen had been killed, and a half-dozen more injured but still walking.

For two days, Ologrin had been focused on surprising and then defeating the raiders. His mind had raced with possibilities, and he had stretched his body to keep up. Now, though his body was exhausted, his mind kept racing, and he could imagine the overwhelming response Lord Wesse was likely to bring once he realized what had happened. The pride and fearlessness of the bisonherders had fooled him into mistaking the battle for the war.

"Word will get back to Madros and Antola," Ologrin said. "You need to get your people away from here. Scatter them through the flats, as far away from here as you can. The arms men will return, and they won't pretend to be Ruhatsi next time."

"You are the Korun. You will protect us."

"No. You must protect yourselves. Move your children and elders to the north. They will be back."

Breeze waited patiently nearby. He had not had time to check her for injuries. Now he did, and found scrapes on her forelegs, but no other obvious wounds. "I have to return to the city. I cannot be here when they come. You should hurry."

The sky was turning blue in the east, where the horizon could be seen beyond the clouds. Ologrin mounted his horse. Marle stood before him and bowed at the waist. For a moment Ologrin thought she was slowly collapsing from exhaustion, but then he realized it was intentional.

"No! You can't do that. I'm not anything. Don't tell them I was here. Don't tell them anything."

Several of the healthier bisonherders walked up and fanned out behind Marle. "You will return to protect us," one of them said, and bowed as well.

Ologrin slipped the staff into the loops on the side of the saddle. "Hurry," he said, and kneed Breeze hard into a gallop.

They had leagues to cover, and he knew Breeze could not run the entire way home. Soon the horse slowed to a trot, which she maintained until they were out of sight of the bridge. The clouds continued to break and re-form, allowing large patches of morning light to warm the land. It was turning into the prettiest day of the entire year. Ologrin struggled to stay awake and not fall from the saddle. Finally, at midday, he saw a milkhouse some distance from the road. They veered off, and Breeze began to trot again as she sensed both food and water. They both drank from the trough. Breeze managed a couple of mouthfuls of drying beans before collapsing to her belly. Ologrin leaned against her and was instantly asleep.

He awoke as the Sun was setting. If anything, the clouds were even more broken. At any other time, it would have been a perfect evening to sit with Vireo, enjoy a meal, and watch the stars come out. A small handful of bisonherders had returned to the milkhouse.

"There are arms men on the road," one of them said.

"How?" he said. "No message could have beat me."

"They are always on the road," the herder replied.

Ologrin felt his control slipping. "I have to get back into the city," he said. "I can't go through the gate. They can't know I was gone."

They stood and looked at each other. Finally, one of the herdsmen muttered "Malach's path."

"What?" Ologrin said. "I've never heard of that."

"That is the way into the city without being seen."

"There is only one way into the city from the west, the Western Gate," Ologrin replied.

They stared at each other again. Then a boy of about twelve pushed his way to the front of the herders. "I know the way," he said.

Moments later, the boy was sitting between Ologrin and the horse's white mane. Ologrin felt more uncomfortable than ever, but Breeze did not complain. They set out at a trot, with the boy guiding them along interconnected paths. The Sun set in the west and shortly thereafter the Sojourner disappeared behind the mountains in the east, but Ologrin could make out the dim paths in the starlight. At first, they traveled to the north, but eventually jogged to the east, and Ologrin could sense the blackened bulk of Arske slowly blotting out stars in front of him. By the time the sun rose again, they were far north and east of the more populated parts of the flats. Here the escarpment became part of the mountain. Numerous draws had been eroded in Arske's base, any one of which looked like it might be the start of a path up the mountain. But Ologrin knew they were all false promises. There was no path up the mountain allowing entrance Antola. If there had been, it would have been exploited centuries before.

But by the time the Sun was directly overhead, the boy suddenly pointed to a small cut in the rock.

"You must be kidding," Ologrin said.

"You climb one direction, then the other," the boy said. "Finally you will come to a spot where you can see the castle and the city."

"The outcrop?" Ologrin asked, but the boy just blinked at him. The cut was just wide enough to admit a horse and rose steeply into obscuring brush. Ologrin had no other choice.

"How will you get home?" he asked the boy.

The boy thumped his chest. "I am a herder," he said, as if that explained everything.

Breeze stepped carefully through the cut. It climbed steeply for about forty hands, then just as it seemed to end in a tangle of branches, Ologrin could make out the path continuing to the left. He dismounted and took the lead. They continued to climb, sometimes on a fairly clear path, then guided by the barest thinning through the trees. At times the path was so steep he feared Breeze would not manage, but she seemed to be part goat as she leapt over boulders and roots. All the while, though, they seemed to be moving toward the north, away from the city. The Sun was getting low. Ologrin worried about being stuck on the mountainside in the dark, with no place to make a camp.

A wide and gentle path opened before them, promising except for the fact it was aimed north, and he needed to head south. But shortly the path steepened and became more rocky, and he felt deceived. Finally, it ran headlong into a steep rock face. Ologrin looked up. At least eighty hands up, he could see trees on the edge of the cliff. It was impassable. The road up the mountain led nowhere.

Quietly despairing, Ologrin assessed their situation. Breeze would have to back down the path before she could even turn around. He tried to squeeze between her and the mountain's flank. That was when he spied the half-rotted push pole leaning against the stone, one end still black from the explosion in the postern yard years before.

He found a foothold and pushed himself up the rock face. Barely twice his height above he felt a ledge and pulled himself onto another path. It had been completely hidden from below, and from where he now stood, the lower roadway would have been equally hidden, were it not for the rump of his horse. Breeze gave a fearsome jump and clawed her way onto the path next to him. The boy had been right. He was on the road to the outcrop. Beyond that was the road to the castle.

It was fully dark, and the Sojourner had once again set, when they rode into the yard next to the chimneys. Ologrin purchased absolute secrecy from the boy in the husbandry with an entire silver coin, then climbed to his room.

28

Ologrin lowered himself into the tub of warm water. One of the advantages of having his own space within the chimneys was the ability to heat considerable quantities of water, allowing him to take a bath whenever he chose. A fire burned brightly nearby, pushing back at the cool weather outside.

He heard heavy footsteps behind him. He did not need to turn to know that Albrect had entered the works.

"We sail in two days," Ologrin said. "This may be the last time I feel the luxury of warm water for a long time."

"You don't mind if I borrow some of your tools while you are gone, do you?"

Ologrin laughed. "The greatest vitachemist of our time needs to borrow a tool? Be my guest."

Albrect stood next to the tub, assuming a familiarity that Ologrin had no choice but to accept. In its own way, it was comforting. Albrect seemed to accept him simply for what he was, head adornment and all. None of it gave the older man pause.

"There was trouble out in the flats a few nights ago," Albrect said.

"What kind of trouble?"

"From what I hear, an uprising of sorts by the bison-herders. They managed to injure a couple of arms men in the process."

"A couple? What do you think led to that?"

"I thought you might have some idea," Albrect said.

"Why would I know what is going on down in the flats? I'm forbidden to go there, remember?"

"Where were you on New Sojourner?"

"In my chambers. What are you suggesting, Albrect?"

Albrect sighed. "This is a dangerous thing."

"Sounds like it was a dangerous thing for some arms men."

"There will be a response, you can count on that."

"A response to a couple of arms men being injured? What's an appropriate response to that?"

"Ologrin, Serenity was Crown for three dozen years before he died. His son has been Crown for half a year. The older had established who he was, and the world was satisfied with that. No one had reason to challenge him. Our new Serenity cannot feel that secure. Any challenge to his authority will be met with a harsh response, to send a message. For every arms man injured, dozens of people on the flats will suffer."

"And the rest of us should do nothing, even if innocent people are doomed to suffer?"

"Does the Sophenary have its own arms men I'm not aware of? What should we do?"

"It's not right."

"Deciding what's right or wrong is a young person's pastime. I have the Sophenary to keep open. Good luck keeping your secret," Albrect said, as he walked away.

Sailing day dawned with the Sun once again obscured by

clouds. Thus far, there had been no word of reprisals on the flats. Ologrin regretted deceiving Albrect. Before leaving the Sophenary, he sought him out to apologize, to no avail.

At the docks, six ships were tied bow-to-oar, with five more lashed alongside. Eleven ships, ready to sail. The *Wasp* floated in the middle of the pack, its twin masts towering over the other ships. Its sister ship sat in its cradle a few gross hands in front of the fleet, still mast-less, and would not be ready to sail until the following Summer. The *Rayfish* rested at the head of the fleet. Though the smallest of the eleven, it remained Ologrin's favorite, and his planned home at sea.

They were lightly loaded. They could easily have taken seven ships rather than eleven. But the plan was to trade value for quantity and return with each ship fully laden with food. As a result, they carried some of Antola's most valuable goods. The storage decks of three ships were filled with bison halves, smoked and salted for the journey, while a fourth was stuffed with stiff, tanned hides. The remaining ships held barrels of burned whitestone, charcoal, and sorghum syrup. And scattered through the fleet, so that no single ship carried all the risk, were fourteen dozen barrels of traditional high-sulfur blast powder. A gift from the Sophenary, Albrect said. *A generous one*, Ologrin thought. Finally, deep within the *Rayfish*, in the small cabin that had once belonged to Terval, Ologrin had hidden the herding staff. Simply knowing it was there gave him peace of mind.

Ologrin was about to take the steps from the Crown's Walk down to the ninth terrace, then cross through the tunnel and take the trestle lift to the docks. But as he approached the palace, two arms men spied him and began walking toward him with purpose. He was trapped, and he knew it. He stopped and waited.

"His Supreme Grace wishes to see you," one of the men said. Ologrin's heart sank. Getting to sea had been his surest way to avoid being interrogated about the events on the flats. He had almost made it, he thought.

The men ushered him through the palace and led him to the Council room, where Serenity worked at his head table. The arms men retreated, leaving the two of them alone. At first, Serenity did not speak. Ologrin decided to wait, afraid his voice might betray his nerves.

"I have something extra for you to take," Serenity said finally, standing and lifting a small pouch. "The Lord Mercantile says there may be a need to sweeten the deal so that we bring back sufficient grain." He handed the pouch over. "There are a dozen gold scarabs and five dozen silvers in here. If negotiations don't seem to be going well, use the coin. I want to be sure all of the ships return fully loaded."

"Thank you, Supreme Grace. That is generous."

"You know, if it were up to me, I would be happy with you calling me by my given name, Serenity."

Your given name is Terval, Ologrin thought.

"I know the Lord Coronet believes it is essential that I maintain appearance. At first, I thought it was a bit ridiculous, but now I'm beginning to understand. When the rest of you sit in this room with me, I feel like I'm the least capable one present."

"We know that's not true…"

"Let me finish," Serenity said. "In here I am surrounded by the smartest minds in Antola. Everyone is an expert at what they do, except me. I sit here wondering when it will all fall apart. Wondering when one of you will stand and say, 'You fool, you have no business being the Crown.' The only thing I really know is that I cannot let that happen. Because once that crack begins to form, not just I, but the entire Crown will collapse soon after. That may be the only understanding I bring to the council, but that I know for sure." Serenity returned to his table. He picked up one of the glowglobes, then sat it back down. *I'm not the only one trying to control his nerves*, Ologrin thought.

"The bridge to Madros was attacked by bisonherders the other night," Serenity added. "Did you know that?"

"Master Albrect told me about it."

"Tell me, and please tell me the truth. Were you out on the flats the other night? Were you there?"

Ologrin looked Serenity steadily in the eye. "I was not."

"They said it wasn't just the herders. The arms men reported there was a sorcerer there as well."

"A sorcerer? There are no such things as sorcerers."

"He caused lightning to pass from his hand, they said. And more than one said it."

"What did this sorcerer look like?"

"It was dark. No one really saw."

"Well, I am pretty noticeable," Ologrin said, running his hand across the horns on his head. "I accompanied Master Vireo into the mountains that evening. She is on a trip to the Polfre homeland. Most assuredly, I wasn't on the flats."

Serenity looked at Ologrin for several moments, as if formulating a reply. Ologrin thought he saw the man's anxiety replaced by a sense of weariness.

"Thank you for coming to speak to me, Lord Commander," Serenity said finally. "I should let you get to your ships. I understand you hope to sail before evening. Best of luck on your journey." He turned his back.

Ologrin paused, debating if he should say what continued to dominate his thoughts. He reached for the door, then looked back.

"Supreme Grace, being Lord Commander of the Fleet is close to a mockery, as I know less about sailing than almost anyone. But I do know that a great wave will mindlessly smash a ship, regardless of the skill of those onboard. There are enough people in the flats to make a great wave. If their

misery grows large enough, they can smash anything."
Serenity did not turn. Ologrin let himself out.

He took the trestle lift to the docks. The clouds were starting to lift by the time he stepped aboard the *Wasp* for one last discussion with Captain Weims. Walking forward to the *Rayfish*, he glanced up in time to see the Sun break through just long enough to illuminate the palace with golden rays. He hoped that his sailors saw it as well, as they would take it for a positive omen. He glanced back at the castle. It stood brooding and dark. He climbed aboard the *Rayfish* and took up a position near the steering oar. He was pleased to see Adept Scaup at his familiar station near the mast. Scaup issued orders, the crew hauled in the lines, and they eased into the bay.

Ologrin had imagined the fleet sailing proudly and in formation out of the bay. In fact, by the time the *Rayfish* was abeam of the Ginney Cliffs, they were strung out in a ragged line and the last of the ships had only just left the docks. They rounded the southern tip of the escarpment and watched the darkness settle around them. It was coming earlier each day. An easterly breeze was waiting for them. The *Rayfish*'s sail billowed forward and they settled into a comfortable run.

A lantern was hoisted to the top of the mast for the evening. The clouds cleared to the south, and the oarsman was able to steer by keeping Ortak off his left shoulder. Ologrin scanned the seas around them and could see only two other lanterns from the closest ships; specks of yellow light that seemed surprisingly close to the surface.

The breeze shifted toward the southeast the next morning, clearing the skies to the north but bringing colder air. The shift had the benefit of bringing the rest of the fleet into view again, and they began to stack together, much like the choppy waves beneath them. Ologrin elected to let the coastline gradually disappear to their right and use his navigation tables to find their position. The wind remained steady, while the waves spread out into broad swells once they lost sight of land. Two and a half days later, the coast gradually reappeared right on schedule. They rounded the broad point marking the eastern approach to the wide Solanon Bay. Another night and another day brought them within sight of the city itself.

The city of Solanon straddled the outlet of the Sestern river. Ologrin knew the Sestern was the largest river in Lhosa, but his imagination had failed to prepare him for its actual size. At its widest and deepest, the Bhin could not accommodate a single sailing ship. By contrast, the mouth of the Sestern was a third of a league wide. Ships were docked on either side, and several more seemed to be sailing upriver. In fact, the river was easily navigable by ship for almost two dozen leagues inland until it was joined by the outlet of the river Brest. Beyond that, the river was shallower, yet still easily passable by the flat-bottomed barges which traveled to and from Dormond, sixty leagues to the north.

Ologrin was impressed by the number of ships before him. The harbor buzzed with activity. Small, rowed craft moved between bigger ships anchored away from the docks, which waited their turn to load or unload. Most of the ships were the size of the *Rayfish*, or even smaller. He had no doubt that heads were turning to watch the massive *Wasp* as it settled into the harbor behind him.

They would have to find someone in charge. He realized they might spend days waiting for a chance to dock and unload. He expected the return voyage to be much slower, tacking their way home against the easterly winds. Every day they were delayed made the return trip seem colder and more formidable. He closed his eyes and imagined being back home in his chambers with Vireo and a great roaring fire. A shout regained his attention.

One of the small boats was rowing their direction. Ologrin pulled the hood of his cloak over his head. As the boat approached, a tall man stood in the bow, balancing despite the boat's rocking motion.

"Hail Serenity!" he yelled. Ologrin waved and the small boat rowed up to a rope ladder dropped over the side. The man took the ladder two ropes at a time. Clearly, he spent a lot of time in and around ships.

"Welcome to the *Rayfish*," Ologrin said as the man grasped his wrist. "Serenity is not on board, but this is his ship."

"It is our custom to greet a new ship in the name of its high chief," he said.

Ologrin had not heard a Solanon accent before and was amused. "How long until we can dock?" he asked.

"We have a space waiting for all your ships," the man said, waving toward the west docks. Ologrin could now see what appeared to be a clearing in the line. "I will guide you."

"Well, this is welcome luck," Ologrin replied happily. He glanced over at his oarsman, who only shrugged.

The wind remained favorable, allowing them to sail the ships in close. Ologrin had the oarsman steer directly toward the docks, then steer hard to the left as the crew doused the sail. The *Rayfish* slid to within a dozen hands of the dockside. Ropes were cast over and a gangway soon fixed. Pleased with the landing, Ologrin decided he wasn't as much a novice sailor as he had previously thought.

He watched as the remainder of his fleet found room on the docks or lashed themselves to their dockside companions. Before long he noticed a small delegation already making their way toward the ships. An older man of considerable girth was in its center, obviously the person of most importance, as he stared at the ships and at Ologrin while his entourage mostly kept their eyes on him. A pair of men dressed in leather breastplates and fingering sword hilts walked with the delegation. Other than the breastplates, they had no uniform clothing. They would have been little more than a nuisance to the Crown's Guard, Ologrin thought. He descended the gangway to meet the man.

"I am Chief Scriber," the man said. "I am a member of the Solanon Elders and am Chief of Ports." He stopped. Ologrin gave a bow, though he was impressed only with how anxious the man appeared to be.

"Ologrin," he said. "Lord Commander of the Fleet for his Supreme Grace, Serenity."

"You are welcome to our hospitality just for the night, unless you have business here," Chief Scriber said.

"We have business with the Elders," Ologrin replied. "We are loaded with the finest goods of Antola. We come to trade for the present, and to extend favor between our great cities for the future."

"Yes, yes. Good. Then I am charged to tell you that, representing the Elders, I will meet with you tomorrow after midday, to discuss terms." And with that, Chief Scriber gave a little bow.

Captain Weims walked down the gangway now fixed to the *Wasp* and joined them. His ceremony concluded, Chief Scriber obviously had continued interest in the huge ship, which dwarfed everything else in the harbor.

"That's a great ship, Captain." Scriber's pudgy fingers went to his smooth-shaven face. "What can you hold?"

"Four gross barrels in the underdeck alone," Weims replied.

Scriber's gaze was captured by the two masts, which he followed to the deck. "And is that a cannon on the foredeck?" he asked.

Weims was momentarily puzzled. "The bombard!" he said finally. "Yes, and adjustable."

"You bring weapons of war into our harbor, supposedly on a mission of peace." Scriber said it in a way that sounded curious, rather than concerned.

"We mean no war," Ologrin interjected.

"Would you like a tour?" Captain Weims asked.

The offer seemed to remind Master Scriber that he had a mission to complete. "No, no. Maybe later. Tomorrow then, after midday." He bowed again, and then the entire entourage backed away.

Ologrin stood next to Captain Weims' side. "We show up from halfway across the land, with the biggest ship they have ever seen, and they act like they've been expecting us," he said. "How could they know?"

Weims sounded unconcerned. "They deal with a great many ships here, from different cities. Perhaps they are used to exotic fleets just showing up and tying to their dockside."

Their crews were released with instructions to check in every couple of days or risk missing their ride back to Antola. Weims had sailed overstaffed, anticipating some of his crew would disappear when they began to consider the more difficult return trip. He seemed unconcerned as his men melted into the city.

Several taverns near the waterfront offered lodgings. Instead, Ologrin decided to stay on board the *Rayfish*. Terval's former cabin on the underdeck was comfortable enough. More importantly, the considerable pouch of coin was hidden there. He did not trust anyone else to look after it, and he certainly did not care to walk about a strange city with it strapped beneath his cloak.

The docks proved to be an active place far into the night. He napped in his cabin until late, then awoke, sensing a change in the weather. The air was still; the cold southern breeze seemed to have blown itself out. Most of the city had finally retired, and only scattered lanterns were left lit, including the one on their own stern. The silhouette of a lone individual stood at the bow. The figure turned as Ologrin approached, two eyes glowing softly.

"I don't like it," Scaup said.

"Too quiet or too dark?"

"I don't like how easy it was. This makes fifteen times I've sailed into Solanon. Usually we spend days looking for a place to slip in, paying this or that person claiming to be harbor chief. They're a touchy bunch. They always find some reason to take offense, then use that to raise their price. They like to play one ship off another. An Antolan ship offers a few silvers to dock first; they just go over to an Ismayan ship and get an offer for a few more. Not today. Today, we just slide right up to the docks; they say we'll see you in the morning."

"Maybe they're just showing respect for Serenity's fleet," Ologrin offered.

Scaup snorted. "This isn't Madros. Solanon's elders don't take anyone's orders. If they thought Serenity was coming in here expecting special treatment, they would likely not have even rowed out to us for a passage or more. Just let us sit in the harbor like fat floating in a pot."

"That one chief seemed impressed with the *Wasp*."

"That's another thing. Biggest ship they've seen, with a bombard that can be directed right at their city, and they don't act a bit concerned."

"Well, if we can trade our goods and be on our way back to Antola in a few days, then I don't care why they're giving us special favor," Ologrin said. He wasn't in the mood for Scaup's suspicions. He paced the length of the ship, then returned to the cabin.

The Chief of Ports returned to the docks the next day with a larger delegation. Captain Weims had prepared a makeshift table on the main deck of the *Wasp* for negotiations, as well as another to one side. Trays were heaped with samples of their goods. Ologrin noted with surprise that Weims had managed to fashion several trays with meat-filled bread pockets. Though they were meant to suggest the Antolan holds were filled with similar delicacies, Ologrin noted the presence of added flavorings that must have been purchased locally.

Weims had been busy through the night. He spied Ologrin and walked over.

"With your permission, Lord Commander, I recommend you let me manage the negotiations."

"It appears you already are," Ologrin replied, feeling vaguely like an imposter once again.

The delegation helped themselves to the food, as well as a considerable quantity of ale. Weims managed to delay any opening discussions until the Solanon delegation appeared quite content, then began laying on the compliments.

"We are honored by Solanon's remarkable hospitality. Never have I and my crew been treated so well. Your tavern meals, Chief Scriber, are as fine as those at the tables of Serenity himself."

Ologrin furrowed his brow. There was flattery, and then there was mockery. But Scriber seemed pleased by the remark. He cracked the knuckles of his short fingers.

"To business, dear Captain," he said.

"Yes. Well, Serenity has charged us with renewing our friendship with your great city. We come with a sampling of Antola's bounty. You have tasted our bison meat. We have eighteen dozen bison sides and twelve dozen tanned bison hides, a sturdy yet soft leather. We have fifty dozen barrels of fine-milled charcoal, and fifty dozen barrels of burned whitestone. Mixed with sand and water, the whitestone makes a mortar stronger than the stones it holds together. And, to show what can be done with the charcoal, fourteen dozen barrels of our finest blast powder."

Chief Scriber's fingers danced on the table. "And you are trading for emmer, is that correct?"

"That is correct."

"Nothing else?"

"Our mission is one of good will. We hope to expand our trade in the future."

Scriber began whispering to a pair of men nearby. Captain

Weims pretended suddenly to have great interest in the shapes of the clouds overhead.

"We have been afflicted by an especially difficult Summer," Scriber said.

"As have we," Weims replied.

"But in the interest of goodwill, we generously offer a trade of twenty-four gross barrels of our finest emmer wheat."

Ologrin felt his jaw go slack. They had brought what he considered an overly generous trade for eleven shiploads of emmer, but what Scriber was offering would not fill half of them. He expected Weims to toss the table and throw them off his ship, but instead the Captain appeared to be thinking, as if he might actually accept the offer.

"So, you have no interest in either the bison or the blast powder, I assume," Weims finally said. This time Chief Scriber was surprised. "Your offer is for the whitestone and charcoal alone, correct?"

Scriber's look of surprise gave way to a smile. "A miscalculation on my part, Captain. Of course we would like the meat and the powder. I meant to offer thirty-six gross barrels for all you bring to trade."

"I think seventy gross is closer to the mark," Weims replied.

"Ridiculous! All your ships together cannot hold seventy gross barrels. They would be hard pressed to hold fifty."

"Fifty gross sounds fair," Weims said. "Do we have a deal?"

Chief Scriber started to splutter, but even Ologrin could see that the man was amused at being out-tacked by the Captain. A smile crept over Scriber's face. "A generous deal for you, I'm sure. But we are generous people. We have a deal. Plus, of course, our cost in coin for the barrels, dock space, and labor."

"Forty silvers ought to cover the costs," Weims replied.

Ologrin thought this was an unreasonably rich offer, but noticed a slight scowl cross Scriber's face, who only gave a short nod in return.

Their negotiations ended, the Solanon entourage took a sudden interest in a tour of the *Wasp*. While a member of Weims' crew showed them the bombard, the Captain took Ologrin aside.

"I understand you have a pouch of coins. I hope it contains forty silvers."

"It does," Ologrin said, "but I think you overpaid."

"We need the grain, and we need to be back at sea by the end of this passage. I hope the extra coin will encourage them to be prompt."

Returning to the *Rayfish*, Ologrin noticed the clouds coming in from the north, like waves stacking up as they neared the shore. *After an endless Winter, finally a Summer storm*, he thought. The west bank of the Sestern river still gleamed in yellow sunlight, but the shadow from the clouds was steadily pushing toward it.

The hatches to the *Rayfish*'s underdeck were wide open. His crew must have assumed that negotiations would go well, as they already had a large fraction of the ship's cargo sitting on the docks. Ologrin checked to be sure things were in order in his cabin, then decided to find someplace ashore to spend the rest of the day.

The buildings reminded Ologrin of the Purse, minus the steep slope. He walked until he could no longer hear the shouts of the docks, then found what he was hunting for: a peaceful looking tavern with a glass-filled window where he could sit and still have a good view of the world outside. He ordered ale and settled into a quiet corner. He suddenly felt very tired. And, as if they had been waiting for this moment, thoughts of Vireo coalesced in his consciousness. He hoped she would be back from the mountains by the time he returned. Another cold Winter would not be so bad, he thought. Let the snow fill the Crown's Walk. There was fire in his chambers and fire in the chimneys. Serenity would be able to relax, knowing that the people of Antola would be fed for the Winter, and he would make a trip to the flats to assure the same was true for the bisonherders. And he would have his Vireo with him again. Tranquility would prevail.

"I knew I would find you in here," a voice said.

Ologrin turned to see Scaup standing next to the table. He began to ask how, in fact, Scaup would have had any idea where he was, but the Polfre tugged his arm.

"Come with me. I have to show you something!"

"It can wait. I'm not going..."

"I know why we are getting special treatment at the docks. I don't think it's good." Scaup grabbed Ologrin's hands. Instantly he was filled with anxiety. Scaup fixed him with a steady gaze. Without saying anything else, Ologrin followed the shorter man out.

They walked back toward the docks. He was tempted to ask more questions, but the intensity of the feeling he had received from Scaup had frightened him. It had been clear and direct, and completely convincing. Scaup led them through an alley between buildings. He paused at a doorway leading, Ologrin guessed, to the kitchen of a tavern. Scaup motioned for silence in the Polfre way: palms almost touching and fingers pointed up. They slipped through the door.

Two cooks glanced their way and then went back to work, as if strangers sneaking through the kitchen was a routine occurrence. They approached a short hall that led to the main room. The tavern was busy, filled with loud, garrulous voices. Scaup motioned for Ologrin to peek around the corner.

Almost two dozen men had taken over the room, standing in small groups or sitting on chairs and tables. The ale was flowing freely. Every one of them had a short sword at his side, and each was dressed in the same short, tight-fitting blue tunic over identically colored breeches. They were absorbed with watching a similarly dressed, shapely woman who seemed to be in the middle of a raunchy tale. Ologrin whipped his head out of sight, then hurried for the back entrance, reaching up to be sure his hood was still covering his head.

"Captain Bana," he hissed, when they got outside. "And a whole room of Antolan arms men!"

"You know the woman?"

"I met her once. She's not just in the Crown's Guard; she's Malacheb."

"There are warhorses out front," Scaup noted.

"This is impossible. There's an entire shield of men in there! Why would Solanon allow armed Antolan arms men into their city?"

"I told you something wasn't right."

Ologrin tried to think. A shield of horsemen might cover thirty leagues a day, if they had fresh horses every half day. Five days from Antola, at an absolute minimum. But the men inside did not look like they had just finished five days of hard travel. "We need to get back to the ships," Ologrin said. He desperately wanted to talk with Captain Weims.

The Solanon dock workers were still unloading the ships when Ologrin and Scaup returned. Ologrin intended to see if Weims was aboard the *Wasp*, but then he noticed two arms men standing on the *Wasp's* deck.

"They're here," he said quietly to Scaup.

They worked their way toward the *Rayfish*. A single blue-tunic stood on its deck as well. "I'm Lord Commander of the Fleet," Ologrin muttered. "I should go up and demand to know why an arms man has stationed himself on my ship."

Scaup grabbed his wrist again, and he felt the same jolt of anxiety. "Obviously, their orders are coming from someone else."

Standing on the docks, Ologrin felt exposed. If he wasn't going to return to his ship, then he needed to find a less obvious perch. They backtracked away from the docks and followed an alley, then found a vantage point in the corner of a tiny tavern, giving them a view of the *Rayfish*'s deck and gangway.

Afternoon shadows began to gather about the docks. Work slowed. Finally, Ologrin saw Captain Weims appear and go aboard the *Rayfish*. After a short period of time, the arms man on the *Rayfish* deck descended the gangway and headed into the jumble of dockside buildings. For a moment, Weims stood alone at the ship's rail. Ologrin jumped up and hurried out of the tavern, then walked along the edge of the docks fast enough to catch Weims just as he descended the *Rayfish*'s gangway and turned toward the *Wasp*. Weims whirled as Ologrin touched his shoulder.

"I have been looking all over for you," Weims said. Ologrin listened for fear or anger, but only heard a touch of irritation. "I didn't take you for an ale-drinker before evening."

"If I have business as Lord Commander that you need to know about, I will share it," Ologrin said, trying to cover the anxiety in his voice. Weims blinked several times at the rebuke.

"My apologies, Lord Commander," Weims said finally. "The Solanons. They have demanded to renegotiate the deal. They say they require more coin than we originally agreed to. I need to know how much coin you actually have."

"How much do they want?" Ologrin said.

"Sixty silvers and now a dozen gold pieces. I fear we are being robbed, but do you have it?"

Ologrin managed to give a slight nod, despite his shock. He had assumed only two people knew exactly how much coin was in the pouch hidden aboard the *Rayfish*: his Supreme Grace Serenity, Crown of Antola, and himself. It appeared the Solanon Chief of Ports knew as well.

"They are coming for it in the morning," Weims said. He started to walk away, but Ologrin stopped him again.

"Why are there Antolan arms men here?"

"I was about to ask you the same thing, but then you said you had business that was none of mine," Weims replied.

"I apologize for that. And I knew nothing of the arms men."

"This entire trip makes less and less sense," Weims said irritably.

Ologrin returned to the *Rayfish*. Scaup was waiting for him on the main deck. Once again, as the Sun set and darkness fell, they were the only ones on board.

"Weims knows nothing more about the arms men than we do," Ologrin noted.

"Something bad is coming," Scaup replied.

"I don't know. Maybe they've always been here, and we didn't know it."

Scaup took a deep lungful of air. "I'm not talking about that. There's a storm coming in from the north."

Ologrin noticed the boat had started to rock gently. Ripples were spreading into the harbor from the south. "It feels like a south breeze to me," he said.

"The south breeze has been slipping under those northern clouds all day. At some point, the north is going to push back. You wait and see."

"Will it pass by morning?" Ologrin wanted nothing to slow the unloading and loading of the ships.

Scaup didn't reply but moved off to busy himself tidying up the deck. Ologrin decided he was done wandering the streets of Solanon. He would stay put until they were ready to sail, and if any arms men had an interest in him, they would have to deal with his staff as well.

He brooded on the afterdeck. The clouds soon obscured any view of the sky. He had not seen the Sojourner since plotting their position the second night of their journey. His

Chapter 28 | 433

anxiety increased, as if Scaup were now sending him nervous energy through the wood of the ship instead of by direct touch.

From the corner of his eye he saw a flicker in the north. He turned and waited, and after several moments was rewarded with another flash from within the farthest clouds. The bunched sail rustled against the spar. He listened for the distant roll of thunder, but instead he heard the *clip-clip-clop* of an approaching horse. He scanned the docks. A single warhorse cantered out of the blackness and headed toward the *Rayfish*. Ologrin hurried to his cabin and returned with his staff in hand.

A tall arms man dismounted easily at the foot of the gangway. Ologrin stood very still. Scaup, he noticed, had taken a position behind the mast where he was partially hidden. Ologrin recognized the head and shoulders of the arms-man appearing over the rail, even in the darkness. He stepped forward, bringing the staff up at the same time. He readied himself to swing the moment the figure reached for his sword and spoke in a low snarl. "Get off my ship."

"I'm just here to bring you a message," Captain Aron said, arms half-raised.

"My entire village died because of you."

"I have no idea what you're talking about."

"You're a murderer and a liar. Remember that day on the flats? You told Lord Wesse what you'd seen, what you thought I was. And instead of killing me, Wesse thought he would make a point by killing everyone I knew. Because you told him."

"Do I remember that day?" Aron said, dropping his arms. "Every waking moment I remember it, because that's the day my life was ruined. I didn't talk to Wesse. I didn't even get to say goodbye to my family. They took me to Madros in ropes. I haven't *seen* Antola since the day *you* decided to pretend to be Lord of the Flats."

For years, the narrative had been clear in Ologrin's mind. Aron the traitor. Aron telling Lord Wesse everything that had transpired in the flats, and Wesse responding by wiping out Halrin's Spur. The Ruhatsi were a ruse. The real demons of Lhosa were Lord Wesse and his Malacheb. Now Aron stood before him, defenseless, and all he had to do was lunge forward. He felt the heat building in the metal ribs surrounding his chest, radiating into the staff.

"What message?" he said.

"You have to leave."

"I am the Lord Commander of the Fleet. I am here under the direction of his Supreme Grace…"

"Wesse is *here*!" Aron cried. "Don't you understand? He's here with ten dozen of his men, and he's coming for you! Serenity ordered him get rid of you. I came to warn you. You have to leave. You have to run!"

Behind him, Ologrin heard what sounded like a sudden restlessness overtake the rigging of the ships in the harbor. A burst of warm wind rolled over them, accompanied by a few drops of rain.

"I'm going back…" Ologrin began.

"You're not going back. You'll be killed. And you can't stay here. Lord Wesse is coming in the morning with an entire shield of men. You must leave tonight. Head for Dormond. Head west on the road for Ismay. It doesn't matter. You just can't stay here."

With a rustling *bang*, the sail on the *Rayfish* fell into place and caught the wind. Ologrin and Aron both stumbled as the ship began to move. The gangway splashed into the water next to the dock. Ologrin saw the lines holding the ship in place were no longer tied to the rail. He watched Scaup grab a sheet and haul the angle of the spar against the wind. The *Rayfish* surged forward.

"You're going to have to steer soon," Scaup yelled.

"What are you doing?" Aron cried at the same time.

"Looks like we're leaving," Ologrin said.

"You can't do this."

"And looks like you're coming with us."

More swiftly than Ologrin thought possible, Aron unsheathed his sword and aimed it at one of the lines holding the spar in position. Ologrin swept his staff around to meet the sword. There was a blue flash where the staff broke the sword in half. Ologrin felt his skin tingle and his hair stand on end. In reply, lightning struck the water next to the ship and set of a crackling web of bolts flashing through the clouds to the horizon. Thunder slammed into them with a god-sized slap.

"Steer!" Scaup cried from the bow. They were headed straight for a ship anchored in front of them.

Ologrin leapt for the steering oar and shoved with all his weight. The *Rayfish* swung to the left, just missing the ship ahead. "Are you coming?" he yelled at Captain Aron.

"You won't make it," Aron said. "They'll hunt you down. You're both as good as dead."

"Swim or grab a line," Ologrin replied.

Then the rain came in a slanting sheet. Aron gave Ologrin a last, desperate glance and dove over the rail.

"I can't see anything ahead of us!" Ologrin cried.

"Don't worry! Steer when I tell you!" Scaup yelled back.

Ologrin stuffed the staff into his left armpit and the steering oar into his right. He pushed and pulled, following Scaup's directions, while the *Rayfish* rocked and bucked in the wind from the storm. About the time he thought he could make out the horizon in front of them, lightning flashed and blinded him again. He caught glimpses of Scaup running from the bow to the mast, attempting to trim the spar and sail on his own. After a while Scaup stopped yelling directions, and Ologrin could see that they were headed generally south into the open water of the bay.

Eventually the rain and wind eased somewhat. Scaup took

over at the steering oar. Ologrin lashed his staff to the mast, and with both hands free he was able to haul the spar into a better angle to the wind. The ship slid more easily over the waves. They both watched in fascinated dread as the mast seemed to come alive. Electrical fire crawled up and down its length, then dropped onto the deck and rolled around in small glowing balls before disappearing in loud snaps. They waited for the mast to catch fire, but it seemed impervious to the display.

They sailed on, surfing across the waves, but to Ologrin it felt like they were sailing into the depths of a cave. He took the steering oar again. Turning his face to the stern, he strained to listen but only heard the roar of the waves. After what seemed forever, he noticed he could more easily see the mast and the rigging, then the length of the ship, with Scaup crouched next to the bow, and finally the seas just around them. But the world stubbornly refused to get larger. Beyond a few dozen hands of sea, they were surrounded by rain and clouds that seemed to reach to the surface.

"Do you think we've cleared the mouth of the bay?" he called forward to Scaup.

The man's voice was surprisingly distant in reply. "We should sail further south anyway. They'll expect us to turn east as soon as we can."

For the first time, Ologrin wondered if they should even turn east. Even if they survived being chased all the way home, he had no idea what they would do once they entered Gosper Bay. Could they disappear into the Purse? Would he even be safe within the Sophenary?

And then a profound sense of despair settled over him. Someone had been trying to kill him since his twelfth year. Had he ever been anything more than tolerated, wherever he had lived? Had he always been just one excuse away from being marked for destruction? He had trusted Serenity, because he thought Serenity loved him, but Serenity was just the latest to want him dead. Had Vireo loved him, or was that a trap as well? The steering oar vibrated in his arms. Pull one way, and head for a city that wanted to kill him. Push the other way, and head for anonymity and a new world, and a feeling of being chased for the rest of his life.

The day finally dawned, the rain lessened, and the clouds lifted. But behind them the clouds were turning black again. He could now see much further in every direction. There was no land to be seen.

"Here they come!" Scaup cried, pointing over Ologrin's shoulder. He peered behind them again. A two-masted vessel was suddenly lifted into view by a swell, then disappeared again.

"Can we outrun them?" Ologrin asked.

Scaup shook his head. "The bigger, the faster," he yelled. "Eventually they will run us down." Ologrin concentrated on the handle of the steering oar, as if he could will the ship to sail faster. "Go hard to the left!" Scaup cried.

"That will only give them a favorable angle. They'll catch us quicker!" Ologrin said.

"We want them closer when that storm hits. It will blind them before it does us. Then we'll double back and try to head west behind them!"

Ologrin saw the logic and pushed the oar. The *Rayfish* began to turn and then rolled onto its right rail as the waves stuck it from the opposite side. Ologrin struggled to find purchase on the steep, slippery deck. Slowly the ship righted itself and began to make way. He watched the *Wasp*, and shortly thereafter it, too, turned, aiming for a point in front of them where the ships would eventually meet.

Ologrin now willed the storm to move faster. Flicks of lightning could be seen striking the water. The *Wasp* appeared distinctly larger. Then a flash of a different sort came from the *Wasp's* bow: a flicker of flame and a puff of smoke.

"The bombard!" he cried. He counted slowly in his head.

At twelve he heard a dull *whump* and shortly thereafter thought he could see a tiny splash behind and to their left.

"They're one league away from us!" he cried. He turned in time to see another yellow flash from the *Wasp's* bow. Again he counted, and at eleven he heard the *whump*.

"Watch for the…"

But the forward rail of the *Rayfish* exploded in splinters and debris. The ship lurched as one of the lines holding the spar snapped. A jagged hole now filled the deck exactly where Scaup had been standing.

"Scaup!" Ologrin tried scanning the waves on either side of the ship but saw nothing. He stared at the hole. There was a hint of red splashed against the tattered remnants of the rail, but no other sign of the man. The spar slammed against its remaining lines and the *Rayfish* rolled again, almost broaching. Ologrin pulled the oar with all his might. He had to run downwind, he knew, or the ship would roll and sink.

Again, slowly, the ship responded, and the rolling seemed less as they began to run with the waves again. He glanced behind him in time to see the storm roll over the *Wasp*. Even if they could get the bombard reloaded in the storm, they would not be able to see him while in its midst.

He struggled to keep the bow pointed downwind. Every few moments it would swing to one side, then the spar would crash overhead, popping one set of lines tight and allowing the opposite set to go dangerously slack. Something groaned deep within the ship. He suspected the bombard's stone had blasted through the hull below the waterline and feared the *Rayfish* was taking on water.

The storm seemed to leap toward him. Lightning flashed, and again the mast shimmered with lines of fire. The gust front slammed into the sail and he heard wood splintering above. Then torrents of rain blinded him. He held on, no longer even feeling like he was steering. He kept hoping the storm would run over him and leave him behind, but it seemed to hold him in its midst.

After what seemed like forever, the entire storm seemed to turn. He felt the wind and rain slowly shifting at his back, pushing the bow of the *Rayfish* toward his right. A sudden wave lifted the ship and then dropped it bow first. The mast's forward stay broke loose and whipped around backward. Ologrin ducked as a huge chunk of wood sailed over his head. The mast began flexing back and forth with each wave.

At last the rain seemed to lessen enough for Ologrin to see more than a few hands beyond the ship. He was surrounded by raging seas, with white spray stripped from the top of each wave by the wind. The *Wasp* was nowhere to be seen.

Ologrin now had the tiniest hope that he might escape the *Wasp*. But the *Rayfish* was slowly being pulled apart beneath him. As best he could tell, the wind was blowing furiously from the east, and he had the ship pointed more-or-less west. The ship struggled to crest the top of each wave, and each trough buried the bow ever deeper.

Nonetheless, in the process of dying, the *Rayfish* seemed to develop a rhythm with the sea once again. Time seemed to collapse. Ologrin did nothing more than hold onto the steering oar, too stunned to think ahead. His life became measured in crests and troughs, rising and falling. After the longest time, the skies darkened again, signaling the setting of a Sun hidden by clouds. He could feel the ship slowing. The bow was burying itself to the base of the mast with each trough. At some point it was going to either break apart or fail to come up again. At that point the end would come quickly, he thought. He would be shoved into waves, his breath forced out, followed by a gasp and lungs full of cold water. If he was lucky, he would be struck by a piece of flying timber, a more sudden and painless end.

The *Rayfish* struggled to the top of another wave, and Ologrin thought he could see a line of darkness ahead. Then it crashed down, he thought for the last time. But the ship came up again and again, and he found himself distracted by the sight of the darkness getting larger atop each crest. He wondered if somehow another storm was coming from the opposite direction. Then he had the idea that he was seeing the edge of the world and laughed. Everyone thought the edge was a cliff, a waterfall over which one would fall forever. But it was a wall instead!

The *Rayfish* dropped into a trough and he heard timbers crack and snap beneath him. He was thrown forward into the base of the mast. The ship lifted and dropped one last time, then hit the wall. The mast bent forward and snapped with a huge tearing *crack*, and a confusion of sail, ropes, and wood crashed down onto Ologrin's head, plunging him into the black water.

FIFTH PASSAGE

Orhal the Crown was mighty and aggressive, and sought to return to the practice of his ancestors. He brought back the Malacheb rituals of the Red Hand. And the people of the riverlands were afflicted with his cruelty.

Now in that time Wysel, most famous Master of the Sophenary, and greatly revered for many deeds and works, sent word to Orhal. "You have engaged in barbarous acts that have been forbidden by the gods. Repent these evils and seek forgiveness."

But Orhal's jaw remained set. "Come to me in battle and see who Malach supports."

So, drawing together great powers, Wysel alone met Orhal and bested him in battle. Then the people of the riverlands flocked to Wysel's side. They came by the gross dozens to the foot of the city, and called out, proclaiming Wysel to be their Crown.

Bemal, Orhal's son, at firsts offered obedience to Wysel. But in his heart he considered himself the rightful heir to the Crown. And then strange and terrible things began to happen in the more distant villages. The Ruhatsi appeared, bringing with them not only bloodshed, but the evil magic of the Lord Sorceros himself. Fear swept through the riverlands. Bemal spoke to the people and said "We have abandoned the will of Malach and allowed Sorcery to become

Crown. Malach abandons us in turn, until I am restored as the rightful crown. Your loyalty must be only to me. I alone can protect you from this scourge."

Wysel saw through the magic fires and apparitions, and spoke to the people of the riverlands. "Do not be fooled. These tricks are well known. They are the tools of Sophenary masters that have been co-opted by Bemal for his own use. They are not the work of the Lord Sorceros."

But Bemal had foreseen Wysel's efforts and had spread rumors that only the Maleugen could conjure such forces. "Wysel even admits to knowing the magic," he said. "Truly this is Maleugen sorcery." And so their hearts were turned.

Then Bemel sent word to Wysel again. He promised safe passage back to Dha-Arenish if Wysel would relinquish claim to the Crown and submit to his protection. But Wysel knew this for another deception and feared being captured and slain. Moreover, without question, the Polfre would never agree.

"I am rejected by my homeland, untrusted by my people, and pursued by my Crown," Wysel cried. "Gods, only you can offer me protection from this world." And the gods heard Wysel's lament. They caused a great darkness to cover the riverlands, and Wysel escaped into the night, and was not seen again, though Wysel's legend continued to grow with time.

—from *The Chronicles of Grebe the Elder*

29

The sensation of being pushed down into icy water so overwhelmed his nervous system that Ologrin could not tell if he was freezing or on fire. His entire body seemed to spasm. He tried to flail his arms, but they barely moved. Something heavy began to wrap around him, causing a panic that helped him break his arms free. He clawed at the thick sail cloth and dragged himself to the surface.

The sail remained attached to the spar, which itself was sufficiently lashed to the broken mast to create an accidental raft of wood, fabric, and rope. Ologrin hauled himself out of the water. For the moment, he was not drowning. There was shoreline nearby; he could sense a vast tract of trees just beyond. Between him and them was a mass of tumbled boulders he would have to climb over. An immense weight of water was thrown up against the rocks and crashed down on him every few moments. With each crash, more pieces of the ship cracked and broke apart.

He reached what was left of the forward end of the *Rayfish* and plunged once again into unexpectedly deep water. He sputtered to the surface just as the last receding wave pulled him backward into the jagged edge of the deck. He felt the corset tear as a fragment of wood jabbed him in the side. Then the next wave tore him loose and he was forced deep into the water again. This time he tried to flatten himself on the rocks, allowing the outflow to wash over him. He pushed with his feet and managed to find a handhold, then pushed far enough to get his head out of the water. He gripped the boulder for dear life as the next wave crashed down, then rolled himself into shallower water on the other side. Another wave, and then he was struggling to his feet. He tripped and smashed his face just as the next wave broke over the rocks, but he felt gravel on his hands. He crawled a short distance and collapsed on his stomach.

A truly tremendous wave blasted into the shoreline and broken ship, sending splintered wood through the air like spears. Realizing he was nowhere close to safe, he struggled to his feet and half-ran, half fell up the shore until he reached the sudden rise that indicated the limit of the waves' reach. A short stretch of coarse grass gave way to something much softer. He fell and rolled onto his back.

He lay there, listening to the waves crash against the remnants of his ship. There was almost no light. The sense of icy cold gripped him and he began to shake violently. Whatever he was lying in was colder than the water. He rolled over and found himself in snow that reached to his elbows. He forced himself to stand. The snow slipped through his thin boots, and his feet, already half frozen from the sea, began to burn due to the icy snowmelt. He was alive, but he was going to freeze if he didn't do something.

He struggled away from the sound of the surf and deeper into the trees. The snow was decidedly thinner the deeper he went, suggesting a heavy overhanging canopy. The ground rose, then dipped slightly. Though damp, the groundcover here was more dense, and nearly free of snow. He scraped an Ologrin-sized hole in the damp clutter, lay down, and tried to protect himself as best he could. Then, though it was now utterly black, he closed his eyes and concentrated.

For long moments there was nothing. Then he felt a tingling in his chest, and eventually a distinct warming. He began to shake again, but otherwise he tried to hold still, as if any movement of his arms or legs would create eddies that would carry away his precious pocket of warming air. Gradually the shaking subsided. Heron had once mentioned that, at the very end, people freezing to death lose their sense of being cold. He did not know if he was managing to warm himself or was simply dying. Gradually the all-over pain subsided, leaving him with coldness in his hands and feet. He was not comfortable, but he didn't seem to be dying, so he waited for morning.

Slowly, he began to make out the silhouette of trees against a brightening sky. He waited until he could begin to see individual trunks in the forest gloom, then painfully raised himself onto his stinging feet. The surf continued to pound a short distance away. He walked back to the edge of the trees. The *Rayfish* was unrecognizable. Every wave pushed it further into the rocks, then pounded it like a hammer, splintering more pieces into kindling. Ologrin suddenly realized that was the best, last use for his ship, and began grabbing as much wood as he could and piling it at the edge of the tree line. Much of the ship was tangled up with the shredded sails and rigging, making it impossible for him to pull away large pieces. He was quickly soaked in freezing water. He tried to dislodge a larger plank, but the next wave caught him and knocked him to his knees. His hands felt something smooth and round lodged in the rocks. He pulled instinctively, then fell back with his staff in his hands.

The *Rayfish* began breaking up more quickly. To his dismay, most of it was being washed out to sea instead of being thrown up on shore. He set to work again, dragging as many broken pieces of wood ashore and up toward the tree line. By the time he felt himself ready to collapse out of sheer exhaustion, he had managed to salvage a pile about thirty hands in diameter and two thirds his own height. Taking some of the smallest scraps and driest surrounding needles, he carefully formed a mound of kindling. There had been a time in the distant past when he would not have ventured out without a pair of flints in his pocket. He had long since forgotten such a useful little habit, and now he greatly regretted it. He dragged the biggest stone he could move next to the pile. Closing his eyes again and concentrating, he picked up the bottom of the staff and swung it as hard as he could at the stone. The stone broke in half in a shower of sparks. He held his breath, but a moment later noticed a stream of smoke coming from the pile of needles. A few moments after that he was rewarded with a tiny tongue of flame. Soon he had a nice fire going. He piled wood and allowed it to burn high for a short while, then die back as the coals at the base of the fire began to radiate red heat.

With his body starting to warm, he realized he was desperately thirsty. He alternated scooping and eating handfuls of snow and rewarming his hands. Snow, it turned out, was a poor thirst-quencher, but after dozens of mouthfuls, he began to feel better. He sat on the warming ground near the fire and quickly realized that next on his body's agenda was sleep. He stoked the fire again, then curled on his side, hoping to take short naps between efforts at keeping the fire going.

When he awoke, the sky was once again getting dim. The fire was nothing but a mound of gray ashes. He poked at the ashes anxiously and was rewarded with a few barely glowing coals deep within. He was able to find more scraps of the ship along the shoreline and got the fire going again in short order. He ate more snow, and then felt well enough to notice the next issue: He was starving. But that would have to wait for daylight.

Darkness descended, and his world shrank to the space lit by the fire. The night was silent. He sat cross-legged until his legs ached, then stood until he felt he might fall over, then fed the fire and sat again. At some point in the night the clouds broke up enough for him to glimpse stars. At first there were too few for him to recognize any, but then a larger patch opened up, revealing a brilliant blue-white star over the sea, unmistakably the star Sautor. Until that moment he had hoped that somehow the *Rayfish* had been twisted by the wind and had been driven up on the southern shores of Lhosa, many leagues west of Solanon. The snow would not have made sense, but his mind had not yet processed that fact. But now Sautor, the brightest star of the north, was shining down from what he had hoped was the southern sky. Which meant—and he was suddenly queasy as his mind whirled to re-orient itself. If that was Sautor, and he knew that it was, then the shore he had been driven up against faced the northeast. The only northeastern shores in Lhosa were on the other side of the continent from Solanon. There was no way he had been driven south and west away from Lhosa, only to end up on its northeastern shore. Which meant he was no longer on Lhosa at all.

He sat and put his head between his knees to stop it from spinning. Since childhood he had wondered if there was anything else out there. He could not have invented a worse way, he thought, to discover the answer was yes.

Sautor arced from right to left and disappeared behind the clouds, just as it should. From that he was able to guess that about half the night had passed. His supply of salvaged wood was dwindling quickly and would not last another day and night. He was going to have to think of something else.

As light once again crept into the sky, he decided to explore the shoreline. It seemed less rocky to the south, so he headed that direction. Though much of the *Rayfish* had been sucked out to sea, it had been broken up and re-deposited along the gravel and rocks. He walked perhaps a half league to where a low bluff appeared to come up to the edge of the water. He climbed the bluff and could see that the shoreline continued to the south in much the same way, as far as he could see.

Discouraged, he walked back to his smoldering fire, picking up another load of wood scraps along the way. He piled them on and allowed the fire to blaze up and warm him. Once again, feeling warm made him more aware of his hunger.

He scanned the shore to the north. It curved, so that if he headed that way he would end up walking east. Somehow, that felt right, as that was the direction he had come. But at the limit of his sight the curve seemed to disappear. He estimated it would take most of a day to walk to that point, too far to return to the familiarity of the fire for the night. He suddenly felt an ache in his chest. Home had been reduced to nothing but a fire surrounded by a dwindling stack of broken wood. Yet leaving it seemed like the last thing he wanted to do.

He decided to spend one more night. The clouds had mostly dissipated, and he had hopes of seeing more stars, or even the Sojourner. He began to look forward to it the way one would look forward to the visit of a best friend. He scrounged as much wood as he could find, then scouted around deeper beneath the trees, hoping to find anything that resembled food. The location where he spent his first night was at the lip of a shallow bowl several dozen hands across. Surrounding it were small trees with black berries scattered on their branches. He debated the risk, but then watched a bird land, examine a nearby berry as if thinking, then pluck it and fly off. Ologrin harvested a small handful of berries and crammed them in his mouth, hoping for the best. They were incredibly sour and distasteful. He forced himself to return to the fire. As he had not become sick by the time the sun was falling in the west, he decided the berries were not poisonous and returned to the clearing to eat several more handfuls, until he began to feel an ache in his stomach. He then stuffed as many additional berries into various parts of his cloak as he could and returned to the fire for another night.

At Sunset, the half-illuminated Sojourner was already high in the sky. He slept fitfully, even though it had been a full day and night since he had last slept. He awoke while it was still dark. The fire was just low embers. He stirred it to life with a few more scraps, then ate several more handfuls of snow and the rest of his berries. The Sojourner was now setting. He walked to the edge of the shore. The sea had settled quite a bit since coughing him up, and he could see broken reflections of the Sojourner on its surface, stretching like a line pointing to the east, beckoning him. He decided there was no value in waiting. Using his staff as a walking stick, he set out along the shoreline. After a long while he looked back, curious to see if he could make out the tiny glow of his fire. The tree line was uniformly black. He swallowed the lump in his throat and continued onward.

Eventually the Sun rose warm and red in front of him, and his spirits rose with it. But clouds slowly returned, and the sky once again became a Sunless gray. The point of land seemed to stretch before him, and he began to think that it was some wicked illusion. Eventually he looked behind him and could see only open water and realized that the shoreline had gradually been curving back to the north again. At last a sharper curve was evident ahead. With the sky dimming once again, he finally reached a point where the land was entirely to his left, and unbroken sea to his right. He had reached the most northeastern point of…whatever place this was. The continent of Lhosa had to be out there, he thought, as he gazed north. Perhaps it was only a few leagues to the north, perhaps just over the horizon. But even as he hoped it was so he knew it wasn't true: Seafarers would have long ago found and plotted this land. Lhosa was dozens of leagues to the north, perhaps farther.

Looking to the west, even as the shoreline disappeared below the horizon, a greater mass of land rose above it. The sky came down and ended against a ragged line of dark grey. Hills, perhaps even mountains, Ologrin thought, depending on how far away they were. Several days, at least. He started walking again. Soon the clouds obscured the distant horizon, and soon after that it began to snow.

He considered just walking on, but realized it was going to be another utterly dark night. The trees continued to parallel the shoreline. He hunted along their edge and fairly easily gathered an armload of driftwood. Soon he had another small fire going under the canopy of trees. He sat with his cloak pulled as high as he could, making himself into a tent. He slept sitting up, then woke to a world of complete blackness. He sat as still as the surrounding trees, listening to the surf, wondering how many days he could walk before he starved. He decided his goal was to reach the distant hills. Perhaps from there he could see Lhosa in the north, and if he died, he could die knowing where he was in relation to the rest of the world. He imagined sitting on those hills and being able to see, far, far in the distance, the tiny jewel of red light Vireo wore in her hair, an impossibly small point on the vast dark continent.

When light came again, the fire was buried under two hands of snow. His cloak had made a pyramid of snow around him. It was peaceful, and briefly he thought it would not be a bad place to stay. But he had made himself a promise; he had set a goal. He stood and shook the snow off his cloak, stepped back onto the gravelly shoreline, and continued west.

The snow made walking slow going. He found it easiest to walk at the very edge of the shore, where the waves had cleared a narrow stretch of gravel. His feet were wet and ached from the cold. Later in the day he came upon a place where the shoreline narrowed between the waves and a low bluff. Several more of the black-berried trees were growing on the bluff, and he was able to harvest as many berries as he could eat. They were no less sour than before, but he decided sour wasn't so bad.

He managed another fire for the evening to warm his frozen feet and was rewarded with the feeling of sharp needles, making it difficult to sleep. Heron would have told him that pain was a sign that the patient was still alive. The next morning he breakfasted on berries before heading out.

Two more days brought him to a point where the shoreline began to curve to the north again, while the hills he had been walking toward loomed above the trees. He had not eaten since the morning with the berries. He found himself contemplating foolish ideas such as wading into the freezing surf in hopes of catching fish with his hands. Just before morning, the Sojourner rose as a glorious orange ball above the hills. He took it as an omen directing him to travel upward.

Climbing the hills proved to be much slower going than walking the shoreline. The forest quickly became thick with undergrowth. He finally found the vaguest of paths. With the increased speed came the disquiet of wondering if some large animal had made the track, and if so, whether that animal was as hungry as he.

After struggling for much of the day, he came to a fold in the land. On one side the forest seemed to fall slowly away into forever, while on the other side a ridge rose rapidly to the height of the trees. The ridge itself appeared mostly free of foliage, making it a natural lookout spot. He decided to make camp below the ridge, where he found an impression in its side that might have been dug out by the same animal that had made the trail. The floor of the impression was smooth and just deep enough for Ologrin to tuck into and have some cover overhead. It seemed luxurious. He hunted around for enough wood to start a fire, then decided to climb the ridge and see what he could see.

Low shrubs dotted with tiny blue berries were scattered across the ridge face. To his delight, the berries were wonderfully sweet. He forgot about the view and was soon on his hands and knees, crawling from shrub to shrub, popping the berries in his mouth as fast has he could pick them. He ate his way to a point where the ridge rose suddenly. There, he found a trickle of water exiting the stone. He sucked at it until he felt his thirst was quenched, more so than it had been in the past several days.

He finally stood and looked to the north. He was disappointed; he had progressed less than a quarter of a league from the shoreline, he guessed, and was only about three gross hands higher. He looked out across the vastness of the sea, stretching from the east to the west. He knew he could not hope to see Lhosa with this slight change in elevation. Still, it was more disappointing than his lack of progress. He picked enough berries to fill one pocket. He was tempted to eat them then and there but chose to save them for the morning.

It began snowing before dark. He positioned the fire in front of his little cave and made himself as comfortable as possible. He was soon in a deep and dreamless sleep.

He awoke suddenly, but something in him told him not to move. The fire was long out. Something warm and odorous was right next to him, snuffling in the near dark. He cracked his eyes. Whatever it was had its head in his lap, and he suddenly realized it was licking the berries out of his cloak pocket. His initial thought to shoo the animal away was quickly overtaken by another, more bloodthirsty instinct. He felt for the staff on the ground at his side, then carefully lifted it until it was gently poking the animal's belly. The animal barely took notice, then went back to stealing berries. Ologrin closed his eyes and concentrated.

The flash was weak, and the animal stepped back, startled. Ologrin tried to raise the staff to clout it over the head, but the animal took one step and crumpled to the ground. He scrambled out of the hollow and crawled over to the body. It gave one last, gasping breath and was still. Whatever it was, it did not appear to be threatening. A large eye stared up at him. He stared back, and felt his own eyes fill with tears. He looked up quickly and tried to focus on his own hunger.

His first butchery was a messy affair. By the time he had the animal skinned and dressed into two halves, he was covered in blood, some of which he had managed to drink. The very act made him feel guilty, as part of his brain argued that he was simply trading one life for another, and what made him more deserving than the animal he had killed? He tried using snow to wash as much of the blood from his face and hands as he could.

In total, he guessed the animal weighed about as much as he did. It had soft brown fur, much like a bison, and hooved feet, also like a bison, and fur covered, branching growths on its head. Even dressed and without its head, it was more meat than he could carry any distance. He was going to be staying, at least for a while.

He roasted meat, ate, and then napped, imagining this is what predators felt after a kill. Then he found some thicker branches and rocks to use as tools and set about trying to make the impression in the slope a little deeper. The ground turned out to be softer than he expected. He was able to make it twice as deep and slightly wider by dark. But he felt energized by the infusion of food, and so he worked late into the night.

The next day he decided to try and bring down a tree. He selected one with a trunk barely thicker than his lower leg, and swung the head of the staff at it, expecting the same shower of sparks he had experienced when the staff met stone. Instead, the tree resisted, and Ologrin felt a shock race back through his arms, as if the energy in the tree had fought him. He gritted his teeth and swung again, and again, finally bringing the tree down, but feeling as if it had required an excess of violence on his part to make it happen.

Over the next few days, he worked at the camp and the cave. Digging straight back was soon blocked by the stone roots of the ridge, so he dug around it, until he had a shallow "front room," as he imagined it, then a narrower passage around the stone to a bedroom just wide enough and long enough to allow him to semi-recline. He felled several additional small trees and stacked the trunks so that they made a sort of front wall to the cave that he could squeeze around to get in and out. He dug a small firepit at the edge of the front room and lined it with small rocks. He found that a modest fire, protected from the snow and the wind, would burn through most of the night, and the warm rocks made the cave almost cozy.

He ate through the meat surprisingly fast and was soon cracking open bones and thinking about how he could capture another animal. He felt safe enough and strong enough to begin venturing farther out. He spied several of the animals as he tromped through the forest, but they ran almost as soon as he laid eyes on them. He would have to trap them. Snow fell nearly every day, which he reasoned was making it more difficult for the animals to forage. So he spent some time foraging for them, building small piles of grasses dug out from underneath the snow, mixed with fungi, softer needles, and the occasional tiny handful of berries. The animals were quite wary; clearly, they could smell him. Nonetheless, he managed to attract and kill two within a few days of each other. He dressed them more carefully and more dispassionately. The days were now cold enough that the meat laid in the snow would freeze, meaning he could try to ration what he ate. The little stream at the top of the ridge froze, too, but he used the top of an animal's skull as a bowl for melting snow. The daylight grew shorter and the nights much longer. He rarely saw the Sun anymore. He tried to keep track of the days but lost accurate count. Still, he figured the Darkest Day had to be near.

The snow deepened, and it became more difficult to move around. He spent most of each day just finding enough wood to fuel his small fire. He managed one more kill before the days turned savagely cold. On the worst days he found it easiest to stay in the cave, wrapped in his cloak and skins, either practicing his knapping skills until he could reliably make sharp edges on rocks, or sleeping away as much time as possible, hoping to survive until the world started to warm again. He had no way to preserve the skins, so they gradually rotted and filled the cave with a stink that he never got used to. His corset reflected back what little energy his body produced, which helped some, especially when he curled himself into a tight ball. He ventured out only long enough to dig up dead needles and dried leaves from beneath the snow, which he packed into the cave's bedroom to give himself more insulation. He worked carefully to prevent the litter from creeping too close to the fire; nonetheless, he remained anxious of being immolated in his sleep.

The snow stopped, but the cold continued. It stung his face and made his feet ache almost as soon as he ventured out of the cave, so he spent as little time outside as possible, scooping snow for water or bringing a piece of meat in to thaw. The skies turned cloudless and brilliant blue, and the nights were filled with countless stars—more, it seemed, than he could remember seeing from his perch above the castle. Long after dark he would climb the small ridge and brave the cold for as long as he could stand it, just for the opportunity to gaze for a few moments at the stars or monitor the Sojourner's backward march through the night. One night he ventured out shortly before Sunrise, when deepest purple had just started to color the eastern horizon. The Red Eye hung low in the east, just starting its half-year journey across the sky.

"Is this it?" Ologrin said. "Is this the worst you have? I'm still here!"

He felt momentarily indestructible. Then the cold forced him in again.

The clouds did not return for three full passages, leaving the sky vividly blue and the air achingly cold. His meat was gone, and scraps of cracked bone littered the little cave, as he has become too lethargic to toss them out. Snow was disappearing fast, though this was a mystery, as it had been too cold to melt. Finally, though, it snowed heavily again, and then the next day the air was distinctly warmer. The day after that it was warm enough that snow turned to rain. He was happy to see the crack in the rocks atop the ridge spring into life again with a burble of icy clear water. But the water only made him realize how desperately hungry he was. He stalked through the nearby forest, looking for anything remotely edible, trying to swallow bits of lichen, bark, and some unfortunate worms responding to the first rain in passages. Despite his hunger, the worms made him retch, and he decided he had to find another hooved animal.

He ranged farther into the surrounding forest than he had ever gone, spending a damp and cold night huddled on the forest floor before finding a half dozen of the hooved animals clustered together. They were lying on the ground, as still as stones, so their dark fur made them look like patches of snowless ground, until he noticed one of the patches watching him. He froze immediately. He waited until they stopped looking at him. Then, as slowly as he could, he worked his way around the animals until he was behind them, where he waited again, until they seemed to accept his presence as unremarkable. Eventually, several of the animals seemed to drop their heads as if falling asleep, and he leapt. All of them bolted to their feet, but he managed to graze the nearest one with his outstretched staff. It stumbled and fell and he was on it, hacking away at its neck until it gushed blood.

This time he shed no tears. He dressed the animal on the spot, then dragged the two halves of the carcass back toward his cave, stopping only when it was so dark that he could no longer keep from running into a tree. He managed a small fire and succeeded in roasting a hind leg, then spent the night awake again, lest something larger steal his prize from him while he slept. The next morning he had not walked far before he recognized his surroundings. He was back at his cave soon after. He cooked and ate his fill, judging that the meat would not keep long if the days were now warm enough to melt ice.

From the ridge above his cave, he surveyed what he could of the surrounding hills. Far above, one of the nearby hills was capped by an area bare of trees. If he could reach that, he could get a much greater view of his surroundings. He waited three more days, consuming a good portion of his meat and worrying that the clear skies would not hold. But they did, and when he was able to pack the remaining meat into a sling to carry over his shoulder, he set out, estimating an all-day climb ahead.

It took longer than that. He quickly lost sight of his target while climbing through the forest, and could only tell himself to always go up, and perhaps a little to the right. On the second morning he reached enough of a clearing to see that the bare spot was still to his right, then he tried to memorize a trail through the woods to his destination. He finally managed to reach the bare area just after mid-day.

It was broad and generally level, with rocks tumbled into leaning platforms. He climbed the highest one and looked around. He could see the shoreline far below. It continued to curve north and west from where he had left it until it reached a point at least a day's walk further west. The shoreline then doubled back on itself to form the eastern shoreline of a large bay, cutting deeply into the land. The bay itself was at least six or eight leagues deep and ten or fifteen wide. He couldn't really see the far shoreline, but he could not miss the mountains that rose beyond it. These were true mountains, not hills like the one he stood on, and were stacked to the south and west, with peaks easily as tall as the flanks of the Adamantines. If he turned the other way and looked to the east, he saw only a sea of treetops sloping gradually downward. Somewhere that way, hidden leagues beyond his view, were the rocks where he had washed ashore.

And if he looked to the north…nothing but water. The sea stretched unbroken to the horizon. Lhosa, which had to be out there somewhere, was still too far to see.

The view, in its own way, was beautiful. He stood for a long time, gazing mostly at the bay and its surrounding hills. The water in the bay was calmer than the seas beyond, and so reflected more of the sky's blue. Though trees grew almost to the water's edge, there were occasional broken patches, revealing a rugged underlying landscape of rocky ridges, similar to the one he currently occupied. There were no fields, no farms, no wisps of cooking smoke. As far as he could tell, he was utterly alone.

Looking at the terrain toward the back of the bay, he caught sight of a brighter glint at the edge of the shoreline. As he watched, the tiny spot steadily grew in brightness until it dominated his attention: impossibly small, and yet bright, as if a star had been captured from the sky and planted on the ground. Over the next several moments the light from the spot peaked in brightness and then changed from white to blue, then green, then red, steadily fading. Several moments later it disappeared into the background.

The Sun was now almost three quarters of the way to the northwest horizon. It was too late to begin the climb back down. Ologrin found a shallow space under the tumbled slabs and built a small fire for the evening. He spent half the night lying on his back, staring upward. The Sojourner was climbing toward its peak by the time it was fully dark. He waited until it set, with half the night remaining, and then huddled under the rock and dozed until morning.

The next day he intended to head down to his camp but found himself lingering. The presence of the wider world was once again working its way into his thoughts. He felt safe in his cave, but it offered little beyond that. He began to think of what it would be like to spend the rest of the Winter there, and then the following Summer. What if he was still there when Winter came again? Was he destined to end his life as just another animal curled in a cave?

The Sun rose, peaked, and began to slide westward again, while he remained deep in thought. He recalled the bright spot he had seen the day before. He settled down and watched, grateful that the sky was once again clear. About the time the Sun was halfway from peak to horizon, he caught sight of the tiny gleam again. And once again, it grew in intensity until it was as bright as the Sun itself, then changed to brilliant colors as it faded from view.

It was a reflection, he decided. What else could cause such a brilliant gleam? It was as if the face of the cliff had been eroded to reveal a mass of pure adamantine beneath. And with that thought he had a purpose in life again. He would find the gleam. If it turned out to be nothing special, then he would have the upcoming Summer and Harvest to figure out if he was pushing on or returning to his cave to stock up for another Winter.

Drawing a direct line, the gleam was about seven leagues from his current position, an easy day's walk on level ground. But the hills rose and fell into black depths between there and where he stood. To set out over the hills meant days of difficult climbing, with no assured route, and a likelihood of getting lost. If he climbed back down and followed the shoreline, he would need to walk almost three times as far to reach the same spot. A half day from the cave down to the shoreline, he estimated, then three days to walk to the point beneath the gleam, and then another day to find it. There was no telling what he could scavenge for food or water along the way, especially as the snow was rapidly disappearing. But then again, there was no greater likelihood of finding food around the cave. The hooved animals were becoming wary of his presence.

He spent another night on the bare rock face, feeling more excited by the thought of an adventure ahead. The next day he started down for his cave. The return trip turned out to be much easier; he spotted his ridge early and was there by nightfall. The next day he scoured his camp, locating his best knapped stones and gathering together anything he could carry that might prove useful. He scouted about and found a collection of mushrooms sprouting on the moist, snow-free ground. They were a warm brown and smelled pleasantly of dirt when he broke them free. He wished he had spent more time listening to Heron describe how to tell good mushrooms from deadly ones. Hunger, however, overruled his caution.

The following day dawned with the Sun once again climbing into a clear eastern sky, but high, wispy streaks filled the west. He hefted the staff and headed toward the shoreline below. Once again, he had the sense that he was leaving home, regardless of how modest that home had been. He reminded himself he could find the cave again if he needed to, but that thought carried with it the deeper fear of a short and bleak existence.

The day was almost warm by the time he reached the shore. The unending Winter appeared to be over. He imagined the excitement that had to be building around Antola as the farmers and herdsmen hoped that the long cold was over and they could hope for a normal Summer again. At least he assumed it was normal for them; that they were enjoying roughly the same weather as he.

He set out toward the west. The shoreline gradually curved until he was walking north. Clouds moved in from left to right, first the high, wispy ones, then a lower, featureless layer that hid the Sun and turned the sky a uniform, featureless gray. Late in the day he stopped to gather wood and decided to build a big fire on the gravel of the shoreline itself. He ate some roasted meat and mushrooms, thinking he only needed a jug of fresh water to be perfectly content. The water came later in the night, first as a light sprinkle, then a steadier rain that soon snuffed his fire. He retreated to the tree line and huddled as best he could. He was able to quench his thirst, but at the expense of becoming uncomfortably damp.

The rain only strengthened the next day, and he had no choice but to trudge on, head down. He pondered trying to shelter in the trees but decided he would ultimately end up just as wet. The world shrank to consist of just him, a few hands' worth of shoreline in front and behind, and the incessant rain. He didn't bother to build a fire that night. The rain seemed to slacken after dark, and then the clouds were light enough to admit some light from the Sojourner, so he decided to walk through the night as well.

The rain finally ended and the sky lightened. He watched his shadow form and stretch into the waves to his right as the morning Sun burned through the residual clouds. He was walking south, apparently having gained the northernmost point of the land during the night.

The vast bay stretched out before him. The gray waters turned blue as the sky cleared. The Sun gradually warmed and dried his clothes. He saw flecks of white peeking through the tree line. He thought it might be bits of un-melted snow, but when he clambered up a nearby ridge to investigate, he found low shrubs covered by mounds of tiny, seven-pointed flowers. They were the same shrubs that had borne the tiny blue berries he had found on his ridge above the cave. The more he looked, the more the shrubs appeared to be everywhere. He felt brighter just thinking about the berries he would have come Harvest.

A fine night followed, warmer than any night thus far. He built his fire and enjoyed the night sky. He could see further to the south, and was now sure that Ortak was distinctly higher in the sky than it appeared from Antola. He hoped to reach the shiny spot by the next afternoon. Only then would he have to decide what to do next.

The next day the sky was brilliant blue, but the wind crossed the bay from west to east and made walking more difficult. At places the gravelly shoreline gave way to long stretches of deep, reddish-brown sand, more difficult to cross. He remembered the trick of walking right next to the water's edge, where the waterlogged sand was firmer. The Sun rose toward its peak. He tried not to think about failing to find the reflective spot. It was distinctly possible that standing on the hill had put him in exactly the right position to see the reflection. What if it turned out to be something small and insignificant? He might never find it, even if he scoured the hillsides for the rest of his life.

The Sun began to slide toward the west. He walked on, having curved from the south to the west once again. He found himself feeling more and more anxious. He was counting steps in his mind: one gross, then three, then twelve.

And then he saw the glint. It flickered at first, then was steady, about a half league beyond where he stood, perched atop a bluff perhaps a gross of hands above the shore. He started to run, keeping his eyes on the spot, afraid it would fade before he could get close enough. It did seem to fade, but also to grow larger so that it was easier to track. Then it slipped behind trees, and he feared it would not reappear. But it did, and now he had memorized the surrounding pattern of trees and rocks and was sure he could find it even if the gleam disappeared. Indeed, as he ran closer and finally found himself standing below the source of the reflection, it did fade, due no doubt to the fact that he was no longer at the correct angle for it to reflect the Sun.

A wall of stones seemed to grow behind the trees at the top of the bluff. Were it not for their uniformity, he would easily have mistaken them for the hill itself. But the stones had been carefully stacked, and they rose even and straight. He could easily have walked past the structure and never noticed it was there. The age of the wall was unguessable; it could have been there for dozens or for grosses of years. It had not been the wall, though, that had caught his eye from the hillside, leagues in the distance. Rather it was the glass set in its upper face: dozens of angular pieces fitted together and filling a window frame, each piece ringed with a rainbow of color. He stared at them, suddenly wondering if someone could be behind the windows staring back.

30

Ologrin stepped to the edge of bluff, suddenly feeling very exposed. There was no movement, except for the sway of branches in the breeze. The only footsteps on the dark sand were his own. He gathered his wits and began hunting for some way up the bluff. It did not take long to find the edge of a smooth-hewn stone barely peeking above the sand. The stone itself was covered with thick vines. Holding the base of his staff with both hands, he swung at the vegetation. To his surprise, the living vines seemed to absorb the energy of the staff. After several swings, he felt drained, while the vine, though smoking, remained tenaciously intact. He resigned himself to a laborious climb over and through the vegetation.

Halfway up the bluff the steps suddenly became less steep. Though the steps were still covered by thickened vines, he found he could simply step around them, if he did so carefully. The stairway followed a curve up the side of the bluff, making it an easier but longer climb than the shoreline steps.

Nearing the top, he caught glimpses of a stone structure in the near distance. He pushed his way through the undergrowth. Smaller windows covered with wood shutters were set in the structure above the height of his head. This was a familiar architecture. It could have been any old stacked stone tavern in any village along the Bhin. He followed the wall forward, where the corner met the wall that paralleled the edge of bluff, the one he had seen from below. The trees and vegetation springing from the edge of the bluff blocked any direct view of the bay from where he stood, but he could see a portion of the sky. Darkness was coming soon. In the wall directly above, the many-paned glass window gazed out over the sea. It appeared dipped in gold as it reflected the setting Sun.

He followed the wall to the next corner. The entire lower structure was about as large as small tavern in the Purse. A second level, containing the large window, was much smaller. Ologrin imagined it served as a lookout, and perhaps a living space similar to his cell in the castle. A large chimney emerged from the lower structure and formed the rear wall of the upper.

Ologrin completed his walk around the structure. The only entrance was a door in the rear wall. A wooden platform, once allowing access to the door, had collapsed into a heap of rotting wood, leaving the door handle at head height. The door itself was still tightly shut. The wood of the door was smooth and remained well-finished, all out of character with the abandoned look of everything else. He reached up and pushed on the handle. The latch clicked beneath his hand as if it had been oiled the day before. The door swung silently out, and he hoisted himself inside.

Unlike the exterior, where the building was slowly being reclaimed by vegetation, the interior was neat and orderly. Ologrin sniffed the air. It was the slightest bit musty, though less so than Heron's dungeon rooms. The door closed behind him with a soft click. With the shutters closed and the Sun setting, the interior was dark, but Ologrin's ability to see in the gloom had not faded, and he could make out distinct shapes. He was in a kitchen. The black mass of a large hearth-grate filled a nearby wall, and pots hung perfectly still. A large table filled the center of the room.

More silent shapes filled the front room. Some were recognizable, such as a reading table and accompanying chair against the far wall. A round shape, supported by a stand, sat on the table. *A glowglobe*, thought Ologrin. He picked up the globe and gave it a shake, but it remained dark. *They don't last forever*, he mused. He could see a small bound book had been left open on the table. There was not enough light to make out its content.

He could make out another door. He felt for the latch and lifted; the door opened as smoothly and as silently as the door to the outside. There was more light in the hall beyond, even though here, too, the windows had been shuttered. Golden light was spilling from the foot of a stairway set against one wall. Three steps led to a landing, then he turned and followed several more steps up to where the last rays of the Sun were slanting through the glass-filled window he had seen from the shore.

He was drawn to the windows. The bay stretched out before him, a spectacular blue bowl filling the lower half of his view. To the west, the Sun was silhouetting the distant high peaks. It was achingly beautiful. He stood there until the Sun was well behind the mountains and the water of the bay had turned black. Reluctantly, he turned around to survey the rest of the room before the light faded completely.

His heart leapt into his chest. Someone was lying on a raised bed in the corner. Gripping the staff, he slowly moved closer. "Forgive my intrusion," he said, and his voice croaked from lack of use. The figure did not move. He crept closer. A finely embroidered cloth covered the form up to the shoulders. Above that, dark skin made it difficult to see features, but silver hair framed the head as if it had been carefully arranged in place. The figure could not see him, he realized, as there were only black sockets where eyes had once been. The dark skin had shrunk around the skull enough to reveal teeth, but otherwise it was intact. A pair of horns rose from the forehead and curled tightly around the skull.

Ologrin sank to his knees. He ran his hands over the thick growths curling around the sides of his own head, trying to process the thoughts flooding his mind. There had been others, Vireo had said. Yet the solitary corpse in this abandoned place struck Ologrin in a way no conversation about the rarity of mosaics ever had. The only known example of the dichotomy that was who he was, who his kind were, was lying in front of him. Nothing to that point, not even a Winter spent in a hillside carve-out, had ever made him feel so alone.

He hurried back downstairs and felt his way to the kitchen, then felt along the shelves. There had to be a way to make fire, he thought. Finally, his hands closed around a small, familiar shape, and a smile split his face. He clicked the tiny mechanism of the ember pot with his thumb. A little flame jumped happily to life.

There was no telling how old the wood was that had been stacked near the hearth. It caught fire almost instantly. The room began to fill with smoke, until Ologrin found the hearthgrate damper and pulled it open. He found candles on a shelf, neatly tied with twine. With a lit candlestick in hand, he turned to explore the open book on the table. A pen sat in an inkpot next to the book. The ink was dried solid, entombing the pen's nib. No hand had touched the pen for dozens of years. He looked at the letters on the page. They were legible, and readable.

Inventory:
Four smoked capreal haunches.
Three jars of blue berries in honey.
Fifteen turnips.

Two flats of smoked fish.

It is enough, I suppose, but barely, and will not suffice if next Summer is late in arriving. I now regret not having planted emmer this previous Winter, but it is a long walk to and from the field, and the winnowing is so tedious. Of course, a warm loaf seems like a treasure now. There still is so much to do.

Regrets:

The disaster, of course. Not the tower, not even the work, but the friends who died.

Never getting the chance again to spend mid-Summer nights with friends in Dha-Arenish collecting dewboats.

No more floating all night in the Tyros, watching the stars.

And, of course, never having gone back again. It haunts me; it steals into my dreams. Sorcery beyond comprehension, but also terrors, and the most profound questions possible. Who were they, these true gods? And even now it frightens me to commit the question to ink: Were they us?

It is a cold Winter. I cannot remember ice so far into the bay. I think I am tired, but I know it is more.

It has taken all day to write this. I am an ember. For a puff of wind to keep the ember glowing. Perhaps more tomorrow.

The remaining pages were empty. Ologrin leaned back in the chair. He had seen that handwriting before, on rolls kept within the library at the Sophenary. Famous handwriting, as it turned out. *Wysel, we meet at last.*

The massive stones of the hearthplace absorbed the heat of the fire, gradually warming the air. Ologrin explored the lower floor more carefully. The front room had thick shelves attached directly to the walls, with dozens of books filling them: leather gems stacked in neat piles. A bin filled with rolls sat in a corner near the reading table. He returned to the hallway next to the stairs. At the far end of the hall was another room, which Ologrin immediately recognized as a workroom. A cold forging furnace filled the far corner. Tools both familiar and unfamiliar lined the walls.

Ologrin returned to the upper room. As soon as he entered, he looked to see if the corpse was still in the same place, realizing even as he did the thought was faintly foolish. It remained as before. He examined it more carefully. There was no way to tell how long Wysel had been dead. Ologrin guessed for as long as it had taken for the yard outside to go to seed and for saplings to grow into trees tall enough to shade the house. With a chill, he realized the house had likely remained untouched for longer than he had been alive. He remembered lying on his mat as a child, eyes closed, flying higher and higher. What would he have thought if he had known this house was already silent and waiting for him, below the southern horizon?

In a corner of the workroom closest to the door stood a familiar enough looking device with a handle sticking out of its side, a bucket chain that he hoped dipped into a rainwater cistern below the house. He leaned against the handle, expecting the entire mechanism to fall to rust at his feet, but after a moment it started to turn. After a few turns clear water poured out of a spout. The water was cold and tasted fresh. He fetched a smallish bronze pot from the kitchen and filled it halfway with water. He swung it on a hook over the kitchen fire, then dumped in what was left of his meat and mushrooms. The room was becoming downright cozy. He had not slept under a proper roof since he had left Antola, he realized. A sense of safety and security enveloped him. He struggled to stay awake long enough to eat his stew.

He awoke early, his mind filling with plans. He lit another fire in the hearthgrate and then sat down to think out a priority list. Water and shelter he now had in abundance, so food was at the top of the list. Then he planned to restore the house to some semblance of its former state. With sufficient resources, he could expand his explorations in a systematic way. Though he had not encountered other people yet, he tried to hold out hope that they were somewhere. There were plenty of landscapes back on Lhosa where he imagined he could be lost for passages at a time and never see any sign of another person. Where there were people there were villages, where there were villages there was trade, and where there was trade there was travel—and hopefully a way back to Lhosa.

But one thing took precedence before all. Armed with tools from the workroom, he cleared a path to the steps and cleared the steps down to the shoreline. He collected as much fallen wood as he could find and arranged it into an elongated pile at the edge of the bay. He returned to the house and wrapped the corpse in the fragile remnants of the bedcoverings, then carefully carried it down to the shore. It was no heavier than a basket of branches. He set it gently on the pile of wood, then lit the wood in several places. Flames quickly spread and roared overhead. *Go home*, he thought, as the smoke was caught by a southern breeze.

Hunger twisted inside him. His next goal was clear, but the path to get there was not. He found several knives in the workroom, some long enough to qualify as short swords, as well as several other hacking and chopping implements of heavy bronze. He jumped with excitement when he found a well-made longbow, but the bowstring was rotted away, and he found no arrows to go with it. He headed up the hill behind the house with a single knife and axe roped to his waist, his staff in hand.

The steep hillside soon gave way to old growth, which was much easier to move through. He found more mushrooms, and threw the axe at a black squirrel but missed. The squirrel had been rooting in the ground, though, and Ologrin was able to steal a small cache of nuts. Fearful of getting lost after dark, he made his way back to the house and had roasted mushrooms for dinner, but it was hardly filling. The nuts were extremely bitter. He crushed them and boiled them, then set the mash out to dry. It was somewhat more palatable the next morning, but made his stomach hurt for most of the day. Or perhaps that was just his hunger.

Two days later he spooked three of the hooved animals. From Wysel he finally had a name for them: capreal. He chased them until late afternoon, trying to get close. One of them had those unusual branched horns, which he assumed made it a male. Just when he was about to give up, the male, which must have been fed up as well, suddenly turned and charged. He had just enough time to swing the axe at the animal's neck as it ran headlong into him. His corset absorbed the blow. He felt the ornamentation atop his own head. Perhaps he looked like a rival instead of a predator.

A thick band of tough white tissue stretched across the muscles of the animal's hind leg. After getting the carcass home, he carefully removed the band and cut it into narrow strips, which he then wove together. He lashed his creation to either end of the long bow. It would shrink as it dried. With food in his belly, he could take some time to make arrows.

Solving one problem led to the next, and the days slipped into each other. Understory trees exploded with pink and white blooms, followed by the higher trees setting leaves in preparation for Summer. The lords of the forest, however, were the massive hemlocks, branches covered with short, soft needles, becoming blue-black silhouettes against the sky. He watched the shifting course of the Sun as it rose earlier each day and farther to the southeast, then wheeled overhead in a great arc before setting above the mountains in the southwest. Often, he fell asleep while the western sky was still purple and awoke to sunlight slanting through the open shutters on the east side of the house.

The longest days of the year had arrived. He had been planning an extended trek, but until the last moment had not decided between heading south into the never-ending hills or west toward the higher mountains. In the end he chose to head west. He decided to follow the shoreline for as long as he could, guaranteeing that he could find his way home again. He rounded the western lip of the bay late the first afternoon and found that the shoreline veered back to the southwest. He spent a pleasant night watching the stars spin overhead and the Sojourner rise just before dawn. Two more days of steady walking brought him to the bottom of a bluff that gradually rose above the water's edge, while the sands disappeared and the shore became rocky and impassable. He climbed the bluff and found open grassland. The nearest flanks of the mountains seemed only a day away. But they deceived him. He spent a third of the next day climbing a long hill, only to find a valley beyond and the mountains just that much further away. He had planned for a journey of one passage. Five days into it, he seriously contemplated turning around, but the mountains beckoned. Finally, the slope of the land steepened, and he realized he had been on their flanks for the past day. The nearest peak shoved its jagged edges out of the ground. His paced slowed as he looked for a path.

He spent the night huddled on the mountainside. There wasn't enough fuel for a fire. With the first light in the east he set out again, focusing on the ground ahead, sometimes finding himself climbing with both his hands and feet. A chilly wind grew stronger. The Sun climbed behind him, stared down from on high, and then raced him for the horizon. He topped a crag and saw that there was just one more above that. With one concentrated effort, he pushed until he stood on what felt like the top of the world.

Not far to the north, the ripples of the Southern Sea broke the Sun's reflection into countless silver arcs, stretching to the horizon. There was no sign of land. As he slowly turned to the southwest, the ranks of mountains stretched away before him, but he could just make out their final stand and the gleam of water beyond. Turning the other way, to the southeast the mountains gave way to high rolling hills, which he guessed were the hills to the south of the house. And if he stared directly south, at the edge of his sight he could just see the dark line of a smooth and straight horizon. More water.

He was on an island. A great island, without question, the largest island he could ever imagine, unless he thought of Lhosa itself as one vast island, with something even larger far beyond its shores. He made some rough calculations. The bay divided the northern shore roughly in the middle. He estimated he had walked at least thirty leagues from his shipwreck until he had found it. He was now at least twenty leagues farther to the southwest, and ten additional leagues of mountains stretched to the westernmost shore. To the south, at least fifteen more rugged leagues stretched between him and the southern shore. The island was fatter where the bay cut into it, such that its greatest width was closer to thirty leagues. He stooped and tried to scratch out a rough drawing in the gravelly dirt beneath a boulder. What he drew reminded him of a slipper. *A sepha*, he thought, the Polfre word for slipper. If Lhosa was a Polfre word, then the island ought to bear one as well. Sepha Island.

"Not everyone gets to name an island," he said out loud.

It did little to cheer him up. In fact, as the Sun disappeared, a profound sense of loneliness once again surrounded Ologrin. There was no evidence of a settlement anywhere on the island. He was completely alone. Somehow, he had known this was true, at least since he had found Wysel's body. She had escaped to exile; he had run from death, but they both had come to a place of utter solitude. *Never having gone back*, she had written. She had changed the world before spending her last years alone. He had merely been struck down by it to face the same end.

He started back, walking by starlight. He made it to the grasslands by the following morning and kept going, finding comfort in the familiar sands of the beach later that day before stopping for the night. Three days later he wearily climbed the stairs to the house and collapsed inside.

He stopped looking at the sky. He cleared the vines and trees from around the house and in the flat yard in the back, creating great brush piles he would later chop into kindling. He worked to make the house neat and cozy. He felled and stripped one of the larger trees, as big around as he was, which proved to be a massive amount of work, but he needed the thicker logs to begin making charcoal.

The days began to get noticeably shorter. He filled each one with work: splitting wood, rebuilding a charcoal kiln, gathering food. He rebuilt the small shed that had been Wysel's smokehouse and smoked as much meat as he could kill and dress. He stripped bark and ground nuts, then brewed them in the largest of the pots and soaked the animal skins in them before stretching them to dry. The berries on the blackberry trees turned from green to purple; he collected as many as he could and cooked them with honey he found in tree hollows, then covered the jars with beeswax. The Sun now rose just north of east and set just north of west. Harvest was only a passage or so away. Then the hills were on fire as leaves turned red and yellow. The bay was beryl blue, wrapped by thick arms of blazing color. Ologrin stood at the windows and understood why Wysel would have gone to such trouble and expense to place them where she did. At times the island felt like his prison, but at others he imagined it must shine like the greatest jewel on the face of the world.

And then the first snow fell. He had been on Sepha for a year. Alone for a year. The great hearthgrate warmed the house. He breathed deep. He was alive.

31

Halfway through Harvest, the snows returned to stay. Clumped flakes fell gently, hiding the muddy tracks in the yard and smoothing the rough edges of his homestead. Then more snow fell, blurring the distinction between individual structures and heaping against the doorway. Winter came early to Sepha.

Ologrin beat a path to the smokehouse and the woodpile. Every morning he kindled a new fire from the embers of the previous day. The massive hearthgrate soaked up the heat and kept the lower part of the house tolerably warm for the remainder of the day. With the shutters closed, the room was dim, but he found he could see well enough by the light of the fire.

Mostly, he read. There were well over nine dozen bound books stored on shelves or stacked neatly in piles, enough to keep him busy for many Winters to come. In addition to the books, he had discovered volume after slender volume of handwritten pages, neatly bound between leather covers, identical to the half-finished book on the table. They had been carefully arranged on a higher shelf. At one end of the shelf the leather was cracking and the writing had faded to be almost invisible, while at the other the volumes were clearly newer, with sharp, dark letters. The letters had all been written in Wysel's bold hand. Starting with the oldest volume, Ologrin began reading, finding himself transported into Wysel's world.

I fault no one, it is not the Polfre way.

I spent a happy childhood in the Dha-Arenish, oblivious to my differences and to the unspoken, ever-increasing pressure my mother felt to account for my existence, and for what it would cost in the future. I think it was pre-determined that I would have to leave no later than my coming-of-age. Nonetheless, that fact was hidden from me for many years, until I entered the upper years of my youth and my childhood friends began to distance themselves from me. No one ever said I could not stay, but in many unspoken ways it became apparent, so that in my twenty-seventh Summer, when I announced my intention to take flight into the world, fully seven years before coming of age, not a single person mourned my leaving. It seemed generally agreed that this was the best and only course for me. I left for Antola late in Harvest, when the ice on the Lake of Skies was still black and sang under the skater's blade.

If the appointed ones doubted my ability to live within the Rha, then I felt no obligation to prove them wrong. I found my place in the Commune, tasked with harvesting trees to be made into boats and ships, for Antola was expanding its interests to include the bay, and had begun to look tentatively, anxiously, out toward the sea. I was tasked with girdling trees, as I could place my hands on the tree and feel how close it was to falling or if there was stress that might cause it to crack in the wrong way.

There was a ferocious demand for wood, not only for boats, but for fuel and charcoal, and most of all for construction within the city. Most city structures were lucky to last a dozen Summers before succumbing to one of the great fires that left swathes of city charred and filled with victims curled in supplication. I knew even then that some other way of building would be necessary if the city was to survive, much less repay its debt to the forest. We felled far more trees than we left behind. The Commune sent excuses on our behalf, but if I previously had hopes of someday being welcomed back to the Dha-Arenish, they were dashed by my labor in the trees.

My affinity for the knowledge within the wood was appreciated, and soon enough I was tasked with working the felled trees. At some point I saw the benefit of fixing the saw to a swinging post. The sawmen were at first worried this would mean fewer of them were needed, but in the end appreciated the increase in speed, as they were paid by the plank. We also needed more saws, which begat more bronzemen, who needed more charcoal, of course. My debt already seemed beyond what could be paid in many lifetimes…

Ologrin was soon lost in Wysel's world. Many things had changed since then: The entire Purse had burned and been rebuilt more than once. In her time the western terraces had been covered in orchards and gardens, rather than shops and houses. The Crown occupied a single stone building at the south end of the city, while the Polfre Commune lived in the north, where the Sophenary castle would later rise. Even then, the two true powers of Antola had claimed their respective corners.

Ologrin read through the evening and into night. He was well into the second volume before stopping to stretch and eat a few morsels. He tried to sleep, but his mind was full of stories and images. With first light he gave up, stoked the fire, and continued to read.

Through my work in the mill I met Runcel. He was first a fisherman, but he spoke often about a ship large enough to go beyond the cliffs and into the sea itself. Together we envisioned and constructed the largest fishing vessel yet. In design it approximated the later shape of the Fearless Heart, *only smaller, being in total five dozen hands from bow to steering oar. Once we balanced the mast, it was a joy to sail. We rode it boldly into the Southern Sea, exploring the coast until we found the outlet of the Bhin. It was then that Runcel conceived of the idea of sailing a bigger ship as far as we could take it along the Lhosan coast—to either find the end of the land or the end of the world, whichever came first…*

The Darkest Day came and went, while Ologrin continued to read. Through Wysel's notebooks, as he had begun calling them, he stood with her on the familiar docks of Antola, only many, many years in the past. Standing with them was none other than the most famous seafarer of them all, Runcel the Navigator, discussing plans for an audacious voyage to the furthest lengths of Lhosa. But gradually the need to keep surviving overcame Ologrin's desire to remain lost in the notebooks. He forced himself to set them aside.

The naked black branches of trees reached like fingers into the low, snow-filled clouds. Devoid of leaves, he could now see that one tree stood higher than the rest. During the Summer he had walked past its straight trunk many, many times without a second thought, but now it captured his imagination. It seemed to command this part of the island. He kicked a path through the snow until he stood next to it. He carefully worked his way around the tree, measuring a circumference of thirty-eight hands. Beneath his bare palms, the tree slumbered in its own dark dreams of Winter. He could see rings extending toward the center, but the center itself remained shrouded.

The days lengthened, the snows ended, and a profusion of flowers sprang up in the woodland, taking advantage of the Sun's filtered light before the Summer's canopy of leaves stole it for itself. Ologrin's supplies had run out; he started another season hungry and cold. But he had learned much in a year, and by SummerTop he was well ahead of where he had been the year before. He had discovered a large area of the forest where all the trees were much younger. Though the trees themselves were hardly worth the effort in terms of their wood, he set about clearing each one, opening up another field-like space on a well-lit northern slope. Soon grasses were growing through the litter, turning the ground green.

One day, as he rested against a trunk near the house, he realized he was leaning against the tallest tree, which he had stopped thinking about once its most extreme reaches were hidden by leaves. He placed his hands on the bark and closed his eyes. Life surged beneath his fingers. The leaves were a profusion of chattering, purposeful voices, reaching deep into the tree's roots to find water and pull it upward. While its blood flowed just beneath the surface, the deeper rings of the tree were also alive, though quiet and more thoughtful. The tree knew he was there. It was no emotion that he could explain, but an awareness the tree had not experienced in a long time. Sixty-two rings separated the bark from the center. With a start, Ologrin realized the tree was the same age as Vireo. In his mind, he kept Vireo in their chambers in the castle, where she was always reading before the fire. But in his heart he knew she was not there. She was no longer at the Sophenary, he was sure, but was somewhere deep in the heart of the mountains, as hidden from him as the heart of the tree had been hidden the Winter before.

The days shortened, and the hills turned red and gold once again. Ologrin felt he had enough firewood now for two Winters, and had smoked more meat than he had managed the year before, as well. Feeling as though his own voyage was well provisioned for the Winter, he allowed himself to return to the notebooks and the Antolan docks, where Wysel had been waiting patiently for him since the previous Winter.

I have tried to be methodical with our preparations, while Runcel rattles around like the lines against the mast, eager to be on the way. But at last we are ready. The Fearless Heart *sits boldly on the water. We have dyed the sails red, and when they are run out, the entire city shows up to watch us depart. Summer storms could begin any day. The time has come for us to depart.*

Wysel and Runcel sailed out of Gosper Bay and headed west along the southern coast, eventually reaching a small fishing village at the mouth of a river, which Ologrin recognized would later grow to become Solanon. Several days later, as they sailed away, Ologrin had the hope that they might continue south and discover his island. He found himself gazing out at the bay, half expecting a ship to appear on the horizon. But Runcel turned west, and soon they were heading toward parts of Lhosa that Ologrin had never seen. They reached the village of Ismay, replenished their stores, and continued westward.

Bomlin, the settlement at the edge of the world, existed even then, but it took longer than Runcel anticipated to sail the remaining length of the southern coast. Finally, after almost two passages, they reached the tip of the cat's paw. Bomlin sat high atop bluffs that plunged into the sea.

Though small, there was nothing rustic about the village dwellings. From a distance, they looked like the hulls of ships rolled upside down, but they were finely constructed, a level of carpentry Wysel had not seen before. Support beams were carved and inlaid with beasts and fanciful scenes, windows had glass, interiors were filled with damasked fabrics and woven carpets. Bomlin supported the largest population of Polfre outside of Antola. Their careful craftsmanship was visible in every small detail.

Wysel devoted an entire notebook to the days they spent in Bomlin. She enjoyed the company of the Polfre, but suspected they were withholding a secret, and they seemed eager to see Wysel and her shipmates be on their way. Runcel, too, was anxious to continue their voyage north before the Winter storms arrived. And he had another reason making him eager to leave: There were those in Bomlin who claimed the lost cities of Faerith and Forought could be found far up the western coast. Even if the riches of the ancient cities were long gone, fame and fortune awaited anyone returning to Antola with evidence of their existence.

After rounding the Bomlin bluffs, the Lhosan coastline ran roughly due east again, and they began to think they had discovered the northern shore of the continent. The sea was treacherous, not for its storms, but for its long stretches of windless calm. Their progress was slow, their supplies dwindled, and they found no abandoned cities. Then, after sailing many gross leagues to the northeast, to their dismay the coastline turned back to the northwest, as if intentionally blocking their way home.

Almost three difficult passages later, they spied broken towers of stone standing sentinel over the thick forest below. The land came to a point again. They rowed ashore in carve-outs carried aboard their ship. Massive, rectangular blocks of stone had tumbled from the forest to the water's edge. They had found the lost city of Faerith.

Wysel filled three additional notebooks with her exploration of Faerith and their further exploration of what turned out to be a vast, half-round bay, at least fifty leagues wide. Runcel named it in honor of Crespe, the Antolan Crown. The far shore, to their delight, contained the remnants of yet another city: They had found Forought as well. These remains, though, were very different from the scattered blocks of Faerith, which, however ruined, still bore a familiarity to their own city.

Where the stones of Faerith bore the marks of chisels and saws, we found nothing of the sort in Forought. We might have missed it altogether had not one of the men decided to examine a humming sound, hoping to find a great beehive full of honey. He found instead several structures unlike anything we had ever seen. We eventually discovered five strange towers scattered over an area roughly half that of Antola. Though the ground was overgrown with vines and vegetation, it seemed to avoid the towers, which grew from the ground on plinths of stone, smoother and seemingly harder than iron. At twice a man's height the plinths gave way to strange wright-works, assuming any hand of man's ever fashioned them. There was an outer structure that at first glance seemed to be a lacework of spiderwebs, but made of gold and woven into complex patterns that seemed to change, depending on where one walked around the column. Other structures were visible within the netting of gold metal, but their construction and purpose were entirely beyond my comprehension. Deepest of all, one could catch glimpses of something that glowed with a bluish-red light. The structures gave off no heat, but they were the source of the humming. I am now convinced they were the source of some great power.

In addition, we found a solitary structure, not quite as high as a man, made of glass and the same smooth, hard material as the plinths. Visible within was the most astonishing piece of mechanical craft I had to that point ever seen. I can best describe it as an assembly of wagon wheels, though without spokes, and made of a very light and smooth material. How the wheels worked together was a mystery, but their combined purpose seemed to be to turn the largest wheel on top, twelve hands wide and two deep, which spun slowly and ever-steadily.

We found no way to stop the spinning or to determine what kept it moving. Fortunately, the entire mechanism was affixed to thick wooden beams by a means we very much understood, and I surmised that those who had placed it here were not the ones who had built it. They had borrowed it from another location. And, since they were long gone, I decided I was well within my rights to borrow it in turn.

Trees were felled and posts fashioned to allow several men to carry the device back to one of our ships. Though it turned out to be less heavy than expected, it was a struggle for twelve men to carry, *as it exerted a powerful force attempting to twist the men in the opposite direction as the spinning upper wheel. Once we had it secured in the hold of the ship, the ship itself began to twist against the anchor line. For the remainder of the journey home, our oarsman had the almost impossible task of trying to prevent the ship from forever turning to the left.*

We shipped the glass box home with us as well. It proved to be harder than quartz and possessed of a wonderful quality of reflecting many colors when light struck it just right. For many years thereafter it sat in my workshops, while I pondered a way to make use of it.

Ologrin thought for a moment, then set the book down and climbed to the upper room. The edges of the jewel-shaped windowpanes refracted the slanting yellow sunlight into reds, greens, and blues. He tapped on one of the panes, realizing she had ultimately found a use and feeling the same rush Wysel must have felt, touching something older than the oldest histories.

He watched as the sea and sky grew dark, until he could see outside no longer and the windows reflected his form as if he were emerging from a black cave. He was taller, he thought, or perhaps just thinner. The ribbed corset hung loosely around his chest; he had already made plans to replace the leather over the long Winter. He was most surprised, though, by the growth of his horns, which swept back from the sides of his forehead fully four fingers thick, then curled tightly around his head to end as points behind each ear.

In the Crespe Sea, Wysel noted, Winter existed on the calendar but not in the weather, which was warm and steamy most days. As the calendar showed the approach of Summer,

Runcel and Wysel turned their ship east for the long journey home along Lhosa's true northern coast. For the most part they had favorable winds and gentle seas. Four passages into their voyage they anchored off the treeless shoreline and hiked inward for a day, until they stood on the sand overlooking the Tyros sea. No greenery crowded its shores; no fishing boats dotted its vivid blue surface. The water was saltier than tears and devoid of any living thing. They floated without effort in the warm, slick water, watching the sky wheel overhead.

Continuing on, they stopped for much-needed provisions at the tiny Polfre outpost of Aeromie, then onward until tall peaks gradually came into view. They had reached the northern limits of the Adamantines. The mountains marched off the end of the continent as if they could not be stopped, forming several steep-walled islands dotting the sea to the north. Plotting them on their map of the continent, seeing them spring from the cat's back, Wysel decided to name them the Fleas. The seas around the Fleas turned out to be treacherous, with mountainous shards of rock just beneath the surface. They picked their way through slowly and managed not to run aground.

And then the coast turned south and they sailed with the majestic snow-covered peaks off their right rail. They moved briskly down the eastern shoreline of Lhosa, rounded the tip into Gosper Bay, and completed their circumnavigation one year and one passage after having left. As predicted, the voyage made them more famous than the Crown himself. Reading the notebooks, Ologrin felt as if he had made the voyage with them and shared in their discoveries.

Wysel had written about the carve-outs they had carried aboard the *Fearless Heart*: shaped from the trunks of trees, with the ends sharpened and the interiors hollowed out. He had thought often about lashing smaller trunks together to form a raft, then fashioning a mast and sail. With a ship like the *Rayfish*, he was but two or three days from Lhosa. A raft and a sail might make the same journey in less than a passage. He was so close. But he had nothing he could use as a sail. A carve-out, however, could be paddled. Provisioned well, it might get him home in a passage. The tallest tree stood sentinel over his camp. Few of Wysel's tools were up to the task of felling a great tree. It occupied his mind, though, as the Darkest Day came and went, snow turned to rain, and he set aside her notebooks once again.

He took his first swing at the tallest tree on a bright morning when the flowers had just started to bloom. A small chip of bark bounced off his arm. He hewed away at the tree for the rest of the morning, having to stop twice to replace the lashings holding the small axe blade to its handle. By the end of the day he had managed to score a thick line through the bark around a third of the tree. He sweated beneath the refitted corset, but it gave him strength and endurance far greater than he could muster without it. Gradually he carved a ring in the tree at the height of his chest. He worked at the tree when he could, but as SummerTop approached, he found he had very little time for anything other than preparing for the next Winter.

The field he had cleared a year before had sprouted several gross stalks of emmer. He was surprised at the vigor of the plants, as they seemed to crowd out other weeds. Within a couple of years' time, he imagined having a field filled with emmer, enough to grind for several loaves of bread. The thought of warm bread made him weak with anticipation.

Just after SummerTop he hiked to the highest point on the island again. From there he could just make out the island's complete coastline. The bay in front of his home was a sapphire set into the island's coast. He imagined, if he stared, that he could just make out a line of darkness on the northern horizon. He half convinced himself it was the southern coast of Lhosa, until the line grew and formed an approaching wall of Summer storms.

By Harvest there was a wide gash around the entire tree, extending almost three hands deep. He pushed on the tree above the gash and could not make it move; it was as firm as a mountainside. Winter was fast approaching. He would have to continue work on the tree the following year. Meanwhile, Wysel's notebooks waited.

It has taken three years of persuasion and hard work to get the trestle lift completed. We felled enough trees to build a fleet of a dozen ships. I am not deaf; for most of that time the talk of the taverns was "Wysel's folly." The wheeled engine was installed, per my instructions, in the winding house just below the Crown's walk. I am quietly proud of the clutch and winches that allow the wheel, which will only turn one direction, to nonetheless be used to both raise and lower the platform. The credit for the ropes, which are the largest by far ever woven, goes to Master Saker.

The engine turns day and night, lifting the heaviest loads from the docks seemingly without effort, and, of course, without fire or fuel. Though I have tried to keep this last fact a secret, it is too much to hide. And in the taverns, they no longer talk of Wysel's folly, but rather of Wysel's sorcery.

Ologrin spent entire days reading the slender volumes, only stopping when there was insufficient light to continue. He followed Wysel as she guided construction of the castle to house the Sophenary, founded from members of the Commune. She built the bridge over the Bhin and supervised the building of the Great Road to Madros, all the while making new discoveries in the practice of physionomy and vitachemy. But she was ever-restless, and after many years, she began planning another journey to the ancient twin cities.

Chapter 31

Deep in Winter, with bare branches black against the low clouds, Ologrin ventured out and placed his hands against the trunk of the great tree, above the gash he had cut. He closed his eyes and focused. There wasn't the slightest murmur from branches far overhead. The rings of the trunk were silent as stone, making him feel guilty and alone.

As Winter once again came to a close, Ologrin reluctantly closed the notebooks and turned his attention again to his own escape. He resumed work on the tree while there was still snow on the ground. By the first of Summer, its bare, dead branches contrasted accusingly with the surrounding green canopy. He tried not to look up at them. He rarely looked up anymore. Whole passages would go by without him glancing at the Sojourner. Time had seemed so important once. Every passage, every day measured. A relentless march toward goals he could barely remember. Then for years that had been reduced to one goal: survival. Now he began to think the goal of getting back to Lhosa might be achievable, and the urgency of time's passage began to nag at him again. He worked harder on the tree, neglecting tasks he would have attended to the year before.

He had worn down one of his two axes considerably. He saved the second one for the work he would have to do hollowing and shaping the tree trunk once he had it felled. But it remained stubbornly upright, despite the wide, deepening groove. The first changing leaves of Harvest caught him by surprise. He abandoned the tree, realizing he had not gathered enough for the upcoming Winter. He had neglected the emmer field, but it had the unexpected consequence of attracting the small capreals, yielding more meat for the smokehouse.

One morning was pleasant, the next bracing cold. Leaves lost their color and began to fall. Ologrin paused late one day to see the familiar gray line of a northern storm rolling in. Late that night he was awakened by a new sound, as tiny ice pellets bounced off the roof and walls. The next morning the ground crunched underneath his feet, and tree branches drooped from the weight of the ice that now encased them. Soon the first branches began to break, sending sharp *pops* echoing through the trees. By midday the ice stopped falling, but the wind picked up, causing trees to sway ominously under their icy loads.

The first loud snaps from the tallest tree caught him by surprise. It seemed to be slowly pivoting about the deep gash but continued to stand tall. He had the sudden, horrible vision of the tree falling directly toward him, utterly smashing the house. But then the tree groaned mightily and slowly tilted directly toward the sea. With one last crack the trunk slid from the stump and the tree fell forward—but instead of falling fully to the ground, it now rested at an angle in the branches of nearby trees. Ologrin's heart sank. Then suddenly the embracing trees gave way and it crashed to the ground, snapping off many of its own ice-covered branches.

He went to work immediately. Switching to the new axe, he stripped away much of the bark covering the top half of the trunk. He hacked a gash several hands long atop the trunk, then dropped glowing chunks of charcoal into the gash. The charred wood was easier to carve away, and he was able widen and lengthen the gash considerably before the persistent snows and cold drove him inside for the remainder of Winter.

I cannot say who I despise more, the bloodthirsty Malacheb, or the parsimonious Polfre. They are equally selfish, and neither can appreciate the value of leaving their old ways behind. And neither appreciate what I have done for them and for this city. Both sequester themselves in their respective palaces, which I built for each of them, where they whisper and plot against each other. The only thing they seem to agree on is a desire to confound my work, and so it has been necessary to waste an entire Summer reinforcing the defenses of the Salient...

Within the first few lines, Ologrin realized he had jumped forward in time. The next notebook did not contain details of Wysel's second journey as he expected. He assumed the notebooks had somehow fallen out of order, but he checked the beginning of the few remaining volumes and found no hint of her second trip. What he did find was evidence of a woman increasingly in pursuit of something she could not quite grasp, which was forcing her into isolation and embitterment. As best he could tell, Wysel had returned from the second voyage obsessed with the desire to create something even greater than the trestle lift. Ologrin found it harder to understand the details of her writings, but had no trouble detecting a sense of an underlying danger.

At last I believe I have enough thorianite to proceed. Never before, I am sure, has such a quantity been in the possession of a single individual: over six cube-weights in total. Considering that a single crystal the size of my thumb sells for ten scarabs in an Antolan shop, I have enough thorianite to trade for the entire city if I choose.

Admittedly, I considered foregoing further investigation once I discovered the compounding heat produced by confining so many thorianite crystals together in an enclosed space. Just to store it, I have to keep it in separate jars holding no more than one cube-weight each. I tried pouring three cube-weights of crystals into a wooden bucket, only to see it get so hot that it singed the inside of the bucket. The vitachemists would sell their little fingers to have a way to produce steam without a fire. But I suspect there is more to the crystals than that. Powdered adamantine mixed with the crystals slows their heating.

. . .

Ologrin recalled his own experiments with adamantine and felt uneasy. Adamantine sought to exert its control over the metalsmith, not the other way around. He at least had the advantage of library volumes telling him what he should avoid. He suspected Wysel of being the source of some of that knowledge, and it was her assistants who likely paid the price.

The work is slow, as none of my Eidos assistants can help me. Too long spent in the presence of thorianite seems to poison them: They cannot eat and their hair falls out. All of this verifies for me that it holds a unique force, and is the key to making power columns of my own. I am now convinced the core of each of the columns in Forought is composed of a single thorianite crystal, as mind-stretching as that may be. The hottest fire I can make does not so much as discolor the face of a crystal, much less cause it to melt. I cannot imagine the abilities needed to forge a single crystal that size.

However, I have found a way to bind the crystals together in an adamantine alloy, allowing me to create a single man-high column. Made this way, the thorianite does not overheat, and it even seems to be less dangerous to the Eidos, though none are allowed in its presence for long. We lack the ability to create the gold spiderwebs surrounding the Forought columns, so we will use hammered gold affixed to tanjium plates.

By late Winter Ologrin was stretching his supplies thin. The corset was once again becoming loose on his frame. But he wore it continuously, as it fed him additional stamina. He resumed work on the trunk as soon as the snow began to melt. He built a firepit under what he judged was the proper length for a boat and used the flames to help him separate and then shape the bow. Meanwhile, the carefully laid coals helped him make progress on carving out the bowl of the trunk. By the approach of SummerTop he had a rough-shaped vessel, now light enough that he could roll it over and clear the remaining bark from the bottom. Once again, he found himself needing to set aside the carve-out to address his need for food. He began to think, though, that he might be able to finish the boat by Harvest. If so, he was determined to press for Lhosa and avoid another Winter on the island.

Days began to shorten. The bow and stern were sufficiently shaped for the task, so he spent his time hollowing and thus lightening the boat. He still had to figure out how to get the thing to the beach; for that reason alone, he needed it as light as possible. After dark he returned to the house and worked late into the nights fashioning an oar. After a nightmare in which he dreamed that he let the oar float away in the middle of the ocean, he decided to make two.

Late Summer storms came again, cracking the air with lightning and lashing the house with rain. The steps to the beach were slick with moss and water. After fretting over the move for most of a year, sliding the boat down the steps turned out to be surprisingly easy. Despite the storm, the water in the bay did not appear particularly choppy. He decided to take the boat out for a test. He shoved it across the sand until the stern just floated free, then hurried to one side to jump aboard. The boat rolled more than he expected. He worked his way up to the midpoint where he had left a band of wood to form a seat. He began to paddle and was pleased to see that the little boat moved quickly away from the sand. The carve-out made headway but rolled and wallowed with each stroke of the oar. The waves were higher than he had thought. Between the rolling, wallowing, and pitching, he fatigued quickly. He couldn't imagine how he would find the strength and balance to row for twelve days straight.

He decided to return to shore. He found he could control the direction of the bow depending on which side he rowed from. He gave several strokes to his left, bringing the boat broadside to the waves. It rolled immediately and tossed him overboard.

He managed to hold onto the oar, giving himself some buoyancy, but had no means to grab for the boat. He kicked toward the shore. Fortunately, the waves gave him and the boat a boost, soon depositing them both on the sand. He pulled the boat to dry sand and lay on his back, staring at the scattered clouds, feeling discouraged.

That night he dreamed he was at sea in the little boat again. The storm rose up and threatened to throw him overboard. But instead of the oar, he held the staff. He reached out and the staff grew in his hands, until it touched the water on either side of the boat. Immediately the waves were calmed, and the boat rode smooth again. He awoke with a smile. He was going to be spending yet another Winter on the island. But he knew what he needed to do.

32

With the decision to wait, Ologrin knew there was time not only to prepare for one last Winter, but to prepare the little house for his departure. Someday he would return on a proper ship with a proper entourage. When he imagined himself returning to the island, he had Vireo beside him. She was the recipient of his tour: here the table where he spent so many Winter days reading; out there the great stump from the tallest tree. He feared in his heart it was a fantasy. In the long and deliberate life of a Polfre, there was no place for miracles.

He would return to the island anyway, though it would prove to be a bittersweet journey. Wysel's notebooks, above all, had to be preserved. He could not risk taking them aboard the carve-out. He planned to store them carefully, hoping to protect them as best he could from fire or destruction until he could return to claim them. Nothing at the School for Servants or in the Sophenary's library matched their comprehensive narrative of the past. Beyond that, they were his connection to what he now embraced as his true heritage. Mosaics occurred only once in dozens of generations. Wysel had been the greatest of any age. She had transformed her world. Though he did not pretend to her level of achievement, he nonetheless felt the cloak and collar had been passed on for him to wear.

Despite his preparations, the Winter passed slowly. The corset hung loosely on his frame once again. He thought about remaking it, but was concerned about his supply of tanned hides, as he had another use for them in mind. He cut them into thin cords and then plaited the cords into a series of leather ropes. When icicles finally began to melt and the snow turned to mud, he ventured out and found four young fir trees, not quite one hand thick and as straight as rods, then cut and stripped them. Given another thirty years they might have made fine masts. Instead, he hauled them to the beach, pulled the carve-out away from where he had tucked it for the Winter, and set to work. He notched the sides of the carve-out in front of and behind the rowing seat, so that two of the trunks fitted neatly into them. He used a leather awl to drill four holes below each notch, and then two of the fir trunks were laced tightly into the notches so that they extended about fifteen hands on either side of the carve-out. Holes were drilled into the remaining trunks, which were then lifted and laced fore and aft to the outer tips of his newly-formed crossbars.

He was eager to test his handiwork. Despite the added weight, the carve-out slid easily over the sand, hard-packed by Winter snow. The water of the bay was near freezing. If he got too far out and the boat tipped him out again, he would be hard pressed to make it to shore before succumbing to the cold, corset or no. Fortunately, the water's surface was calm.

Pushing off and then stepping into the boat, he yelped as the water soaked his moccasins and stung his feet. The carve-out bobbed to the left, but then the fir trunk on that side contacted the water and prevented it from rolling further. Ologrin smiled. He worked his way to the rowing seat, while each outrigged trunk prevented the carve-out from rolling too far to the right or left. He then tried rowing. At first, each stroke tended to make the same-side trunk contact the water, slowing his motion. But within a few moments he was able to counterbalance and largely prevent the outriggers from touching. His smile broadened. The carve-out skimmed smoothly across the water. He then tried to turn the boat. It turned clumsily but did not roll. He looked back and was surprised at how far he had rowed. The bluff at the base of the house seemed small. The myriad glass pieces in the upper windows sparkled in the morning Sun. He rowed back and pulled the boat ashore, then sat heavily on the sand. He was exhausted. He needed food if he was going to have the energy to row for days at a time.

He spent the next passage hunting and gathering fulltime. Within days he had two of the capreals skinned and curing in the smokehouse. He found and dried edible fungi. Berries would not appear before SummerTop, and emmer would not ripen until closer to Harvest. He planned to be gone before then.

He worked to preserve the house, stuffing cracks between shutters and doors and hunting diligently for leaks in the roof. He set aside those things he wanted to take with him, then set about reducing that pile to the most necessary items. He leaned the staff against the hearth, as if he might forget it if he did not see it daily. He carefully wrapped Wysel's journals in his best remaining skins, then wrapped them again and placed them next to the hearth. He planned to cover them with the great cooking pot when he left, affording them the most protection he could devise.

He stacked the remaining books on a single set of storage boards near the hearthgrate. After removing the last book from the bottom board next to the writing table, he noticed the board itself rock slightly. He got onto his knees to look closer. Unlike the other boards, this one was not fixed to the supporting stiles but seemed to have its own supports underneath. He wiggled the shelf and managed to work it free. Underneath was a small pocket of space. In that space was a skin-wrapped bundle, similar to, but far older than the one he had made for Wysel's journals.

Sitting on the floor, he unwrapped the bundle. The skins were brittle and cracked as he tried to separate them. Inside were two additional volumes of her journal. The clean and vigorous writing of Wysel's middle years faced him once again. Forgetting his other chores, he started reading.

Though the distance is greater, the winds and currents are favorable for us to travel once again along the southern coast, pass the point of Bomlin, then work our way back east. Solanon and Ismay have grown large, and we will be able to take on provisions there more easily. This time we shall take two vessels, though the treasures that await would fill many more.

The self-sustaining engine that now powers the lift cannot be the only device of its kind. I hope to search Forought more fully this time; our last voyage gave us only a few days there. We will fill one ship with the remarkable crystals, as well as the gold netting we found in the towers. There is tanjium in that netting, I am certain. If I can bring a portion home and find a way to extract it, we can greatly enrich the existing tanjium supply. There may be enough netting in those towers to double the Polfres' current supply, which they would value more than the remaining wealth of the continent.

Ologrin knew Wysel had documented her life too thoroughly not to have kept a record of her second voyage. He had been certain there was more, and he had found it at last. He sat and read, oblivious to the soreness creeping into his legs or to the light sliding across the floor.

. . .

The gods are but quarreling children compared to the ancient builders of these wondrous structures. I know now it was something not meant for us. I cannot help but feel I have awakened a thing that should have been left to sleep much longer.

We set out, simply enough, to find a road. We were convinced the road leading east from Forought eventually met up with a road returning west to Faerith, connecting the two cities. But once we reached the edge of the mountains, the road became more difficult to follow. Despite this, we pushed on, climbing with the Sun at our backs, we thought, until we realized we had begun descending and were now to the east of the bulk of the mountain ridge. For another passage we slowly pressed forward, seeking the road back west. But days passed with the sky, and even the tops of the mountains, obscured by clouds. When we finally experienced a cloudless day, we could no longer see the mountain range. We were hopelessly lost.

I climbed the highest ridge, trying to regain my sense of location. The land was buckled into numerous ridges and troughs, covered with nothing but trees, which made the four black stone columns towering in the distance that much more obvious and out of place.

The Sun was already setting toward the west when we finally reached the base of the nearest column. The rough ground gave way to a smooth and level platform, raised ten steps above the forest floor, about sixteen dozen hands across. The columns defined the corners of a square at the edge of the platform, which were connected by arches rising from each column and meeting above the center of the platform, higher than the platform was wide. The stone of the columns was like black glass, impossible for any light to penetrate. The platform itself was the same smooth stone that formed the plinths we had seen in Forought. The surface was completely free of dust or leaves, as if swept clean on a daily basis, though the surroundings were completely wild. There wasn't the slightest evidence of anyone having been at the platform for a long, long time.

In the very center a disc of gold metal had been inset with no visible seam. The only adornment in the disc was the vague impression of two hands, each with six fingers. Of course I placed my hands in the impressions. Who wouldn't have?

A ball of light formed before my eyes, so bright that I had to stand and take several steps back. It was bright enough that it hurt to gaze directly at it, but there was no heat from it whatsoever. I turned to see if any other change had occurred. Two steps away, floating over the platform and slowly revolving around the central light, was another sphere, much smaller and not nearly so bright. It was perfectly round, covered in blotches of brown and green, surrounded by a beautiful blue. Wisps of white whirled across the entire surface, like clouds. And I knew that they were in fact clouds, and the blue was sea, and the rest was land. Spreading my hands apart, I discovered I could make the sphere grow and move before me. I did, until a familiar brown shape was beneath my hands. It was Lhosa, or rather a depiction of Lhosa, made completely of light.

No god has ever had a clearer view of their lands. I found myself looking upward, fearing that I might see my own hands stretching to the horizon, but the sky remained blue.

I manipulated the map to trace our voyage thus far, moving it until I could find Bomlin perched on the end of the Carpan peninsula, and then along the southern coastline until I was back at Antola again. I pulled the city closer, my heart pounding with anticipation, until I could even see the terraces and the Purse.

And then, of course, I looked farther, for beneath my hands was the answer to the question every sailor had ever asked: Was there anything beyond Lhosa? There was. Of course there was. Lhosa, in fact, was the smallest land on the world. A smaller island was several leagues south, beneath Lhosa's belly. And a few gross leagues to our north, I judged, was the southern coast of a land vastly larger than Lhosa. It contained mountains twice the height of the Adamantines, and great long lakes, and huge tracts of grassland and forest and even desert. I could see many areas that appeared similar to Faerith and Forought, once having been cities, now disappearing beneath the forests. Nowhere I looked, though, did I find anything that appeared to be a living city.

There was a third great land, not as large overall, but long, like a fat snake stretching from near the top of the world to the bottom. The seas themselves were interconnected, such that one could sail anywhere on the surface of world, given sufficient time, except for the very top and bottom of the world, which appeared covered in snow. Small enough caps of snow, it seemed, until I realized each was larger than Lhosa itself.

Lhosa then, was the smallest land, except for the scattered islands. And yet, as far as I could tell, it was the only land harboring living cities and people.

"Lhosa," I said out loud. In response, whether it was from the wind or in my mind I could not tell, I heard a distinct voice fill my head and say, "Eia."

"Lhosa," I said again.

"Eia," the voice said.

"Eia," I repeated, and the voice was still.

"Who are you?" I asked, looking for any source of the voice.

"Who," it said, within my head.

"Did you hear that?" I said to my three companions, but they looked at me quizzically.

"You," the voice said.

"What is this place?" I said to my companions.

"This place," the voice said. "You must leave this place."

"Why?" My scalp suddenly tingled. "Are we in danger?"

"It is not for you. You are not ready."

The images of the world and the Sun vanished, and I found myself sitting on the smooth stone. And as the thunder follows slowly after the flash, I finally understood what this place implied. The world did not begin and end with Lhosa. People had been here before, people with powers and knowledge far beyond my own, people who were long, long gone. The Polfre were not the first. We, and everyone else on the world that I knew, were the only ones left.

Not willing to give up, I placed my hands on the impressions once again. "I want to know more," I said. But the voice did not return. "When will I be ready?" I asked, but there was no answer. "I need to know!" I screamed, looking upward. The arches were silent.

My companions had neither seen nor heard a thing. They each pressed their hands into the impressions but heard nothing. We stayed for two days, while I fashioned every question I could think of to get the voice to answer me, all without success. At last, reluctantly, we knew we must find a way out or starve.

Climbing the nearest ridge, we could see the mountains in the far west, the first time we had seen them in days. I tried to estimate the distance, and thus where the platform was in relation to them. I was reluctant to the point of immobility to leave. I had every intention of returning.

The skies remained clear, and for three days we made steady progress toward the mountains, until they loomed above us. I estimated another three or four days would be required to cross, after which I hoped to spy the Crespe Sea once again.

We were high on the mountains when we first saw the raptor. It swept toward us from below, flying just above the treetops, and before any of us could shout, grabbed Berla in a claw—just like a hawk snatches a mouse from the grass. It was gone as quickly as it came; we had only a moment to gape when it flashed past. What I remember most beyond its huge size were the wings: bones visible under the skin, like those of a bat, spread as wide as a ship was long. We hunted the side of the mountains but found no trace of our companion.

Two days later we saw it again, circling high in the sky. We tried to stay under cover of trees as much as possible after that.

At last we crossed over the mountains and could see the Crespe in the distance. Over three more difficult days we made it to the shoreline. From there, we knew we could simply follow the shore until we gained our ships once again.

At first, I vowed never to speak of the place to anyone. The Astrarium, I called it, a name that seemed to come to me without effort. But by the time we had sailed to the Fleas, I was already thinking of when I could return. I needed to know.

Then another raptor appeared, as if it been waiting for us. For reasons I don't understand, it attacked the other ship while leaving mine alone. I was able to clearly observe its horrible appearance. It had a beak, like a great bird, over a third as long as its body, and a cord like, barbed tail. It snatched men from the deck and either split them open or hurled them into the sea. In the time it took us to come about and return, the other ship had capsized and was sinking bow down, while the raptor had disappeared. We searched the water but found only dead sailors. My companions, those who had seen the Astrarium with me, had been on the second ship. I was the only one left who had been there. The remainder of our journey home was uneventful, which gave me much time to reflect.

The only honorable way to lose companions at sea, it seems, is to die with them. Anything else marks you for suspicion. I was never asked to take another voyage, and I never volunteered.

But for years I dreamed about going back, even as in my mind the raptors became the guardians of a forbidden place. I was haunted by the thought that it was waiting for me, known only to me. That place knows our past, and perhaps even our future. Who would not give most anything to know those things? Even now, I am torn between the jealousy I feel thinking the secrets should belong to me, and the terror of knowing what will happen to the next person who stumbles onto it. So it remains my secret, and my obsession.

Ologrin uncurled himself painfully from the floor. The light was failing. He stepped outside. Ortak was already visible in the darkening sky. To the east, the Red Eye of Lord Ruhax stared at him, and he stared back. "I know where to find you now," Ologrin said aloud. It was laughably arrogant, he knew. But knowing the secrets of one's enemy was a step in figuring out how to defeat it. And the Red Eye, whether a god or just a star in the sky, had become the embodiment of his enemy.

He could not possibly do it alone. So much everyone

would have to learn anew, and he had no sense of what those things were. Wysel had been right to hide the volume. Having read it, he was now infected with her obsession, and he knew it would grow. He knew where he needed to go.

He ate and he prepared, and the corset began to fit more snugly. He practiced rowing the carve-out to the mouth of the bay and back, building his arm strength. The woodland flowers bloomed; the trees filled themselves with leaves. He packed primarily food and water, but the water would be most problematic, as he did not have many waterskins, and wax-sealed clay jars would be too heavy. He would have to hope for rain along the way.

The house, at last, was as tidy as he could make it. He re-read the secret journals one more time before replacing them in their hiding place. Wysel's return journey had been more grim than he hoped his would be. Scaup's story had been true: black raptors were real. One more thing he would have preferred to remain a myth.

It was New Sojourner, and the air was warm. SummerTop, and the onset of the stormy season, was less than three passages away. It was time to go. He hefted the staff, stepped out, and sealed and barred the door. He made his way one last time down the steps to the beach, where the loaded carve-out waited. The staff slipped through a hole in the rowing seat he had made for it, lying snugly along the inside of the boat. He pushed off and stepped in. The water of the bay shone brilliantly. He waited until he was almost to the mouth of the bay, where the smooth blue water gave way to the gray Southern Sea, before looking back. A few glints of light caught his eye. Then he looked north and rowed for home.

The swells were gentle and ran from east to west. He soon got into a rhythm of strokes to match the swells. He rowed until the Sun was high overhead. Sepha was sinking behind him, though the central and western mountains were still visible, dark against the sky. He rested, drank some water, then rowed again, trying not to think too far ahead. He had days to go, he told himself, and land would come when land would come.

The Sun set, then the Sojourner rose beside it, a great sliver of orange, quickly turning white and becoming fat as it rode higher. The Red Eye was somewhere over his right shoulder, he knew, but he refused to look. He rested again, then awoke with the Sojourner and the Red Eye having switched places. His arms and back felt as if they were on fire, but he started rowing again, and the fire slowly subsided to a low ache.

When the Sun rose, he found that the last peaks of Sepha had disappeared. He was alone, with nothing but sea surrounding him. He took comfort in calculations he had made prior to leaving: He would have to have rowed ten leagues before the highest peaks of Sepha disappeared behind him. With luck, Lhosa was little more than thirty leagues further north. His heart rose to think he would be home in as few as three more days.

The second day passed as did the first. With rationing, he would have just enough water to last two more days. He ate some dried meat but felt little hunger. The aches in his shoulders were less as well. The Sun set, while the Sojourner did not appear until after the first stars were visible.

The next morning he imagined he saw a dark mass in front of him, but the mass turned flame red as the Sun rose and the clouds drew nearer. They formed a haze overhead that seemed to shrink the horizon and made him feel as if he were rowing in a great pot, with swells slapping him on the side, rowing but not moving. It was a discouraging day, unbroken in its monotony. He tried to cheer himself up by reminding himself that tomorrow was the fourth day. With luck, he would see land. The Sun was a flat yellow disk behind the haze, falling toward the sea. To the east, though, the sky was darker, as heavier clouds seemed to be heading south.

The swells picked up in the night. He was awakened by a rhythmic knocking, and by the light of the Sojourner he could see that one of the outrigger crosstrees had come loose from the boat and was rising and then slamming into its groove. Timing his moves to coincide with the swells, it took longer to retie the tree than he expected. The boat creaked much more than it had when launched. He hoped for land the next day.

Day broke, but the swells did not let up. The wind was picking up from the east as well and was starting to blow froth off the top of the swells. He worried that he was being pushed too far to the west. Beyond Solanon, the Lhosan coastline veered to the northwest. His journey would become considerably longer if he missed the wide bay of Solanon by much.

Clouds began to build ominously directly to the north. *Too soon for a Summer storm,* he thought, and then he yelled into the wind, "It's too early!" The waves were beginning to push the bow of the carve-out toward the west. He felt it was all he could do to keep the little boat pointed roughly north, and feared he was no longer making headway.

The first oar broke around midday. He had been digging viciously at the water, attempting to keep the bow pointed in the right direction. As soon as it snapped, the boat spun to the west, but the ride eased. He allowed himself to rest, sitting deep in the carve-out, and drank the last of his water. Left on its own, the little boat seemed to fly over the surface of the waves.

The clouds built but then collapsed, and by evening they were breaking up, revealing the earliest stars. He was starting to feel thirsty and had hoped the clouds would bring an easy rain. The Red Eye spied him and glared at him unceasingly. Darkness became complete; he could not see the front of the boat from where he sat, but the motion of the waves was too great to allow him to relax and sleep. Toward the middle of the night the Sojourner rose at last. Ologrin's spirits rose, too, and he pulled out the remaining oar and began pushing the boat slowly north again.

The Sojourner crept higher, causing the Red Eye to fade. But its movements seemed slow, and Ologrin began to think that the Red Eye had finally figured out how to push back. He rowed, then looked over his shoulder, willing the Sojourner to reach the top of the sky so that it could slide toward the horizon again. He suddenly realized that the hissing of the waves contained voices. "*Wessse, Wessse,*" they said.

"You don't control the waves," he croaked with his dry tongue, but he was no longer sure.

The sky began to lighten; in the north and east it turned purple, then erupted into red fire. A weary-looking Sun crept above sulking gray clouds. Still the swells lifted and dropped the little boat. Ologrin tasted the salt on his lips. He opened his mouth to catch the spray, but it, too, was salty, and he tried to spit it from his dried throat. Once again, the clouds began to build in the north. Ologrin tried to imagine who might be behind this bit of treachery. Did Lord Wesse control the clouds as well?

The storm toyed with him until late day. Then blackness formed in the northeast and raced toward him. Lightning flickered, revealing towering masses of clouds. The swells began to loom over him. He heard a crack but saw no flash, then realized the forward crosstree had snapped between its two lashings. The ends began grinding and popping against each other violently, and he had no choice but to turn the boat again and allow it to run before the swells, easing the flexing motion on the outriggers.

The wind blasted him, then the rain arrived. He stowed the oar and sat as low as he could again, holding on to either side. The bow of the boat crashed into the swells, while rain fell in torrents. The carve-out was awash in water, but he feared the water was full of salt, and so he did not lower his face to drink. He tried opening his mouth into the lashing rain, which seemed to cause the rain to pelt every part of his face but his mouth. Lightning flashed again, close, and thunder boomed over the water. He gasped, realizing the enormity of his mistake. There was no land to sail toward. Lhosa was a cat; she had finally stretched and leapt away.

The rain lessened but the wind howled. With a *pop*, the leather ties holding the forward crossbar gave way. Almost immediately the left outrigger was bent away from the boat, and the rear crossbar snapped. The left side of the rig vanished into the waves. The boat immediately rolled onto its side. Ologrin stared at the right outrigger as it towered over him, then smashed back down into the waves. He flung himself out of the boat's bottom and onto the remainder of the rear crossbar, leaning outward as far as he could and wrapping his legs around the bar, trying to counterbalance the missing rig. The boat ceased trying to flip itself over, but he found himself half drowned every few moments as waves crashed over the boat. He craned his neck to see the clouds break and scatter before the glare of the Red Eye. It burned into him; he felt its fire deep inside his chest.

"Where are you!?" he cried, looking the other direction. He desperately needed the Sojourner to rise and save him from the Sorcerer's fire. "My only friend! Where are you!?"

But in the end even the Sojourner abandoned him. He hung on, spluttering through the waves, and after some time thought their ferocity might be lessening; the rhythm returning.

This is my only chance, he thought. Timing the motion, he flung himself into the bottom of the carve-out and grabbed for the staff. He raised it and even tried standing, but the Sorcerer slammed him to his knees. It did not matter. The waves behind the boat seemed to be reaching new heights before breaking over into a crash of foam. He reached deep inside himself for his last remaining energy. He raised the staff, aiming it directly at the Red Eye.

"For Vireo!" he cried, and a bolt of energy burst from the staff into the clouds. "For Tobin!" he cried, and another bolt lit the sky and energized the air. The Sorcerer responded with a blinding flash and a deafening crash. Ologrin was flung forward into the depths. Water thundered overhead. He craned his neck to see a wonder of light crackling and skimming across the surface of the water above him. Then the blackness of the water claimed him.

SIXTH PASSAGE

Adamantine, rarest of metals, hoarded by the Polfre, is nonetheless not coveted in the same way as gold or silver. For one, its properties make it a difficult metal to work with. A small amount of pure metal, worked into a flat disc, will not stay flat but will curl and warp. Adamantine's true value can only be realized when it is alloyed with other materials, where its unique properties can safely be harnessed. A small amount, for example, melted in the glass furnace, will impart to the glass a red tint not seen in the raw ore.

The raw stuff of history, the emotional recollections of those who were there, are, like adamantine: rarely encountered by the archivist. And when they are found, they need to be worked with other evidence to make them into something durable. Like glass, they must then be tempered with heat and time to become valuable. Only then does a useful, historical narrative become apparent.

The archivist is aware, of course, that the heroes and villains of history are not the actual persons they portray. The tyrant, in life, may have been a tender and devoted lover. But that fact, unless it explains how he came to be hated by an entire world, is not important. At best it may impart a slight tint to the final story.

—From *The Invention of History* by Robin the Archivist

33

A smallish individual sat in one of the front corners of the tavern, stirring a bowl of stew with the heel of a loaf, occasionally taking a small bite, then returning the bread to the bowl. From his seat he could see the approach to the door of the tavern, though the ripples in the window glass made it impossible to make out someone's features before they entered the room. Any new visitor would automatically stop in the doorway to gain their bearings, which gave the seated figure ample time to study the newcomer before being spied. The corner was dim, even in the middle of the day. Nonetheless, out of habit he kept his head down and only made careful glances upward, lest the stray beams of some light source reach his eyes and cause them to glow like tiny lanterns.

    A shadow passed by the window. Pausing briefly outside the door, the shadow then entered the tavern and stopped to look around, just as expected. The figure wore a common traveling cloak with a deep hood, thoroughly blocking his face from view. The man rolled his head, seeming to take in the entire room in a single glance before settling his hooded gaze on the front corner of the room. He walked over purposefully.

"Robin, am I correct?" the man said. "Unless for some reason you're using a false name."

Robin gestured for the figure to sit in the chair opposite his. "Considering the rarity of Polfre in this part of the world, a false name wouldn't do me much good."

"I am Voreno," the man said, sitting.

"I am flattered you asked for me specifically," Robin said. "I would ask how you knew to do that, but it turns out we know many of the same people."

The man's face was dimly visible, and Robin could see him smile thinly. "How old are you?" Voreno asked.

Robin hesitated just a moment before answering. "Thirty-eight. For some reason, I think you already knew that, too."

"Thirty-eight. Barely of age. But life doesn't always have the patience to wait."

Robin regarded the man silently. He had not removed his hood. It made him more conspicuous in the warm tavern, not less. The cloak itself was well-worn and appeared to be made of a soft leather, with an intricate pattern stitched into the edges of the material. *It must have taken a highly skilled tailor several days to complete that kind of work*, Robin mused.

"So. Did you find the answers to my questions?" Voreno asked. His voice was pleasant enough, but there was a no-nonsense tone to it.

"I have answers bidden and unbidden," Robin replied. He saw the man's eyebrows rise slightly in an otherwise impassive stare. Robin felt his discomfort rising in turn.

"Do you need to see my coin first?" Voreno finally asked.

"Oh. Of course not," Robin said. "You're the Amir Voreno. The master of Voreno Works Chimneys. I know you have the coin. I just wanted to be sure you are ready. And that you want the information here."

"Here is as good as any place."

Robin realized he had pinched a hole in the heel of his bread. He dropped it in the stew and pushed the bowl away.

"Very well. First the things you probably already know and are asking me simply to see if I am reliable. The arms-commander in Madros is a man named Aron. He has held the post for seven years. He is very much trusted by Lord Governor Saelis."

"And what do they say about the former governor?"

"Wesse? That he lives in a house larger than the Crown's Palace. And that he lives in peace and raises oranges." Robin tried to discern any change in expression under the hood. "Did you think there might be more, perhaps?"

Voreno ignored the question. "What else," he said.

"Well, Moran remains Lord Priest of the Panthea. Again, that is common knowledge. Moran seems to be Serenity's closest advisor. Perhaps closer than just advisor, some say."

Voreno nodded but said nothing.

"Albrect is no longer at the Sophenary," Robin said. This elicited a small movement of Voreno's head, and Robin knew he was beginning to deliver virgin information.

"Is he dead?" Voreno asked.

"Retired. After three years as Dodecant, he said he'd had enough and went back to work in the Sophenary's chimneys. For years he kept a horse that no one was allowed to ride, that lived like a chief until it died contentedly of old age. Master Hammei took over Albrect's chambers just last year. Master Heron, by the way, has been Dodecant for over a dozen years now and shows no evidence of slowing down. There aren't many willing to cross her publicly."

A brief smile played across Voreno's face. "One more," he said.

"Yes. The only one you probably can't find out about for yourself. The one you needed a Polfre to find. Yes, I found her. Vireo left the Sophenary for the Lake of Skies a year after you disappeared, and never returned."

Robin watched Voreno carefully. He had taken great care, this man before him, to hide his past. Robin guessed he was taking a risk divulging he knew the man's secrets, however hushed their conversation. How great a risk he might not know until a knife crossed his throat in the dark of the night. The Amir Voreno was said to be not only very wealthy, but very dangerous.

"How is she?" Voreno finally asked.

"Fine, as far as I could tell. I only spoke with her briefly. I was afraid asking her more might make her suspicious, might make her start wondering why someone was inquiring of her."

"Thank you for being discreet," Voreno said.

"Just to be clear, I was careful for her sake, not yours. She is at peace with her history. Why would I want to upset that balance? She lives alone, if that is your next question. That is the Polfre way."

Voreno carefully pulled a purse from his cloak and formed a half dozen stacks of silver coins containing six coins each. "When did you figure out it was me?" he asked.

"It took most of the year. I never said my reputation wasn't deserved. What interests me is why?"

"You said you have answers unbidden as well?" Voreno said, ignoring the question.

"I do," Robin said.

"For which you expect to be paid more," Voreno added.

"Oh yes, but not in coins."

Voreno froze, and Robin took a moment to consider how precarious his position might be.

"My price is a story," Robin added slowly.

Voreno remained unmoving.

"Tell me about the Korun," Robin said.

Voreno snorted and began to stand up.

"Just one part of it, for now," he said hurriedly.

"Foolishness from the past," Voreno replied. "I left it behind long ago."

"But it hasn't left you behind, I'm afraid. There are plenty of myths. The truth behind them is harder to find."

"What truth is that?"

Robin paused to gather his words carefully. "You know, not everyone died in the butchery of the riverflats, after you disappeared. A fair number of people escaped into the Highland Hills, west of the Bhin. They are independent folk now, but full of superstition. There are lots of stories about the Korun. My interest is in the truths behind the stories."

"You said just one story," Voreno reminded him.

"Yes. One story. The Battle of the Bridge. They say the Korun called lightning from the skies and killed two dozen men with a single stroke, then he cracked the bridge in half. Astonishing, if true. I just want to hear the story from someone who might have been there."

Voreno sat down again. "I had plenty of help," he said. "And I may have blasted a hole in the bridge, but I didn't crack it in half."

"But the lightning? Is it true?"

"Call it what you want. I don't know what it was."

"How did you call lightning from the sky?"

"It doesn't matter. I made a foolish choice, and lots of people later died. That's the story. The Korun was never a god."

Robin tried to see through the darkness around the man's face. It was not the face of an old man, but Voreno had lived an entire life before this one. So many stories remained.

"Not everyone thinks the Korun is a godly creature," Robin said. "There are some who say he is a demon of Ruhax. They say he started the war, then disappeared while the Crown's arms men laid waste to the flats."

"I never intended to disappear. If you know as much

about me as you suggest, then you know that my ship was destroyed."

"Yes. Drowned at sea. And yet here you are."

"Here I am. But that is another story. You have yet to keep your end of the bargain for the first. What else do you know?"

Robin spoke carefully. "I know where to find the Child of Alera."

Voreno leaned forward so suddenly that Robin's head hit the wall behind him. He had a vision of a striking snake.

"Where. You will tell me where," Voreno demanded.

"I will show you where," Robin said, feeling as if he had awakened something menacing. "I have a map." He pulled a small roll out from his own cloak and smoothed it out onto the table. The map was smudged, and spaces were filled with notes written in a tiny hand.

Voreno scowled and stared at the map for a long moment. But as Robin looked on, he began to recognize the loops and curves of a meandering thick line running from the top to the bottom near the right margin—the River Bhin—including the peculiar bulb of land that once had supported his childhood village. Overlying what geographic features were recognizable, the map was covered with gentle arcing lines, coming together and then diverging in many places.

"The people you seek have become nomadic; they move along these lines," Robin said. "Study the map and the land around you. It will guide you to where you need to go."

"Have you been there?" Voreno asked.

"No. This was given to me. I trust those who gave it to me, and they say it is used by nomads. It will get you where you want to go."

Voreno's intensity seemed to soften, and he sat back in his chair. "If this map is accurate, then I owe you far more than a pile of coins."

"You cannot travel the Great Road," Robin added. "There is no way the Amir Voreno could travel in secret for long.

And the closer you get to Antola, the more that name will elicit jealousy and anger. They will discover who you really are. And they remember."

"How should I go?" Voreno asked.

"You must go north. Leave from Wheatberry, then travel north into the High Grasses before heading east. You ride, I assume?"

"Whenever I can."

Voreno stood to leave. Robin smiled and pointed a single finger at Voreno's head. "I should really like to see that crown of yours, the one you keep hidden."

"Someday, I'm sure," Voreno replied, pulling his hood tighter. "I suspect we will work together again."

Robin nodded hopefully.

"Do you know the story of Farus and Lord Ruhax?" Voreno asked suddenly.

"Well, there are many versions. I believe I've heard most."

"Then you know about the Temple of Ruhax, where Farus finally meets the Sorcerer?"

"Of course."

"Someday, perhaps, you can help me find that, too."

Robin furrowed his forehead. "You're not serious, are you? That's just an old children's story."

"You suggested yourself," Voreno said, "that there are truths behind the myths." He pulled a small object from the folds of his cloak and set it on the table, a coin as golden as the Sun. A small pair of bison's horns had been struck into the coin's face.

"What's this" Robin asked.

"You can spend it or keep it. Some day it may have greater value than you can imagine."

Robin carefully placed his finger on the coin, as the taller figure turned to leave.

. . .

Late the same night a horse and rider stopped to exchange quiet words with the guards at one of Dormond's gates, after which they settled into a slow trot on the road north, roughly paralleling the Sestern river toward its headwaters. The Sojourner would not rise until daybreak, so the night was as dark as ink, but both horse and rider had no trouble staying in the roadway. The horse, which answered to Smoke, was the embodiment of his name, with a dark gray coat and black mane. The rider, who now answered to Voreno, rode with the ease of an experienced rider. Few could see or hear them pass. A long staff, black as the night, was secured across the rider's back. Any highwayman unfortunate enough to molest either horse or rider would likely encounter the staff and experience a memorably bad evening.

They rode until daybreak, then rested a few hours near a tiny village. Voreno purchased a few supplies, even though he was well stocked. They were riding again shortly after midday. They rode through the evening and night again, and the cracking dawn put them in sight of Wheatberry, the last decent village on the road. Beyond were the High Grasses, too far from Dormond for farmers to safely settle, even if people discounted the stories of the wild creatures who made it home.

Voreno paid in advance for two nights in Wheatberry's only tavern. Except for his meals, he stayed in his room that night and the next. Before daybreak the following morning, the tavern owner was surprised to find room empty and the horse gone from the stable.

Two leagues beyond Wheatberry, the road ended at the foot of tumbled stone ruins. The ruins were very old. Long before there had been modern tools, stones had been painstakingly selected and stacked to form its buttresses and defensive walls. Generations had spent themselves in its building, generations more in its occupation, and even more generations had passed since it had been abandoned to its ghosts. *The sojourn of an entire people is just a brief moment in the expanse of time,* Voreno mused.

Smoke broke into a slow trot, which he maintained without slowing until the Sun was well past midday. He finally slowed as they approached a shallow gulley. They descended into the washout and drank from a tiny, meandering stream. Then they were on the move again, occasionally slowing to a walk, but always traveling north and east, through grass that reached to the horse's withers. The Sun set, leaving the Sojourner high in the eastern sky. Only after it dropped below the horizon and the world was truly dark did they stop for the night. Voreno guessed they had covered at least twenty-five leagues from Wheatberry.

On the second day of riding, the grasses thinned and the ground became cracked hardpan interspersed with tufts of spikegrass and grey sage. Late in the day they rode the length of a gradual rise until they crested a ridge and looked down on a bleak, empty bowl of red sand and exposed rock, extending to infinity from the northwest to the northeast.

"The edge of the Great Desert," Voreno said out loud. Smoke nickered in reply.

They followed the ridge for many leagues and again did not camp until after the Sojourner settled in the east. The remaining night was short. The stars, however, were so thick and so bright Voreno did not sleep but allowed himself to rise up into them, where he scooped them into his cloak, then flung them out like seeds to grow new patterns in the sky.

On the fourth day they bent their path toward the south. The grasses returned and soon shared the rolling hills with sumac and scaly-leafed junipers. They rode further, and valleys began to be filled with dense woodlands, though the ridges remained clear. They rested early on the fourth night, and Voreno fell asleep immediately, hidden in the fragrant cedars.

On the fifth day they gradually began climbing higher.

They were riding toward the highest point of the ridgeline, beyond which the world seemed to disappear. But the crest seemed to move away from them as fast as they approached, until the edge of the world revealed itself to be an illusion: The ridge finally leveled out and the ground dropped gently away beyond. However, it continued to descend slowly for dozens of leagues eastward until it became the broad plains of the river Bhin. Beyond that, just at the edge of his sight, Voreno could see a jaggedness on the eastern horizon, the highest peaks of the Adamantine mountains. A steady breeze rose from the valley and ruffled his cloak, then flipped the hood off his head.

He was now on the edge of the map. The lines were bearings, he realized with a smile. The distant peaks matched those drawn on the opposite edge of the map. Those who had made the map used the mountains to navigate the grasslands just as he had used the stars to navigate the sea.

Late in the day, he followed a map line into an especially broad and long valley, through woods composed mostly of tall poplars with fluttering leaves, and into a meadow of vivid wildflowers. In the distance, a small collection of huts was nestled in the grass. From where he sat, the cluster of huts looked like simple structures of sticks and skins. But as Voreno drew closer it was evident their construction was more sophisticated. The supports were evenly finished, intricately interlinked arcs of wood, and the thick, skin-like coverings were fitted without wrinkle or seam. Each was craftmanship equal to anything in Madros. Near the center of the camp, several of the structures had been linked to form a single, larger structure, and the various domed and peaked tops reminded him of a chain of mountains. He picked up tantalizing odors as he drew closer and could make out a thin line of smoke rising into the sky.

Three men appeared from the huts and walked toward him. Voreno noted the way they spread themselves out. Each carried a spear with a broad metal blade, and each had a long knife belted to one side. He could hear the laughter of children beyond the huts. Smoke walked toward the center man. Too late, Voreno realized he had not pulled his hood back up.

"May I rest near your people this evening?" Voreno asked.

The center man looked at him for a long moment before answering. "You are the Korun," he said, holding his spear across the front of his body.

Voreno did not answer. He thought about the staff slung across his back and decided to leave it right there. These men would have been there, he thought. They might have even prayed to the Korun, then been dismayed when he never came as they watched their families die. If they sought an opportunity for revenge, he would not deny them. He only hoped to first find what he had come so far to find.

"I seek the Child of Alera," he said softly.

The center man slowly lowered his spear to point at the ground and stepped to one side. Voreno dismounted to stand beside him. The man turned and walked toward the huts. Voreno followed, and Smoke trailed behind of his own accord.

They walked through the huts. Voreno's stomach rumbled from the delicious smells. Beyond, in a grassy space, a dozen children had arranged themselves in a circle. They were busy: squatting, then standing, whispering, laughing, and occasionally jumping to a different part of the circle, but still seeming to direct most of their attention on a single figure seated in their midst.

Voreno's guide pointed to a man in the center of the group. "The Child of Alera," he said.

The children noticed them then, and they ran screaming and laughing toward them, leaving the central figure to slowly and painfully stand. One leg bent abnormally outward compared to the other, causing the figure to lean to one side. A few tufts of white hair seemed stuck to a weltered approximation of skin on the old man's head, divided by an indented crease along the left side of his skull. In contrast to his battered appearance, he wore a cloak of fine material, fastened with a pin of three entwined rings bearing three colored gems. He looked their direction but could not see, as the center of both eyes was as white and opaque as the edges. He took a couple of limping steps.

Voreno stepped forward as well.

"Tobin?" he said.

The wounded figure came to a stop.

"Tobin? It's me, Ologrin. It's Olei."

The old man turned his head to the side and seemed to concentrate. The children returned to rally around him, touching his arms and gently guiding him forward.

Ologrin stepped up and took the man's forearms in his hands. "Tobin, it's me, Olei. Do you remember me?"

"Olei?" the man said slowly. "I had an Olei."

"I know. That's me. I'm Olei."

The old man appeared to be resurrecting a long-lost thought. "Where have you been, Olei?" he said finally.

"I went away. To school, remember? And I came back to visit."

"But where have you been?"

"I was in Antola, remember? At the Sophenary."

"Where...where have you been?"

Ologrin paused and looked beyond the man to the hills, blinking the tears from his eyes. "Well, I've been to sea. And I've been in love, but I lost her. And then I was alone for a long, long time. And then I came back, and I've been busy for several years and I've met many people, and then I heard about a child who blessed the land wherever he walked, and so I came to find you."

"Olei, is that you?'

"I'm sorry I took so long to come back."

Tobin reached up with both burn-scarred hands and

placed them on Ologrin's cheeks, then carefully wiped away the tears. "Olei," he said. "Who are we going to serve today?"

Ologrin took one arm while the children took the other. Together, they walked to the central cluster of huts, where they sat and let the late day Sun warm them. Someone served small berries from a tray, and then a short time later cheese and bread and tender roasted meat. Clay pitchers gurgled as they dispensed cool water that reminded Ologrin of freshly melted snow. The Highland Hills cast long shadows. Finally, Ologrin separated himself from the gathering and walked to the top of the nearest rise. Colors faded to gray, and then the waxing crescent of the Sojourner lifted itself into the western sky.

"Never again," Ologrin murmured, turning and staring toward the distant, shrouded river valley.

The Sojourner rose majestically behind him, becoming fatter and brighter until it shone down white and full onto the quiet land below, embracing it with soft, silvery light.

ACKNOWLEDGMENTS

Thanks to Jasmin Kirkbride for her unapologetic editing and conceptual notes, and to Claire Maby for her careful line editing and insistence that I learn the difference between *which* and *that*.

Thanks as well to Alejandro Colucci for his spectacular cover art.

Special thanks to friends who read drafts and provided feedback. In particular, to Denise Gribbin, who didn't let a few bad spots get in the way of glowing praise, and Rebecca Crosbie, who didn't let praise get in the way of an honest and much-needed critical reading.

And, of course, thanks to my family for putting up with the many months spent hearing me say "it's almost done!"

ABOUT THE AUTHOR

Carey Allen Krause lives, works, and writes in Grand Rapids, Michigan. This is his second novel.

For more information: **www.lhosaworld.com**

Made in the USA
Columbia, SC
20 February 2020